JAKE'S
TALE

MIKE HODGKINS

JAKE'S TALE

DB
PUBLISHING

Also by Mike Hodgkins: 'Better Red than dead'

This edition published in Great Britain in 2013 by DB Publishing, an imprint of JMD Media.

ISBN 9781780910796

Printed and bound by Copytech (UK) Limited, Peterborough.

Contents

Introduction   7

About the Author   8

Acknowledgement   9

Chapter 1   11

Chapter 2   17

Chapter 3   23

Chapter 4   29

Chapter 5   35

Chapter 6   45

Chapter 7   51

Chapter 8   57

Chapter 9   61

Chapter 10   67

Chapter 11   73

Chapter 12   77

Chapter 13   89

Chapter 14   93

Chapter 15   101

Chapter 16   107

Chapter 17   109

Chapter 18   125

Chapter 19   131

Chapter 20   133

Chapter 21   147

Chapter 22   153

Chapter 23   157

Chapter 24   169

Chapter 25   173

Chapter 26 179
Chapter 27 185
Chapter 28 189
Chapter 29 197
Chapter 30 207
Chapter 31 223
Chapter 32 227
Chapter 33 239
Chapter 34 245
Chapter 35 251
Chapter 36 257
Chapter 37 261
Chapter 38 271
Chapter 39 275
Chapter 40 281
Chapter 41 285
Chapter 42 295
Chapter 43 299

Introduction

In writing 'Jake's Tale' I have scratched the itch I have had for a long time. I think that there are many people who see the fire engines thundering around the streets of their town and wonder where and what the emergency is. The possibilities are of course endless; it could be a fire in someone's house, or a car that has suddenly burst into flames. Maybe a dog has got stuck in a hole in the ground, or banks of LPG cylinders are exploding.

The people who ride the fire appliances are not heroic; they are ordinary people, just like the rest of us who, just occasionally, are required to do extra ordinary things to save a life or protect the public's property.

For many years, I have loved the Derbyshire Peak District. It is located within a short bus or train journey from where both my friends and I were brought up, so it was a place we frequented when we were young, going on long walks and learning the skill of rock climbing. Those early experiences have stayed with me.

The Volunteers who live and work in the Park are largely unheralded, the Mountain Rescue teams and The Ranger Service all do sterling work rescuing people in trouble, helping to maintain footpaths and stiles, their only reward being the satisfaction of helping the public to enjoy England's busiest and oldest National Park.

About the Author

Mike is 69 years old and lives with his wife Carol in Chesterfield. They have two children and six grand children. He spent almost 30 years as a fire fighter, serving in both Hertfordshire and South Yorkshire. Mike joined the fire service in 1968 in Hertfordshire, where he and his wife Carol lived at that time. In 1974, he transferred to the South Yorkshire Service where he spent the next four years, during which time he gained promotion. In 1978 they moved back south where Mike re joined The Hertfordshire brigade as an instructor in the service training centre. He was further promoted, ending his career in the fire service as a Station Commander at Bishop's Stortford, the station where he'd begun his career.

After his retirement, he moved with his wife to live in Norfolk, and four years later they moved to Derbyshire where he began training to become a Peak Park Ranger. He also became a guide at Chatsworth House. After his subsequent final retirement, he now fills his time writing and walking in the peaks.

Acknowledgement

'Jake's Tale' was in many ways an easier book to write than my first book 'Better red Than Dead' in which I set out the characters who inhabit both books. Jake's Tale is the second in the series of books about life in the Fire Service and the Peak District.

My task has been made infinitely easier because of the kind assistance given by Bob Graves of the Edale mountain rescue team, also my friend Andrea Pedley who advised me on matters relating to the Ranger Service, and my friend Dominica (Mimma) Cardullo who advised on all matters relating to Italy and its language, and also for her valuable advice on classical music. I must also thank Steve Caron, my publisher, for his continued faith in me as a writer. Finally to Carol my wife for who has endured the many hours I have had to spend sitting in front of my computer.

Chapter 1

Jake sat quietly, fingering the handle of his coffee cup. The phone call had taken him by surprise. He'd hardly given it a second thought after the initial interest had died down, but the call had re-awakened the thoughts and memories he'd stored away in the back of his mind since the incident.

He stared vacantly at the blue emulsion painted wall of the small café where she'd asked to meet him. Inside, it was warm and quiet, just one other customer, who sat three tables away and focussed on reading the newspaper. The windows were grubby and running with condensation. He'd agreed to meet her, and now the memories of that night had re-asserted themselves in his consciousness.

His mind placed him on the staircase again, blinded by the pungent hot smoke; the heat drying his skin. Then the pain as the temperature began to toast his body and the desperate need to breath. His hands trembled as he searching the room again, certain that he was going to die along with the girl he was trying to save. He remembered the weight of her body as he dragged her, stricken by panic for the stairs, he remembered the air bursting from his lungs and the response of his body as he sucked in air, contaminated by acrid poisonous smoke. He remembered coughing and the mucus pouring from his nose, and then falling. He remembered a light in his face, the nurses in the Hospital, his mother by his bed weeping. Then the reception from his colleagues at training school who treat him as a hero.

He sensed the door swing open, and felt the draft of cold air waft in from outside, but took little notice, and then he was aware of a presence close by his left shoulder.

'Hello' the voice said. Jake knew instantly it was her, the gentle northern accent, the light, almost nervous tone. 'Hello, Jake, I'm so glad you came.' Jake turned and saw the girl, he guessed her to be about his age, or maybe a year or two older, and he sensed her nervousness. She was pretty, about five foot two he thought. She wore a Denim jacket and jeans, her hair was long and black and tumbling down her back. He looked at her face, the faint remnant of her injuries just visible; the left side of her face still slightly reddened and scarred, she turned her face to make the scarring less obvious.

'Hi' Jake replied, 'take a seat, can I get you a cup of something?'

'A coffee would be nice' she said, smiling nervously.

Jake motioned to the girl behind the counter.

He looked at her; she glanced at him, they both knew in that moment there was an understanding; a bond, forged by chance in desperate circumstances a few months earlier. Jake had saved her life and had almost died in the process; no words were required, they looked and said nothing.

Brian lay back in bed, his left arm stretched out and Jane's head rested heavily on his powerful shoulder. He looked at her, the mother of his child. The holiday together had gone well; the family had come together again. He had almost tricked her into coming with him; their young daughter Jill had almost blackmailed her into coming. The days that followed were relaxed and happy. Feelings which had not existed for a long time began to emerge. Brian had often thought of the past with Jane, feeling regret at the mistakes which lead to their separation and his self imposed exile from the home. Now he felt another chance had fallen at his feet, he looked at her and his head tumbled with a mixture of feelings. He felt grateful, and hoped that maybe their life together could be re-assembled. Over the past few days they had all relaxed and the times had been fun. Jane seemed happier than he had seen her since their acrimonious split some years ago. She'd relaxed and looked at him with the old look, which he recognised from their past. The animosity and bitterness had receded, and the quiet evenings playing cards and dominoes with their daughter Jill was drawing them closer together again. On the fourth night they sat on the sofa and finished off a bottle of Australian red. They could hear Jill in her bedroom gently breathing. They were all tired after a short visit to the beach where, after being driven away by the cold wind, they escaped to the warmth of the car. They then drove around the island in search of interesting things to occupy them all.

Jane leaned against him. He lifted his arm and put it around her shoulder; the most natural thing in the world to do. He did it without thought or motive, he turned and kissed her cheek, she turned and put her arm across his stomach and kissed him on the mouth. They made love; it seemed the natural thing to do.

'This is so good.' Brian said. 'I couldn't have imagined we'd ever get together again.' They parted and looked at each other, both sensing that this would change everything; the start of something good; this wouldn't be the end of it.

'It's a shame it's taken so long for this to happen.' Jane said quietly.

'I just think we were too young and a bit immature, not ready for a relationship' Brian said, 'when we were together, I guess I was so busy thinking about other stuff that I didn't see what was right under my nose.' he paused, 'but I'm glad we've done this, I never thought it could happen,' he said with a serious tone in his voice, 'I reckon I've always had feelings, even when things got bad between us, I just buried them. I was immature I guess.'

Jane let out a laugh, 'There were times when I absolutely hated you, but despite that, there was always something about you. I missed the times when you made me laugh and you always were a good dad.' She paused for a second. 'It's been a nice week, I've really had a good time and I know Jill has loved having you around.' She paused again and spoke quietly, 'I'm dreading going back to how it was before, everything is a struggle, I'm permanently tired and worried about everything, Jill's always asking when she's going to see you again.'

'We don't have to go back,' Brian interrupted, 'I feel the same, we've all had a good time, we just need time to talk and maybe see if it would be right to have another go.'

'That would be nice, but let's not rush it, it's still early days,' she said cautiously.

Brian took her hand. 'I'd really love us to be a family again, I'm sure Jill would like that.'

Just then the bedroom door swung open. They were both naked on the bed. They scrambled to pull a sheet across themselves.

'Mum?' Jill said, standing in the bedroom doorway, illuminated by the light which shone from the landing.

'What is it my darling?' Jane replied, pulling the bed sheet tightly up beneath her chin.

'Are you and dad going to get married?' she asked, the fingers of her right hand twisting a curl in her long brown hair, the other hand gripping a large teddy bear.

'Let me just say this my lovely; Daddy and I are in negotiations as we speak,' she said turning her head to look at Brian.

Brian was sat bolt upright, pulling the sheet across him attempting to hide his exposed parts from the curious eyes of his daughter. He glanced back at Jane, grinned, and winked his eye.

Jock stood on the touchline; the wind howled and carried flecks of snow across the football pitch. His feet were frozen, and he was beginning to have reservations about his self imposed determination to watch every game that Fraser played for the Sheffield United Junior team. Through all of Fraser's life it had been football. Jock would have loved it if his son was on the books of his beloved Celtic, but he figured that the Blades were a good second best. He'd given up his part time job as a bouncer to free him up to drive him to wherever he had to be to train or play.

Fraser had always been seen as a defender; powerful for his age, but also a terrier in the tackle, with boundless energy. The club had recognised this early on, and he was soon a key member of the team, operating in midfield. He'd developed a reputation for toughness and a dogged will to win. This had been spotted by the scouts of several other league teams, who had expressed their interest in him; he was seen as a good prospect.

The ball floated into the United penalty area from the left corner flag, the centre half, only fourteen but over six feet tall, headed the ball powerfully out of the area. It dropped at the feet of another defender who hoofed it on the volley away from danger. Fraser backed away; the ball coming from height allowed him to adjust. He stunned the ball on his chest, the ball dropped perfectly at his feet, he turned, blind, realising that he had only one defender to beat. He dropped his shoulder and barged powerfully past the slim, smaller boy. With just the keeper to beat, he looked up. The keeper was in two minds; stay on his line or come out to narrow the angle. He began moving out and Fraser clipped the ball with his right foot causing the ball to soar up into the air. The keeper, knowing he was beaten, turned in time to see the ball drop gently into the goal behind him. In that instant, Jock knew for sure his son was going to make the grade.

Janet Clark was up early; today she was doing an extra shift to cover for illness at Edale Ranger station, located at the base of the Peak District's highest mountain, Kinder Scout. She poked her head out of her kitchen door and noticed that the temperature had dropped; the puddles in the courtyard of her farm house were frozen solid.

I'd better put on an extra layer today she thought, the wind biting at her cheeks. *It looks like it's going to be a cold one.*

Chapter 2

Paul Bates, his wife Alison and nine year old twins Toby and Kelly threw their rucksacks across their shoulders. They were well prepared for the day; they were experienced walkers. Although they had never been on the Scout before, they knew of its reputation and took the challenge seriously. Their route would take them alongside the stream which gave the name to the route they were to ascend, Grindsbrook, the most common and accessible route onto the plateau. The path was deeply scarred from millions of booted feet which had trod the route over many years, and was the original start to the Pennine Way, which, because of the erosion, had been changed. Once on the plateau they would follow the path around the southern edge of the escarpment, a great route giving impressive views all the way, then they would cut north and have lunch by Kinder Downfall, a spectacular waterfall and a honey pot for people who have the stamina to get there. Then they would return on a bearing from Kinder Gates, a prominent outcrop on the Kinder River, and again hit the edge of the escarpment then back to the holiday cottage for supper.

The ground reared up before them. They were alone on the rough muddy path, and the further they walked the steeper the terrain got. They stopped for a breather.

'When we get up onto the plateau, we'll find some shelter, have a breather and a nice hot cup of coffee,' Paul said.

'Sounds good to me,' his wife replied, 'this track is a bit steeper than the ones we normally walk, we'll be ready for it.'

Mac sat in his armchair with his feet up on a stool, a hot cup of tea on the coffee table and the Sunday paper wide open. This was what Mac considered to be a civilised way of wasting time. The clock on the mantelpiece showed ten o clock. Val sat; waiting for what she knew would be his next action.

'Well, girl, what shall we do today then?' He said looking at Val, who already knew he'd decided what they would do.

'Well it's bitter cold outside, so shall we go out in it?' she said, a hint of irony in her voice.

'Good idea,' Mac retorted. 'Where do you fancy?'

'We could drive out to Castleton, if you like, maybe have a stroll up Mam Tor?' she said, with a light smile on her face. They often went through this process, and she knew that Mac, in his mind, would already have decided to do a walk, and where they would go. She played along. It was part of the James ritual; it would seem strange if some day they didn't do it.

They threw the rucksacks into the back of the old Volvo. Mac had noted the cold wind and the potential for snow, but it would take more than that to stop them.

'Come on then, Mac, where are we going?' Val asked.

Mac turned to her and grinned. 'We haven't been up on Kinder for a couple of years in the snow. Thought it would be a bit of an adventure; you know, before we get too old. Reckon we could soon be past it. I've put the ice axes and crampons in the bag just in case. It'll be warm fire and slippers soon enough,' he laughed.

'Don't you think it'll be a bit chilly up there today? It's perishing now and we're in the car.'

'I know love, I'll see if I can fix the heater tomorrow.' He laughed.

Val knew not to worry; all of their life together had been one of doing things that were slightly out of the ordinary. When the girls were only eight and ten, Mac had them walking the Pennine Way. Just to make it more interesting, they camped and took their dog, Morris the Jack Russell, who by midday each day ended up being carried in Mac's rucksack. At night he insisted on sleeping in one of their sleeping bags, which often made for uncomfortable and sleepless nights.

Janet pulled the car into the small area at the side of the Edale Ranger station, where there were already several cars. *That's good,* she thought, *hopefully we won't be too short handed.*

'Hey up, love.' The powerful baritone voice emerged from the kitchen, 'long time no see. What have you been up to? It's good to see you; you've picked a good day for it.'

Phil Brown, Edale's Chief Ranger, was a huge man, only five foot eight but was built like an Ox with a broad chest and powerful tattooed arms, and a face permanently creased with a smile. Because of his size he looked unfit and cumbersome, but looks didn't tell the story; there was no other ranger that could match him. Physically he could walk twenty five miles, then spend the night on Kinder, searching in appalling conditions, and then patrol the next day with no signs of tiredness.

Phil had been a Collier in Rotherham for many years. When the pits closed he took his redundancy money and bought a bungalow in Tideswell. Then he joined the Rangers as a volunteer. Phil loved it and soon his personality, strength and natural aptitude for the service was recognised. He was offered a full time position, an offer he grabbed with both hands.

'So what have you been up to, Mrs Clark?' Phil asked. 'Has that grizzly old bugger, Stan Gregg, been looking after you all at Brunts Barn?'

'You know Stan,' Janet replied, 'he never changes, just like you; he's married to the job.'

'Me? Married to this? You must be joking; I could walk away from this tomorrow if I wanted.'

'Yeah, Phil, I'm sure you could, but you don't want to do you?' Janet laughed.

'It seems to me lass that you know both me and Jack too well.'

'Best part of the job,' Janet said. 'What would I do if I didn't have to spend my time with pedantic old sods like you two?'

There were four other Rangers, sat in an arc along one side of the briefing room. Janet knew all of them. She'd done patrols with some, and met others at social occasions, and they briefly exchanged pleasantries. Phil emerged from his office, clipboard in hand.

'Today looks like it could be difficult. The weather is due to take a turn for the worse, heavy snow is due to hit after lunch, we can't stop people going up the hill, but we can advise them of the risks. So if they look under-dressed, you know; lightweight gear, party frocks, high heels etc, advise them strongly to go somewhere else.' Phil looked serious, 'I think today could be interesting.' He paused momentarily. 'Look, this is the plan for today,' he said, bristling with confidence.

The Edale Mountain Rescue Team had received the weather forecast early, and made a decision to do an exercise on the plateau in light of the potential for problems. They thought it best to be in the vicinity if the weather turned really bad. It was Sunday and you could be sure there would be plenty of people wanting to go onto the plateau.

Kinder Scout is a special place, almost mystical, not high when compared to the peaks of Scotland, Wales or the Lake District. But its topography made it a dangerous confusing place, especially when the weather turned bad.

Many people underestimate Kinder Scout; its relative low altitude and the fact that it has no obvious peak, but it does have a summit which covers many acres of peat which is scarred by a vast maze of deep channels which make navigation almost impossible. There are no land marks, resulting in people becoming lost, sometimes perishing. The hill has a mystique which is difficult to fathom.

'Hey kids, let's get in here under this rock out of the wind,' Paul said as they crested the escarpment. The walk up, especially the last four hundred feet over a surface of steep uneven boulders had been tough; they were all ready for a breather. Paul got the flask out of his sack and poured each of them a cup of hot coffee. The wind was gusting and carrying occasional flakes of snow into their protective little cove. The temperature had dropped. Paul peeked out of the cave-like dwelling, which gave a view directly back down the route they had just walked. He realised that they were on their own; no one else was on the trail below them. It didn't seem important at the time.

Janet had heard and understood Phil's message. He'd chosen to station Ranger Eric Suggs at the base of the hill to discourage walkers from going up onto the plateau, a sensible precautionary measure. Phil realised that if things went bad, he'd need his strongest team on the hill. Janet and the other Rangers were making their way to the top by various routes to give the best coverage of all the options on the plateau.

Mac parked in the railway station car park and decided they'd go via Jacob's Ladder on the southern edge of the escarpment. A steep climb to the top followed by a shorter walk to the Downfall.

'Are you happy with that?' Mac asked as they strode along the base of the hill.

'Happy as I can be, you know Kinder always gives me the collywobbles, I've seen too much bad weather up there,' Val retorted.

'We'll be fine,' he said optimistically, 'any problems and we'll come down, you know me, I don't take risks.'

Val smiled to herself, Mac really had no idea of what he was like; he was probably the least cautious person she had ever met. That's what had always made him the most attractive of men. He was the one to get stuck in, a doer. It made her laugh to think that he considered himself to be cautious.

She'd never thought that Mac was the most handsome man she'd ever met, but he wasn't entirely ugly either. He had something that set him apart from the regular bloke, something that others also saw; he was down to earth, completely reliable, honest, and that's what she loved about him.

Within three quarters of an hour they were sitting against Edale Cross, a carved stone high on the southern slope of Kinder, having a breather. Mac had noticed the drop in temperature and the few snowflakes in the air, but he was happy and relished what the day was to bring. 'Come on we'd better get moving, we'll be at the Downfall in an hour; we'll have a cuppa and a bite to eat when we get there.'

Val sighed, 'Yeah I've heard that one before, look at the weather.'

'It'll be OK; we'll come down if it gets too bad.'

That was a small concern to Val. She realised that her idea of bad and Mac's were probably poles apart. She decided that she would have to be insistent if she got too worried about the weather.

Janet had hit the summit of the brook and felt the drop in temperature, but still feeling fresh she donned another layer beneath her jacket.

Phil's instructions to her had been pretty specific; there was nothing left to chance. 'Go via Grindsbrook, across by four Jack's cabin, then cut across to Seal Edge, have a look over there, see who's come up from the snake. Then get over to the Downfall.'

Other Rangers had used other routes to the top, one doing the anti clockwise route via the Druid's Stone and another doing the southern route via the Hog's Back. Phil was going to patrol the area between the top of Grindsbrook and the Downfall, the area most likely for trouble to occur. A blast of cold wind almost blew Janet off her feet as she turned north and headed for the deep peat gully that would send her into the unforgiving heart of the Kinder Scout plateau, the most disorienting forbidding area of the Peak District.

Chapter 3

'It's really good to meet you at last,' she said, drawing the chair up close to the table, opposite Jake.

Jake looked at her, remembering the night when the two of them had met. The scarring to her face was hardly visible, and he felt sure that with time it would be almost invisible.

'Same here,' Jake replied, 'I was wondering how you were going on.' He was lying It wasn't that he didn't care, but his mind was so full of his life that those peripheral things like the situation with her, and getting his laundry done, just weren't important.

'How are you then?' Jake asked.

'I'm fine now, the burns were mainly superficial, there was just one small bit on my cheek that needed a bit of plastic surgery, other than that it's been great.'

'You look well, the doctors have done a good job, you'd hardly know,' Jake replied.

'Anyway,' she said, 'I thought we should meet. Since that night I've wanted to meet you to thank you properly for what you did.'

'No problem, anybody would have done the same.'

'No, you're not anybody, you're Jake and you saved my life. I'll always be grateful, I'll never forget what you did,' she said, her voice cracking. 'And, oh, by the way I'm Tracy Jameson; I'm at University in Sheffield.' They chatted for about twenty minutes, both comfortable in the other's company.

'Where are you living now?' Jake asked.

'After the fire my mum and dad decided that it would be better for me, and them, if I got a room in the halls at University, so that's where I am now. It's OK, but I preferred my own space, you know. In halls there are always people milling around, you don't get much peace, it makes study difficult sometimes.'

'Yeah I can imagine,' Jake replied.

'Well I'd better get back, I've an essay to produce by tomorrow so I'd better make a start,' she said. She took Jake's large hand, her hand seeming minute as she gripped it lightly. Jake felt that their history, albeit short, almost required him to ask.

'How would you feel about meeting up again sometime?'

'I'd like that a lot,' she replied, her face transformed by a dazzling smile.

The wind bit into Janet's face as she ploughed up the long dead stream beds which created the maze of gullies. She was passing close by an old and now ruined stone shooter's cabin, known as The Four Jacks. The sides of the gullies in some places were fifteen feet deep, the walls black and glistening, almost vertical and impenetrable, creating a terrifying and oppressive environment for the uninitiated or inexperienced walker. A strange, deadly landscape bereft of landmarks, unrelenting, tough, and dirty but also exhilarating.

Janet walked quickly, the route through the peat had reached bedrock in parts, sometimes a couple of inches of water flowed either east or west. With it being the Pennine watershed and the direction of flow, in bad conditions it can be a useful navigation aid in an area where a compass is almost useless. After a couple of kilometres she took stock, sat on a rock, escaping from the fierce wind, and pulled on the balaclava from her rucksack, attempting to protect her face from the worst of the wind. She poured herself a small cup of black coffee and turned her mind to the problems the day may bring. She heard the vague crunch of a gravel footfall and turned her head; she hadn't expected to meet anyone this early in the day, especially in these weather conditions. The deep gulley twisted and turned away from her. After a short while she could hear the stumbling sound of boots and a vague curse; a male voice. She pricked up her ears. About twenty yards away a dark shape appeared trudging tiredly along the gulley, his appearance telling Janet that he was worn out and wet.

He caught sight of Janet and stopped sharply.

'Thank goodness,' he said, 'what sort of a place is this? I've been walking around in circles for the past three hours, how on earth do I get out of here and down to civilisation?' he said, sounding exhausted.

Janet stood up. 'Come over here and sit with me out of the wind for a minute,' she said, 'how long have you been up here? Have you got any more clothes in your bag? Have you got a warm drink?'

The man looked at Janet, his face creased with relief. At last he'd managed to make contact with civilisation again.

'No, all my clothes are wet through; I got caught out last night and had to sleep up here, not that I got much. It was freezing; all my drink was finished yesterday.'

Janet rummaged in her rucksack. 'Well it's your lucky day,' she said as she delved deeper into her bag, dragging out a bright orange plastic sack. 'This is what you need.' The man stared in disbelief. Out of the sack she then drew a thick blue cotton shirt and an old worn brown jumper. 'Now quickly get your wet stuff off, use this towel to give yourself a quick rubdown, and put these on, they'll do you until you get off the hill,' she said casually.

The man continued to stare, 'I can't believe it, do you always carry spare clothes in your bag?'

Janet gave the man a wide grin. 'On Kinder Scout you need to carry the kitchen sink. All Rangers carry extra food and clothes just for such occurrences as we find you today.'

'Oh I see,' the man blurted, 'Ranger, I should have realised, I can see now,' he said, noticing the badge on her coat.

'Yep,' Janet said, we all wear these uncomfortable red waterproofs, they're a pain, but up here an absolute necessity in these conditions,' she said, fingering the sleeve of her red Gortex winter wear.

The man quickly ripped off his jacket, jumper and shirt, and at speed in the biting wind rubbed his torso with the towel that Janet had given him, not pausing for a second. He quickly pulled on the heavy crumpled shirt and jumper, then gingerly put his saturated coat back on over the top.

'Here, slide into this survival bag; it'll help you to get warmed up,' she ordered. He quickly slid his body into the orange windproof bag.

The man now began to look more comfortable. Janet could see that he was probably in his mid thirties. If he'd shaved she would have considered him to be quite good looking, his long dark hair plastered to his forehead, his waterproof over trousers caked in the finest black sludge that Kinder could produce.

What's your name?' Janet asked.

'Bill Staples, I'm on a relaxing weekend away from all the stress and strain of everyday life,' he said with an ironic smile on his lips.

Janet had always had a fascination for accents, and this man's she found particularly intriguing. 'Are you a Geordie?' she asked.

He looked at her and smiled. 'Na bonnie lass, I'm a Mackem, straight from the dirty streets of Sunderland. It's funny; most people ask that, I suppose the accents are similar.'

'Right- now we've sorted that out let's get you warmed up. Let me give you a cup of coffee; you look as though you could do with one,' Janet said cheerfully, 'then I'll put you on the right track to get you down to Edale.'

Bill Staples lay back, resting his body against his rucksack, sipping the steaming coffee, in his mind a feeling of great relief that he had stumbled upon the person probably best served to help him. His eyes were heavy, and his body ached from the tension of walking blindly, lost, in an area he had vastly underestimated.

'I don't think I've ever walked in such a confusing place,' he said, blowing out a thick vapour from his mouth. Janet saw the vapour, and realised that the temperature was dropping fast.

'Yeah it is confusing, but after a while you get to know and love it,' she said, fondly. 'Anyway, we'd better get you out of here, the weather is turning naughty,' she said, a tinge of anxiety in her voice. 'There's no point me giving you directions from here,' she said, I'll walk you back to the track and it will be easy enough from there.'

'You're an angel, I can't believe it, I'll be writing to your boss to tell him what brilliant people he has working for him.'

Janet gave him a wide grin. 'Yeah, tell him we should have a big pay rise, that would be a day to write home about.' She laughed.

Mac had spotted the dark heavy cloud heading for them from the west and took the decision to forge on at even greater speed. He planned to get to the Downfall, then make a rapid exit straight across the plateau.

'I'm not happy Mac,' Val said, her demeanour and body language telling Mac that she had almost had enough.

'We'll be OK love, trust me, ten minutes we'll be there, a quick cuppa and then straight down.'

In the thirty years they had been married, Val had rarely questioned Mac's judgement. Today, however, she felt it was different, but decided that she would go along with him; he'd never let her down before. She leaned into the wind, the snowflakes now getting bigger and wetter. She pulled the muffler on her jacket across her face, gritted her teeth, and stuck tight up behind Mac, who was marching determinedly on.

Chapter 4

'You did well today son,' Jock said, looking across to the passenger seat of his car where Fraser sat, his hair still damp from his shower in the changing room block. 'You took the goal well, and your overall performance was great, you worked really hard.'

'Yeah, I enjoyed it. Tony Drury came in to the changing room after the game and said he thought we played well, and he said to me he would have been happy to score the goal I got.'

Jock's heart swelled with pride. He'd never been much of a player himself, but he loved the game. Tony Drury was a Blades legend, so if he was impressed, then Jock was even happier.

Jock was keen to know everything that had gone on, but at the same time didn't want to be one of those parents, who bathed in the glory of their kids. His view was that he would support Fraser every way he could, but wouldn't push him. If he was going to do well, it would be through his own effort and desire to succeed.

'What did the manager say in the dressing room after the game?'

Fraser slumped back in his seat and put one trainer clad foot up on the car dashboard. 'He said we played OK.'

'Whoa just a minute son, you're not a star yet, this is my car, get your foot down off the dashboard, have a bit of respect.'

Fraser leered at his dad from the corner of his eyes, but said nothing. He respected his dad, and he knew that some things really irritated him. If you knew that, then you avoided it like the plague; his dad when irate was not a pretty sight.

Mac and Val sat on the summit rocks overlooking the Downfall. The wind was tearing in from the west bringing in snow. At the moment it was quite light, but at this height that could change very quickly. 'Just look at that,' Mac said to Val. The water from the Kinder river flowed over the deep rocky outcrop. The Downfall; forming the highest waterfall in the Peaks, and in conditions like today the wind catches the water and blows it vertically upwards.

'Time to go,' Mac called to Val.

'Thank goodness,' she replied, immediately standing up and pulling her hood firmly over her head.

'Shortest way back I reckon,' Mac shouted as the wind gusted into his face, 'straight along to Kinder Gate and off,' he said, his voice exuding confidence. They set off smoothly, the snow beginning to turn the landscape white, heavy flakes soon covering their jackets.

'We'll go across through Kinder gate then cut across from there,' Mac shouted into the wind which was now howling across the plateau. 'Look there,' Mac said, 'footprints, we're not on our own, there's another group gone through here recently.'

A few minutes ahead, the Bates family were struggling to make progress. Paul, the father, had left his compass in the boot of the car. The visibility was closing in and the snow was getting thicker. The children were beginning to complain about the cold.

As they walked up a deep gulley, they had little idea of which direction they were travelling. There were no footprints to give them any indication that they were on the right track. Paul found a sheltered place and told his family to wait; he would do a short foray forward to see if he could work out their location.

Each channel offered several offshoots, the majority of which lead him into dead ends. Then some offshoots had further junctions. Paul, in trying to retrace his steps, found that he had become completely disorientated and was soon following his own footsteps in the snow. He began to panic, almost running through the deep channels shouting out to his family as the wind howled above his head. It began to dawn on Paul that he was hopelessly lost. Forty yards away his family were huddled together against the biting wind and driving snow.

Mac and Val walked briskly, pushed along by the strong wind from the west. There was no problem. Mac was enjoying the challenge; they were both well versed in the conditions that Kinder can throw at you. The secret was familiarity and having the ability to read a map and compass. Mac's plan was to travel along the Kinder River bed and at some point to cut off and walk on a bearing for the top of Grindsbrook. Not as easy as it sounds though; it's necessary to cross gullies, some shallow some deep, but all steep and slippery. This was very tiring, but it was the most direct route. Any attempt to find the way by following the base of the gullies would be impossible.

Janet had guided Bill Staples to the top of the track and waved him on his way. She stood and watched as he descended the steep rocky outcrops which led to a well defined track some hundred feet below, and walked on rapidly down hoping to get to the Nag's Head public house in Edale before it closed.

Better get over to the Downfall. Janet said to herself. She hadn't seen Phil who reckoned that he would patrol the plateau between the brook and the Downfall. *Wonder where he's got to?* She mused. She retraced her steps to the point where she'd met Bill, then cut off right and made rapid progress and was soon on Seal Edge, looking over the Snake Pass. She stood looking at the view. It had been quite a while since her last trip over to this part of Kinder, and it always, even in good weather, felt remote and a bit forbidding. She could see that there was little traffic on the Pass, and from her elevated position she could see that there was no sign of any hikers heading on to the hill.

She breathed a sigh of relief. *Sensible people* she said to herself, *it's only idiots like us up here.* She quickly threw off her sack, rummaged in the pocket of the bag and pulled out a bar of chocolate, knowing that it would give her the energy she'd need. She wouldn't stop, she'd eat it on the move. *Right, direct to the Downfall.* She took out her OS map and compass and quickly plotted a bearing. *I should be there in half an hour* she told herself.

Phil Brown had forged a rapid path onto the plateau and made a bee-line, following the rocky base of the gulley, to a point where he knew he would have to leave and plough a furrow across the peat. He had done it a thousand times; he knew historically that if there was any trouble this would be where it was. A few minutes earlier he had been in radio contact with the Mountain Rescue team on the northern edge of the plateau, and they'd reported that there was no activity in their area. Phil asked them to stand by in case they were needed.

For the first time in his life, Paul began to feel real fear. He was lost, cold and tired; he had no idea what he should do now. His usual calm demeanour was being fractured... he was worried about his family. How would they manage? He hadn't seen any evidence of other people on the plateau. He felt helpless as the snowfall increased, driven by an increasingly violent wind. Desperation forced him to stand up and face into the wind, but he wasn't sure in which direction he should walk. Paul Bates began to panic, he felt light headed, he needed to sit down and rest for a minute.

Phil stopped; he thought he heard a strange sound, a child crying. *It can't be* he thought. He listened again; all he could hear was the sound of the wind tearing across the peat, pushing the bilberry and gorse in a crazy dance as the wind gusted around it.

Then he heard it again and strained to identify the direction the sound was coming from. He shouted loud. 'Hello,' he waited, 'hello.' Deep in the gully, not twenty yards away, Alison and the twins lay, covered in an orange plastic sheet. The wind howled and the snow swirled around them; they were getting very cold indeed. Alison was terrified; Paul had left them twenty minutes earlier and hadn't returned, so she began to think the worst. *Should we move or should we stay?* Keeley was painfully cold and let out loud shrieks as the numbness in her hands cleared momentarily and the pain returned. 'Hello-Hello.' She heard it quite clearly, Paul had found them. *He was back. OK thank god!* She stood upright, pulled back the hood of her jacket, the wind gripping her face as she called as loud as her voice could manage. 'Hello Paul, we're over here.' She looked up at the rim of the gully, ten feet above her head. She saw the red of the jacket and her heart sank. *That's not Paul* she thought.

Janet forced her way on the bearing, up and down the greasy channels. It was slow and exhausting walking. She reckoned maybe twenty minutes to the Downfall. Her radio crackled. *'Peakland Edale1 to Mountain Rescue, and Peakland Edale 3, how are you receiving over.'* Janet heard the instant response from the Edale Mountain Rescue team. *'Edale Rescue receiving you loud and clear, over.'* Janet pressed the button on her radio. *'Peakland Edale3 receiving you loud and clear also.'* Janet waited. The radio came to life again. *'Edale 1, I'm at SK 0873 8890. I've located a family of three, lost and in difficulty, a fourth member of the family is missing, I need you over to me ASAP at this GR over.'*

The leader of the mountain rescue team, Jack Greenstock, quickly plotted a course to Phil's location,. *'Edale Rescue to Edale 1, your message received we will be in your vicinity in 20 minutes over.'* Phil switched the radio. *'Thanks boys, look forward to seeing you.'* Janet had located Phil's grid reference on her map, and a line to walk to get to him. She called him. *'Peakland 3 to Peakland 1, Phil, if you like, what with the rescue team on the way to you, I'll work my way around, see if I can locate the missing family member, it may save a bit of time.'*

Mac was walking comfortably, Val close up behind him as they walked east. The snow being driven from the west was plastering the backs of their waterproofs. The wind prevented any conversation, and anyway Val wasn't in a mood to talk much. They rounded a curve in the gulley and saw a group of people with one large man in the familiar red jacket, *He's a Range,r* Mac thought. As they approached the group, Mac could see a small group of people huddled tight together wrapped in an orange plastic sheet. Phil heard their footfall and turned to face them. 'Hello, are you two lost?'

'No, we're fine,' Mac said, looking around at the group of people covered in plastic sheets.

Mac looked at the group and quickly realised that there were three people, one adult and two youngsters. 'Is everything OK, can we help?'

Phil looked at Mac. He quickly sized him up and realised that here was someone who could help. 'I reckon you can. I've got the Mountain Rescue making their way here, they'll be about fifteen minutes, and I have another Ranger who is, as we speak, searching east of here. The father wandered off about twenty minutes ago and hasn't returned.'

Mac quickly summed up the situation. 'I know this area well, how would it be if I left my wife Val with you, she can help with these people, she knows first aid, and I'll disappear east and see if I can help your colleague with the search?'

Phil breathed heavily, the trudge across the peat had taken it out of him. 'If you're happy to do that then do, but be careful, OK.'

Mac quickly scrambled to the top of the peat channel, trying to get a view of the surrounding terrain. He also hoped that he would spot the other Ranger. The snow was blinding. Mac opted to get back down into the channel, assuming that the missing walker would probably have taken as much shelter as possible from the wind.

Jack Greenstock and his team were carving a direct line toward the position Phil had given them. He had his team strung out in a line about ten yards apart, attempting to cover as much ground as possible on their way in. Andy Jackson had the rescue dog on a long leash, and the group were moving swiftly. They'd done this many times, but not often in such severe conditions. Jack called across to Andy. 'Why don't we let Jag off? Let him run about a bit, he may pick something up. 'This was more of a decision than a question. Andy, realising that the walker should be found, quickly let Jag loose from the lead. 'Go on Jag, find him, good boy.' The dog raced off along the snow-covered base of the gulley, occasionally springing up the side and diving over into another channel.

Chapter 5

Jake started his car and pulled up the stick to operate the wipers. The screen was flecked with heavy drops of rain. He peered up into the sky. Above the dark stone buildings he saw massive clouds coming. *Looks like the weather's going pear shaped* he thought.

On the drive home he churned the conversation he had just had with the girl through his mind. For sure she was attractive, in fact he believed he could quite fancy her. Or was it just the circumstances of their first meeting? Certainly it was emotional, meeting the girl he had almost died for. He noticed the way she looked at him, almost a desperate gratitude. It wasn't something that Jake wanted, but could understand where she was coming from. *Yeah, probably if somebody had rescued me, I'd be pretty pleased* he thought to himself.

The traffic was light as he made his way through the city centre. He passed close to the central Fire Station, and he saw the large red bay doors were swinging open. He saw two pumps and the turntable ladder pulling out onto the roundabout amid a cacophony of horns, wailers and flashing lights. He pulled up to allow them direct access onto the main drag, the wheels of the machines screeching as they took the small roundabout and headed off at speed, in a cloud of grey diesel fumes. *I wonder where they're off to?* He mused. Almost unconsciously he followed; they were going in his direction anyway. The machines sped off accelerating rapidly; soon they would hit the up slope of the city road.

Mark Devonshire was in the first pump, he fought to drag on his heavy fire gear as the machine dodged between cars and bollards. His heart pounded with anticipation, he was still excited by his new life.

Central was busy, and Mark was settling in well in his new life and loved what he was now doing.

'Jacko and Mark, get rigged, it looks like we've got a job.' Mark lowered his head to get a view forward through the windscreen. He saw a plume of black smoke boiling out of the steelworks' roof, and his heart raced. 'When we get there, let's have a jet out fast; put your tallies in the board, no hanging about. Chas, you chase them up with water and let's have the hydrant in quick as you like.' No one spoke, just focused on what they would have to do in the next sixty seconds.

'Right, let's go,' Station Officer George Collier shouted as the appliance pulled up sharply, close to the burning factory. The old large brick building housed a vast amount of machinery, oil tanks and the paraphernalia of the steel making industry. George was met by a suited manager, who informed him that a large oil tank was alight and the flames were threatening the building next door. The smoke, driven low by the weather, was rolling low across the roads and railway lines which fed the city and was causing traffic chaos.

George peered into the building, its dirt floor encrusted with grease from a hundred years of traffic. He peered under the layer of oily smoke.

'Christ almighty,' he called, 'you two, back to the machine, high pressure hose reels here quick.' The words spat out and hit Mark who almost jumped. *Oil fire, hose reel? He must be joking* Mark thought.

'Chas; George here, I want the other crews here, I want four high pressure hose reels up here now. OK.' George spat into his hand held radio.

'Will do boss, will have to use the crew off the TL, will that be OK over?'

'Chas, I don't care how you do it, just you grab the O.I.C of the other pump and get it sorted, don't hang about.'

George looked at his BA men. 'Don't suppose you've ever done this, Devo?' He said, using Mark's new name on the watch.

'What are we going to do boss?' Mark asked nervously.

'We're going to put this fire out the old fashioned way, I think you'll like it,' he said, a wicked smile crossing his lips. 'Just hold on until the other three hose reels get here then we'll sort this bugger out.'

Mark stared incredulously. Inside the factory was a fire, larger than any fire he had ever seen, raging and crackling, almost like fireworks exploding, and he was going to put it out with a hose reel. He had a lot of respect for the boss who, after nearly thirty years in the job and an old timer, still thought that some of the old methods were better. The boss sometimes had difficulty adapting to the modern methods that the job now required. A minute later a group of men, wearing BA and flash hoods to protect them, were ready. Some of the group were experienced men, which gave Mark confidence.

'Look now boys.' George said. 'Just quickly for the benefit of the new boys, this is what we're gunna do.'

Jake sat in his car across the road from the blazing factory, wishing that he were in there. He realised that Mark was on duty. *Lucky buggers*, Jake thought.

The snow was blinding as the team headed south, and Jag the search dog was covering the area fast.

'Stop, listen a minute.' Jack Greenstock had heard Jag barking excitedly.

Paul Bates had lost the feeling in his hands. At some point a glove had come off, he'd tried to find a place which offered him some relief from the driving snow, but this was impossible. So, out of sheer tiredness, he had laid with his back to the wind, and had gone to sleep exhausted. He stirred, his face felt warm and wet, and consciousness began to force its way into his brain. *What the hell's going on* he thought, as he opened the lashes of his eyes with difficulty. Snow had been driven into his face and covered his eyes. He heard a dog bark and saw black and white flash across the front of his face, he heard the bark again and then the face of a dog up close to his, its warm pink tongue licking his cheek. Paul Bates began to understand what was happening to him. Within seconds a group of men had surrounded him. They pulled blankets around him and gave him warming tea. Paul's head began to clear; he remembered his family and began to panic. 'My wife and children are here somewhere, has anybody found them?' he pleaded.

'Ranger Edale 1 from Mountain Rescue over.'

Phil heard the call sign and pressed the button of his radio. *'Go ahead, Jack, over.'*

'Yeah Phil, we've found the missing husband, he's OK, but a bit cold, we're warming him up, should be with you in a few minutes, over.'

'Thanks Jack, well done. His family will be relieved to hear that, out.'

Paul Bates was cold, he'd never felt so exposed. He'd made a mistake and he knew it, and had found a new respect for Kinder Scout. It was a lesson he would never forget. His overwhelming feeling was one of relief and gratitude to the men who'd found him.

'Don't worry, we've got your wife and children, they're fine. You'll be with them in a minute, then we'll get you off the hill, so don't worry,' Jack said to Paul, patting him gently on the shoulder.

'Right boys, you're clear what we're doing?' George said to the crews.

'Yes gaffer,' they nodded, the youngsters looking apprehensive. George had arranged each team so that each young fire-fighter was paired with a more experienced older hand.

'Remember lads, if you're positive and brave, this fire will be out in twenty seconds, OK?' The crews nodded again. 'Right let's get to it, just wait for me to give the word.'

The four teams, each of two men, found their position, each team covering one corner of the huge rectangular tank. The heat was intense; forcing them low beneath the worst of the heat and the filthy black smoke that rolled from the boiling surface of the oil.

The pump operator, Chas Brewer, waited for the word. When the order came he would hammer down the throttle and deliver gallons of high pressure water to the hose reels. Forty bars; six hundred pounds of pressure per square inch, the velocity of the water will have a very rapid cooling effect, and turn the oil into an incombustible emulsion. But this was a technique which had long since been superseded by more modern techniques. George however was not modern, and he had not been superseded; he thought it would be a nice interesting thing for the young lads on the watch to experience.

George stood by his crews. He had sight of Chas on the pump. Chas had spotted George raise his right arm above his head. George pressed the button on his radio, *'Chas you ready, on my signal; go.'* He dropped his arm, Chas slammed down the throttle, the engine screamed, the thick black rubber of the hose reels which ran twisting into the factory tensed and straightened as the pressure blasted its way up the tubes. He signalled to his crews. 'OK boys, set the spray on the nozzle.' George once again dropped his arm. 'Hit it,' he shouted, and went up close behind one of the teams. Simultaneously, all four teams lifted the spray and turned them vertically onto the oil, which by now raged in the tank. The water instantly became a vast cloud of boiling steam as it pounded the bubbling surface of the oil. Each team crouched low and walked slowly towards their counterpart at the other end of the tank. The oil sizzled and spat, the flame recoiled in shock, overpowered by steam and the high-powered water forcing its way into the oil. The teams met in the middle having covered the whole of the tank's surface with the cooling spray. In less than ten seconds the fire was out. Mark looked, amazed, at the surface of the oil tank: the flame had gone, the oil was still dangerously hot. It bubbled and spat as the water, which had been forced below the oil's surface, boiled, expanded as it turned to steam, and blew out droplets of boiling oil

'Right lads, well done, make up two of the reels,' George said to his crews, a broad grin splitting his craggy features, 'we'll keep the other two here for now to help cool the tank.'

Mark stood completely bemused; he had never in his life seen anything remotely like it. He looked across at the boss, who seemed oblivious to what Mark was feeling. Mark's heart raced; the other rookies all seemed to be in a state of euphoria, whereas the older hands that had seen it all before looked at their younger counterparts and chuckled. Old Jack Blakemoor, who had done it many times, twenty nine years at the same station on the same watch and for most of the time with the same boss, slapped his filthy gloved hand on Mark's shoulder. 'Now that's a bit of proper fire fighting, like in the olden days, none of the Health and Safety then lad.'

Mark turned his head to face Jack who, since his arrival at his first station, had taken Mark under his wing. Mark spluttered. 'That was fantastic, I was almost crapping myself when the gaffer said hose reels, I couldn't believe it. It was just fantastic.' Mark was almost breathless with incredulity.

'You just listen to the boss and us older hands, we'll point you in the right direction. There's a lot to learn, even I'm still learning, but isn't it good fun?'

'You can say that again, I absolutely loved it, I can't wait now for the next one.' Mark's chest heaved with satisfaction and relieved stress. He looked around for his pals from the watch who were in a tight group laughing, all bursting in awe at what they had just achieved.

Across the road a hundred yards away, Jake sat in his car. He'd watched the action from afar, men scuttling at speed running out hose, the black oily smoke, the flames leaping skyward, then suddenly it was gone. No smoke, no flame, only vast clouds of steam. *What's happened there then?* Jake mused, surprised that such a large dangerous looking fire had just evaporated, into thin air. *I'll go round and have a chat with Mark tonight* he said to himself.

The group of rescuers had formed a plan to get the family off the hill. Phil and Janet were to help the children across the plateau, Mac and Val were to help the mother and Paul, who was feeling tired and a little embarrassed. They'd also be supported by the Mountain Rescue team. The snow was beginning to drift and visibility had worsened. Phil and Janet would lead, walking as much as possible on a bearing for the edge of the escarpment. This would be tough walking, but they'd decided it would be the quickest and safest way to get everyone down from the hill. As the group began forging their route across the plateau, the wind increased and the snow quickly got deeper. Phil reckoned that if there were no major problems ahead they would be out of trouble in about forty minutes. They soon reached the point in the stream bed where they had to cut to the east and take a direct line. This would mean a lot of difficult terrain to be crossed and a lot of encouragement to keep the youngsters going.

Phil stopped and got the group together. The wind howled and the temperature was falling rapidly, so he realised the need for speed.

'Now look, the next half hour is going to be tough, but trust us, just stay with us, and it will be OK.' The kids pulled their hoods tighter over their heads and nodded.

'Right, let's do it.' Phil shouted into the wind, a broad grin splitting his face, more to reassure the children than a feeling of certainty that all would be well; he knew Kinder and just what it was capable of. Janet looked at him and though all of the things she had heard about Phil were true. *He's something else,* she thought.

Mac and Val were close behind; the walking was hard but Mac was in his element. Even Val had taken on board the good fortune of their being in the right place at the right time.

'Are you OK, Alison?' Mac turned and asked. Alison looked up, relief etched in her face that somehow they were all going to be alright. She'd felt sick at the prospect of her husband being lost, it had been the hardest thing to bear. The feeling of absolute helplessness and her inability to help her family had brought home just how vulnerable they had all been.

'I'm fine Mac, thanks to you all, we're all so grateful, we'll never forget today.'

The Mountain Rescue team were on autopilot, one man in the lead watching the compass, the others supporting Paul as he half walked half stumbled across the rapidly whitening and freezing plateau.

Phil began to recognise the ground now; they had bisected the plateau and met the main artery leading onto the plateau from Grindsbrook. He looked around, he could see that about three inches of snow coated the ground, *No one else around* he thought, *not a single footprint in the snow, not often you can say that; the plan to keep people off the hill had worked.* Minutes later they had reached the edge of the hill, the snow wasn't falling so heavily. Lower down the eastern slope, the visibly was clear.

Everyone breathed a sigh of relief. It had been an interesting few hours and there were no real casualties, just Paul Bates whose pride had taken a massive blow. He'd always prided himself on his ability to manage the conditions and look after the well being of his family. Today had been a big lesson; he'd learned that sometimes things go badly wrong and they hadn't survived because of his efforts, but because of the courage and hard work of others. He would always be grateful, but had told himself that it would make them all the more determined to master all the elements needed to manage the environment, *We will be back up here, next summer,* he said to himself.

An hour and a half later they were all in the village of Edale. The Bates family, grateful for the efforts of the Rangers and the Mountain Rescue service, had recovered sufficiently enough for them to leave and go to their cottage. Mac and Val, and Phil and Janet, sat quietly in the bar of the Nag's Head, relieved that the day hadn't proved even more serious.

'Thanks for your help up there Mac, you both made life easier for us. It seems that you know the terrain pretty well?'

'Yeah we've been going up for years, I thought today would be interesting, and so it proved,' Mac said wistfully.

Val looked at him and smiled. 'Yes Mac, next time you want to drag me up there, I think I'll be busy washing my hair.'

Phil tapped his glass on the bar. 'Right, it's my round, as a way of thanking you for your help, what can I get you?' he said, a broad smile creasing his face.

'Nothing for me,' Val said, 'I think the excitement of today has got to me, I feel a bit light headed, so no thanks.'

'Not for me either,' Mac said, 'back on duty in the morning, wouldn't want to be drunk in charge of a fire engine.'

Phil looked at Mac. 'I just knew there was something about you . . . . A fire fighter, it figures, most people in the conditions we were in up there would have had a problem. I thought you looked pretty unfazed by it all.'

'Well I suppose being in the brigade I'm used to dealing with stress, so it's not a problem, and in a funny way I enjoy the test.'

Janet spoke up. 'We could do with your type in the Rangers. We need people who know and love the Peaks. Things are a bit stretched these days, like me today doing an extra shift, because Edale were short,' she said, looking across at Phil and grinning.

Mac's brain clicked. Val spotted it, a sort of quizzical look crossed Mac's face, she'd seen it before, and realised straight away that Mac's interest had been roused.

'It's not something I've ever considered; I've always been too busy at work and doing the house up, but I retire soon so I'll have to give it some thought. Yes, that could be quite interesting,' he said.

Janet put her hand on Mac's arm. 'If you fancy it, you could have a wander around with me on one of my patrols. I do every other Sunday usually about fifteen miles, I reckon you'd both enjoy it.'

Val looked at Mac. She could sense that he'd been enthused by the prospect. 'Why don't you, Mac, I think you'd love it. It would be ideal for you, I quite fancy it myself,'she said, smiling at him. They sat comfortably in the pub, talking about the day's events and the prospect of Mac and Val joining the Ranger service. 'So are you on duty next Sunday, Janet?'

'Yes, I'll be going out of Brunt's Barn at Grindleford.'

'How about it then, me and Val, walk part of the day with you, just to get a taste of what you do?' Mac said enthusiastically.

'Yeah, that would be fine, I'll just have to clear it with the boss at Brunt's, Stan Gregg, he's a crusty old so and so, but I'm sure it won't be a problem.'

Mac and Val climbed into their car. A light sprinkling of snow was settling on the ground, their breath creating clouds of vapour around them.

'It's a good job those folk got off the hill this morning, it would be a more serious prospect if they were up there now. Reckon it's a good three or four degrees colder than when we went into the pub.' Mac pulled the car gingerly out of the station car park and headed carefully along the narrow winding road. He glanced up to his right and looked at the Mam Tor Ridge, its slopes glistening white as the snow settled along its length, the summit obliterated by thick low lying clouds.

'Next day off that might be a nice walk along the ridge, what do you reckon?' he said, looking at Val.

'Tell you what I reckon, I'll definitely be washing my hair, you do it if you want,' she said, punching his left shoulder.

Chapter 6

George Collier slumped into the padded armchair he'd installed in his first floor office, He figured that at his age he deserved a bit of comfort. He'd left the crews to sort out the machines and dirty gear; his Sub Officer was sorting out the paperwork from the job. It was George's style to give his lads their head, let them have some responsibility, that's how he was trained and how he matured to become an officer. He loved all of his lads; if he got one he didn't like for whatever reason he didn't stay long. George was not a man to mince his words or suffer fools.

He rested his head on the back of the well-worn armchair, closed his eyes, and let his mind drift. His time was coming to an end. He wasn't overly sad about it; he had always loved the job, but things had changed. It wasn't as free and easy as it used to be; now he felt stifled by regulation. Sometimes he would break free, as he had today, and put the fire out the old way. The new way was just as efficient but much less exciting. George knew that if the boss heard about it he'd be in for a bollocking, but over the years George had had so many that they had little impact. He thought about the early days and some of his buddies. Some, in fact most, were now retired, or even dead. His old gaffer Billy Brett, a one off, an absolute madman, had the nickname Barmy Brett. The guys loved him, he was fearless, irreverent and had an easy way with the women, but was a hell of a fire-fighter. He died two weeks after he retired, the demon drink finally getting him. His funeral was the wildest the brigade had ever seen. Some of the boys screwed a Tetley's Ale sign to the side of his coffin, in line with his wishes, and his ashes were scattered in the garden of the Red Lion Pub, Billy's favourite watering hole.

He remembered shifts with Mac James. They were always in trouble with the gaffer; they spent a lot of time together doing a window cleaning round on their days off to make ends meet. They both served at Darnall Road station; even then Jack Blakemoor was on the watch. Jack was a steady man and completely without ambition. He liked his job and plodded along in his own comfort zone; he seemed to have followed George around. George was happy about that. Jack was steady and sat quietly in the background, but George knew if you needed someone to trust your life with, he was the one. He never lied and had never been heard to swear, which was a rarity on the watch. He never spoke behind anyone's back, although if he had a problem with anyone he'd tell them in his own quiet way, directly to their face. They knew you didn't argue with Jack.

He missed those days. Life was fun. These days things were so much more serious with Health and Safety rules, and George didn't like it.

'Do you want a cuppa George?' The words swiftly brought him back to reality. 'They've made the tea on the mess deck, but if you want I'll get one of the guys to bring it up here for you.' George pulled his hands across his brow stretching the tension from his body.

'No I'll come down for it, Jack, it'll give me a chance to have a chat with the lads before we knock off.'

'OK boss, I'll tell the boys to put a couple of sausages in for your break.'

Jake was exhausted. It had been a strange day, and nothing had gone the way he'd expected. Meeting the girl had been a worry and it had brought up the trauma of a few months ago. All the painful memories, the fear that he was about to die, but on the plus side he'd met the girl again and it made him feel proud. He was now living a life where, if he did well and worked hard, he'd have an impact. That would mean something, something much more important than mixing cement and hauling bricks. He breathed in deeply, shaking off the negatives from the meeting, his mind quickly switching to the job he'd seen Central attend. It had looked like a great job and Jake, like any firefighter, wanted to go to big fires. He reminded himself to ring Mark and get the lowdown.

'Jacob, your tea's ready.' His mother's warm voice brought him back to the present, and he could smell onions. *Hope she's got some liver with that*, he thought, as he tripped lightly down the stairs.

The night was dark, Mark's mind was filled with the images of the fire, and he was tired; a tiredness borne out of tension rather than physical stress. He slowly drifted into a deep sleep.

He was in the appliance; the boss in the front was twisting to pull on his fire coat. His crewmates alongside him were chattering as they slipped on their BA sets. He heard the sudden sound of the whistle as the air to the sets was turned on. He could hear the clinking of the equipment as it rattled in its housings in the cab. Every sound was in sharp relief, he felt the sweat dripping down his face; stress he reckoned. How would he perform? He heard the guys talking about oil fires and how they can go wrong, then he thought about the gear the boss would tell him to get. He did the mental exercise, his mind visualising the content of each locker. Will I be up to it? This was unlike anything he'd experienced before. He could see the plume of black smoke in the distance; he felt his heart racing and the sense of anxiety which seemed to paralyse his body. The boss was laid back, relaxed, talking quietly into the radio. He could hear the flames as they crackled, spitting out boiling oil. He felt terror in his heart, he was scared, more scared than any of his time in the Navy. He'd done fire fighting on board ship but this was different, this fire was like a huge uncontrolled monster. He felt the searing heat even through his anti flash hood, but the boss was unconcerned. Mark's mind swirled. 'Right Devo, this is what I want you to do. You're going to put water on the fire, OK?'

Mark's stomach churned. Water on the fire, that's bloody stupid, even I know that will kill me. I'm not doing it, he can sod off, bollocks to it, don't know if I want this job anymore, working with a stupid old fool like that. I'm not going to let him kill me; I've got a family, doesn't he realise that? I'm going tell the idiot.

He saw his mates in the distance, crouching. There were long tongues of red flame erupting from the tank, creating orange sheets above their heads. He saw the gaffer pointing across at him, his mates turned towards him and laughed.

'Typical Southerner, no balls, scared he'll mess his hair up,' he could hear them shouting over the roar of the burning oil. 'You just stay where you are you big southern puffta, we'll manage without you.'

There was a loud crack and a massive eruption; a volcano of burning, boiling oil spat high into the air and descended in a thick black burning soup over his crewmates. They were silent, their blackened bodies burning; eight blackened piles of charred clothing.

Why are you here and your mates are over there, Mark? Why is that? He turned, it was his wife, she's somehow found out and followed the appliance. Mark was wracked with guilt, how did this happen? It's my fault, I should have been there for them; maybe it would have been OK if I'd been there to help. I'm going over now. He said this to his wife, guilt wracking every fibre in his body.

A bloody bit late now isn't it, they're all dead, and you stood here watching, some hero you are, I'm leaving you, and I'm taking the baby, I don't want him knowing his dad was a bloody coward.

He walked; almost stumbled across to the devastated area, his eyes sore and filled with tears. These guys were my life, and I let them down. I'll have to leave the job and get work where nobody knows me.

He stood close by the smoking remains of his watch. He looked down and saw the blackened face of Jack Blakemoor, the old hand. He'd been to hundreds of oil fires and survived them all, until he came onto the watch. He felt a surge of pain and grief, and suddenly he was sobbing like a baby. Through the tears he could see Jack's face. The eyes opened and then winked, a broad smile appeared, his mouth moved. We got you there Devo, the mouth said. The best wind up for ages. He looked around, the black smoking bodies were all standing up and laughing. He looked across at his wife. She waved and laughed, and he realised it was a joke. He hadn't failed, he was happy again. Then he was on the floor as the fire raged above his head. The pain he felt in his legs paralysed him. He was afraid to move, but he had to move or die. The timber floor he lay on was burning, but he couldn't move because, the heavy beam had him trapped by his legs. The low-pressure warning whistle on his BA set was blowing; he knew if he was to survive, something needed to happen soon.

Hang on in there, Mark; I'll have you out in a sec. It was Jake. Where did you come from Jake?

We came in on the first make up message. We know you central crowd can't handle these tricky jobs without us. Mark felt faint. He could see blood seeping from the top of his boots. I'm gunna die, he thought.

Listen to me you silly southern sod, I know what you're thinking and it's not gonna happen. You'll be OK, trust me, have I ever let you down? Jake said. You just need a bit of determination. Remember on the tests at training school, when you thought you'd had it, you found it from somewhere. Well this is another of those days. You'll be OK because I'll make it OK.

OK Jake, Mark agreed just before passing out.

Mark was floating above the fire. He could see himself pinned down by the huge beam, and he could see Jake who was taking his own BA set off and putting the mask over his face. He saw Jake scramble around, coughing and swearing. Among the rubble which covered the room, Jake found a large baulk of timber. He had a plan, he just hoped it would work; he hoped he had the strength.

Mark looked down. Jake had used the timber as a lever and somehow got rubble under the beam, which was holding Mark's legs. It gave enough leverage to give him space to drag Mark out. The smoke was thick; he could hear Jake coughing and spitting out mucus. Come on you silly sod this isn't the time to give up, get a grip, Jake shouted to himself. I need you to help me, Mark. Mark looked on like a spectator at a football game. Jake had dragged Mark out from under the beam; he now just needed to move him to a safer place. The timber floor was on fire. It creaked and groaned under the impact of the heat. Jake stood beside Mark and grabbed the BA set waist strap and part lifted part dragged Mark's limp body across the floor toward the door, which would take them to the staircase and safety. The floor screeched, the wall began to fall outward and the floor began to *collapse. Flames poured through the floor, engulfing Mark and Jake. Then silence. Mark looked dispassionately down at the gaping hole in the floor. He realised he was dead and his great friend had died trying to save him.*

Mark's wife was disturbed. She turned over in bed to face him. He was sweating and talking gibberish, and suddenlysat bolt upright in bed, was crying and shouting.

'No, no not Jake, not Jake.'

Mark felt an arm around his neck, and a soft voice found its way into his tired brain.

'Come on love, it's OK, you're at home with us, you're dreaming.'

Consciousness slowly began to penetrate his head, *I'm not dead, I'm at home, thank Christ,* he thought.

As Mark lay there, his mind ran through the dream. He'd spoken to Jake earlier in the evening, Jake had rung and told him that he'd followed the machine to the fire, and how he was a lucky sod, picking up a good job like that. Mark told him about it, and the unconventional methods of his governor, how he'd been terrified but elated, and how the older guys had dealt with it so nonchalantly. He remembered how his heart had quickened just telling the story to Jake. Obviously this was the source of the frightening dream that had just woken him from his sleep.

Mark slept better now. The dream seemed to have disposed of the fear, stress or tension he'd felt at the fire. Trish lay quietly by his side, unable to get back to sleep and more worried about Mark than she was prepared to admit.

The room was still dark when the alarm rang waking them up, Mark stretched out, still feeling tired after the disturbance to his sleep, Trish turned to face him and put her arm across his waist. 'How are you this morning?' she asked, looking at his tired face.

Mark smiled. 'I'm fine, I think the job yesterday was such a surprise it had obviously played on my mind; I feel a bit of a wimp now.'

'You're no wimp, but if you have any worries about work, you've said how good the boss is, have a chat with him.'

'Yes, maybe I'll do that,' he replied.

Chapter 7

Pete Jacks resisted the sound of the beeping from the alarm clock for a while before finally giving up the fight to remain unconscious. He was shattered; his wife Trudy, ill with multiple sclerosis, had needed him several times in the night, and the effect of broken sleep had left him drained. For years he'd worked as a fire-fighter, managing to survive on little sleep, doing extra jobs to try to make ends meet. The cost of getting the car adapted and child care when he was at work had left them on a very tight budget. Today he had just about had enough, and he could see no end to it.

For months now Red Watch had been his salvation. They'd changed his life in so many ways; he now loved his work. Both he and his Trudy, for the first time, felt part of the fire brigade family. The guys had supported him and made him welcome on the watch, they'd pulled him up to their standard by his boot straps, and he was so grateful to them all.

The pounding in his head made him feel for a second that he could go sick, have the day with his wife and relax for a change, but this new philosophy had grabbed him; he'd be letting the boys down. A feeling of guilt rolled over him, *I* couldn't *do that* he thought. He clambered out of bed as his wife looked across at him

'Are you OK love?' she asked.

'I'm fine, I'm just a bit tired, I'll be alright when I get going.'

Pete loved his wife, nothing was too much trouble, but Trudy could see the toll it was having on him and she felt the pain of guilt. This wasn't what she wanted or expected when they got married and started a family. It in no way met her expectations, but she and Pete were close. Not once had he given the slightest inclination that her condition was any trouble to him. Pete went to work, did the shopping and did his other job. He sorted the kids out, Pete was a great husband, and her guilt became even harder to bear.

'What's on the agenda at work today, love?' she asked. It's not a question she would have asked a couple of months ago, but since Pete had moved station he seemed different somehow; different in all sorts of ways. He got up earlier, ironed his shirt, polished his shoes, shaved, and he was also more attentive to her. She asked him what had changed, and he told her that he felt re-born; the new station with new mates and a new philosophy. He was a changed man, and he could not be happier.

'I'm not sure, but you can bet Mac will have something up his sleeve. I'm the cook today, so it will be Shepherd's Pie. It's about the only thing I can cook. They seemed to like it last time, so I'll be out shopping first thing.'

Pete slumped out of bed, stretched, and went into the kids' bedrooms to get them out of bed. 'Luke, Jason, up you get, time for school.'

Clive Botham turned over in bed and gazed at his fiancé, the sheets stretched across her expanding waistline. She was four months pregnant and he was going to be a Dad. He was terrified and excited in equal measures. Helen was always telling him to relax but he couldn't, he could only focus on what would happen in about twenty weeks time. He turned over towards her and let his arm lay gently across her stomach, feeling her breathing, looking at her face. She looked lovely, blooming and relaxed, he rolled back and slid quietly out of bed, then padded silently on the new carpet downstairs. He filled the kettle and stood looking out into their garden waiting for the kettle to boil. The ground had a thin coating of frost. Two blackbirds sat patiently huddled on the low branch of a tree in the garden. They'd become accustomed to being fed scraps of bread and bacon fat most mornings, so Clive knew that the second he put out the food the birds would descend and begin the feast, pecking frantically trying to gulp down the booty before other birds realised what was on offer.

He moved silently back up the stairs and put a mug of tea on her bedside cabinet, standing for a moment to watch her breathe, her blonde, shoulder length hair spread untidily across her pillow. He leaned forward, gently stroked her forehead, and kissed her on the cheek.

Taff felt unusually light. He'd woken early, and was somehow different- he knew why. For years, his and his wife's lives had been dominated by the desire to have a family. They'd tried almost everything and it hadn't happened for them. It caused them a lot of pain, worry and stress, and worst of all it was beginning to form a barrier between him and his wife. It had got to the point where he doubted his own masculinity. Soon, a rift began to form, and in desperation they sat down and had a heart to heart talk and said all that was on their minds; things which had gone unsaid for a long time. They'd spoken to Mac and Val whilst out together for a meal. The consensus was that as important as having a family was, it shouldn't be allowed to destroy their life. Maybe fostering would be a sensible route to try. After a long and painful discussion, and several pints of bitter, it was deemed to be a good idea, something that they'd look into. Suddenly the pressure was off and Taff looked forward to going to work today.

Jock Mclean was up early; his son Fraser was now in serious training for the young Blades and had somehow managed, much to his mother's surprise, to get his dad out two mornings a week for a forty minute training session in the local park. Jock was also surprised; he had thought that he would hate it, but found the opposite. He enjoyed every minute. OK he jogged whilst Fraser ran, but the session always ended with a kick about with a football and a gentle warm down. The other benefit was the relationship between Jock and his son. Once fractious, it was now healthy and very slightly competitive, but overlaying it was a realisation of mutual love and respect.

Maddie was coming to the end of night shift. It had been busy, but now she was going home for three days of rest. She needed it; it had been hectic, several new patients had been admitted into her ward. She'd recently moved into a new phase of her career, and she now worked in the coronary care unit. It had five bays with six beds in each bay. There were very elderly men who were mostly pretty sick needing a lot of nursing, and then a younger group, some serious some not, but all needing her time during her shift. After the initial surge at the start of the shift, doing observations, taking blood and blood pressure, her time then was mainly spent attending the more serious cases, issuing medicines, changing sheets, sometimes sitting by a bed holding a hand and talking and re-assuring the patients; being a surrogate friend. She found it very satisfying and rewarding. She gained great pleasure seeing her sick patients improve, smiles coming on their faces, and sometimes listening to their worries or a joke. She loved it, but she was now ready for a rest.

Jim had turned his life around. It seemed a long time since, as a security guard, he became bored and disillusioned with his life to the point where he experimented with the life of an arsonist. He was lucky. He got away with it, no one was killed, and he was never caught. He breathed a sigh of relief; had he not met Madeline in the pub at Edale, he was sure things would have been very different had fate not smiled on him that wonderful day.

Now prompted by her, he'd resigned from his job as a Security Guard and had enrolled on a course which would give him a basic qualification in Plumbing. He enjoyed the work and the learning. He spent time with men of his own age who wanted to learn; something that he never experienced during his life at school.

Maddie was the love of his life. He'd never understood why she liked him, but she did, and this had propelled him into another life. She gave him purpose, ambition, and a reason to achieve; something that he would never have considered before. Every weekend, when Maddie was available, they drove out into Derbyshire and walked. Sometimes they would walk for just two or three miles, and sometimes he would sort out a route that would have them walking all day, maybe ten or twelve miles. He liked the challenge of working out the routes from the OS maps, always with the intention of making them interesting. Part of Jim's style was to read up about the areas they were going so he could tell Maddie facts about the areas they were in.

Jim lay in bed. Recently he'd been up early at weekends ready for their weekly walk, but today Maddie had to catch up on her sleep. He was sure that within the next half hour his phone would ring. It would be her, his life and the focus of his being; she would almost certainly say something that would make him laugh. Laughter was a commodity he'd not found much use for in years. Then along came the Mad woman and shone a light into his little world and turned it upside down. She gave him love and gave his life some purpose where none had previously existed. She'd made the boy into a man; Jim now saw life with a new maturity. Suddenly he was studying in an attempt to get a career, having abandoned his previous life. He read books, mainly about the Peaks, but this was all very different from his life just a few months ago, and he relished every minute of it. However, all of this was insignificant when compared to the earth shattering events which took them both by surprise. After a walk in the hills and their first real intimacy, things changed. It was serious, and he knew Maddie wouldn't just get casually involved with anyone. The realisation that this relationship, love, he had, was the real thing for her also, the gravity of it all, had somehow invigorated him; motivated him into a new phase of effort. He hoped for achievement, he now felt that he was a worthwhile human being. She didn't deserve a waster in her life, she deserved a good man, and he was determined to become one.

Chapter 8

Mac pulled the Volvo into the station yard; he saw that the night crew were still out on a shout. He grabbed his bag and sauntered into the watch room. The Tele-printer message was there, it had sent the crew to a house fire on a nearby estate. *It looks like they'll be in for a bit of overtime* Mac thought, thumbing through the station log book. *Phew they've had a busy night, six shouts, and all fires, just like the old days* Mac chuckled to himself.

The watch room phone rang, it was control. 'Hi, Mac,' the control operator said. 'When you get your crew in, will you get over to this job and relieve them.'

'Yeah will do, I'm the only one here at the moment, I'll call you when we're mobile,' Mac replied. Fifteen minutes later Red Watch were all present; they'd clambered into the station van and were en- route to relieve the night crew.

They pulled the van up behind a row of shops just off the High Street; the atmosphere was heavy with the damp smell of smouldering wood and cloth, and there was a fine fog of blue smoke and steam drifting above the neighbouring shops. The night crew were turning over saturated cardboard and piles of charred wood and paper; they all looked weary and jaded.

'Hi Alan,' Mac called to the Officer in Charge of Blue Watch. 'Looks like you've had a busy shift?'

'Yeah, been up and down all night, we're all pretty knackered now. It'll be good to get home and get some sleep.'

'Have you got a cause yet?' Mac asked.

'Well it's supposition, but they've had a few problems with vandals lately; they've been firing rubbish at the back of the shops, we came down last tour and told the shopkeeper to keep his excess rubbish locked away until collection day, but I reckon the kids have put burning paper through a broken window. Anyway, the damage is pretty extensive, but we caught it before it got into the roof space and the other shops, a good stop I think.'

'Yeah reckon you're right; if it'd got into the roof you could have lost the lot.'

Alan and Mac did a quick tour of the shop; Mac could see what still needed doing. He called his crew. 'Right guys, let's take over and get cracking. OK Alan, I have it, you and your boys get away.'

Pete was sweating. The shop was still hot and steamy, he was working, turning the hot debris over with a large rake. Mick Young was damping down with a hose reel and steam engulfed them both.

'Phew, it's like a bloody sauna here,' Pete called, as he wiped the black stained sweat from his forehead. Mick laughed and coughed.

'We should be grateful, it'd cost a packet if we had to pay for this down at the massage parlour.' Pete leaned heavily on the handle of the rake. 'It'd be worth it, the staff there are better looking than Jock and Taff.'

'You're right there, perhaps we should go and have a look sometime.'

'It'd be nice, but I don't know what the wife would think of that,' Pete said with a wry smile creasing his face.

Mac lifted the radio hand set. *'Control from Alpha zero one zero over.'*

The female controller's voice came back. *'Alpha zero one zero go ahead over.'*

'Alpha zero one zero stop message. From Sub Officer James; stop for the same address, a two storey shop, ground floor severely damaged by fire, first floor damaged by smoke, two BA, one jet and one hose reel.'

'Alpha zero one zero your message received, out.'

'Right guys let's get back to station and get ourselves fed and watered.'

Jock pushed hard on the throttle and soon skimmed through the gears. 'Your wish is my command, leader,' he said as he flew around the round-about at the end of Graveton high street.

Red watch sat around the mess table. Mugs of coffee and a pile of bacon sandwiches dripping with brown sauce were being devoured at record speed.

'What were you up to at the weekend, Jock?' Mac asked.

'I took Fraser to football, he's doing well, he scored the winner; I'm really pleased how it's going for him.'

'He's turning out to be a good lad,' Mac replied, 'you'll have to let us know when his next game is; we'll all come and watch, give him a bit of support.'

'Yeah I'll do that, he'd like to see you guys anyway, he still remembers you from when he was a kid, dressing up as Father Christmas at the kid's party.'

'Don't remind me, the damned beard was too small and it kept falling off.'

'Yeah and the trousers were split at the crotch, we all had a good laugh,' Taff said.

'Right you lot, let's get out, get the cylinders recharged and there's loads of hose to wash, and Jock, let's give the machine a good clean. I've a report to do.'

Chapter 9

Alan Goodchild had farmed all of his life, his father before him had started it up. He'd drifted into farming having lost his job in the steel-works. He'd seen the job advertised, so walked the six miles to ask the farmer if he could have the job. He got it, and after many years he bought his own small holding which has grown into what it is now, a small farm concentrating on crops. Potatoes and cabbages mainly, also a few hens and a couple of pigs. When his father retired, Alan took over the farm and his life seemed settled; he had a wife and two children to support. It was hard work with long hours, but there was a lot of joy when he saw how his two girls loved life on the farm. His wife Jules would take the girls to school, and then she'd be home running the house and sorting out the chickens.

He'd had the usual busy day, sorting out the tractor's brakes, replacing a broken window in the barn, and then he'd driven into town to get animal feed. His last job before the night came in was to take the tractor to the bottom field and bring up the trailer and put it in the barn. Then he could relax. Jules would be getting the dinner ready, the kids would be doing their homework, and he was ready for a rest.

In the dim light, he picked out the track back to the house in the headlights of the tractor, the puddles of water were now frozen solid in the holes in the track, a mist was developing, and he felt the chill of the winter evening through his heavy jacket.

Mac jogged lightly down the stairs from his office along the corridor and through the swing doors into the appliance room. The boys were finishing off the day by leathering the machines and mopping the bay floors.

'Good job boys, leave it sparkling for the Blue Crew.'

Jock looked across at Mac and grinned, 'yeah, just like they leave it for us- not!'

'Yeah well,' Mac said, 'that's why the Reds are the best; the standard setters.' He laughed and turned to leave. Then there was the clunk, then the lights, then the alarm.

'Oh hell, bloody typical,' Clive shouted, 'why doesn't it happen before we clean the machines?'

'Because you love it laddie,' Jock called, clipping Clive's head as he climbed into the back of the machine.

Taff ripped the message from the printer. 'What have we got?' Mac asked.

Alan drove slowly up the narrow dirt track. He saw vague a movement off to his left, he peered into the gloom and saw a pair of illuminated eyes, belonging to what he thought was probably a deer in the field. He felt a jolt as the bank of the track collapsed into the deep ditch. The front wheel drove down, the weight of the tractor pulled the front over dragging the back wheel into the ditch, it rolled, and in a second it lay upside down in the water filled base of the ditch. Alan half fell from the seat, his body almost clear, but his legs were trapped and he guessed were broken. The pain was intense. He lay still for a few minutes gathering his thoughts through the pain. He was wet and cold, he quickly realised that there was no chance that he would be able to extricate himself; he needed help. *Where's the bloody CB Radio* he thought to himself. He only ever used it when he was working some distance from the house to call his wife. He scrabbled around and after a short and painful search located it still locked into its holder in the tractor cab. He fumbled, and prayed it would still work.

'Jules are you there over?' He *waited. 'Jules pick up the bloody radio will you.'?*

Julie had gone outside to gather in the kids who were playing in the barn. As she walked back across the farmyard she thought she heard Alan's voice, so she went into the kitchen, and heard the CB radio blaring.

'*Jules for Christ's sake pick up the bloody radio will you.*' She instantly recognised the pain and panic in Alan's voice.

'*I've had an accident in the tractor, just off the track to the bottom field, call the Ambulance and the Fire Brigade quick.*'

'*Will do love, you hang on, I'll do it straight away.*'

The appliance sped along the bypass, heading for the farm. Mac turned to his crew.

'When we get there, I want lifting gear and lighting to start OK.'

Jock dragged the wheel around to his right to negotiate the farm entrance. In the distance they saw the lights of the farmhouse, and a minute later Mac had climbed out of the machine and was getting directions from Julie.

'OK love, you stay here with the kids, we'll go and sort it out. Try not to worry, give him a call on the CB and tell him we'll be there in a jiffy. And look out for the Ambulance, it should be here any time now.'

It was dark now and it would be hard to find the tractor, as it had almost completely disappeared into the ditch, which was overhung with trees and bushes. But despite the tractor being almost buried in the steep ditch, a glow was emerging from the headlights and this was what Mac spotted as they made their way cautiously down the narrow stony track.

'Right guys, lets have the lights set up. Clive get the shears and saw, start clearing some of the woodland around the tractor. Pete, you and Jock get the First Aid Kit, Airbags, and get the Winch set up, OK.'

Mac scrambled into the ditch, shining his heavy torch into the gloom. He could hear a voice, and muffled groans.

'Hang on mate; we'll be with you in a second,' Mac called, attempting to calm Alan down. Alan groaned, and with an effort began talking. 'I'm pretty sure my right leg is broken. Other than that, and it being trapped, I'm OK.' He attempted a chuckle.

Mac shone the torch into the ditch. He could see that the tractor was on its side, and also a badly deformed leg projecting from beneath it. 'You'll be fine, you've got Sheffield's finest here now; the Paramedics will be here in a mo, so they'll be able to deal with the pain.'

Mac quickly worked out a plan. 'Alright mate; I'm Mac, what's your name?'

'Alan Daft Prat, that's me, I made a real balls up of it.'

Mac grinned to himself, sounded like a man after his own heart. 'Don't beat yourself up about it; we'll be with you soon.'

He could hear the activity above him. Clive had made fast progress with the saw, and the area around the ditch appeared more accessible. He heard Jock, 'Mac we're pretty much set up here and ready when you are.'

'OK Jock, I'll just get up there and let you know what we'll do, any sign of the ambulance yet?'

'Just heard the siren and it sounded close, it should be here soon.'

'Pete, I want you down here with me. Jock you stay aloft and operate the generator, Pete you do the airbags, and Jock, when Clive's done the woodwork, get him to help you set up the winch.'

The ambulance jerked to a halt behind the fire appliance and the Paramedic soon appeared at Mac's side.

The ambulance man, George Godfrey, thirty five years of service, winked at Mac. 'Shall I sort him out for you then Mac?' he said; a mischievous grin crossing his well worn face.

'If you would be so kind George, I'm sure the gentleman would be very grateful,' Mac retorted.

Alan felt the gentle surge of gas around his face and soon the pain began to dull, delivered through a simple plastic face piece; the gas was beginning to work. 'Thanks George, we'll get this thing off him now you've done your bit,' Mac said, winking at the aged ambulance man.

'We're all set to go when you're ready, Mac,' Jock called down.

'OK Guys just slide me down a couple of big wedges and let me know when you're starting.' The appliance engine increased its revs and the winches' heavy wire took the weight of the tractor, relieving the pressure on Alan's legs. Mac saw his chance, and as the side of the tractor lifted he jammed a large wooden wedge to bridge the gap; there was no way now the weight could fall back. The airbags inflated and assisted with the stability of the machine as it was steadily lifted and dragged away from the ditch. Thirty seconds later Alan's legs were free, the surge of the now unrestricted blood into the legs made him wince.

'Bastard,' Alan shouted. 'Sorry guys, not you, it took me by surprise, sorry.'

'No worries Alan, some of my guys feel pain like that if their coffee's late.'

'Ha, bloody ha,' Jock called down into the ditch.

Mac was now satisfied that everything was safe. He got the crew into the ditch and in rapid time they got Alan onto a stretcher and out into the ambulance.

'Well once more George, we have to thank you for your brilliance, how could we manage without you?' Old George chuckled, and with a broad grin stretching his leathery featured face, he clipped Mac around the ear and let out a laugh. 'The truth is, you fire bobbies couldn't manage without us.'

Mac grabbed the diminutive Ambulance Man in a bear hug, lifting his feet off the floor.

'Come on now George, you go on and get this young man off to hospital, it'll be your bedtime soon, mustn't miss your beauty sleep now.'

Mac and George had known each other for years. Their friendship began when, following a serious fire, the side of the house had collapsed. Mac suffered a broken leg. George was there and fixed him up; it was a long lasting friendship based on mutual respect and a shared sense of humour. Mac once related that old George was taught how to care for shrapnel wounds by Florence Nightingale when he did his training for the Ambulance service.

Chapter 10

Saturday morning was Clive's favourite time of the week; he'd get out early on his mountain bike, or go for a run. His life had changed lately, with the future mapped out. The wedding was coming soon, Helen was pregnant, and he knew he had to change some things. Boxing had been part of his life from being a boy but now it had become time consuming and expensive, given all of the circumstances in his life. It seemed to him to be almost an irrelevance, so he gave it up without a second thought.

Today he and Helen were driving out into the Peaks to have a couple of hours riding their bikes along a disused railway line; a popular spot for walkers, bikers, and horse riders.

'Are you ready yet love?' Clive shouted up the stairs of their terraced house.

'I'll be with you in a minute,' Helen called back.

'That's what you said ten minutes ago,' Clive replied with a laugh.

'Woman stuff, you wouldn't understand, you being a man,' she emphasised, 'you blokes get life so easy.'

Clive heard her coming down the stairs; he hid behind the stair wall and as she reached the hall he grabbed her from behind.

'Come here you gorgeous lump of female,' he whispered in her ear.

'As I said before matey, its woman stuff. Because of you my trousers don't fit properly so I had to move the button to get them on.'

Clive put his hands on her expanding tummy. 'You're getting to be a big girl,' he said, pulling her up close to him. "Do you think we should forget about the bike ride and maybe go back to bed?' he said, hoping for a positive response.

'Not a chance mate, I need the exercise and you need to let off steam, and the bike is the only way it's going to happen today.'

'Oh wonderful, now you've got me on the hook all the other stuff disappears does it?' he said, kissing her neck.

'It's alright for you, you just get the good bit. I have to carry this lump around for months, looking and feeling like a beached whale. While you just swan off on your bike or have fun with the watch, little old me gets all the hard work.'

'Yeah, but remember, I have to go out hunting and killing for food, it's not all fun you know, it can be dangerous work.'

'Yeah I've seen some of this dangerous work you talk about, playing volley ball, having water fights in the drill yard, very dangerous,' she laughed, 'now get me out of here and let's get some exercise.'

Brian parked his car behind the supermarket and walked the short distance to the shops. He was on a mission. Since he and Jane had rekindled their relationship he was doing everything he could to rebuild bridges and catch up on all that had been missed over the preceding years. He looked in the shop window. He could see that inside it was busy with mostly young women and teenagers foraging through the racks of clothing. It was years since he had bought clothing for anyone other than himself.

The shop interior was dark with little natural light to brighten it; it was dimly lit with a variety of small coloured lights, and the overbearing sound of pop music blaring out of some unseen speaker. He found a likely looking rack, jammed with dresses of a variety of styles and colours, and soon realised that he was well out of his depth. As he leafed slowly through the mass of fashion he shook his head with confusion. 'Can I help?' A voice came from behind him.

Brian looked round, and saw the young female shop assistant. She was slim, with beautiful long dark hair. She looked directly at him and smiled.

'It looks like you're struggling,' she said, 'do you need any help?'

'Well yes, I'm trying to find a dress for a girl about so big,' he said, indicating with his hand how tall he thought Jane was.

She turned and began looking through the rack close to where he stood. Brian couldn't help but notice the tightness of the blouse being pushed and stretched as she moved; the curves of her hips and the length of her legs which appeared from beneath a short black skirt, and the strong aroma of her perfume as she moved closer to him.

'What about these?' she said, pulling two dresses from the rack.

Brian was distracted, and was pulled back by her voice.

'Sorry, what was that?' he said, unable to completely remove his eyes from the vision of the girl.

'Do you think these will be suitable?' she said.

'I'm sure they'll be fine,' he said, unable to grasp how he was feeling. He caught her eye again and felt his heart begin to race.

This is stupid, he said to himself. *She's just a girl, I'm over forty.*

'I need a dress for a woman about so tall,' he indicated again, using his hand as a guide.

'What size is she?' she asked sympathetically.

'Oh I don't know.'

'Well, is she about my size do you think or maybe a bit smaller or larger?'

Brian felt strange. 'Well she's not as slim as you,' he mumbled.

'What bust size?' she said, a faint smile crossing her red lips.

'Oh I don't know, quite large I think.'

'Larger than me?' she said again, smiling at him.

'Well yeah, a bit I guess,' he said, being almost compelled to look at the woman's breasts and beginning to feel embarrassed.

'I reckon sir,' she said again looking into his eyes, 'you need to bring her in, and let her try something on.'

'Yes maybe that would be the best, thanks for your help; I'll take these two dresses to the till and pay for them, thanks again.'

She turned away. Brian found it hard to take his eyes off her as she walked slowly away to look after another customer.

Clive pulled his car into the rough dirt car park, just off the road close to the A6. He unhitched the bikes from the rack on the back of the car, and they were soon pedalling gently through an avenue of low trees, stripped bare by the recent strong winds. The ground was hard, the area had until recently had a light covering of snow which had cleared but remnants were still clinging to the underside of the walls and bushes. It was a still but cold day. They pedalled steadily along the flat old track bed of the now disused railway. The landscape opened up before them, then the ground to their right fell away and the hills were still green. It was a bright, typical winter day. Clive positioned himself behind Helen and watched her as she pedalled effortlessly along the smooth track, her breath condensing as it came into contact with the cold air. He could see that from behind her waist had thickened and he felt almost over-come with pride that this girl had chosen to spend her life with him. It was something that he had never taken for granted. He'd been the prod-uct of a broken marriage, his parents were both good people, but were unable to live together without fighting. When Clive was eight years old they split up and his father moved away with work, so his mother raised him and his younger sister. He rarely saw his dad after that.

The track was fairly busy with groups of walkers and cyclists.

'Look over there,' Helen called, and half turned to Clive, pointed sky-ward. Clive looked, following Helen's pointed finger. In the distance he could see a low flying helicopter.

You've seen a helicopter before, he was about to say, when he heard a metallic crash. He turned again to see that Helen was on the floor and the bike was entangled with her legs. His heart stopped. Clive jumped off his bike and threw it into the long grass and in a second he was kneeling alongside her.

'Are you alright love?' he said calmly, his brain fighting the desire to panic.

'I think so,' she said, sounding shocked. 'I caught my stomach on the handlebars as I went down, but I think it's OK.'

'You just sit a minute, here put my jacket over your shoulders, it'll keep you warm while you recover.'

Clive's mind raced. 'Are you sure you're OK, does it hurt anywhere?'

'I'm sure, I'll be fine, just give me a minute and I'll be ready to carry on.'

'No, no, we'll get back to the car and get you home, do you think you'll be OK to pedal back to the car?' he said as he adjusted the jacket around her shoulders.

'Stop fussing, I'll be OK,' she said, her face a mask of determination.

'OK but we're going back to the car,' Clive said, trying desperately to remain calm.

Thirty minutes later Clive was driving fast down the motorway, which was busy. He was still worried, and an overwhelming feeling of guilt hung over him.

'We'll be home soon,' he said, smiling weakly across the car at her. He noticed her grasping her stomach; her face had become ghostly white, and was screwed up with pain. Clive's heart thumped loudly in his chest and his mind was in turmoil.

'How is it?' he said, already in his mind working out the quickest way to the hospital.

'I think we're going to have to go to the hospital, it's hurting like hell now,' she said through gritted teeth.

'Just hang on; I'll have you there in five minutes,' he spat, treading hard on the car's accelerator.

Mac loaded the half dozen plastic bags into the boot of the car whilst Val took the trolley to the trolley park. She climbed into the car and clicked the seat belt into position.

'When we were out on Kinder the other day,' Mac said, 'what did you reckon to what they said about joining the rangers?' he paused, 'I've been thinking about it a lot.'

'It seemed interesting to me at the time, but I'm not so sure now. But I think it'll suit you down to the ground,' Val replied.

Mac hesitated for a second. it had always been his plan that when he retired he wouldn't commit himself to anything for a while; they'd have a break, take some holidays, and not get bound up with anything, but the thought of joining the rangers had really made him think hard.

'You know Val, I think I'm going to go for it, I reckon it will be really interesting.'

'Yes I reckon it will, but count me out though, I'd like to spend more time with the girls. You go for it if that's what you want,' she said, knowing that he'd already made the decision to do it.

Chapter 11

Jake put the key in his locker door and the grey metal door swung open. Brian peered over his shoulder. 'What you got in there, Jake? It looks like the inside of Tesco's.'

Jake's mother had packed his bag with biscuits and fruit, shaving foam, a tin of shoe polish, and several pairs of underpants and socks. Jake turned to him, and almost apologetically said, 'my mum thinks I'm going to starve, so she piles stuff into my bag. I haven't the heart to tell her not to.'

'That's mums I suppose; still, be grateful, you've only got one and they don't last forever.'

Jake thought about that for a second and imagined his mother, and the pride she had in him now he was a fire-fighter, and smiled to himself.

'Duties for the today are,' Mac called out to the watch as they paraded in the appliance room.

Red Watch were on duty, their positions for the day had been allocated. Jake was middle man, he would sit on the back seat of the appliance between Taff and Pete Jacks. Mac sat in the front next to Brian the driver. Jake had mixed emotions, he was desperate to see some action and prove his worth, but he was also nervous, worried whether when he was needed, he would do OK. Pete called across to him.

'You check the lockers on the driver's side, I'll do these,' he said. Jake nodded and slid open the locker doors, checking the gear against a check list. Seventy millimetre hose, standpipe key and bar, crowbar, light pump, large axe. There was the smell of petrol permeating from the locker, he absorbed the aroma and breathed out with a silent sigh, feeling completely happy.

'Right,' Pete said, 'all done, you go and tell the watch-room man and get it entered in the log book.'

Brian had finished his vehicle checks, the machine was fuelled up and ready to go. Pete and Taff set about checking their BA equipment. Now they were set, ready to go when called. Jake could barely contain his excitement.

'Right you lot of hooligans, up to the mess deck, a quick chat and a cuppa,' Mac shouted from the watch room.

Five minutes later they had gathered around the table on the mess deck. Jake was promoted to tea boy; unusually no one was critical of the outcome, normally newcomers were always given stick when they arrived, almost as a matter of principle.

'Keep this up young Jake and you'll get the job permanently,' Brian said with a hint of joviality in his voice.

'Right guys, let's get started.' Mac spoke and they fell silent.

Mac's face was serious. 'There are a couple of things I need to talk to you about.' He took a sip of tea. 'You'll have heard already, but just to reiterate, Clive won't be in for a few days. Sadly Helen lost the baby, so he's going to be with her for a while. Manning wise, Taff I'm going to have to cancel your bank holiday, normally it would be covered by standbys but the Division is running on minimum so it'll have to be like this, are you OK with that?'

'It's not a problem Mac; I was only taking it to get rid of it. It wasn't for anything special. How is Helen?'

'They're both alright; Helen is obviously sore and pretty upset, but otherwise healthy. Clive is really upset; he feels it was his fault. I've spoken to both of them and the Station Commander's been round as well.' Mac took another sip of tea. 'However they both say to give them a ring and go and visit; they'd like to see you. Ideally, though, not all at once.' Mac paused again. 'The other thing I need to mention is the lad from West Midlands who died. We ought to think about sending someone to the funeral, and doing something to rise a bit of money for his widow. If you've any ideas let me know. The Station Commander has said we should send a couple from the station so let me know if you want to go. OK, that's it, let's have you back to work.'

The watch made their way out of the recc room; no one saying much, none of what Mac had said had been good news.

The bell on the front door of the station rang. Brian got up from his seat in the office to see a middle aged man standing by the door.

'What can I do for you Sir?' Brian asked.

'My mum's asked me to come round and ask the firemen.'

'Well, Sir, how can we help?' he asked.

'There's been a couple of fires near where she lives, she lives on her own, and gets a bit worried. She saw something on TV about the firemen fitting smoke alarms and giving advice, she wondered if she qualified.'

Brian said 'Come on in we'll go into the watch room and I'll take some details, I'm sure we can help.'

The day was over. Jake lay on his bed, from where he could hear the TV downstairs. His Mother had made him tea and he just wanted to relax. They'd only had the one call but he felt exhausted. After speaking to Mark a couple of days ago, and seeing how enthusiastic he was about everything, Jake found himself envious of him. As yet Jake felt he'd been left behind; he was still waiting to be tested on the fire-ground. The guys on the watch realised that he needed to see some action, if only to prove to them that he would fit into the watch so Jock had had a word with him. 'Don't worry boy, it will happen soon enough.'

Mark had been lucky, his time would come. *The sooner the better* Jake thought.

Jake's bedside radio played quietly. He'd dozed off, he was floating lightly, he heard Tracy Jameson's voice. *I'm so pleased to meet you, I owe you my life, it would be nice to meet up again.* Suddenly Jake was crawling at speed up the smoke filled staircase, he felt the jab of pain as his head hit the wall at the top of the stairs, he tasted the almost glue-like black smoke as it penetrated his nostrils. His hands were hot, he was trembling, on the verge of panic. *Need to breath, got to breath, don't breath, breath and you're dead,* he felt the bundle of rags by the window.

He half lifted half dragged the smoking bundle, he crashed into a desk and felt the heat on his skin.

Got to breathe, he felt the hot rawness of the acrid smoke passing into his lungs, the violent spasm as his lungs vented the noxious smoke, and then nothing, oblivion.

Jake woke with a start, gasping for breath, hot and sweating, his pillowcase saturated. He sat bolt upright, dragging air into his lungs. He heard his radio, saw the picture on his wall illuminated by his bedside lamp. He realised that he'd been dreaming.

He half stumbled down the stairs, his mum had fallen asleep in front of the TV which was playing to itself. Question Time had just begun. He put the kettle on in the small kitchen and made himself and his Mum a cup of tea. He thought of the dream and made a decision; tomorrow he would get in touch with Tracy.

Chapter 12

The dawn broke with a dull light piercing the curtains of his small bedroom. Jim had been restless; his head was filled with thoughts that he had couldn't remove from his mind. He pondered his life with Maddie, he thought about their trips onto the moors and the pleasure he felt just being in her company, but he was still unable to fully grasp how his life had changed because of this one small, beautiful girl. He remembered the brain starving routine he'd endured for years as a security guard, the problems he'd had at school. Deep in his mind he'd wanted to learn, his mind craved information, but to expose that to his classmates would have made him an outcast. So he took the easiest option, he conformed, and learned very little. He thought about his parents who'd died in a car crash when he was young, his memories of them now fading. He tried hard to recall the sound of his mother's voice, but it had somehow evaporated from his memory. He turned over in his mind the fateful night when, out of boredom and frustration, he'd taken a match to rubbish stored behind a factory in the next compound to where he did his work as a security guard, and then the almost disastrous consequences when the building collapsed almost killing several fire-fighters. The guilt from that night continued to haunt him. Jim shuddered at the memory.

Maddie stirred, stretched, and made a beeline for the bathroom. She stood in the shower, allowing the hot water and soap suds to soak her body. She rested her back against the tiled shower wall and relished the warmth. She thought of Jim and their meetings, and the times when his body would be close to hers, it was almost dream like. *Come on gal, stop dreaming and get yourself ready.* She stepped out of the shower and quickly towelled herself dry.

'Are you going to be in there much longer, Madeline?'

'I'll be out in two minutes dad, just hang on.' She smiled as she said it, knowing her dad had a prostate problem, and sometimes his need to get to the bathroom was urgent.

As she stepped out he pushed past her. 'Got to get in quick, sorry,' he said apologetically, 'where are you going today?' he called through the now closed door.

I think we're doing a walk along some Dale or other, I'm not quite sure, Jim's got it arranged.'

'Well you take care, it's getting pretty cold, make sure that you're well wrapped up.'

'Yeah I will do, I'll just have my toast and fill my flask then I'll be off.'

Jim was up early again, on the days they were going out he couldn't sleep in. He wanted to be up, prepared, pack his rucksack and sort out the map, sandwiches and drink, then he could relax for a while before leaving to pick Maddie up from her house.

Tracy Jameson lay, still half asleep, still feeling tired. This wasn't unusual for her, since her accident she'd had nightmares about the fire. The dreams were usually about the prelude to the fire. She'd been working on her computer for a few hours when she dozed and was woken by rawness in her chest and violent coughing. Then there was the sudden awareness that her room was on fire. Disorientated she stumbled panic stricken through the smoke unable to breathe. She soon collapsed, and she knew that she was going to die. Then she dreamt of voices and lights and waking up in hospital with a mask on her face. Then the clicking of a valve as oxygen was pushed into her raw lungs and the pain across her face and arms. She roused herself and her mind put a picture of Jake before her, the man who'd risked everything to save her. She thought about the recent meeting in the café. She was surprised at how young he was, but she was pleased to recall that she thought him to be good looking in a manly way. His short dark hair contrasted with his pale skin, and she remembered his large hands as they engulfed hers. She thought she could see gentleness in him, or maybe she was viewing him from her own perspective. She knew that she would see him again; she'd felt a mild electricity between them when they spoke. Jake had a knack of looking directly into her eyes and seeing beyond her outer layer.

A light tap on her door brought her back from her imaginings.

'Cup of tea,' her father called through the closed bedroom door.

Come in dad,' she called. Her dad had always respected her privacy, never barging in on her.

'How are we this fine morning?' he said cheerily.

'I'm fine; a bit tired though, had the dream again last night.'

'Don't worry sugar,' he said, 'it's understandable; it was a tremendous shock. Things like that are hard to forget,' he said trying to sound reassuring.

'It's nearly nine o clock; shall I run you a bath after I've taken mum's tea in for her?'

The phone rang in the hall. 'I'll go and get that,' he said as he trotted down the stairs.

Tracy sat up in bed and began sipping her tea.

'It's for you, Trace,' he called up the stairs, 'I'll bring the phone up for you.'

That's unusual, a call for me on a Sunday morning, she said to herself.

'Hi Tracy, it's me, Jake, hope you don't mind me calling you at home. We said we'd keep in touch, and I wondered if you fancied meeting up today? Sorry it's such short notice.'

'No that's alright, I was just a bit surprised, I don't get many calls at home, but yeah, I'd love to go out.'

'OK, shall I pick you up in a couple of hours, say eleven o'clock? We'll have a drive and go for a drink somewhere.'

'Yeah, great, look forward to seeing you.'

'OK then, I'll see you at eleven, bye for now.'

Jim had studied the OS map and committed the route to memory. It was a place that neither he nor Maddie had been before. He dropped into third gear as the car began to slow on the steep hill leading out of Bakewell. He soon entered a series of narrow twisting lanes which were lined by complex patterns of limestone walls. The road dipped and turned and Jim took his time, being careful not to miss his turning. The road was now lined by high trees which cut out the daylight. Then suddenly they were there, a sharp hair-pin bend signalled the starting point for their hike today.

'So James, where are we?' Maddie asked.

'Today, wife to be,' as he said it he glanced at her and grinned, 'we are going to do a short walk up Lathkill Dale. From the pictures I've seen it looks beautiful.'

They were soon striding steadily, their fingers entwined, along a track bounded by dense bushes. After a few minutes they emerged into a clearing with a river bisecting the base of the valley; the far side of which was covered by trees which were bereft of foliage. The river sparkled in the bright sunlight and its shallow waters cascaded over a series of low weirs. There was the occasional fisherman standing knee deep in water trying to seduce trout with a fly, selected to be the one the fish would take today.

Despite the chill in the air, there were groups of people sitting close by the river bank absorbing the atmosphere of this idyllic place. Children were playing football with parents. Jim and Maddie slowed their already gentle pace, enabling them to spend time taking in the beauty of the dale.

'This place is very pretty,' Jim said, giving Maddie a knowing glance, 'but also it has a very interesting history, which I will tell you about when we stop for a break soon.' Jim put his arm over Maddie's shoulder as they continued the slowest of walks.

The steep grassy hillside towered above them; the surface was intermittently broken by small escarpments of dazzling white limestone.

'Do you know what I think?' Maddie said, out of the blue.

'What?' Jim responded.

'I think we should shorten the walk a bit today and have a nice pub lunch somewhere, just for a change.'

'Why would you want to do that?' Jim queried.

'No reason in particular, I've just got this fancy for a nice dinner and my legs are a bit tired after the last few days at work.'

'Well OK, if that's what you want, that's what we'll do,' Jim acquiesced.

Maddie folded her arm through Jim's and they continued their snail like pace along the track, occasionally stopping to look at the wading birds foraging for food in the river.

'I guess we cut up to our right here,' Jim said, pointing upwards toward a narrow lane which disappeared between high trees. 'I think there's a pub in the village where we can get something to eat.'

The river at this point was shallow, just a couple of inches deep. The water was crystal clear, and ran over smooth limestone, with sporadic patches of luminous green weed. 'Look Jim!' Maddie exclaimed.

'What?' Jim replied, surprised at her sudden outburst.

'Look, there's a beautiful trout,' she said, pointing excitedly at a spot in the river, close to the bank.

The fish lay almost motionless facing into the flow of water, with only the gentle movement of its tail giving it away.

'OK young lady, now that you've seen the fish the birds and the flowers, shall we make our way to the pub? I'm ready for something to eat.'

'That sounds good to me,' Maddie said enthusiastically. 'Thank you for bringing us here Jim, it's a very beautiful place, I love it.'

Jim put his hand on her shoulder and pulled her close to him. 'A beautiful woman and a beautiful place, what could be better, now come on let's see if we can get a bit of a sweat on going up this hill.'

Jake steered the car into the busy car park at the rear of the pub. It was thronged with people setting out on walks and climbers with their bodies strewn with ropes and what appeared to be small mattresses strapped on their backs.

'I think I know those guys,' Tracy said, looking across the car park towards a group of four young men. 'I've seen them at Uni. I think they're part of the climbing club. I'm told they're all nutcases. They even tried to get me to go with them once, but I've never fancied it, how about you?'

Jake gave her a twisted grimace. 'I don't know; there was a time when I thought I would have a go, but the gear was a bit expensive, and it seems a bit cliquey, so I didn't do anything about it. Shall we wander up by the rocks and watch what they get up to?'

'OK, that sounds good to me,' Tracy said, 'we can make the best of the sunshine.'

'OK then, we'll have a quick lunch then do it,' Jake replied, ushering her into the pub, which was busy with walkers.

They sat in the dim light of the pub eating their meal and chatting about nothing special. 'You know Jake, I'm very grateful for what you did.'

Jake turned and looked at her, her pretty face, one side lit by the light from the window, the remnant of the scar hidden on the other, shaded side of her face.

'Think nothing of it, what I did was automatic, I didn't have time to think. I suppose training to be a fire-fighter has put me into that sort of state, so I am glad that I did what I did. I would have reacted before I joined the brigade, so it's a good thing it helped me as well as you.' He paused. 'The other positive thing to come out of it is that I got to meet you.'

That surprised Tracy; she'd assumed that she was the only one keen to meet up.

'Well for me it was a double blessing, I got my life and I got to meet you too,' she replied, her face now an expressionless mask. It was almost as though their conversation was making her re-live the experience.

There was a silence, neither spoke. Jake drew a pattern in the dew around his beer glass. Tracy half turned and sipped her glass of wine, both of their minds mulling, computing what was being said. Was there some hidden meaning behind this albeit innocent conversation, or were they misinterpreting what had been said. Things had taken an unexpected turn, something which neither of them had planned for.

Jake gulped his beer. 'Do you fancy going out again, on a date some-time?'

'You know what, you've just taken the words right out of my mouth,' she replied.

'After what we've been through it would be a good idea. You know nothing about me and I'm the same.' She paused. 'But you know what?' she said, looking him straight in the eye. 'I like you, but there's no great surprise in that is there,' she said, a smile crossing her young face.

'I'm the same,' Jake said. 'I'm not experienced at this sort of thing, me and girls. Well put it this way, I've not really had a girlfriend before; I've just got my mum at home. I've never had a lot of friends, I've always been happy in my own company.'

Tracy put her hand on Jake's and squeezed it. 'I don't want you to think I'm flirting or anything, but it would be nice to go out, and see how it goes.'

'I'd like that; mum's always telling me I should get out more. She's on her own and I guess we've been company for each other since dad died. I don't mind though, I don't feel I've missed out, she's been really good. And now I've got the lads at the fire station, they're great and you now as a friend, so everything's looking good.' Jake took another mouthful of his beer.

'Tell me about you, Jake,' Tracy said.

Jake shuffled in the softly upholstered seat.

'There's not much to tell. I'm eighteen, I live at home with my mum. School was OK, but I was pretty average. I enjoyed sport. I tried a lot of them; football, rugby and athletics, but none of them really grabbed me. I was always better at the practical stuff, but the theory, maths history and chemistry, well I was hopeless.' Jake took another sip from his glass. 'When I left school I got a job labouring on a building site, the money was ok but it was hard work and I found it pretty boring.' He stopped and looked at Tracy. 'I knew that I wanted something better, but didn't know what.' Jake paused again and took another sip of his drink. 'Then, about six months ago, I came out here on the train. I was just out walking on the moors, when I met this guy called Mac and his wife. He was trying to resuscitate an old man who had collapsed and he asked me to go off and call for an ambulance, which I did. The helicopter came and we probably saved the old man's life.

Mac really impressed me, of course. I haven't had a dad so in a way meeting him and him trusting me seemed to make me want to be like him. He told me he was a fire-fighter.' Jake paused again. 'And that was the spark; I knew then that was what I wanted to do. So I joined the brigade, I did my training, and now I'm a fireman on Mac's watch and I love it, it's the best thing I've ever done.'

'So you haven't got a girlfriend?' she said, smiling.

'No, I've never bothered. I was never very good at mixing when I was younger; I think since I joined the brigade I've come out of my shell a bit, but no, no girlfriend.'

Tracy smiled; this was something more than gratitude, she really liked Jake, he was nice.

Jake lifted his head and looked at her. 'Fancy that stroll then?' he asked.

'Love to,' she replied, getting up from the table.

'Then let's go and have a look at the lad's climbing shall we?'

They walked down the narrow track alongside the road, soon arriving at a small car park where half a dozen cars were parked and their occupants having left to walk the moors or climb the rocks. The track now trended right and climbed steeply through dense gorse and jumbled rocks heading for a quarry, where already they could hear raised voices. They emerged close to a massive overhanging crag. In the quarry the small group of the climbers they'd seen earlier had gathered, and were busily scrambling up one of the easier routes. They stood and watched for a few minutes before Jake spoke. 'Let's move on a bit further shall we, and see what else is happening?'

As they walked they talked about work, parents and holidays, both feeling comfortable in the other's company.

'What do you think, Jake?' Tracy asked, right out of the blue.

'What do I think about what?' Jake replied, wondering what she was talking about.

She stopped and looked at him. 'What do you think about everything? You know the state of the world. What you'll be doing in ten years time? Will you be married, have kids; you know general stuff like that.'

Jake looked back at her, wondering where the conversation was heading.

'I don't know. I don't think ahead too much, I just think about today, you know, what's happening now. What about you?'

She wrinkled her brow and thought for a second. 'Me; I'm not sure, I think that girls are programmed differently to you boys. I think we look for different things from our days. I think about my studies, about boys, you know. What will my husband be like? If I have kids what will they be like? Who will they marry? Will I have grandkids? What will it be like when mum and dad aren't here anymore?'

Jake was shaken. 'That's some list you've got, I just think about my mum, work and the guys at work, not much else really.'

'What about your mum?' She said, 'haven't you thought about what you'll do when she's not around anymore?'

Jake suddenly felt very uneasy. 'No, I can't imagine a time without my mum, she's always been there. If I lost her I don't know what I'd do,' he said, an obvious tenseness in his voice.

'Me too, but I often think about it. It makes me sad when I do,' she said.

'Perhaps you should stop thinking about it then,' Jake said, a grim feeling coming over him.

They walked a little further and chatted about nothing in particular. Jake stopped, a sudden feeling of worry or was it sadness began to take him over, he wasn't sure. 'Let's head back to the car shall we?' he said, his demeanour now much less relaxed. 'I've lost my appetite for the walk, and I've got a bit to do at home before the night's over.'

Tracy began to realise that the subject of his mum had caused a change of mood. 'I'm sorry Jake, I hope the conversation hasn't upset you. I guess it's being at Uni, we're always being prompted to think about all sorts of things, I didn't mean for it to upset you.'

'Don't worry about it, I really can't be late, I've got things to do at home. I'll drop you off at your place if that's OK.'

They travelled back to the city barely exchanging any words, and feelings of regret hung over the two of them like a dark rain cloud.

Jake parked the car by the pavement outside his house, and went into the home he had shared with his mother every day of his life. He was shaken by the earlier conversation he'd had with Tracy. It had suddenly made him think about something he hadn't dared consider before. His mum was sat watching the television. Jake looked at her, and he felt a wave of emotion gathering in his chest.

'Hi mum, be back in a minute,' he said, choking back the tremor in his voice. He walked out of the room into the kitchen and put the kettle on.

'There you go mum, a nice cup of tea from your favourite son,' he said, attempting to sound cheerful.

'Well thank you, I thought you were going to be out a bit late tonight with Tracy, weren't you?'

'Well I thought I'd come back earlier and spend some time with you.'

'That's nice,' she said. 'What have you been up to today then son?' she asked.

'Not too much. I met Tracy and we had a drink, we did a short walk on the moors then came home.'

'Is that it?' she said, sounding surprised.

'Yep, that was it; I decided I wanted to spend some time at home with you.'

'Well Jacob, that's very nice of you, but you should be out having a nice time with your friends; you work hard, you deserve time to relax and have some fun.'

'I know, but to be honest, I like being here with you, you spoil me and I love you.'

She turned and looked at Jake and saw his flushed face and the tears welling up in his eyes. 'Oh what is it son?'

Jake stood by her chair, his head bowed. his mother stood up and put her hand on his arm.

'Come on son, what is it?'

'Oh it's nothing really, Tracy just asked me if I'd ever thought what it would be like when you weren't around anymore, and it got me,' he said, trying to keep control of his voice.

'You shouldn't be concerning yourself with stuff like that Jacob, I'm still a youngster; I'm as fit as a flea, so don't even think about it. I'll probably still be ironing your shirts in twenty years unless you get yourself married.'

Jake looked up and smiled. 'I'm sorry mum, it's just when she said that, it threw me. You know, you've always been here, and I'd never even thought that far ahead.'

'Well let's forget about that, I'm planning to be around to see my grandchildren married,' she said, trying to lighten his mood.

Jake lay on his bed. He had his headphones on and was listening to his music. He thought about the day and the trauma it had caused both him and Tracy. She'd unwittingly brought about the early finish to the planned day, and was probably feeling guilty about it. *I'll give her a ring later; let her know it's all right now,* he thought.

Chapter 13

Mac parked his car and walked the half mile to the Ranger Station. It was a nice day; he'd dropped Val at their daughter's house, and was now on his way to meet up with Janet Clark, the woman who had encouraged him to do a patrol with her following their meeting in the snow on Kinder Scout.

The low, single storey stone building nestled at the end of a rough lane with a tree covered rising bank to one side and a steep fall down to the river at the base of the valley on the other.

Mac entered the small foyer and beyond into a dim corridor. He could hear muffled voices beyond a door, so he tapped lightly, and almost immediately a deep voice called him to enter.

'Hi, come in, you must be Mac. Janet here said you might come along. Welcome, do you fancy a cup of tea, whilst we do the briefing?'

Mac spotted Janet sitting in the corner and moved across and sat alongside her. 'I'm glad you came, I've told them all about you,' Janet said, smiling widely.

Mac sat quietly sipping his tea and listened intently to Stan's briefing.

After the brief, Stan singled Mac out. 'It's good to meet you, do I call you Mac?'

'Yeah that will be fine,' Mac said, smiling broadly. 'I'm looking forward to seeing what it's all about.'

'Well you'll spend the day with Janet doing a patrol and I'm sure she'll tell you anything you want to know.'

Twenty minutes later, Mac and Janet were striding steadily up a steep slope leading into a dense patch of woodland, which hid the remnants of the now defunct quarrying industry. The industry was long dead, but had become a perfect playground for walkers and climbers. There was mass of silver birch which hid from view the crags known as Lawrence-field. In the distance, they could hear the occasional clink of climbing hardware, and conversations between the groups of mainly young people. Mac and Janet emerged from the trees close to the edge of a quarry. A small group of climbers were looking up at a young man in blue shorts and tight fitting rock shoes. He was thirty feet up the almost vertical rock, and was beginning to show signs of fatigue. His rope was threaded through a metal belay, designed to keep him safe in the event of a fall, and this was now his saviour as he leaned away from the rock, the belay taking his weight, his arms dangled tiredly by his side. Mac could hear him blowing air through his strained lips.

'I don't think I can do it, Tom,' he called down, 'I'm knackered.' As he spoke, his foot slid from the minute hold on which he had placed his right foot. He shouted, 'I'm off.' He plunged six feet before his second, the man entrusted to hold him if he fell, managed to take the strain. His friend rebuked him. 'Give me a bit more warning before you peel off will you, you were taking so long I was beginning to doze off.' He laughed.

'Well maybe we'll see if you can do any better soon,' he retorted.

'Maybe I will, but got to have a cuppa before I have a go,' he said as they walked the ten yards back to the place where they had dumped all of their gear.

'I reckon we'd better move on a bit,' Janet said, turning to Mac.

'Yeah, good idea, the problem here is that it's such a lovely spot and, being so warm, there's a temptation to sit and just let the time go by.'

'You've never been tempted to climb have you, Mac?' she asked as they passed by another group climbing a rock face which emerged from the base of a small pool.

'I dabbled when I was younger, but once I was married and kids came along I seemed to be at work permanently, so I never had the time.'

They had both stripped down to their T shirts, the rising ground making them sweat. 'Tell me about the Rangers then, Janet,' Mac said as they continued climbing up towards a prominent ridge; the smooth line of the ridge occasionally broken by prominent boulders.

Janet stopped close by some low lying rock. 'Let's have a breather and a drink and I'll tell you.' She rested a minute to re-gain her breath. 'I've been doing it about ten years and I really enjoy it. I love the walk; it's usually between ten and fifteen miles, and it can be hard sometimes, especially when the weather's bad. I like to think I'm doing my bit for the park, and the people who use it.' She paused a moment. 'It gives me a lot; I loved it from the start. There's a lot to learn, there's a lot of focus on navigation of course, that's something that if you decide to join us you'll have to do a lot of.'

'Yes, I thought that. I saw when we met up on Kinder Scout that it must be an important part of the job'

'You'd be surprised how often when we're out on patrol we come across people who are lost. Often poorly equipped; no maps or if they have a map they don't know how to use it. Some think a compass will save them, which it will if they understand how to use one, but it won't if you don't,' she stressed. 'It's a big part of our ongoing training. Then there's the other stuff; knowing something about the geology. The plants the trees and the history, it's all there to give us the tools to help and advise the public. I just love it.'

'I can tell you do,' Mac said, 'It stands out a mile.'

'I suppose you love what you do as well?' Janet replied. 'It must be interesting and frightening at times. I remember going into a fire station with school. The firemen showed us all the equipment and let us squirt the hose, I've always remembered that.'

'Yeah we still get loads of schools come around,' Mac said, sensing that Janet was genuinely interested in what he did for a living. 'The questions are usually the same, but it's a nice thing to do. They get a lot from it, it's a change from the classroom environment, and it's a change for us too,' he said, with a sense of pride in his work.

Pete Jacks loaded the wheelchair into the back of his car, and then he leaned into the passenger side and made sure that his wife, Trudy, was strapped in and comfortable. 'Come on Pete, where are you taking me?' she asked.

'I'm going to take us over to Buxton, and have a nice stroll around the park,' he said, 'then maybe have lunch at the Pavilion. I thought that would be just the ticket for us, it seems ages since we last went out for a bite to eat.'

'That will be nice, we've not been over there for years. I just hope the weather stays nice for us.'

Pete pulled the car into a vacant space at the roadside and quickly got Trudy into her chair. The day was mild for the time of year, but nevertheless he'd come prepared and had a blanket ready to lie across her legs. They headed gently through the park then stopped on a low bridge to look at a gang of Canada Geese who were fighting over scraps of bread left by visitors. They moved slowly along the serpentine river to a spot close by the bandstand where the a band were in the early stages of their performance. They sat a while listening to the music, Trudy nodding her head and tapping her hand on her knee.

'Have you had enough yet love?' Pete asked after about twenty minutes.

'Yeah, I think so; let's go and get a bite to eat shall we.'

Chapter 14

Monday Morning. 0905.

'Red Watch, fall out. Do the routines. Jake, you make a cuppa then we'll get out for drill.'

'Yes Sub,' Jake responded, before jumping into the back of the machine and placing his fire gear neatly in the centre of the seat.

On the mess deck there was the usual noise of men who hadn't seen each other for a few days and were keen to share their thoughts with the others. Jake sat quietly at the end of the table listening, and remembering that only a few months ago his life had been so different.

'Crew, get to work,' Mac shouted. The crew scrambled from the appliance and in a whirl of activity a ladder was thrown up against the third floor window of the tower. Jets of water streamed across the concrete of the drill yard accompanied by the sound of revving pumps obliterated all other sounds in the area.

Jake slung the hose over his shoulder and sprinted up the ladder quickly followed by Pete, and soon the water was streaming down onto the yard from the tower.

Above the noise of the pump there came the sound of the Station alarm telling the men they had a call. Jake and Pete scrambled back down to ground level; the hose was abandoned on the ground. The pump was closed down and the ladder quickly re-stowed on the roof of the machine. Brian ran out to the machine with the message on paper delivered from the printer. 'What have we got, Brian?' Mac shouted.

'A job in the city, eight pump make up,' he called breathlessly. Mathew Street, an old warehouse, well alight.'

Mick Young swung the wheel of the machine into a wide arc and slowed before joining the heavy traffic on the main road into town. Mac hit the switch turning on the appliance wailers.

'Do you know where we're going, Mick?' Mac asked, a smile crossing his ruddy face.

'Yeah Mac, I know it well, we went there a few times when I was standing by at Central, it's a big place.'

'Yeah, I've been there a few times myself; I often wondered why it's not burned down before now.'

As the machine descended to the city they could see the plume of black smoke rising from among the cluster of high rise buildings. Jake's heart was pounding. Brian and Jock who sat either side of him were getting rigged in their BA sets and testing that all was operating correctly. Jake was aware of the sound of their whistles sounding as they charged the sets with air. The appliance braked and swung around bends in the road, jumping the tram track, then there was the sound of equipment rattling in their cab. Everything resonated with Jake. He was beyond excitement. Adrenaline flowed through his veins, his senses razor sharp. He looked around at his friends, fellow fire-fighters, ready to go into battle; Jake felt proud. He was amazed at the nonchalance of his crewmates; their sense of the normal surprised him. He could see the smoke, he knew he would soon be doing what he'd trained for, he loved the feeling of excitement that was fizzing in his blood.

The street was lined with several appliances, and there were men running out hose and setting into hydrants. Water was flowing like a river down the gutters and into the drains; Jake noticed that entry control had been set up about twenty yards away from the building. He looked around; it was huge, maybe four floors in height and maybe eighty meters long by about forty meters wide. He noted that there were two points of entry into the warehouse that were both in use; this was a big job.

'Pull up over there, Mick,' Mac said, 'behind that pump. You lot wait here until I get back.'

Mac walked swiftly across to the ADO who he figured would be in charge of the job. He recognised him as one of his lads from a few years ago.

ADO Paul Davis had flourished on Mac's watch, and had shown that he had good practical sense, allied to a sharp mind. Mac always thought that he'd do well.

'Hi Paul, Graveton in attendance with a crew of five, what do you want us to do?'

Paul grinned widely. 'Well Mac, you can see we've got a little cracker going here.' He looked around the area surveying the scene.

'Can you get your guys to help get a good water supply going, and then I could do with you and one other inside in BA, I've not got a lot of experience in there, it would help a lot.'

Brian and Jock were disappointed to being taken off BA duties, but Mac explained the reasons behind it, so they got on with giving the other crews a hand in securing a good supply of water to the pumps, because for sure they were going to need it.

Mac got hold of Jake. 'Right Jake, you and me are going in, get a set checked and started up, we're going in from the second entry point over there,' Mac said, pointing at the entry point over to their right.

Jake's brain bubbled with excitement. This was it, what he'd joined the brigade for, and he was almost dizzy with adrenaline. He quickly donned his BA set and tested all the operations in just the way he'd been taught; this was his first proper BA job, and it was a good one.

The officer who was running the BA entry control board took Mac and Jake's tallies and checked they were correct, before giving them their instructions.

'Right Sub, I need you to clip on and follow the guide line up and along the first floor, relieve the team along there. Their whistle time is approaching. When the fire's subdued enough we have to extend the line further into the building, is that clear?'

Mac had started his set and spoke though the face mask in a distorted heavy voice. 'Yeah we've got that, we have a guide line. Right Jake, clip on to me, I'm on the line, let's go.'

Several lines of charged hose passed through the doorway and disappeared in different directions, each one fighting the blaze in a coordinated way. Mac slid the small karabiner like clip along the length of the guide line, along which small pieces of thin nylon cord were tied functioning as a reference if the crews were in thick smoke. Being able to feel these chords would tell them which way to go to get out of the building. Occasionally he, Jake, would have to remove the clip to get past a point at which the line had been tied to a radiator or a column, then clip on again at the other side of the knot. They kept low, below the smoke, giving them a good view of their location. They were moving fast, unhindered by having to drag hose behind them.

'Right, Jake, let's take a breather, not far now,' Mac said, 'are you OK, no problems?'

'No Sub. I'm fine,' Jake said as the sweat ran down his face and gathered in a shallow pool in the bottom of his facemask.

All around was the sound of fire; burning, creaking, cracking, rumbling, shattering. A cacophony of sounds, added to the sound of raised voices and rushing water. Jake looked across at Mac, he had absolute trust in him, in fact he felt privileged to be in the fire with his hero. If Mac said to do it, then it would be done, no discussion. He remembered once that Mac had said during a talk he'd given to the watch on the night shift, that fire fighting is an autocratic process and has to be so; on the fire ground, democracy doesn't work. The O.I.C has a plan in his head; he needs co-operation not conflict. Trust his judgement. And it was true now, Mac was doing what he'd been told to do. Jake knew he had to do what Mac decided in the job, no discussion, just do it.

'Right Jake, let's go again, keep the pace up.'

They moved swiftly over piles of debris, boxes and machinery, following the pre laid guide line. Soon they were there; a team of two men crouched low beneath the heat band pouring water onto the fire. 'OK guys, you get off, we'll take over' Mac said as they relieved the rapidly tiring team. The two fire fighters clipped onto the line and soon disappeared into the thick smoke. Mac handed the branch to Jake.

'There you go Jake, let's give it a go shall we?' Mac said, smiling to himself. Still remembering how he felt at his first big job, and the sense of danger and excitement, it evoked even now. Jake took the branch in his gloved hand. He felt the weight of the hose and the power he had in his hands. He took an arm lock around the hose. This was something he would always remember. He turned the valve on the aluminium branch, he heard the hiss of the water as it shot from the nozzle, he felt the hose recoil like a shot from a high powered rifle as a jet of water shot into the hot smoke laden atmosphere.

'Get low Jake, less heat and a better sight of what we're hitting.'

Jake crouched, but could still feel the heat through his anti flash hood. Above their heads the smoke swirled and ran like liquid tar, heading out of the building, driven by the expanding heated atmosphere, and the incoming rush of fresh air that was feeding the fire. Mac looked around surveying their position. They were exposed, a long way from their entry point. If anything were to go wrong now it could be a problem. They were close to a heavy stone wall, but there were no windows to help illuminate the rooms or give any sort of direction.

Mac was tense, he'd done this many times, but today he had a rookie with him, and he felt the weight of responsibility on his shoulders. There was also a realisation that the only way to develop and become experienced was like this, dive in head first, get your boots dirty, feel the heat and survive it.

Mac was aware of a significant rise in temperature; he could feel the heat through the soles of his heavy rubber boots. Jake was pouring a narrow spray jet through an open doorway onto the visible fire, and the volume of sound had increased also. Mac was tense, sensing that a problem was about to raise its head. He looked up into the thick smoke and saw flames dancing horizontally above their heads amid the smoke.

'Right Jake, listen to me,' he said. Jake turned to face Mac; he could tell immediately that Mac was concerned about something and his heart began pounding.

'I'm not happy Jake, I reckon it's going to kick off, if we leave we lose it so here's what we do.'

'*Control from Sub Officer James over.*'

Assistant Chief Officer Alex Battle had just arrived at the fire ground, and was in the control unit being briefed. Alex had served with Mac many years ago and was defined by many who had served with him over the years, as a crusty, belligerent bastard. Some would agree, others not. But everyone respected him as a first rate fire fighter. Alex had been orphaned and brought up in a children's home from being six years old, and this made him tough, so he got wherever he got through hard graft and determination. He was not a man to tangle with; those who tried had lived to regret it.

'*Go ahead Mac over.*'

'*Control, I'm not happy, the heat is rising, we need to really hit this hard or we're going to lose it. It's really bloody hot in here and the signs aren't too clever. Can we blast it with the TL at one end, and get reinforcements where we are? If not I think we'll have to abandon ship soon, over.*'

'*Mac; this is the ACO here; If you're worried it must be bad, we'll get it sorted. Stick in there OK? We'll get the T.L. and re deploy more at your end ASAP, out.*'

'Right ADO you heard the man, let's get to it,' Alex shouted to the men around him.

Mac glanced at the young man beside him, remembering the first time they met. He knew then that he was made of the right stuff. As Jake turned to face him, Mac guessed there was a smile on Jake's face behind the semi misted heavy plastic facemask he was wearing.

'Jake; open the spray wide, remember your flashover training, we're going to do that.'

Jake's heart skipped a beat, but he was high on adrenaline and felt no fear; he was with Mac and felt sure that everything would be OK.

Over the next ten minutes Jake opened and closed the wide spray of high pressure water into the super heated smoke in a series of pulses, designed to rapidly absorb the heat, with Mac close behind him, his leather gloved hand resting on his shoulder, encouraging him, cajoling him to keep going in the energy sapping heat. Jake felt no fear. The pump operator could tell what they were doing, the gauge on the pump registered wildly as Jake opened and closed the nozzle. Above the clamour of noise, Mac could hear distant voices and high pitched engine noise, then there was a strong draft of air shooting over their heads at speed, the smoke billowed around them, the temperature rose, Mac realised this was the effect caused by a massive injection of water onto the fire from the turntable ladder.

'Keep going Jake, I think the cavalry has just arrived,' Mac shouted to Jake above the rumble of noise surrounding them. Mac trying not to appear too relieved at the pressure being lifted off them.

Minutes later two more crews were working in their area, and lead by Mac, yard by yard, they managed to force their way forward, squeezing the fire between the gushing river of the turntable ladder and the numerous jets which were now slowly overpowering the fire.

Mac called across to Jake. 'Gauge check.' They lifted their gauges, shone their torches, and saw that the time was fast approaching for them to withdraw before their cylinders of compressed air activated their low-pressure whistles.

'*Control from Sub Officer James over.*'

'*Go ahead Mac over.*'

'*We're getting low on air, we're ready to come out, are there reliefs around? The fire is OK with the three jets already in situ, over.*'

'*OK Mac, well done, the reliefs have already been sent, over and out.*'

The fire now seemed to have been subdued and in no time Mac and Jake were relieved by another crew, Mac briefed them before handing the job over to them.

'Right guys,' he said, his voice distorted by the BA mask he wore, 'it's well down now, it's just a matter of damping down and keep your eyes open for fire travel above, it shouldn't be a problem.'

Minutes later Mac and Jake were picking up their tallies from entry control and taking off their BA sets.

'How did you like that then, Jake?' Mac asked, knowing already what the answer would be.

Jake's face was red and running with sweat, steam erupting from the space around the collar of his fire coat. A broad grin stretched across his face, his dark hair plastered to his head. He stretched his body and lifted his arms, linking his fingers behind his head. He shook his head from side to side, his smile seeming even bigger now.

'You did well Jake, but you will have tougher jobs that are not so much fun, and more dangerous, so enjoy this, it won't always be as easy as this,' Mac said, hiding a smile.

Chapter 15

Mac sat back, relaxed in his office chair, and there was a tap on the door.

'Come in,' he called.

'I wondered if I could have a word Mac,' Pete Jacks said, standing framed by the door.

'Of course, come in Pete, sit yourself down,' Mac said as he removed his tie from around his neck. 'What can I do for you?'

Pete ran his hands through his thinning hair and looked tense.

'Well Mac,' he said, struggling to get out the words. His body language seemed strained. Mac sensed that something wasn't right.

'What can I do for you Pete, what's the problem?'

Pete's face was flushed. 'I've always tried to keep my problems to myself,' he said, his voice trembling. 'Trudy's not been too good these past couple of weeks, her tremors have increased, she's slurring her words and she can't remember anything for more than a few minutes.' He paused, clasped his hands across his face, and his voice cracked. He tried to speak again but his voice became a sob. 'I'm sorry.' He shrugged and composed himself again. 'That's why we were at the doctors, she had some tests the other day and her results didn't look good. Later, after I took her home, I rang the Doctor again. He told me that her condition seems to have deteriorated, he thought maybe another six months.' Mac was shocked. He sat looking at Pete, not quite sure what to say. Pete sat with his head in his hands trying to hold himself together.

The station alarm operated again, and almost instantaneously both Pete and Mac went onto auto pilot, the conversation of a few seconds ago relegated to the back of their minds.

'What have we got Jock?' Mac shouted as he climbed smoothly into the front seat of the machine.

'Wouldn't you just bloody well believe it, twenty to six and we get a helicopter crash, I don't believe it.'

'Where?'

'Big Moor just over the border, we're backing up the local retained crew. Chesterfield's pumps are already out on a job, so we've got it.'

Mac twisted to put on his heavy fire coat; he looked back at the crew in the back seats and saw Jake looking intently out of the cab window.

'Are you set Jake?'

Jake looked at Mac and a huge grin crossed his face.'

Mac smiled. 'OK you don't have to answer that, I can see for myself.'

Jock gunned the machine up the steeply angled road which led into Derbyshire. They were soon leaving behind the heavy traffic and the tightly bunched buildings of the city. At the huge roundabout which formed the county boundary, Jock slammed the wheel first to the left and then right, the heavy rubber tyres screaming in protest. Jake sat in the back grimly holding on to anything that was fixed to stop him being propelled across onto Brian's knee.

'You hang on tight young man,' Brian said above the roar of the diesel engine, as once more Jake crashed into his space.

'Sorry Bry, it's like being at the fairground on the dodgems.'

The road now descended gently, it had long straights with a series of sharp bends, the height of the road giving distant views to the north and to the west.

Mac caught a glimpse of blue flashing lights in the distance.

'It looks like we're almost there,' Mac called to the crew. A few hundred yards away the local fire appliance, manned by part time fire fighters, had already arrived and its crew were disgorging. Lead by their officer in charge the crew were making their way across the boggy ground to the sight of the crash, three hundred yards from the roadside. The helicopter had landed heavily and struck the only rock of any size in the vicinity, and smoke was issuing from its engine compartment. Jock pulled the appliance to a halt behind the Derbyshire pump.

'You boys wait here, and I'll go across. Get ready to get some gear across. I'll let you know what we need by radio.'

Mac struggled across the heavy mud soaked terrain, and on arrival at the crash scene he spoke to the junior officer in charge, a man he had never met before.

'Hi leading fireman, I'm Sub James from Graveton. The junior officer looked relieved that some help had at last arrived.

'I'm glad you're here Sub, I've never had one of these before. Have you?' he asked.

Mac patted his shoulder. 'Not recently, had one about ten years ago. It's your patch, it's your job, we're here to help, give your lads the first go at it shall we. We're here if you need us.'

'That's fine by me,' he said, looking relieved.

'I see your guys are getting a foam branch ready just in case, and some cutting gear, how are the helicopter crew?' Mac asked.

'Just had a quick look, they don't look too good to me, but I have to say I'm no expert.'

Mac gathered his thoughts. 'OK L.F, you and me should go and have a look inside."

The helicopter was on its side, its rota blades bent at sharp angles and what had looked like smoke was in fact steam. 'Call me Mac, what do I call you?' Mac said to the fraught looking junior officer.

The man, relieved at the help, and somewhat in awe of Mac's experience said 'I'm Derek Miles.'

'Hello Derek, how long have you been in the job?'

'Three years, no one else wanted to do the job when Dave Perkins retired. He'd done thirty five years, so I got it; I've never had a fatality, so this all scares me a bit.'

'Don't worry about it; we'll get by together OK,' Mac said, his tone reassuring.

'That sounds good to me Mac,' he said, looking as though a ton weight had been removed from his shoulders.

Mac lay on the floor and squeezed into the damaged cockpit. 'Come in here Derek,' Mac called. He realised this could be tough for the young man, but guessed that this was the right time for him to get into the nasty side of things. A couple of minutes later,

Derek almost reluctantly joined Mac inside the badly damaged cockpit.

Before them were the bodies of the pilot and passenger of the helicopter. The impact with the huge rock had driven most of the side of the cockpit inwards, squashing the pilot as he sat braced in his seat. The passenger had been almost decapitated by one of the rotor blades, and his right arm had been severed close to his shoulder. Mac checked the pulse of the pilot. 'I'm pretty sure they are both code one, will you send the message from me. But first let's get out of here; have you got your notepad with you?'

'*Control from zero one zero; informative message. From Sub Officer James, at Big Moor. One helicopter crashed and badly damaged. No fire situation, two passengers believed code one, crews making the area safe, awaiting arrival of doctor and Ambulance. Crews standing by over.*'

'*Alpha zero one zero, your informative message received, and understood control out.*'

The ambulance crew arrived and were soon at the site of the crash.

'We've had a look in the cab; we've had a close look and we are pretty sure that both the people in there are dead,' Mac said as the ambulance crew approached him.

'Thanks for that, but we'll still have to have a look, the doctor should be here soon. It sure looks like there was one hell of an impact on the rock,' the ambulance officer said looking carefully through the shattered Perspex of the windscreen. The doctor arrived shortly after, and after a cursory look and a check for a pulse quickly certified both of the crew dead. Mac and the leading fireman gathered the two crews together and made to extricate the two men from the crushed cabin.

'Well Derek, it's been good working with you and your guys, they all worked really well together. I'm sure they'll have gained a lot from the experience. Good luck with the job, your crew did well today.'

'Thanks for your help, Mac.'

'No problem, if you're on your way to the city passing Graveton, pop in and see us, it'd be good to meet up again.'

Derek smiled, and felt grateful that Mac had taken him under his wing.

'Sure, will do; once again many thanks.'

'Right Mick, let's get off back and don't spare the horses,' Mac called across the cab. 'The night crew will be desperate to take over from us.'

Jake pushed the brass key into the lock of the front door of the house he'd lived in for almost every day of his short life. He walked into the narrow corridor from which the staircase ran. The familiar smell of his home assaulted his mind. *Could that be meat and potato pie?* He mused. The house had a familiarity about it; he couldn't imagine living anywhere else. It was the one place where he'd always felt safe, confident and happy; a familiarity brought about by real happiness. He loved his house and his mother; it was stacked with things and memories dating back to his very early childhood. His mother had nurtured him through the trauma of the loss of his dad. Difficult as it was for her to lose her husband, she recognised Jakes pain, so she devoted everything to make up for his loss. Yes, no one else could ever replace his mum.

'Hi, it's only me,' Jake called.

'Hello son,' she called back.

Jake walked into the kitchen; his mum was leaning up against the sink, her floral pink pinafore tied around her waist. 'What have you been up to today?' she asked.

Jake had lightness in his demeanour that she'd rarely noticed before.

'Well Ma,' a term Jake used only when he felt really good, 'I've had a great day. We had a fantastic fire.'

'Oh yes what was that then?' his mother asked.

'Well we had this old warehouse alight in the city centre; I wore BA with Mac. He let me do the fire fighting; it was really hot, like being in a dream. It was just what I hoped it would be like.'

'Sounds exciting son, and if I may say a bit dangerous?' she said, looking quizzically at Jake.

Jake scratched the back of his head. 'No, I was with Mac, it was great. He kept telling me what to do, and saying I was doing well. It was brilliant; I can't wait for the next one now.'

She smiled outwardly, but inside her stomach churned. 'Well son I'm glad you had a good time, but please don't go doing anything stupid will you?'

'Well then, we got back to the station and only just finished clearing up when we got another shout out in Derbyshire; we had a helicopter crash on the moors.'

'It sounds like you had a busy day.'

'Yeah it was fantastic, the two men in the helicopter were killed, and I had to help the boys carry their bodies off the moor to the ambulance.' Jake was buzzing, and his adrenaline flowed again as he relived the experience for his Mother.

'No, no Jacob, it isn't fantastic. Two people were killed.'

Jake, suddenly realising that what he was saying sounded callous, quickly re-phrased what he meant. 'I mean mum, it was a fabulous day, it was really interesting and I learned loads of stuff. Everyone tells me it's good to get your first fatality out of the way, there's no way Mac or the lads would take these jobs lightly.'

'I know son, I understand; always remember though that life is very precious, especially yours, and the public's as well so respect it, and look after yours. That's the most important thing to me.' She stopped and wiped the back of her hand across her eyes. 'I know you love it, but I don't ever want you losing yours. I think I'd die if I lost you,' she said, her voice cracking. Suddenly, her little boy was a man doing a man's job, and she was terrified of what could happen to him.

'I'll be OK mum; I promise I'll always be careful.'

'OK, now sit down and I'll get your dinner on the table for you,' she said, managing to regain her composure.

Chapter 16

Brian arrived at his semi detached house on the Park Estate, about a mile from the fire station. He quickly stripped off his uniform and ran a hot bath. Tonight he felt in need of a good soak and a book in the bath. He'd pop out later and get a takeaway, a couple of tins of lager, and watch some TV.

He lay in the bath reading his novel and it wasn't long before he dozed off. The phone rang. Brian was startled, the phone jolted him instantly back to consciousness, and he looked down to see his book floating amongst the bubbles.

'Oh shit!' he said to himself as he clambered out of the bath, attempting to get the phone before the answer machine cut in.

Hello, sorry I can't get to the phone right now, leave your name and number and I'll get right back to you, leave your message after the beep. 'Bugger it,' he said, moving as fast as he could across the landing and into his bedroom, leaving a trail of bubbles on the carpet. He leaned across the bed to grab the phone, and the towel that he'd quickly wrapped around his waist fell to the floor. Mrs Dean, his elderly neighbour, was taking washing from her line in the back garden. She looked up at exactly the moment Brian became detached from his towel and she caught his eye, smiled a toothless smile, winked, and gave him a thumbs up. Brian gave up; he picked up the phone ignoring the towel and smiled back at his neighbour.

'*Hello,*' he said.

'*Hi Brian, it's me,*' said the now familiar voice of Jane, his ex partner and mother of his daughter Jill.

'*Hello, how are you?*' he replied, surprised at the call.

'*I'm fine, but you sound flustered,*' she said, sympathetically.

'*Well if you'd been in the bath and accidentally exposed yourself to the old lady next door, I reckon you'd be a bit flustered.*'

'Sorry.' She laughed. '*Did she get the full Monty?*'

'Yeah, I reckon so.'

'*Don't worry; it will have made her day,*' she said, almost laughing out loud.

'*It's good of you to ring, is everything alright? How's Jill?*'

'*She's fine, so am I,*' Jane replied, '*I just phoned for a chat and to ask you something.*'

'*I'm glad you rang, what do you want to know?*'

'*Jill said to me yesterday that she'd like to see you soon. We wondered if you fancied coming and staying for the weekend, it is your weekend off. If you've not got anything planned, we'd love you to stay over, if you know what I mean.*'

Brian picked up on the hidden meaning, and his pulse jumped. '*I'd love to stay, especially seeing you both. And the staying over bit sounds perfect,*' he said, his heart beating a little faster.

'*Can you come over tonight?*' she said, '*I need,*' she paused.

'*What do you need?*' Brian asked.

She paused for what seemed an age. '*I need.*' She paused again. '*I just need you; I want to get close to you, close like the Isle of Wight, you know.*'

'*I've just got out of the bath, I'll be there in half an hour. Wait for me, don't start without me,*' he said, his heart now racing.

'*I won't, but hurry up. See you soon,*' she said. '*Bye, love you.*'

Chapter 17

The sky was darkening rapidly, just the dull orange glow as the sun finally disappeared like a hot ball of steel dipping into the sea behind the distant hills. The temperature dropped; a frost had been forecast with the possibility of light snow on the higher ground of the Pennines.

The small group of Scouts had made their way onto the plateau from Fairfield via the Kinder Reservoir an hour earlier, and were now heading for a sheltered spot somewhere in the middle of the large upturned dish shaped boggy surface of the Kinder Scout plateau. Their leader, head scout Alex Burgin, was eighteen years old, and had been a scout since he was young. He was now leading in an area where he'd been many times, but always before had been lead by a more experienced scout. He was happy and confident; this area was familiar to him, and he saw it as an opportunity to prove to himself and his peers that he could do it. He was however slightly nervous about controlling eight lively teenagers. They were young but pretty sensible for their age, they were good lads.

He remembered the lessons he'd learned and the pleasure he'd had doing just what they were about to do. This was these boys' first great adventure; away from the constraints of their parents, practising lighting fires and tying knots, building shelters, cooking their own food, and practising their navigation skills. And of course there was the singing of the traditional scout songs. He'd always felt this created teamwork and bonding, it was something he'd loved doing as a young scout and wanted to pass this on to these young boys.

They arrived at their camping spot at nine o clock in darkness; their only light was from their head torches.

Alex gathered them together. 'OK boys this is it, so let's get your tents put up and we'll get a brew going, then we'll make toast and jam before you go to bed.'

Alex quickly pitched his tent and watched the youngsters racing around chattering excitedly whilst they got to grips with getting their tents sorted out, and laying out their sleeping bags and bags of sweets for the inevitable midnight feast.

Brian pulled his car into the drive of Jane's small semi detached house. He lifted his overnight bag from the rear seat of the car and rang the doorbell. A few seconds later Jane opened the door. Jill ran past her and flung her arms around Brian's waist.

'Hello dad, I'm glad you could come round, I've missed you.'

'I've missed you too sweetie,' he replied, running his large hands over her head and gently squeezing her shoulder.

'Me too,' Jane said. 'Now let dad get in the door, best not let all the heat out.'

Jane looked at Brian and smiled. 'Come on through, get yourself sat down. Do you fancy a drink?'

'I'd love a cuppa,' he replied.

'Have you eaten yet?'

'No, I was going to do something after my bath.'

'Fancy a takeaway?'

'Yes, love one, what shall we have?'

'What would you like?' Jane asked Jill.

'Can I have fish and chips?' Jill said as she jumped onto Brian's knee.

'Tell you what, I'll take Jill with me to the shop while you make the tea and bread and butter,' he said, tousling Jill's hair.

'Sounds like a plan,' Jane called as she walked out into the kitchen.

'Do you know what young lady, I think they were the best fish and chips in the world, especially when we poured the mushy peas and the salt and vinegar on to them,' Brian laughed, 'and also because you picked them,' he said.

'Yes they were lovely. I like mushy peas; mum says they give her wind.'

Brian looked at Jane and a smirk crossed his face. 'So that's why you didn't have any was it?'

'You do say some things madam,' Jane said, 'you really do know how to embarrass me don't you.'

Brian had washed again and had a shave; he lay on Jane's bed in his pyjama bottoms, exposing his muscular hair covered chest. Jane came into the room in a sheer nightdress. Brian's heart quickened; this was much more than he could have hoped for. She climbed into bed, pulling the sheet over her chest. 'Are you going to get in then?' she said, a subtle smile creasing her pretty face.

Brian got off the bed. 'I just want to go and see Jill before I settle down, OK?'

'Yeah OK but don't be too long.'

'No I'll be just a minute.'

He padded quietly across the timber-boarded landing and silently opened Jill's bedroom door. The light was dim, just a dull illumination from a small night light by the side of her bed.

He leaned over her to kiss her forehead.

'Can you read me a story dad?' Jill said, opening her eyes and smiling.

Brian sighed silently. 'Of course I can Sweetie, now you just close your eyes.' He then read a chapter from one of her collection of the Roald Dahl books that she had lined up on her small bookshelf. When he'd finished reading, he paused and looked down at his daughter who was by now sleeping soundly.

The wind was changing direction and now came from the north; the temperature was dropping significantly. Alex shrugged in his sleeping bag. The boys were all quiet, but he was still awake. He pulled up the zip of his tent and peered out. It was cold and he shivered, the wind seemed to be gathering speed. The canvas of the tents began slapping rhythmically, and Alex was certain it would wake the boys. The moon peeped out from behind a cloud as it raced across the sky, illuminating a huge bank of cloud which was approaching from the north. Alex shivered and calculated that so far things would be OK, he'd have to monitor the conditions every half hour or so.

Brian crept back into Jane's room. The planned short visit to see Jill had taken longer than he'd anticipated. He could hear Jane breathing, a slow gentle rhythm; she'd said earlier in the evening that she was tired. It had been a hard week. Work every day, shopping, washing, ironing, running Jill around to the various clubs she belonged to. It was too much, and now she was paying the price; exhaustion. Brian realising that she was fast asleep, so slid silently beneath the cotton sheet and lay still, not wanting to disturb her.

Alex lay quietly; the sound of the wind straining the tent walls and the guy ropes preventing him from sleeping. He lay with his head torch lighting up his tent. He picked up the folded O.S. map of the Dark Peak, and marked their location on the map with his pen. Something inside him, a sixth sense perhaps, told him that he should be concerned. He looked again at their position on the map and began calculating routes to get them off the plateau should one be needed.

A loud high pitched noise startled Alex, the sound of sleet driven by the high wind pinging against his tent. The wind speed increased again, straining even further the ability of the tent to withstand the stress.

Peter Phillips was woken by the sound of tearing canvas and a sudden inrush of freezing wind. Alongside him, but still asleep, was Jason Grainger aged eleven, a boy with health problems. He suffered from severe Asthma, and often an attack was induced by stress.

Peter lay shocked, shaken to his core as the wind ripped the tent from over their heads. Jason was by now awake and struggling to get out of his sleeping bag. The wind tore across their camp site and now all of the boys were awake. Alex scrambled out of his tent and was shocked at their predicament. Of the five tents, three were now ripped and in danger of being completely blown away. Alex quickly gathered his group together.

'I want you all out of this,' he said as the wind roared and the icy sleet pummelled their faces.

'All squeeze into my tent, get your clothing together, ignore every-thing else,' he said, trying his best not to appear scared. But deep inside he was terrified. Alex knelt down and peered into his tent which was now jammed tight with eight worried young boys.

'Right lads, I don't want you to worry; this is an adventure I hadn't anticipated, but let's make the best of it shall we?'

He felt the wind driving the sleet, which was now beginning to turn into snow. It soon began to cover the side of his body. You stay there boys, I'm going to see if I can get anyone on my radio, just stay calm OK.'

Alex walked quickly away from the tents, not wishing to unduly alarm the boys, and tried for several minutes to make contact with someone on his radio but to no avail. His mind began to churn, he realised they were in a difficult spot, he just had to work out the best course of action, something he'd never had to do before.

Jack Greenstock was restless. He could hear the rain splatter against his bedroom window; he'd seen the weather report earlier in the evening. Reports like that always made him nervous, snow on the high ground was pretty, but not if that was where you were, and un-prepared. Over the thirty years he'd been in the Mountain Rescue Service, there had been many situations where he'd found himself and his colleagues out on the moors or the high ground in these condi-tions searching for missing people. Usually there was a happy end-ing, but on a few occasions there had been tragedies and it was these that had got to Jack and made him very sensitive about the weather. He switched on his bedside light and turned on his work radio, fully expecting silence. He left it switched on, and soon began to drift off to sleep again.

The conditions on the hill were getting tough. The snow was falling fast and the temperature had dropped even further, causing the boys and Alex to start feeling very cold.

You've got to make a decision Alex, What do you do? Stay put, or move to somewhere less exposed? He argued with himself, unsure of his best course of action; his inexperience was now beginning to show.

What would William, his old scoutmaster do? He made the decision, one made out of desperation and fear. One last try on the radio, he changed the band by turning the large dial and spoke.

'Hello, can anyone hear me?'

Jack almost jumped out of bed. The message came again.

'Hello can anyone hear this message?' The voice was now sounding desperate.

Jack picked up the radio. *'Hello, I'm getting you loud and clear over.'*

Alex thought he heard, amid the noise of the wind a distant voice from the radio.

'Hello, can you hear me please?' Desperation was coming from every fibre of his body.

'Yes, I'm hearing you, who are you and where are you over?'

Alex turned his back to the wind and huddled into a low crouch.

'Hello, I'm Alex Burgin, I'm a Scout Leader. We're on Kinder, the wind has shredded our tents, it's snowing, and I'm not sure what to do.'

Jack now turned into positive mode. *'Now listen to me Alex, how many of you are there, over.'* The feeling that now he wasn't alone, and that help was there, made him snap into a positive mode.

'There are nine of us, myself and eight youngsters, aged from ten to thirteen.'

'Right Alex, I can help, just give me a map reference if you have it and we'll be with you. What is the situation as of now?'

'Well we're OK, I've got all the lads in one tent, that's all that's left, the others are shredded and blown away. Our camp site is at SK 09180 87172, who are you?'

Jack paused and got his map from his bedside drawer. His wife, before she died, often commented on his habit of keeping maps in the bedroom. His stock answer was always 'you never know when you'll need them.' *'Just hang in there Alex, I'm just checking my map, I'm the leader of the Edale Mountain Rescue Team, once we've got you located on the map we'll be on our way.'* He quickly found the map reference and spoke again into the radio.

'Alex, listen in over.'

'Yes I can hear you over.'

'Now Alex, this is what I want you to do.'

Brian had fallen asleep; he was lying on his side when he felt movement beside him. In his semi conscious state he thought it was Jane, so he turned onto his back, the light from the landing streaked across the room.

'Can I get in with you and mummy, dad?'

Brian was suddenly wide awake. He looked up and saw Jill sitting on his side of the bed, holding her Teddy Bear.

'Are you OK, sweetie?' he asked.

'I had a bad dream, it scared me,' she said, lifting the blanket.

'OK, just this once then, squeeze in between mum and me.'

Brian smiled the happiest smile he had had for a long time. This was real life, what had gone before was just a pale imitation.

'Alex, this is the plan, you can't stay where you are, you'll be stuffed if the last tent gets shredded, so listen.'

Alex held the radio close to his now frozen ear.

'Now, I want you to calmly tell the boys that this is what you're going to do. Make sure they're all in their waterproofs, get their rucksacks if that's possible, make sure you have survival bags, then walk due South together. Have you got a length of rope available?'

'Yes.'

'Get the rope and tie yourself on to it, then get your strongest boy, tie him onto the line at the back, then get the rest of the boys between you and the lad on the back to hold onto the line. You're going to walk South, with you leading, use your compass. The Woolpack Rocks are about a quarter of a mile to the South. When you get there, I want you to call me back on this frequency, OK Alex?'

'Yes I've got that, thank you.'

'Alex, just hammer in to them the need for them to stay together, hold on to the line at all costs, we'll be on our way as fast as we can.'

Jack quickly called the police and gave them the information he had. They then informed the Mountain Rescue controller.

Pat Ford had been a controller for eight years. Previously she'd been an active member of the rescue team, but as the years progressed she'd been affected by Arthritis, and now this was her way of continuing her contribution and staying involved. Pat activated the team's alerters and gave out details of the location of the incident.

Andy Jackson climbed quickly into his car; he was heading direct to Upper Booth at the base of the plateau to get a fast start with his dog. He was barely awake after doing his afternoon shift at the factory in Sheffield. He'd noticed the chill in the air, and anticipated a cold couple of hours.

Jag, Andy's rescue dog, danced around in the back of the car, hopeful that he was going to have some fun.

The team's headquarters in Hope was a hive of activity; groups of men and women scuttling around gathering gear together, checking radios, preparing for a fast getaway. Many of the team however had made their way direct to Upper Booth and the grid reference that Pat had supplied.

Jack Greenstock lived just a couple of hundred yards away from where their cement works H.Q. was located, and he had wasted no time turning in.

Amanda Ridgewell and Paul Blake usually acted as the team's snatch squad. Although in her forties, Amanda was tall and slim, listing her interests, after the mountain rescue, as fell running and rock climbing. She was fit and strong; much more so than her slight build would seem to indicate. Paul was an ex Sheffield Harrier and a long time athlete. When called, they would often go off first using their speed and fitness to get them to an emergency fast.

Jack called across the garage to Tony Yeats.

'You come on in the Custard Bus Tony; I'll take DM 1 with the rest of the lads.'

He knew that some of the team would make it to the location given to them by the controller in their own vehicles, and they'd be getting prepared to go by the time they arrived on the scene. The Custard Bus, as it was affectionately known, was a bright yellow Transit Van that had served them well for a good few years, but as usual there were the ongoing problems of keeping it running. Fortunately, one of the team was a mechanic and tried his best to keep it serviceable, but they all knew its days were numbered. That would be a sad day for the team, as it was held with great affection by them all, most of whom had cut their teeth using the yellow peril.

DM 1, or Derwent mobile 1, was the unit's other vehicle, a Land Rover with a trailer that carried the bulk of the equipment they would likely need. Now that both vehicles were fully crewed, they shot out of the garage into the cold night. As Jack looked forward from his cab he could see that the top of the ridge was swathed in a thick blanket of cloud, which didn't bode well for the summit of Kinder Scout. He shuddered; he'd done this trip many times before, often without the warmth of success.

Alex was worried. All of the group were up and dressed in their waterproofs, he knew he had to be quick, and as the wind roared, tearing at their clothing, he could see that the smaller boys were scared. He quickly gathered them together.

'Right boys this is what we're going to do. I don't want you to worry; we'll soon be under cover. Stay close.'

Initially the group moved well together with Alex leading, Chris Clark, the oldest of the boys, tied on to the back of the line, and the remainder holding the line following in Alex's footsteps. The ferocity of the wind soon began to take effect; many of the boys were literally blown off their feet as they tried to wade through the ever deepening snow which gathered in the channels of the Kinder summit. The strength of the wind slowed down their progress more than Alex had anticipated. The cold was desperate, and was made even worse by the freezing wind-chill.

Jason Grainger ploughed on, but the extreme cold and the stress of their predicament began to effect him. The constant inhalation of cold air, along with the massive effort needed to keep up the pace of the others, was causing him difficulty, his lungs were becoming tight and he began to feel light headed. Frequently he fell into the drifting snow, but Chris Clark moved forward each time and dragged him back onto his feet.

'I can't breathe, Chris,' young Jason gasped, and almost fell again.

Alex turned and looked back, checking that they were all still together, and realised there was a problem when he noticed that Chris was struggling with Jason. He stopped.

'Right lads, have a rest a minute out of the wind.' His mind was racing. 'Jason, take off your rucksack, have you got your inhaler?'

Jason patted his pockets, 'I've got it somewhere,' he gasped, struggling to remain standing.

'Just stand there; let me look for it for you,' Alex said as he began to forage through Jason's pockets. There was no sign of the inhaler Jason so badly needed.

'Hello there, can you hear me Jack?' Alex called on his radio, desperately hoping that it would get a reply. All the time the wind tore at them and the little group were becoming cold and frightened.

The Land Rover roared up Winnat's Pass, its tyres screeched as Tom Sanders dragged the wheel round to take the bend at the summit of the pass. He noticed that ice was starting to form on the road and the occasional flurry of sleet pounded against the windscreen. Tom jammed the vehicle into the lowest gear and pressed hard on the accelerator pushing on steeply through Mam Nick, a wedge of land sculpted from the ridge allowing the passage of the road. They descended steeply, twisting snake like into the isolated village of Edale. They could see that conditions on the hill were bad, and began to mentally brace themselves for what was about to come.

'What do you reckon guys?' Jack called to the rest of his team on board. 'Jacobs's Ladder or Crowden Clough?'

After a short few seconds the answer came.

'If they're going to be at the Woolpacks, our best bet is Upper Booth and Crowden Clough.

'I agree,' Jack said. 'The Clough it is then.'

'DM1 to DM3, Amanda, are you receiving over?

Amanda and Paul had just arrived at Upper Booth. *'Yeah Jack we're receiving you over.'*

'Amanda, we're going up to the Woolpacks via Crowden, will you make it to Jacob's Ladder and do the snatch, direct to the Woolpacks over.'

'Yeah will do. That's a tough run, will be in touch.'

'Yeah, good luck, one other thing, they have a serious asthmatic with them, make sure you have the inhaler with you over.'

'Hello can you hear me, over.' Alex was making desperate efforts to get contact again.

Jack heard the call above the engine noise and could tell that Alex was stressed. *'Hello Alex, is that you, over?'*

'Yeah, we're in difficulties, it's terrible up here, it's very cold, deep snow and one boy struggling. He's asthmatic, reckon we're a couple of hundred yards from the rocks over.'

'We're on the way Alex; a bit of psychology may help, tell them it's only a hundred yards, but get them moving. When you're at the rocks give me another call.'

Tom slammed the gear lever down to help brake as they approached another sharp bend in the road, he felt the slide coming, the back end of the vehicle swung out several feet before he could correct it and he just managed to avoid hitting a roadside tree.

'Phew that was a bit too close for comfort,' Jack called above the rasping roar of the engine, whirring as it was used to assist the brakes.

They slid under the rail bridge and moved left along the narrow metalled road leading to Upper Booth.

Brian stirred, Jill had shuffled and was now taking up most of the bed, and Brian was just hanging on to a small portion of the blanket that covered them. His bladder called. He slid out of bed and as he did he pulled the curtain to one side and was surprised to see that snow was falling outside.

He slid back under the covers.

'Dad,' Jill was awake. 'Can I have a drink please?'

Brian smiled. 'Of course you can, water?'

'Yes please dad.'

Brian slid out of bed again and filled a glass tumbler in the bathroom. Jane stirred.

'Hi, you're awake then?' Jane said blearily, rubbing her eyes.

'Yep, we have a visitor.'

'So I see, madam,' Jane said, putting her arm around her daughter and squeezing her tightly.

'Shall I go down and make us all a nice cup of tea?' Brian said, rubbing his fingers through his hair in an attempt to bring himself back to full consciousness.

Jane released Jill from her grip. 'What time is it?' she asked.

Brian squinted at the clock beside Jane on her bedside cabinet. 'It's ten to four. I suppose we're all awake, we may as well.'

'Are you going back in your own bed now?' Jane said, looking at Jill. 'You need to get back to sleep; you'll be worn out when it's time to get up.'

'But I want to stay here with daddy,' she implored.

'Well OK, but only if you go back to sleep.'

The Land Rover and Transit pulled up in the narrow lane. The teams gathered around Jack.

'Look boys, they're still not at the Woolpacks, I'll get back to them. Let's get the gear together, the space blankets, first aid kits, and take the casualty bag, just in case we need it. The usual stuff, any questions?'

Andy and Jag had preceded the rest of the team by about five minutes and he was well prepared.

'Andy, they're still not at the Woolpack but I expect they will be by the time you get there, so if you can head up in front of us and do what you do with Jag, we'll be after you ASAP. I want you to aim off to the right and come into the rocks from the east. We'll be behind you. Alison and Paul are heading up from Jacob's, so there's a good chance they'll be there first; they'll approach from the west.'

The teams soon loaded their back packs and tested their radios and indicated that they were ready to go.

Jack called across. 'Tom will be the base contact with us, and linked to Control, so keep in touch, it looks like things could get a bit difficult.'

The team set off and were soon lost to sight. Within minutes they were at the snow line and heading steeply upwards alongside the rapidly freezing stream.

Andy was well in front of the main group. He'd released Jag who was quartering the hillside, stopping frequently to try to pick up a scent in the hard blowing wind. Jag's experience and time served on the hillsides of the Lake District and Scotland were serving him well, and this was, for him a very familiar and fun job, despite the appalling conditions.

Alex stopped momentarily, the conditions had worsened, he wanted the boys out of the wind fast, but also he had to be sure they were kept up close together.

He called above the noise of the wind. 'Is everyone OK?' He received a unanimous 'we're all OK Alex.' The short rest seemed to have helped them all. Jason seemed to have got his second wind and had recovered from his asthmatic episode without his medication, and the rest of the boys, despite the difficult conditions, seemed to be enjoying the challenge. Alex had worked out that they should be at the rocks within a few minutes if they managed to keep going without any further problems.

'Right lads, we're nearly there, let's move on again, you're all doing really well,' Alex said to the boys who were now feeling confident that they were going to be all right.

'Hello Alex, are you receiving over?'

Alex felt somehow stronger being in touch with the outside world, the radio message sent a surge of optimism through him.

'Hello, yes receiving you over.'

Jack felt relieved that they were still able to reach them.

'Give me a progress report Alex over,' he said, trying to sound calm.

'We're going well, Jason seems to be less troubled by his asthma than before, and we're all still together, should be at the rocks in a few minutes over.'

'Good lad, you're all doing well, we'll be with you soon. We're on our way up. When you get to the rocks get straight into your survival bags, keep together, and put on your head torches, this will help us locate you over.'

'Will do Jack, hope to see you soon.'

'You will. Look out for the dog, he likes biscuits and he's called Jag.'

The wind had eased but the snow was now falling heavily and lay deep in the grough's, making the going hard and slow.

'Keep going lads, nearly there.' Alex said. 'Are you all OK?'

Quite suddenly they were out of the channels close to the steep edge of the summit. Now, unprotected by the high sides of the groughs, the wind speed picked up and was battering them, but the snow didn't lie so deep on the ground, driven by the wind and accumulating against any contour or rock, making their progress less arduous.

The rocks, I think this is it, Alex said to himself. Suddenly all of the fear dissipated from his body, he was now certain they would all be safe.

'We're here lads; can you see the big rock over there?' he pointed, indicating a large boulder about thirty yards away. 'Get round the leeward side and get into your survival bags as quick as you can.' The sense of relief in the boys was obvious as they staggered across to the boulder and collapsed to the ground.

'Hello Jack, glad to say we're here, all intact and all behind one huge boulder, no injuries, over.'

'Well done Alex, you've done well; someone will be with you in, I guess, ten minutes, keep your eyes open and head torches on, out.'

Alison and Paul were moving fast despite the conditions; Andy Jackson and his dog Jag were leaping forward in front of the team. Jag had been given his head and was doing what these dogs do. He was catching the wind and systematically searching the side of the mountain.

Quite suddenly, Alison and Paul hit the summit plateau. 'OK, let's head east, she called to Paul.

'Jack, are you receiving me over.'

'Loud and clear Alison.'

'We're on the plateau, now heading east, should be at the Woolpacks inside ten minutes over.'

'Well done girl, you must have got a shuffle on,' Jack said, struggling to get his breath. His team were moving at a pace that was just beyond

comfortable for him, his sixty years now beginning to tell. *'Did you pick up my chat with Alex?'*

'Andy did you get that over?'

'Yep, got it, Jag is running around demented; I don't think it'll be long before he finds them over.'

'Yeah, hope so; we're just coming up onto the top now, I reckon we'll meet up with you in about ten minutes over.'

'Jack; Jag's disappeared at speed, I reckon he's got the scent, will be in touch, out.' Andy, once again, felt proud of his dog.

Jack and his team crested the plateau; Jack was now beginning to understand the torture the boys must have endured, the wind was ferociously driving the snow hard into their faces.

Alex and the young Scouts huddled together; they watched the heavy snow being driven horizontally by the fierce wind from their relatively protected spot in the lee of the large rock. Suddenly, without warning, a black and white shape careered around the rock, it spotted the group of boys and leapt on them barking furiously.

Alex laughed out loud, and then there was the sudden release of tension as Jag came among them which brought about a round of wild cheering from the boys.

'DM 1 from Andy over.'

Jack heard the message over the sound of the wind which ripped around them as they made their way across the plateau.

'Go ahead Andy over.'

'I reckon Jag's found them, he ran wild a minute ago and I can hear him barking, so it looks positive. Will get back to you in a sec.'

Jag was jumping around licking the boys' faces as they remained cocooned in their survival bags.

'Come here boy,' one lad said, having rummaged around in his rucksack and found the remains of a cheese sandwich. Jag accepted it gladly and then continued his quest to extract as much food from the boys as he could before Andy got to him.

Within five minutes the rest of the teams met up around the area of the rock and were busy checking the health of the group. Despite the trauma and being cold and uncomfortable there were no injuries to report.

Jack pulled Alex to one side. 'You did a good job there son, I couldn't have done it any better myself, well done.'

Alex was exhausted through the sheer effort of moving the boys and the stress of the situation. He'd survived on adrenaline and now it was virtually over. With everyone safe, the flow stopped and tiredness began to overtake him.

'Right boys this is what we'll do now.' Jack spoke to the group briefly, not wishing to extend their time out in the cold. Each boy was fully kitted out in waterproof clothing carrying his own rucksack, and was accompanied by a member of the Mountain Rescue Team to the base of the hill, then transported to the HQ in Hope. After several phone calls had been made to their parents, arrangements were made to pick the boys up and take them home.

Jack and Alex sat together in the kitchen of the Hope headquarters.

'Well Alex, you did well there, and the boys all seemed to have enjoyed the experience.'

'Well it's thanks to you and the team that we survived. My mind went blank; it was only when I managed to get you on the radio that I seemed to get my head straight.' Alex took a large gulp of hot tea. 'So thank you very much Jack, we're all very grateful that you switched your radio on tonight.'

Chapter 18

It was eight thirty when the alarm sounded; they were still fast asleep with Jill curled up in a tight ball between Brian and Jane. Brian sat up with a start. Jane stirred; Jill remained untouched by the shrill ringing. 'Well what a pleasant night, sorry about that,' Jane said apologetically.

'Don't worry about it; it was nice, just what I needed, time with my two girls.'

'Well, maybe we'll have to arrange the next visit when Jill's at school,' Jane said, a wicked grin crossing her face.

After parade, Red Watch did the routine checks then went to the mess deck for a cup of tea, before their drill session.

Jake was on tea making duty again. 'This time young Jake, put a bloody tea bag in the water will you, the last effort was like gnat's pee,' Jock shouted through the hatch where Jake was foraging through the cupboards looking for the mugs. A few minutes later, he emerged with a tray of tea, which he put down in the middle of the table, then sat down next to Mick Young. 'Well that looks about the right colour, but what does it taste like?' Mick said.

Brian spoke. 'Jake, this is your chance to be the mess man for this tour, so may I suggest that you start thinking about what you need for the meals to come this week.'

Jake looked at Brian. Cooking had never been a thing that had interested Jake, let alone planning meals and buying the food, he was nervous. He looked around the table hoping for someone to come forward to offer a helping hand or even some advice, but none came.

'What do I have to buy?' Jake said, a light sweat beginning to appear on his forehead. His predicament, noticed by the watch, was ignored.

Jock intervened. 'Well young Jake, erstwhile hero and general good guy, winner of the coveted silver axe, I'll tell you what you have to buy.'

Jake thought for a second that Jock was his saviour and breathed a silent sigh of relief.

'Ye go out laddie, to the supermarket, ye get yerself a trolley, but make sure you have a pound coin for the trolley, then you push the trolley round the supermarket and you buy food. Simple as that OK?'

'Yeah,' Jake said ironically, 'but how do I know what food to buy?'

Taff butted in. 'Listen Jake, take no notice of these idiots, it's easy, you just have to decide what to cook and then you go and buy the stuff, nothing complicated OK?'

Jake listened and heard but couldn't understand. *Was he missing something or are they taking the Mickey?*

'OK, what do you want to eat?' Jake said, beginning to get the drift.

'Well young Jake, you're the mess manager, you don't want us to do the job for you do you? That's your job. You decide, you buy, you cook, we only eat, we're out of the loop.'

'Yeah but what if I cook stuff you don't like?'

'The advantage of being the mess man is that while we're out in the cold and rain doing tests etc, you're in here in the warm listening to the radio, doing the cooking.' Brian paused. 'The disadvantage of course is that if we don't like what you cook then it changes. We are in here in the warm and you are out there in the cold and rain,' he said, not allowing a smile to emerge from his ruddy cheeks.

Mac came onto the mess deck. 'OK, you shower, let's have you out on the yard and get a bit of exercise shall we?' he said, a broad grin spread across his face.

'Crew, as detailed, get to work,' Mac shouted from the rear of the appliance.

Jake sprang from the back seat of the machine. Quickly slamming the locker door open, there was a general melee around the lockers. Taff, Jock, Brian and Mick slid the thirteen point five metre ladder from the roof of the machine and began pitching it into the fourth floor of the drill tower. Jake sprinted around the yard, running hose and setting the hydrant in; then he grabbed a line bag from another locker and slid his arm through the canvas loop. He was now ready to climb the ladder. His objective; to get into the fourth floor window assisted by one other crew member, the task then to lower the twelve stone dummy from the window by using the lowering under foot technique, a skill he'd learned and perfected whilst at training school.

'Rest.' Mac's voice barked across the yard, the crew stopped everything instantaneously.

'I don't want anyone entering this burning tower until we have water on a branch. Jock, you get on the pump and let's give Jake some protection from the fire. Taff, once he's in there, you go up and support him. Crew, get to work.'

Once again, the crew sprinted around the yard with Jock operating the pump, supplying water to the covering jet. Jake began climbing the ladder. Brian was standing with one foot on the base of the ladder to give it stability whilst Jake climbed rapidly upwards. Mick had the water now crackling from the branch; he followed Jake, spraying the water onto the wall of the tower whilst he climbed.

Mac stood back to give him the best view of the drill, he smiled; he had a shrewd idea that something was about to happen.

Jake climbed quickly and soon stepped into the window, he pulled the line bag from his shoulder and undid the clip which secured the bag. He then tipped out the line which he quickly tied to the guard rail, then tied the knot, a double bowline which would be used to lower the dummy to the ground. He heard the change in the tone of the engine but nothing registered with him, he was focussed on getting the knot tied correctly onto the dummy, so he barely responded. Mick lifted the branch, and now the water was aimed directly into the window. Jake was completely unprepared so took the full force of the jet. Instantly he was soaked by a river of cold water, and when he caught his breath he laughed. *I should have seen that coming!* he thought.

'Knock off make up,' Mac shouted above the noise of the pump. Jock slammed up the throttle and quickly disconnected the hose from the pump. Jake untied the line and threw it out of the tower window. 'Stand from under,' he called. Brian stepped away from the base of the ladder and watched as the line smacked into the saturated concrete close by his feet. Jake climbed out onto the ladder and quickly descended, the water still dripping from his boots.

The crew lined up at the back of the machine. 'OK lads that was pretty good. The ladder pitch was slick, Jake your hose running was fast. Jock you were on the ball on the pump, so no problems. I know Jake got wet, but other than that, it was good. Let's get the kit sorted, then on the mess deck for a chat. Jake you get in now. Make sure you're dry then get on and make the tea and sandwiches.'

The crew sat round the table, making inroads into the cheese and onion doorsteps that Jake had prepared for them.

'You've done a good job here Jake, they just needed a bit more brown sauce and they'd have been perfect,' Taff said. Jake grinned; he was happy being part of the team.

'Right guys, 'Mac said, 'I wanted to talk about next week. Jock, you and Brian are off to the West Midlands to the guy's funeral. Full undress uniform and you've got to be at the church by ten thirty. I've got the cover arranged so there are no problems. Remember you're representing the brigade and red watch, so stay sober and don't get into any trouble.'

'Come on Mac; are we likely to get into trouble?' Brian laughed.

'Well if the last time you were let off the lead is anything to go by, yes.'

'No, it'll be fine, we'll come straight back after the service, we promise.'

Mac stretched his aching body before slumping into his padded office chair; he pulled open the drawer and took out a small buff folder. He got up and shouted through his door.

'Brian, is Pete there? If not, find him, I want to see him in my office.'

Pete had been in the hose room doing repairs to damaged hose. He walked into Mac's office.

'Come in Pete, sit down. How are things?'

Pete sat down opposite Mac, he looked up, his face looking tired and grey.

'No change since we spoke the other day, of course she knows, and she's obviously worried about me and the boys, it's understandable I suppose.'

'Well, you know the score, we'll do whatever is needed to help. If you need time off or help in any way, let us know.'

'Yeah, thanks Mac, I may need it.'

Mac lifted up the folder and opened it. 'I've had a word with the Station Commander and the Divisional Benevolent rep, I've not given them any great detail, but it seems to us that it would be good for all of you if we could fix it up for you to go for a break up to the Benevolent Fund place at Penrith. I'm told the amenities are first class, it would give you all a break and be a nice change for Trudy and the boys. Give it some thought, have a chat with her, and come back to me OK?'

'OK Mac I'll do that, I'm sure that she'll like that.'

Chapter 19

Mac and Val sat having their evening meal. 'How's things?' she said, 'you seem a bit out of sorts tonight.'

'To be honest love, I'm worried about Pete Jacks. I spoke with him today. He says Trudy isn't too good, he's pretty upset about her.'

'What did he say?' she replied, her face showing her concern.

'He said she's deteriorated, and the doctors aren't too optimistic about things.'

'I've suggested we try to get them up to Penrith, to give them something to look forward to.'

'Yeah, I'm sure they'd like it, I've heard it's superb.'

Mac scrubbed his fingers through his hair, a sure sign he was upset about the situation. 'I just wish I could do more to help,' he said.

Val stood behind Mac and rubbed his shoulders. 'Why don't we have them over for a meal?' she said, out of the blue. 'We said ages ago that we should do it.'

Mac sighed. 'That could be nice, how about you giving Trudy a call tomorrow, I'll speak to Pete at work in the morning.'

Chapter 20

It was nine thirty in the morning; Albert Jenkins stood at the lathe that he had stood at for over fifty-five years. It had been a lifetime of work and sweat to raise his family. He'd taught his six children the rights and wrongs of life and the value of family. He was a proud man.

His wife Jeannie had died two years earlier from cancer; it had been a long torturous process that had tested the fabric of the family to breaking point. But true to the principles he'd instilled in them from their earliest years, they rallied around him. Despite great personal sacrifice, they supported him at the time of his greatest need.

William his eldest, a Major in the Parachute Regiment. His oldest daughter Doreen, a PA to the director of a London bank resigned from her job and came home to live with her mum and dad until the end. Two others, Bernard and Lizzie, living abroad visited; Bernie travelling from Sydney and Lizzie from Montreal, the two youngest Eric and Catherine still lived in the city and gave all their time to supporting their parents.

Albert was a craftsman; he'd been brought up in the trade, the craft that had made Sheffield famous around the world. He was a Little Mester or Little Master, a master of the craft of cutlery making, one of the last of a dying breed. He had a small factory on the outskirts of the city, from where he'd plied his trade since he was a boy; his DNA was embedded in every centimetre of the unit. The building, now old, was in need of some repair. The windows were badly in need of new frames, the floor still comprising of dried mud, fifty years of grease was absorbed into the timber bench that bore the scars of his years of labour. Years ago, when the children were young, he'd bring them to work with him on a Saturday morning; they'd do colouring and play around the site in which other Little Mesters worked.

He'd been busy, fulfilling an order for several sets of cutlery, all made by hand. The swarf had built up from the dozens of bone handled knives he had formed on his lathe. The shallow heaps of bone dust lay like a carpet around the workshop.

Albert made himself a cup of tea, boiling the water on his old gas ring, resisting the temptation to buy a new electric kettle. He sat on his stool listening to the music being played on the local radio station. As he sipped his tea, he reminisced about his wife, who in his mind still lay by his side every night, her nightdress still neatly folded beneath her pillow. He thought of the kids; always as six or seven year olds, cheeky and full of energy. How he'd loved those days. Still, they texted him or rang him every day, they'd bought him a computer, something that he had never got to grips with. He finished his mug of tea and pushed the button on his grindstone, he was going to sharpen his chisels, something he'd done virtually all of his working life.

The grinding wheel spun and whined. Albert lay the edge of the chisel against the stone, the familiar sound of steel on stone, he saw the sheet of sparks flying from the stone across his arm. He didn't see the sparks settle in the small pile of swarf dust by his feet. He didn't see the embryonic swirl of dust like a micro tornado gathering around his legs. Seconds later, he did see the dust gathering rapidly around him, the sparks still flying from the stone. In the final seconds of his life, Albert saw the sparks ignite the cloud of dust which was now hovered around him; with the perfect conditions of flammable dust and the correct ratio of oxygen in place to create a dust explosion. He saw the flash as the dust ignited, he heard the beginnings of the bang as the rapidly igniting dust particles flashed around him. He had no time to react; he was blown violently across the lathe he'd used safely for over fifty years. In his final second there was a time in which the realisation of what was happening hit him and then a momentary vision of his wife and children flashed through his head before he died amid the dirty dusty debris of his wrecked workshop.

Red Watch had finished parade and fully engaged doing their customary daily routine of checking appliances and equipment. Mac had taken Pete into his office for a chat.

'Well Pete, a couple of things. How's Trudy today?'

Pete looked slightly happier today than the last time he had spoken to Mac.

'You know what, Mac, it's like a miracle, she's great today. She had a good night's sleep; I wasn't disturbed at all, which is unusual.' Pete sat up straight; Mac spotted it, a sure sign that he was feeling happier about things.

Mac smiled. 'You've settled in well, and I'm very happy with you, the guys like you and are confident you fit in. For me that's important.' Mac paused. 'What are you Trudy and the kids doing next Thursday night?'

'Not sure without looking at the diary, but I doubt we've anything on, we don't get out much these days.'

'I spoke with Val last night; she said she'd love you Trudy and the boys to come round for a meal with us.'

'That sounds good Mac, I'm sure it will be OK, but I'll have to just check with her.'

'Good, let me know and we'll get it arranged, do any of you have anything you don't like to eat.'

'No, the boys eat anything and everything. Trudy struggles a bit with steak and some meats; chicken she loves, and eats it easily.'

'Good, one last thing. Have you thought anymore about Penrith?'

Before Pete could answer, a loud explosion shook the building.

'Christ, what was that?' Mac said as he jumped up from his chair. 'I think you'd better go and get rigged Pete, sounds as though we've got a shout.'

Taff pulled the appliance off the station forecourt as the traffic slowed to allow them onto the road. Mac pushed the button that set the wailers going, heightening the tension Jake was already feeling. Brian looked across the back of the machine at Jake.

'You'll be fine Jake, stick with me; get your set on and make sure your tally's filled out properly.'

Jake knew it was but checked it again anyway. Realising that he was going into a job made his heart pound as the machine swerved and switched its way through the traffic.

'Looks like a good one boys,' Mac shouted to the back of the cab.

A dense cloud of dusty black smoke surged into the atmosphere about four hundred metres away. Mac pushed the button again and the siren wailed, cars slowed and pulled to one side. Taff gunned the machine forward, feeling the water slosh back and forth in the tank behind them.

Another explosion and an eruption of flame shot into the sky, and Jake's heart fizzed with excitement. 'Settle down Jake, remember; composure and calmness.' Brian smirked; he remembered his younger days when a job like this would have sent him into an adrenaline fuelled frenzy.

The building, mainly of brick and timber, was badly damaged; most of the roof at one end had been lifted and deposited a hundred feet away.

'*Control from Alpha zero one zero make pumps four over,*' Mac said over the radio.

'*Alpha zero one zero your make pumps four received, out.*'

'Taff get the hydrant in. Jake, Brian, get started up, I want you in straight away.'

'Mick, you set up BA control over there,' Mac called, as he pointed to a point close to the building but protected somewhat by a solid wall. 'Brian, I want a guide line putting in OK?'

'Yeah OK Mac,' he replied almost casually. 'Are you about ready young man?' Brian said, as Jake completed his starting up procedure. Mac threw the bag containing the guideline to Jake. 'Get that fixed on to Brian's belt, Jake.'

'*Control from Alpha zero one zero over.*'

'*Go ahead over.*'

'*Informative message. From Sub Officer James at Jenkin's cutlery works. A building of two floors approximately seventy five metres by thirty five meters well alight, one jet two BA in use over.*'

Taff pushed the throttle lever slowly down, increasing the pressure on the jet that Brian and Jake had taken into the building. They clambered over the rubble which had formed part of the now devastated gable end of the building, dragging the hose with him them. Jake had secured the guide line close by the entry point, and fed it out across the ground, whilst Brian knocked down pockets of fire as they moved deeper into the building. Jake was sweating hard, dragging the hose to give Brian the freedom to move with the jet of water. He also had the task of securing the guideline to anything which would allow secure anchorage which was tough; smoke had reduced their visibility to a couple of metres.

Brian stopped and turned to Jake.

'How are we doing Jake?' he said, looking at his young inexperienced colleague, his voice distorted by the thick rubber of his facemask. Jake's face was red with effort; the sweat poured from his face and gathered in the dead space of his facemask.

'I'm OK,' Jake panted through his tortured breath. The heat and the difficulty of manoeuvring himself and the hose across the rubble strewn ground and the sheer effort of dragging the hose was tough on Jake. Brian recognised the problem he was having. 'We'll take a breather here; let's rest a minute.'

They crouched low with broken brickwork and shattered timbers lying around them. Jake could hear the crackling of the fire and the splitting bricks as the building moved and groaned, and then the sounds of the action outside the building. Pumps were running; they could hear the voices of men as they got more jets of water to work on the fire. Jake looked up and saw the smoke moving at speed out toward the entrance through which they'd entered.

'Are you ready to move on, Jake?' Brian asked.

'Yeah, I'm fine now, thanks,' Jake responded.

'OK sunshine, let's go and smack its arse shall we?' he said, lifting up the branch and beginning to drag the hose through the smoke which flowed like a river a few inches above their crouching bodies. Jake smiled; this expression was one he'd not heard before.

There was a tearing of timber and cracking of brick and part of a wall collapsed behind them, at the spot where they'd rested.

'Bloody hell, it's a good job we moved,' Brian chuckled.

'Yeah,' Jake replied nervously. His senses were as sharp as a needle, hearing and seeing everything.

Brian moved forward. Jake stuck close behind tying the guideline to a loose piece of girder. A rumble penetrated the smoke. Brian cocked his ear.

'Get down Jake.' The urgency was obvious in Brian's voice. Jake responded instantaneously flattening himself against the floor. The smoke evaporated, driven by a ball of fire which incinerated everything in its path.

'Stay low,' Brian shouted above the roar of the oncoming torrent of fire. Brian raised himself up onto his elbows, dipped his face to his chest and quickly opening up the jet of water from the branch, turning the nozzle until a high-pressure wide spray formed a curtain of water in front of them.

The ball of fire was upon them in seconds; it screamed past and over them, the water boiling around them in dense clouds of steam. The ceiling above turned to ash and fell like filthy rain, covering them in a veil of hot grey slurry. Jake gritted his teeth as the temperature climbed to almost unbearable levels; he forced his eyes upward and saw Brian in front of him. Brian was being almost boiled alive; the water which had soaked and protected him now was scalding him inside his tunic.

The fire was developing fast; Mac had now been relieved of his command by ADO Paul Davis. A young go getter, who served his apprenticeship on Mac's watch.

'Mac, can I leave you to look after the entry controls? Keep in touch by radio. Any problems let me know, alright?'

Since the fire had developed, the number of appliances had escalated and so had the entry control procedure. More men in the building meant more control was needed; now there were three entry points and this vital function had to be managed carefully. There were five teams of two men operating inside the building. The appliances were supplying water to eight jets; three hydrants were being used to supply the necessary water to the pumps.

Alex Battle screeched to a halt behind the rearmost appliance. Although not on call, having heard about the fire, nothing was going to stop him *going for a look* as he would say. Almost simultaneously, Divisional Commander Ian Blain pulled up at the job.

'How goes it Ian?' Alex said on seeing the DC arrive at the fire ground.

'I thought you were off duty tonight Alex?'

'Yeah well you know me, can't resist having a look.'

Ian looked at him. 'Are you taking over?' he asked.

'No, that wouldn't be right,' he emphasised, 'I just wanted to have a look; if you want any help just ask, I'll just watch and keep my eyes open for you, and to be honest I forgot to put my fire gear in the car.' Ian laughed. Since his miraculous re-birth a few months earlier, he'd relished the chance to get out and get to see the crews on the fire ground, something he'd previously avoided where possible, he'd developed a new respect for the men in his division, and they for him.

The Control Unit trundled into the yard at the front of the building.

'I want all OICs not directly involved to the control unit now. Over.' Ian called into his personal radio. He needed information to allow him to devise a strategy to put the fire out, and no one better than the men on the ground to help devise the method.

They stood in an irregular group in the control vehicle. Ian spoke.

'Right guys, give me a report as you see it.'

Sub Officer Pete Grainger from High Storrs station spoke up. 'I've got two teams in on the first floor. They tell me that it's pretty damn warm up there, but they seem happy that they're holding it.'

The next officer spoke. 'I've got my men on two jets at the north end, and they tell me they think they're making good progress.'

Mac spoke up. 'I have a team of two in BA. The latest report says that they are struggling to hold it. Seems to me we need to get at least one more jet in and really get after it before it gets after us.' The rest of the officers nodded their heads in agreement.

'How's the water supply holding up?' Ian asked, writing notes on a note pad attached to a clip board.

Paul Davis was monitoring this. 'So far it's OK, we've got the water company to increase the pressure but I reckon if we need more jets we'll struggle,' he said.

Alex Battle spoke up. 'I'm sorry to interfere, but it seems to me if we reduce the number of jets by a couple at the North end, and just hold the fire there then re-deploy those jets at the South end and squeeze it, that could work.'

Paul looked around the unit, there seemed to be a general agreement that it could work.

'OK lads, we'll do just that. Just let the teams in the building know what we're going to do OK? Let's get to it.'

Jane had dropped Jill off at school, and got to work in plenty of time before she was due to start her work at the local solicitors office where she worked as a legal secretary. She looked up at the ancient clock on the wall opposite her desk and noticed the time. It was nine fifty. She didn't know why she noticed the time, it was nothing of significance. She felt her heart beginning to race and her body growing warm. Too warm, even hot. Perspiration began to flow from her face; she felt ill. She got up from her chair and walked into one of the partner's offices.

'I'm sorry Matthew; I feel a bit poorly. I'll just have to have a sit down in the tea room.'

The elderly solicitor looked up at her from his desk. 'You look awful Jane, you go and have a sit down, get yourself a drink, relax for a while.'

Jane turned and stumbled against the door frame, almost falling; she grasped the edge of the door to support herself. Matthew got up from his seat, put his arm through hers and helped her through into the small room they used for lunch breaks. It had two comfortable arm chairs and a settee.

'You just sit there for a bit; let me know if you don't feel better in a few minutes,' Matthew said, concern shadowing his gaunt features.

Jane lay back on the settee, her head flopped back. Her eyes were almost turning back in their sockets, and her arms were draped loose.

An image of Brian came into her head; she saw his face blackened and sweating, the face said, *don't worry love, it'll be alright.* She sat up with a start. *Had she just received some sort of message, or was she dreaming?* She began to worry, she sensed that somehow she'd foretold something almost telepathically, and she was frightened.

She got up from her seat and went to Matthews's office again. 'I'm sorry, Matt,' she said, 'I don't know what's wrong, but I've got to go home.'

'OK Jane,' he said, realising that she was going through some sort of crisis. 'I'll drive you, I don't think you're in a fit state at present, just hang on a second, I'll just let the other partners know what's up.'

The fire had not abated, and it was now desperate for the crews to hit it hard to subdue it. Brian's movements were becoming sluggish. Whereas before he'd been brash and confident, now he was quiet and introvert. Jake had noticed that his effort to protect them from the fire-ball and the massive rise in the temperature seemed to have drained all the fuel from his body.

'Are you OK Brian?' Jake asked, concerned for the welfare of his col-league.

'Yeah, I'm alright, just a bit weary. You take the jet, just keep it going; I'll be alright in a minute,' he said. His words had become slurred, and his face was a mask of exhaustion.

'Are you sure?' Jake asked, still worried about the change in Brian.

'Yeah, I'll be OK, I just need to rest a minute, there's no problem,' then he slumped sideways onto the floor. Jake put down the jet and went to him. He'd passed out. Jake quickly guessed that it could be heat exhaustion; he took Brian's radio from his belt.

'Control from Fire-Fighter Higgins over.'

'Go ahead over.' was the instant response from the control van.

Jake wasn't sure what to say, but after a few seconds to compose him-self, he spoke into the radio.

'Control, Leading Fire-Fighter Parks has been taken ill, I think I need to bring him out.'

'Fire Fighter Higgins; Jake. What's the problem?'

'Control, he's unwell, I think it could be heatstroke.'

'OK, you hang in there; I'll have a team in to relieve you, out.'

Matthew held Jane's arm as he guided her to the door of her house. 'Are you sure you'll be alright?' he said, 'give us a ring later; let us know how you are.'

'OK Matthew I will, don't worry about me, I'll be OK soon.'

She closed the door behind her, threw her coat onto the stairs, went into the lounge, and picked up the telephone.

'Hello; Graveton fire station. Leading Fireman Jefferson speaking.'

'Oh yes, I'm a friend of Brian Parks, is he there please?'

'No, I'm sorry, they're out on a shout in the city, we're here on stand-by, do you want to leave a message?'

'No; can you tell me where they are?'

'Well I'm not really supposed to, but for you, they are at a job in the old cutlery works, it sounds like a good job.'

'Thank you very much,' Jane said as she placed the phone back in its cradle.

Jake was struggling to hold the branch and support Brian. The fire was still roaring around the building and the temperature was still high, but Jake now seemed to have adapted to the conditions. He felt calm. He looked at Brian and removed a glove, feeling for a pulse in Brian's neck. It was there, strong, beating fast. Brian stirred.

'What are you up to young Jake?' he said, smiling through the heavy plastic of his facemask.

'Phew, Bry, I thought for a minute you were dead, thank Christ you're not.'

'Well young Jake, it takes a bit more than a little fire to kill me off, you know me, indestructible.'

'Well, anyway, there's a team coming in to relieve us, it's about time. I've checked our gauges and it's heading soon for whistle time.'

Jane had walked unsteadily around to her neighbour. 'Hello Jean,' she said, 'I wonder if you can do me a favour, I need a lift now! Down into the city.'

'Is it urgent? I've got a lot on at the moment,' she said.

'Yeah, I've got a real bad feeling. Brian's at a fire, and I just got this sense that something's wrong. Will you take me? I'd be very grateful.'

'Of course I will, just let me get the dog in from the garden and I'll leave a note for the kids, I'll just be a minute; then we'll get off.'

'As the car reached the top of the rise, the view over the city opened up, and they saw the plume of smoke rising into the sky being carried along by the wind.

'Bloody hell,' Jean said, 'I hope that's not where we're going; it looks like a bloody disaster area.'

'I think it is,' Jane said, her voice wavering with fear.

Jake was just about holding the fire with the branch delivering its liquid load at its heart; but it seemed to be making little difference.

Jake heard the crunch of boots behind them, then the voices.

'We're here to relieve you boys, is everything OK? How's it looking?'

'Brian turned his head and looked vacantly at their replacements.' We're OK, just holding it,' he said, feigning normality.

'Well I think they're about to bring in re enforcements any time, so we have it, you're relieved, get yourselves out.'

Jean managed to get her car close to the scene but most of the surrounding roads were closed, so they quickly parked up on a yellow line and walked the remaining distance to the fire. Jane walked quickly, almost running towards the fire. They came across police tape manned by a young policeman. 'I need to go in there,' Jane said.

'I'm sorry madam, but because of the situation, no-one is allowed in there,' he said, looking sternly at her.

'My partner Brian Parks is a fire fighter in there and I've got a bad feeling, I just need to know that he's alright,' Jane spluttered, trying hard not to cry.

'Just hang on there a second, I'll speak to someone.'

'Thank you, I'd be very grateful.'

The message from the Police got to the control unit. Ian Blain got on to the radio.

'*Control to Sub Officer James over.*'

'*Go ahead control.*'

'*Mac, come to the Control Unit ASAP over.*'

Jake clipped himself onto the guideline, and Brian clipped onto a chrome ring on Jake's BA set. 'OK Bry, let's make a move, just hang on to me and we'll be out in a jiffy.'

The route out was easier, with no jet or guideline to tie off, so Jake made rapid progress. He was almost dragging Brian out by his belt buckle. He reckoned that they were getting pretty close to their exit point from the changes in sounds outside of the building. He heard a thump behind him and a dead weight dragging him back. He turned and looked, he felt panic rise in his chest, then was forced to gather himself. *Right Jake, we're nearly there, let's not mess about, just do it.* He said aloud to himself. He crouched over the prone bulk of his comrade, the man he admired. He gritted his teeth and hauled him upright; then pulling Brian's arm over his shoulder and jamming his powerful hands through his BA straps he physically manhandled him over the debris. This soon used up Jake's last resources of energy. *Come on Jake, bloody do it,* he said to himself. He saw the light a few feet in front of them and summoned up one last effort, before collapsing through the hole in the wall through which they had entered thirty minutes earlier.

Mac jogged the one hundred yards to where Jane stood, she looked worried, she spotted Mac moving quickly towards her.

'Oh Mac, I was worried, I had this awful premonition that Brian was hurt, I just had to come and see for myself, is he OK?'

'Last I heard from him about twenty minutes ago he was fine, but I'll check up, just hang on here a bit, OK.'

'*Control from Sub Officer James over.*'

'*Mac get up here we've just got one of your boys out, he's in a bit of a state, over.*'

Mac turned to the girls. 'Look Jane don't worry, I'll let you know what's up.' He grabbed the young policeman. 'Can you just sit these girls in your car? I'll be back in a minute.'

Mac ran back to the control unit, he heard the sound of a siren. He looked, and saw it was an ambulance. 'What's going on?' he said as he approached the Control.

'We've just pulled a couple of guys out, I reckon they're suffering from too much heat, we've got the ambulance here to check them out.'

There was a gathering of men around Brian and Jake. Brian was sat on the ground with his head between his knees. Jake was standing at his side looking exhausted. When Mac arrived, he pushed his way past the crowd.

'Are you OK?' he said, looking straight at Jake. Jake looked up at Mac and tried to smile but the effort was just too much. 'Yeah Sub. I'm OK, a bit tired. I think Brian's OK; it was really hot in there.'

'You both did well, I'm proud of you,' he said, kneeling down in front of them both knees and looking into Brian's eyes.

The paramedic stood up, 'I'm going to take them both to hospital just to be on the safe side. It'll be the Northern General.'

'Well done boys, I'll catch you later,' Mac said to them. Brian lifted his head again, his face almost scarlet. 'Sorry about this Mac, this young man did well,' he said, looking at Jake. 'Don't worry about it Bry. Jane heard about the shout so she's come to have a look, I'll tell her you're OK, I think you can expect a visit from her later.'

Mac grabbed the Paramedic. 'If it's alright with you, no sirens or flashing lights when you leave, it'll frighten the life out of Brian's partner.'

'No problem,' he said, 'they're OK, not serious.'

Mac made his way back to the police cordon where Jane and Jean were sat in the police car. They saw him coming and were out of the car by the time he arrived.

'What's the score, Mac?' Jane asked, concern written across her face.

'I've just seen them. They're OK, they've had a bit too much heat I think. The ambulance is taking them to the Northern General for a check-up, don't worry, they'll be fine.' Jane breathed a sigh of relief. 'Thanks Mac, I'll get Jean to take me to work to get my car, then I'll get up there to see them. Who else was it?'

'It was young Jake; they both did a good job in difficult conditions.'

'You know Brian,' she said, 'it's not worth doing if it's not bloody difficult, it's his favourite saying.' Signs of relief spread across her face.

The crews worked hard, managing to re-deploy the jets, and after an hour of fierce effort the fire was beaten, but the building was devastated.

A young couple arrived at the police cordon and spoke to the Officer, then made their way to the Control unit.

'Hi, I'm Eric Jenkins, this is my wife,' he said, 'I think that my father was working in the factory when the place exploded.'

'Are you sure? I have to say that we haven't come across anyone whilst we've been dealing with the fire.' Ian replied, realising now that another phase of the incident would probably have to start.

'I know he came to work about seven thirty, I rang him about half past eight and we spoke briefly. I've tried to call him again and his phone was dead.'

Chapter 21

The ambulance pulled in close to the Casualty Department of the hospital. Both Brian and Jake were now fully aware of their surroundings. The paramedic took them into casualty on wheelchairs where they were checked over by a young doctor. Jake was fine; just tired. Brian, though, had suffered steam burns through his tunic; his upper body was scorched red and sore, and he would have to spend some time on a ward to get treatment for his scalds.

Several teams of fire fighters were deployed inside the crumbling building searching for the missing man. Within ten minutes, in what remained of the devastated workshop, the remains of Albert Jenkins were found beneath the lathe which had served him so well for so many years, his wrecked body buried beneath a small mountain of broken timber and bricks.

Maddie left work, still dressed in her nurse's uniform. She climbed into her red Ford Focus, the luxury she loved; it was her real treat to herself. Jim had upgraded his car to a second hand Peugeot. It ran well, and he could afford to run it, which he thought was important, it made their lives much easier.

They had arranged to meet tonight. The wedding which had been talked about but not yet planned was up for more discussion with Maddie's parents, who, now having met Jim a few times, had begun to realise that despite his lowly circumstances he was actually a decent young man. It was clear to them that he loved their daughter from the way he looked at her and talked about her to them. Jake was in fact a surprise. On their first meeting they'd judged him by his appearance; he appeared to have neglected himself as his clothing looked worse for wear. Understandably they were concerned about their daughter's choice of partner, and they talked to Maddie about him after he left. She told them how they'd met, and the way they reacted together, and how Jim was working hard to improve himself. But most importantly how she loved him. This was enough for Maddie's parents to re evaluate their view and look again at Jim through slightly different eyes.

At eight thirty, Jim pulled his car to a stop outside of Maddie's parent's house. He looked across the garden. The curtains were drawn closed but Jim could see the room was illuminated. He walked nervously to the house and rang the doorbell.

'Come on in, Jim' Maddie's father said as he opened the door and smiled broadly.

'Hello Mister Brookes, thanks for letting me visit,' Jim said, trying not to let his nerves show.

'Before we start, Jim, let's have no formalities,' Maddie's father said, 'call us Bill and Wendy.' Jim was relieved that they seemed to be relaxed about him coming to visit. 'Madeline thought it was time we got together to talk about some of the future arrangements. Take a seat, Wendy's going to make us some coffee.'

Jim and Maddie sat together on the heavily upholstered leather settee.

'It's good to see you again, why don't you tell us a bit about yourself Jim? Maddie's told us a bit, but it would be better to hear it from you.'

Jim wriggled in his seat. 'Well, as you probably know, I'm doing a course trying to qualify to become a plumber. My last job was working as a security guard, but it was boring and the wages were pretty poor. I lived with my grandmother for years after my mum and dad were killed in a crash. She looked after me until she died about a year and a half ago.' Jim paused as the memories re-surfaced. 'I've been living in a small flat on the Green Acre Estate. My Nan didn't have much money, but she always said you have to have self respect, so you must have a job. Being a security guard made her happy, and it helped out with the expenses.' Jim sighed, talking about her had brought back many happy memories of his life with her; she'd been the one permanent feature of his life.

'Then I met Maddie in Edale.' The memories of that day came back into Jim's mind and he got the same overwhelming emotion that he always did when he brought it to mind. He flushed, and his eyes welled with tears.

'Until then I had nothing, I was just sort of stumbling through life,' he said, his voice almost cracking with emotion. 'Maddie has given me everything. She's made me realise that I'm not a waste of space; she's made me like myself a bit more. It was the luckiest day of my life.' He stopped and wiped his sleeve across his eyes. 'She's the best thing that has ever happened to me. She's beautiful, I can't believe that she even likes me, let alone is prepared to marry me. I just feel so lucky.'

Maddie's parents were dumb struck for a moment.

'Well Jim, I have to say, we like her too. She is lovely, and it's good that she's motivated you to improve yourself. For the record, we like you as well.' They both beamed with pleasure. 'Now, let's get down to business shall we?'

The hospital A and E was busy. Jake and Brian were taken to a small side ward where Jake was examined by a nurse who, after a brief examination, concluded that he was fine and wouldn't have to stay in overnight. Brian was also checked over by a nurse who thought it best that the doctor should have a look to determine the treatment he should have.

The doctor was middle aged and from Nigeria, a man with an obvious sense of humour. He looked at Brian. 'Well sir, it looks to me as if you have been out in the sun too long, just some mild reddening of the skin on your back and shoulder. There are a couple of small areas where it is a bit more of a problem.' He smiled, 'So how do you feel about the prospect of spending some time in hospital?'

Brian looked surprised. 'Well Doc, I hadn't really thought it was that serious, so staying here isn't something I would want or expect.'

'Well, that's good,' he said trying to look serious, but failing to rid himself of the huge smile which adorned his chubby features. 'You have been very lucky, you don't have to stay, we just need to put a couple of dressings on two small areas then you can go home. But you will need a bit of time away from work, say seven days, how's that?'

Brian breathed a sigh of relief. 'Thanks Doctor, that's good news, I thought you were going to say I could go straight back to work.' They both laughed out loud.

Jake lay in bed and ran the events of the fire in the factory through his mind. This fire had tested him to his limit; Brian had kept him going through his exhausted state. Then the fire ball came, moving fast like a rocket. That was when the penny dropped in Jake's head. Brian, in doing what he did, almost certainly saved their lives. He'd laid flat, his face buried in the dirt and debris. But not Brian, he'd raised himself up, almost placed himself as a barrier between the fire and Jake, and delivered a protective curtain of water between them and the fire. That was why Brian got the scalds and collapsed on the way out. This sudden realisation hit Jake hard; it hadn't registered at the time, probably because he was also exhausted. He tossed and turned, unable to get off to sleep, the images of the fire still dancing in his head.

Jane managed to manoeuvre Brian into her car. His back was sore from the scalds but she was just happy that he was alive. Jane's neighbour was sitting in, looking after Jill.

'You know, you really scare me sometimes, I thought you were going to die today,' Jane said.

Brian looked across the car at Jane. 'I'm fine, you have to expect odd things like this in the job, it's the nature of the beast,' he said, lifting his arm gingerly and placing it gently on her shoulder. 'Anyway, a week off work will be nice; the DC and Mac both popped in and told me to take it easy, so that's me for the week, feet up reading the paper. How's your cooking these days?' he said, a wicked smile creasing his reddened face.

'You cheeky so and so, I've got a job to go to. If you're staying at mine for a while you'll have to look after yourself.'

'OK, I know where the remote is, and the tea bags, I'll be fine,' he said, grinning at her.

Jim lay on his bed. It was half past eleven and he wasn't tired yet. The evening had been spent speaking with Maddie's parents about the proposed wedding plans. His head was filled with so many thoughts, that no matter how he tried he couldn't switch off. He was taut with excitement. There was still no firm arrangement or date set, but a general agreement that it would happen this year, and an acceptance that they thought Jim was a good man and they were happy for their daughter to marry him.

Chapter 22

Jake woke before the alarm; he was on the night shift, so the day was his to do with as he wished. He walked quietly down the stairs, the third from the bottom step catching him out again as it creaked. For the past ten years Jake consistently tried to avoid it but always forgot. It stemmed from the time when his mum had told him that there was a magic angel under the step and if it creaked that was the angel complaining that her back was aching. Ever since, he'd tried to avoid the creaking step, even now, when he had long time realised that it was just his mum putting a little bit of magic into his life. The kettle whistled and he made a cup of coffee, switched on the television, and sat watching the early morning news.

Jake hadn't realised that the fire had become a minor item on the local news channel. The news presenter, Joan Taylor, was speaking over a report of the fire; it showed the devastated building. Wisps of steam were still rising between the charred and blackened rafters of what had once been the roof of the factory. Fire-fighters were rolling hose and stowing gear back onto the fire appliances. The fire was out, but the on-site reporter was saying, *'the factory owner, Mr Albert Jenkins, aged sixty six had died in the fire. He'd worked as a cutlery manufacturer for all of his working life; he left behind six children and several grandchildren. The cause of the fire at this time was unknown and being investigated by specialist fire officers.'*

This was Jake's first fatal fire and he'd not been aware of it till now. The thought of someone dying in the building saddened him.

I must go and see Brian. Jake decided.

He put the kettle on again and put bread in the toaster

Jake silently opened the door to his mother's bedroom. The room was dark, just a small slit of light against the far wall. 'Morning mum, here's a nice cuppa and some toast,' he whispered. His mother stirred and replied blearily. 'Good Morning son, what sort of a day is it?' Jake pulled the heavy curtain back a few inches. 'It's still raining, but the forecast is for it to improve as the day goes on.'

'And how are you today, after the fires yesterday, have you got your strength back?'

After Jake had told his mother what had happened at the fire, she'd made him sit down and relax for the whole of the evening until it was time for him to go to bed.

'Do you know son?' she said.

'What mum?' Jake asked.

'I'm very proud of you,' she said, smiling the smile, which to Jake was the face he always pictured in his mind's eye when he thought of his mum, which was something that he often did.

Jake sat on the bed close to her and stroked her hair.

'I'm proud of doing what I do mum, I love it, it's the best thing I've ever done.' Jake paused for a second, almost as if he was deciding whether to say any more.

'I've been thinking about yesterday's fire a lot. You know, I didn't realise it at the time, but I think that Brian saved our lives, that's why he got burned.' Then Jake related to her what he'd done, the risk he'd taken.

She sat up in bed resting her head against a pillow sipping her tea. 'I think, son, you should go and have a chat with him. It'll help put your mind at rest, he'll probably be glad to see you anyway.'

'Yeah, I think that's a good idea, I'll give him a ring later.'

Jake tried to call him on his home phone and got no reply, so left a message on his answer phone. *I'll try his mobile, see if that gets him.* Jake said to himself.

'Hi Brian, it's me, how are you doing? Where are you? I just tried you at your place.'

'I'm at Jane's; I've got a week off work.'

'Can I come and see you?'

'Course you can,' he replied, 'sometime this morning would be best, we're busy this afternoon.'

'Yeah, that will be fine, does eleven o-clock sound OK?'

'Yeah, well I'll see you then,' Brian said, before clicking his phone off.

Mac sat at the dining table, examining a map of the Dark Peak. He wanted to get out for a walk with Val again, and thought it was time that he started doing a bit of work on map reading. He traced an imaginary course from the car park below Mam Tor along Rushup Edge and down the Chapel Gate track into the hamlet of Barber Booth, then a steep climb via Harden Clough up to Mam Nick and back to the car park. He studied the route, not very long, maybe six miles, but a tough route with steep ascents and descents. He decided that he would do that on his next day off.

'What are you planning?' Val said, looking at the map he'd spread out on the table.

Mac looked up from the map. When I was out with Janet the other day, she set great stall on navigation and map reading. I know my way around, but I've never really studied the maps much, so I thought maybe I should start. I'm just looking at a little walk for us on our next day off, how are you fixed?'

Val looked at him. Well, after the last episode I ought to say on your bike mate, but on the other hand why not, I need the exercise. So put me down for it. Where are we going?'

A short six miles, Rushup Edge, a circular walk, should be good; we've not been along there in a while.'

Jake parked his car outside of Jane's house and rang the doorbell. After a few seconds, Brian opened the door.

'Hiya mate, come on in,' he said, grasping Jake's hand. 'How are you today?'

'I'm OK, what about you, though?'

'I'm alright, just a bit sore, it feels like I've had a couple of hours in the sun without putting suntan cream on. I'll be fine, seven days off; they're the first days I've had off sick in fifteen years.'

Jake spoke. 'I saw the news this morning on the telly; it seems there was a man killed in the fire yesterday.'

'Yeah, I heard that too.' Brian sat up straight, attempting to alleviate the soreness in his back. 'I have to say though, that explosion was massive, it's a miracle that it was just one fatality.'

'Yeah, you're right.'

Jake sat down opposite Brian and looked him in the eye.

'I just realised how you got burned, I think we would have both got roasted if you hadn't done what you did.'

'Don't go fussing about it Jake, I did what I had to do, there was no real decision to make.' Brian looked at Jake like a father looks at his son. 'I understand how you feel, but I was the experienced one there, I was looking after you, some day you'll do that for someone else; it's the job, it's what we do for each other.'

'Yeah I know, but I wanted you to know that I know what you did.'

Brian leaned forward and patted Jake's knee. 'Look Jake, there were two of us there, I did what I did, you did what you did, end of story. I was struggling and you helped me, just like we all do for each other. It's the code of the job and it's the code of the watch. Be proud, you did well.'

Chapter 23

Jake sat at the table with his mother having a meal before setting off to the fire station for his night shift.

'Do you know what mum; you make the best egg and chips in the world.'

His mother laughed 'I bet you say that to all the girls, you little monkey.'

'No, you're my only girl, I'm not interested. Girls cost money and hide the remote; at least that's what Mark said the other day when we talked.

'How is Mark, I've not seen much of him recently, and what about that girl you met the other day, you know the one from the fire?'

Jake sat back in his chair. 'We went out and had a nice time, and we'll probably meet up again sometime, but I'm not expecting it to develop into anything serious. She's a nice girl, but she's busy studying for her degree, so I don't think she'll have a lot of time to socialise.'

Jake set about mopping up the egg yolk from his plate with a piece of bread.

'And Mark, he's OK, he loves it at Central. They're really busy and they've settled nicely into their new house, his wife's got a job in town at Boots, so yes, they're all settled.'

'Why don't you ask them across here, perhaps at a weekend. We can have a nice lunch, it would be nice to see them all again.'

'How long is it since you had a night out mum?' Jake asked as he sipped his tea from his mug.

'A proper night out? I reckon about ten years she said, with no hint of it being a problem. 'Why do you ask?'

'Because,' he said, 'I've got a surprise for you.'

'Oh yes, what's that then?' she laughed.

Jake got up from his chair, stood behind her, and placed his big hands on her shoulders.

'You mum, or should I say we, are going to London. We've got a nice hotel and we're going to the theatre to see Les Miserables, then afterwards we'll have a nice meal out. And if you're good, we're going on a river trip. How does that sound?'

'Well Jacob, it sounds wonderful, when are we going?' she asked, her face stretched in a huge smile.

'We go on the twenty sixth, the Saturday morning. The coach picks us up at ten in Fitzallen Square.' Jake laughed. 'That's got you going hasn't it; you'd better arrange to get your hair done.'

'So son, what brought this on then?'

'You know I never know what to get you for your birthday, well this is it, sorted.'

But Jacob, it's not my birthday for a couple of months yet.'

'Look mum I don't want to get into technicalities, for the purposes of this trip; it's your birthday, alright?'

Mac had changed into his uniform, packed his holdall, and was ready for work.

'OK Val I'll get off, I'll see you in the morning.'

'Alright love, you take care.'

He climbed into his car and drove on his usual route to work, the routine for the past thirty years, day shifts, night shifts, days off, back on the day shift. The continuous cycle of work and rest. Mac had been mulling his life over for several months, unsure of how his life would change once his work wasn't such a massive segment of his life. He knew that he'd miss it a lot, but he also realised that all things come to an end, so he'd mentally readied himself for the inevitability of his retirement. The day he'd spent patrolling with the rangers had opened a new field of interest, he'd enjoyed the day and learned a lot, and had decided that he would go again and almost certainly apply to become a volunteer ranger after his retirement.

He pulled into the station yard, noting that as usual he was the first of his watch to arrive for the shift. He also saw that the day shift were out, presumably at a job.

He packed his holdall into his locker and wandered into the watch room, looked at the tele-printer, and saw that they had in fact got a shout about half an hour ago.

'Hello control Mac James, how long do you expect the day shift to be, do they need a relief?'

'Just hang on one second, we'll call them up and find out.'

'Hello Mac, we've talked to them, they should be back by six or there-abouts.'

'Thank you control,' Mac replied before replacing the phone in its cradle.

The night shift began drifting in. Pete Jacks was the first, and went straight to the boot room and began polishing his boots and shoes. Mac saw him and followed him in.

'Hi Pete, how's things?'

'Fine Mac, all is well at the homestead.'

'How's Trudy?'

'She's OK; she seems to have got a new lease of life.'

'I know we haven't had much chance,' Mac said, 'but I was wondering if you managed to talk to Trudy about Penrith.'

'Yeah, well we have talked about it and I was surprised, she quite likes the idea,' Pete said, looking happy and relaxed. 'The only thing is the kids, we can't easily take them out of school, but if it's possible we'd all like to go.'

'I'll get on to it for you then, I think it would be a good thing for all of you,' Mac said. 'It's probably a good idea to go to the school and talk to the teachers, I'm sure they'll be OK about it.'

Taff wandered into the watch-room 'What have they got, Mac?'

'Car fire; should be back in a few minutes.'

'Ah that's good, didn't feel too energetic tonight. Let's hope for a quiet one.'

'Well I reckon that's put the curse on it Taff, we'll probably be out all night now.'

Mac turned in his chair. 'Have you spoken to Brian?'

'No. I tried to ring him but he wasn't picking the phone up.'

'Yeah, well Jake rang me yesterday, said he'd got hold of him and he was staying at Jane's for a bit.'

'Yeah, and knowing Brian I can guess what bit he's staying for.'

Mac smiled. 'You, young Evans, have a very dirty mind. What I was about to say was, have you sorted out your arrangements for the West Midlands funeral yet?'

'Yep, we're going down in my car. We're not hanging about, we're coming back straight after the service.' Taff smirked. 'She's been in a really good mood recently, so I could be on a promise. I'm taking her out for a bite to eat that night so I mustn't be late.'

The day shift returned from their car fire and handed over the reins to Red Watch for the night.

'Have a good shift Mac,' Alan Wilson, the officer in charge of Blue Watch said. 'Not much for you to do, just recharge a couple of cylinders and that will be about it.'

'Thanks Alan, you have a nice evening.'

After parade, Mac sat with the crew on the mess deck drinking tea. 'What have we got for supper, young Jake?' Clive asked.

'I cheated, I got my mum to give me a hand, we've made a couple of Shepherd's Pies at home, I hope you like them.'

Mac spoke up. 'Well Jake, I call that using your initiative.'

The lights came on with the familiar clunk and a second later the alarm sounded. Jock ran to the watch room and ripped off the message from the printer.

Jock called out of the watch room door. 'Chimney fire. Mount Pleasant Avenue.' In seconds, the machine flew out of the door. Jake was sat between Clive and Jock on the back seat, Mac used the siren sparingly. Chimney fires, whilst they can sometimes be serious, usually were not a threat to human life, so risk taking en route was not essential.

Mount Pleasant is the wealthy part of Graveton, large Georgian styled houses in the main, occupied by professional people. The well heeled of the community.

They could smell the fire before they arrived at the address, the strong smell of burning soot hung around the area. As they got closer, a thin layer of smoke hung low like an autumnal fog.

The house was large, red brick with a red tiled roof, large multi paned windows; it looked like a very expensive property.

Mac walked up the pebbled drive to the house. The house owner was in a state of hyperactive panic. 'Thank God you're here,' he said. His voice was effeminate, as were his rapid movements backward and forward across the front of his large doorway. 'I thought that we were all going to die,' he said brushing his coiffure'd silver hair back from his well-polished forehead.

'OK sir, don't worry, we'll sort it out for you,' Mac said, trying hard not to show the smile which was on the verge of erupting from his face. 'I'll get the boys in and it'll be sorted in a jiffy.'

'I'm so grateful that you came so quickly, my guests are all ensconced in a back room away from danger.' Mac smiled to himself.

'Really sir, don't worry, it will be fine.'

'Well I've never had an emergency before. In fact I've never even been close to a fire fighter before.' Mac winced.

'You can help sir.' Mac suggested.

'How?' he replied enthusiastically.

'You have a big house here sir; I need one of my men to get up into your loft, just to make sure that there is no problem up there, will that be OK?'

'Of course, bring him to me, I'll direct him,' he said theatrically.

'Clive, you go with the gentleman and have a look in the roof space. Check for the usual, smoke etc, and have a look at the rendering on the chimney up there make sure that its sound.'

'OK Mac will do.'

Clive could be described as a handsome young man, and this had not gone un- noticed by the householder. As they climbed the several flights of stairs Clive, in his fire gear holding a large yellow plastic hand lamp, closely followed the man, who introduced himself to Clive as Hubert Styles. There was a small door at the head of a narrow staircase which led into the roof space. Hubert entered and switched on the light, illuminating the whole of the huge area, which was filled with what appeared to be years of artefacts from another age. There was a stag's head with part of one antler missing fixed to the wall, and a series of romantic age sepia prints in gilt frames which leaned against the wall. Several manikins and suitcases could also be seen, and a wardrobe with the doors missing, filled to bursting with exotic women's clothing, including a fur coat. The area was huge. Several other rooms could have been installed in the space. Clive found it fascinating.

'Where will I find the chimney, Sir?' Clive asked politely.

'Follow me,' Hubert said, suddenly excited and seeming proud to be of assistance, before striding quickly along a planked gangway between several timber units. *Filled with what, who knows?'* Clive thought, as he hurried to keep up with Hubert.

The chimney, as it passed through the roof space, formed a large rectangular bulk in the centre of the loft space. Clive looked around it and felt it for hot spots, and quickly worked out that there was no problem there to worry about.

'Well Sir,' Clive said, 'I'm pleased to tell you that there is no problem at all up here.'

'I'm so grateful to you young man, you're all so brave, we're so lucky to have men like you to look after us. I've always admired firemen, the bravest of the brave.'

Clive felt surprisingly comfortable in the man's company, he relaxed.

'This is a beautiful house, how long have you lived here, sir?'

'My partner and I, well we moved here from London in nineteen seventy, so we've been here almost twenty years. Yes, that's when I opened my first salon.'

Clive looked interested. 'So you're the Mister Style of the Style's Hairdressers in town?'

'Yes, it was a good move from the smoke, we love it up here, there's so much fresh air, and the social life is incredible,' he said, with some emphasis.

Clive turned to face him. 'Do you know Mister Styles, I think that you were my partner's first employer.'

'Oh yes, what's his name?'

'Her name,' Clive emphasised, 'is Helen Casey, soon to be Mrs Botham. I'm sorry to say that we have just lost our first child. Helen miscarried after an accident.'

'Oh dear,' Hubert exclaimed, 'is she alright now? I'm sure that I remember her, isn't she tall and slim with long blonde hair?'

'Yes, that's her. She's fine now; we get married in about four weeks.'

'That is absolutely wonderful news,' Hubert replied theatrically.

Hubert put his hand on Clive's shoulder. 'I hope that you will both be very happy, and if she needs a job after the wedding tell her to get in touch with me.'

'Thank you sir, I'll tell her.' Clive smiled at Hubert. 'This really is a beautiful house, you are very lucky.'

Hubert gave a pale smile, almost not a smile, but a sad looking change of facial expression.

'Not so lucky really, we worked very hard to buy this house and we have loved it here, but life isn't perfect.'

Clive felt a certain empathy with this stranger. 'Well, Mister Styles, it seems perfect to me. A dream house, I could only dream of having a home like this.'

'You know young fellow, you have a happy life; cherish your wife to be. Have a nice life. But don't take it for granted, I did, and now it's not so happy.'

'I'm sorry,' Clive said.

'Yes well my partner, Raymond, he hasn't got very much longer on this earth, he's already exceeded the time that they originally predicted that he'd live, but lately he's deteriorated and the doctors have said it will only be a matter of weeks now.' Tears began to flow down Hubert's cheeks.

Instinctively, Clive put his arm around Hubert's shoulder, as a gesture of sympathy towards him. Clive quite surprisingly felt a connection with him.

'I'm so sorry to hear that sir,' Clive said. 'If there is anything I can do, just let me know, will you?'

Hubert stood up straight and tried to compose himself. 'Thank you for that, I'm sorry, what's your name?'

'I'm fire fighter Botham, Clive Botham, and it's been a pleasure talking to you sir.'

'Likewise young man, I thank you most sincerely.'

'Now Sir, if you don't mind, I'll have to go and help my colleagues downstairs.'

Clive entered the large lounge. It had four heavily upholstered sofas, and a series of leather chairs. There was a huge TV set in one corner. The walls were hung with a variety of modern paintings, the windows hung with heavy brocade curtains; this was the room of a rich man. Clive was impressed.

'How's it going down here boys?' Clive asked. They'd moved along well whilst he had been busy in the roof space.

'We're doing OK, got the rods up, but the chimney stack has quite a few twists and turns, so getting them up there has been difficult.' Jake and Taff were pushing the rods skywards, Mick was operating the stirrup pump, and Mac was outside looking up at the chimneystack. There was a small group of guests loitering around the room, obviously fascinated by the process of extinguishing the fire; one man caught the eye of Jock. He leaned over to Mick and said, 'see the guy over there?' He was speaking quietly, trying not to let it appear that he had noticed anything. 'The guy with the yellow cravat, over near the window.'

Mick casually looked round and saw the man Jock was talking about; he was half standing half leaning against the wall, sipping what appeared to be a glass of whisky.

'Yeah, I see him, what about him?'

'I reckon that's Peter Swanson. You know the actor guy, he was in one of the soaps for a while, married to that Irish bird. You know, the one that ran off with that other guy, the one that got done for shop lifting. Peter what's his face. What was his name?'

Mick looked up at Jock. 'I don't care Jock, I don't watch the soaps and I don't give a toss if they're actors or royalty, they're just people, like you and me.'

Jock gave Mick a hard stare. 'You're right, but they've got more money than us.'

The last remnants of fire and burning soot had been eliminated and Mac got the boys to clear up, sweeping all of the loose soot and charcoal. They then removed the protective sheets from around the fireplace, put there to protect it from the dust and grime.

Hubert came into the room looking very relieved. 'Well gentlemen, I think you have done a magnificent job, thank you all very much.'

Mac went across to him. 'It's been our pleasure sir, you shouldn't have any more problems with the fire, and may I suggest that you get the chimney swept every year.'

'That, young man, is what I will do, I'm very grateful.' He reached into his pocket and pulled out a bulging wallet.

'Now men, I want to make a donation, do you have a society or club or something?'

Mac spoke. 'Sir you don't have to do that, you pay for us on your rates, we're a free service and we do it happily. It's our job.'

'I'm sure you do, and I'm sure it is, but I would like to donate to your charity if I may. It would make me happy to do it. It has been a most surprising pleasure having you all here on our special night. And you have created some excitement for our guests.'

'Well sir, we do have a charity, one which looks after injured fire-fighters and their families,' Mac conceded.

'Then that is where my donation should go.'

He pulled out a wad of notes and stuffed them into Clive's hand. 'This young man, Clive, has been an absolute treasure; he has done your service proud.'

Mac spoke again. 'We thank you sir, your donation will help a lot of people. May I ask, what is the special occasion you spoke about?'

Hubert's eyes began to fill with tears. 'This is a farewell party for our friends. Raymond and I,' he said, gesturing to the middle aged man who sat looking ill on one of the sofas, 'are taking our leave of England. I have a home in Spain, and we are going to spend some quality time, maybe our final time, in the sunshine.'

Clive went across the room and put his arm across Hubert's slim shoulder. 'Good luck to you and your friend, Mister Styles, God bless you both; it's been good meeting you.'

Taff pulled the appliance out onto the main road and drove along the tree lined avenue towards the fire station.

'Well Clive, what was that all about then?' Taff said, a slight mocking tone in his voice.

Clive had been moved by the experience and was reluctant to say much. 'You do realise that they were gay don't you Clive?' Taff responded.

'Of course I knew. It was pretty obvious. I had quite a chat with Hubert when we were up in the roof space; he is a really nice man. He's offered Jane a job when she wants to get back to work. His partner is dying, he's only got a few weeks left, and he was pretty upset. We sort of connected, I liked him.'

Mac turned and looked at Clive. 'Well Clive, I'm proud of you, you have a good heart. Now what about your wedding?'

The rest of the shift was quiet. Jake warmed up supper for the watch, and because Jake's mum had been involved in cooking, the Shepherd's Pie was consumed without a single detrimental comment. Jake smiled to himself. *Thanks mum* he thought as he and the watch set about washing all of the pots.

It was ten thirty, and some of the watch were preparing to get their heads down for the night. Mac sat in the TV room in a comfortably upholstered chair and Jake and Pete wandered in. 'What's this Mac, having a bit of quiet time?' Pete said.

'Yeah, all the paperwork's clear, there's nothing worth watching on the box, so I thought I'd get in here and read a book, it's nice and quiet.'

'Then we came in and ruined it,' Jake said.

Mac looked up and put the book he was reading down on the coffee table.

'No you didn't, this time for me is the best time. When I retire I'll miss this. Quiet nights, talking with the boys and swinging the lamp.'

Pete stood up and walked across to the window and sat on the windowsill.

'You know when I came here I was a right mess.'

'Peter, that is an understatement, you were a disgrace,' Mac responded with a smile on his face.

'Yeah I know that now, I didn't realise it then.'

'You've turned it round Pete, and that's a lot of credit to you.'

Jake sat quietly watching the ebb and flow of the conversation, not saying anything, trying his best to store this away. He knew Mac was heading for retirement and he wanted to have times like these packed away in his memory bank. Mac was one of the last of the old timers, men who did the job before regulation began to swamp it.

'It's a funny thing. The state I was in before seemed normal, even the fact that my watch over at Halifax road were what you'd call decent blokes, good firemen, it didn't register with me that I'd let myself go so much.'

'Well Pete, you had a lot to contend with. A sick wife and two kids, it must have been hard to give your time and effort to anything outside of your family. I think that since you came here you have done brilliantly.'

'Yeah, that's down to you and the lads, and the thing that surprises me most is that I actually like being the way I am now; it feels like I'm doing a proper job.'

Mac sat back in his chair, stretched his body, and yawned.

'You are doing a good job, Pete. Your improvement in the short time you've been here is remarkable. See what I mean? Here we are, no TV, having a serious chat about stuff that matters to us. Yes I'll miss these times when I go.'

Jake stirred. 'What's happening about the Penrith trip?'

'Well, the arrangements are made it's just now up to Pete to sort the finer details out, and they'll be off.'

Pete looked at his two colleagues and smiled, he was beginning to realise just how good things had become since his move.

Chapter 24

Janet was up early. Justin had gone to London on business. She'd planned to meet a group of deaf people and assist in guiding them on a walk around Chatsworth Park. She drove down the narrow track from her house; the day looked promising. There was a bit of a chilly breeze, but nothing that would deter her or the group from doing the walk. Brenda Allsop, another Ranger was to be there also. Janet knew of her but they'd never worked together before. However, she did know that Brenda was a veteran of guided walks for the deaf and blind, and was well versed in sign language which, from Janet's perspective, was a great help.

She pulled her four by four into the Carlton Lees car park on the edge of the Chatsworth Estate. A group of adults stood about twenty yards away from where she'd parked, the group were all very animated and were chatting away furiously, talking in signs and laughing and slapping each other on the back. Janet smiled. *That must be them,* she thought, *they look like a good happy bunch.*

Brenda was there already, happily signing with the group as Janet arrived. They looked across and waved at her, Janet returning their friendly gesture.

Brenda had assumed command, and Janet was happy to go along with her. Janet had no experience of dealing with the deaf; therefore she was happy that Wendy was to be the leader.

'Now Janet, have you ever done one of these before?' Brenda asked.

'No, I'm afraid I haven't,' Janet said, almost apologetically.

'Well don't worry, they're great fun, but we do have to watch them.'

Janet looked surprised. 'Oh yes, why is that?'

'Well Janet, they're free spirits. They talk with each other using sign language, they stop for a chat and often lose track of the rest of the group, so now I like to have a rear gunner; you if you like, just to ensure we don't lose anyone off the back.'

Janet grinned, 'Yes I can imagine that could be a nightmare.'

'Believe me, it can, but I love these groups, they are such happy people. I think that you'll love it.' She paused. 'Would you like to be my rear gunner today?' she said.

The group moved slowly away from the car park, their progress frequently halted by their conversations requiring them to stop and explain. Brenda was out front, happily chatting away to some of the group. A small bunch of the group began to fall behind; they said nothing to each other. The two men, and one grey haired elderly lady, who appeared to have recently had a hip replacement, moved slowly along. The gap between what was now two groups was slowly growing wider. Janet began to feel that something was not quite right. The lady with the hip was clearly finding it difficult.

After a mile, the main group were almost out of sight beyond a group of trees. They walked slowly on. Janet was becoming more concerned; she wasn't absolutely sure which route Brenda had planned for them to walk. They passed an old farmhouse and began a gentle climb between trees and dry stone walls. At the top of the rise the track split, Janet had managed to catch a glimpse of the back end of the other group and fortune smiled. 'We have to go to the right here,' she said, taking care to move her lips and pointing her arm to the right so they could easily understand what she was saying.

The lady with the hip turned to Janet. 'No love, we're going off to the left,' she said in a broad Birmingham accent.

'You're not deaf?!'

'No love, it's been nice of you to walk with us though. We thought it would be nice just to tag along at the back.'

Janet panicked. *Oh bloody hell, she'll kill me,* she thought.

'Look, I've got to go. I'll have to go quickly to catch up the other group, you enjoy the rest of your walk.'

'Goodbye then dear,' the elderly lady said as Janet started to run as fast as she could in the direction that the other group had taken. Janet turned and waved to them as she disappeared over the crest of the hill.

The sun came out and suddenly it felt warm. Janet jogged along the well-worn track, peering forward in the hope of catching a view of the group. She rounded a bend in the track and a hundred yards away sat the group, chatting and laughing, eating their lunch. As Janet approached they spotted her, and immediately gave her a round of applause. Janet stopped to get her breath, and she bowed as an acknowledgment of their appreciation of her effort to catch them.

She slumped down next to Brenda. 'I told you these walks were interesting didn't I,' Brenda laughed.

'I'm sorry. They tagged on the back, I thought they were part of this group, they never spoke so I assumed they were deaf.'

'You sit there and get your breath back, have you got a flask?'

The group progressed steadily downhill towards the rear of the village of Edensor, skirting right to avoid a large herd of belligerent looking cows who seemed determinedto accompany the group as they strode ever faster in an attempt to discourage them from getting too close. Eventually, after several hundred yards of high-speed discouragement, the cows lost interest and began to disperse. They soon crossed the tarmac road and descended towards the front of Chatsworth House. It was busy, throngs of people were milling around on the stone flagged front of the house. Cars were coming and going to and from the car park. Brenda gathered the group together and patiently explained the need for them to keep together. *I really would be most upset if I lost any of you,*' she said, both mouthing and signing to the group who clapped their hands and signed back to her saying that they would take care not to lose anyone.

They moved smoothly now, the crowds growing thinner. The road sloped steeply upwards, and some of the group were puffing freely.

'OK gang,' Brenda said, 'let's have a two minute breather.'

Refreshed, the group climbed further beyond the farmyard and then followed a steep dirt track heading towards the Hunting Tower, one of the last remnants of Bess of Hardwick on the estate.

There was a sudden mad shuffle and rapid activity. Janet, who was still bringing up the rear, paced forward to see what the fuss was. Brenda was laying prone on the path, having tripped on a timber step.

'Are you alright?' Janet asked as she reached the front of the group.

'Yeah, I'll be OK, I just felt a bit weird and light headed.'

'Have you hurt yourself?'

'No I don't think so, just my pride, I feel a bit stupid,' she said, standing up and dusting herself down.

After a couple of minutes, Brenda had recovered her composure sufficiently to get the group up and moving again. They stopped briefly to examine the outside of the Hunting Tower, Brenda giving the group a brief explanation of its history, then they walked smoothly through the woods along a broad track, to a point where the water from the lake was channelled down to the house to feed the Cascade and the Fountains in the park. They stood on a huge rock watching the water descend, and Brenda explained to the group that the huge stone aqueduct which stood proudly before them was designed and built by the famous Joseph Paxton in the 19th century. They strolled further, eventually descending through the fields into Beeley Village. They continued across the park following the river, then made their way wearily into the car park, all of the group still chattering excitedly.

'Well Janet, thanks for your help today, I told you it would be interesting.'

'No, thank you, I really enjoyed it. These people are a pleasure to be around, they're all so happy.'

Janet said her goodbyes to the group before climbing back into her car and waved as she drove out of the car park, heading for home with a broad smile on her face.

Chapter 25

The London trip

The coach rumbled its way down the motorway heading for London. Jake sat next to his mother. They talked about the schedule for the weekend, the theatre and the boat trip.

Jake felt happy. He'd been so pre occupied with work these past weeks that he felt he'd neglected his mother. It gave him a lot of pleasure to see her so happy and excited by this special weekend away together.

The coach dropped the passengers off in the centre of London close to the theatre, and told they were to meet back there in four hours time. The driver explained to them where to meet him on their exit from the Theatre; then he would then take them to their hotel.

'Come on mum, let's go and find a coffee shop shall we, I think a latte for you and I'll be having an Americano.'

'Oh yes, and what are they, some foreign coffee is it?'

'You'll love it mum, and we might have a sticky bun as well, if you behave yourself,' Jake said, putting his arm around his mother's shoulder.

After the coffee, they meandered slowly to Oxford Street. It was busy; the street was filled with tourists all seemingly laden with shopping bags.

After half an hour of gentle meandering along taking in the sights, Jake's mum stopping to look in the shop windows, Jake noticed the many pretty girls who seemed to be everywhere.

'I'll tell you what Jacob, the prices are astronomical. I couldn't afford to buy anything here,' his mother said, once again threading her hand inside Jake's arm. Jake was happy, he was content; doing something good for the woman who had always done her best for him.

The street was crowded with tourists and required that they moved from side to side to avoid the onrushing hordes of people.

Jake stopped, he listened, something caught his ear, he thought he'd heard a distressed call. He listened again; he looked but couldn't see through the crowds jostling around them.

Then he heard a scream. It sounded like a foreign voice, clearly in trouble. Jake stopped. The voice called in desperation. *'Ehi! Lascia! Ti ho detto!'* The cry stopped momentarily then sound again. 'Brutto vigliacco! Via via! Via.' The cries of desperation rang in Jake's head.

Jake felt the hairs on the back of his neck rise, and felt his heart begin to beat faster. A gap in the crowd opened up in front of Jake. He looked, and couldn't believe what he saw. A young woman was being attacked and nobody was intervening, the attacker was dragging at her handbag. She was on the ground, he was shouting something, and she was responding, *'Brutto vigliacco.'* The attacker finally ripped the bag from the woman's hand and sprinting away in the direction of Jake and his Mother. No one attempted to get involved. Jake's mother was furious. 'He can't just do that; he's just a big bully,' she said, her face a mask of anger.

Jake turned to his mother. 'Don't get involved mum, it's not our job; the police will deal with it.'

'Well it's disgusting; who does he think he is.?' The man approached, running fast. He barged past an elderly man just in front of Jake and swerved to within reach. Jake said nothing, his gaze never faltered. The attacker was four feet in front of Jake, his eyes focussed beyond, searching for the quickest escape route. The man was slim, athletic and fast. As he approached at speed he didn't see the blur as Jake lifted his right hand and spread his fingers, he saw nothing. But he did feel the steely grip of a very large hand grip his throat. His reaction too slow, his body continued moving forward, but his neck was stopped dead by the power of a younger, stronger man. He crashed on his back to the floor, Jake's hand following him down but not releasing its grip.

The man's face was distorted with shock and surprise, and his eyes bulged as Jake tightened his grip around his throat. The face began to change colour to a dark shade of purple. Jake knelt by his side, peering directly into the eyes of the stranger. 'You, mister, are a thieving coward, and I don't like you.'

The man thrashed around, his body contorted in panic, but Jake held his throat tight like a vice against the ground.

'Now mister, you have a choice,' Jake said, his voice quiet and calm. 'I can loosen my grip and you will just lie still until the police arrive, or I crush your throat beyond repair.'

The police siren was fast approaching. 'Blink your eyes rapidly if you want me to loosen my grip,' Jake said, looking hard into the man's contorted purple face. The face gurgled and twisted and his eyes blinked in desperation. Jake loosened his grip. The man exhaled and inhaled, his breath ragged, as the air was sucked past his damaged vocal chords.

'Now you just lie there like a good boy, the police will be with us in a minute.'

The man, in desperation, lashed out with his fist, catching Jake on his jaw. Jake's face hardened, he peered into the face of the criminal through the slits that his eyes now formed, he tightened his grip once more, and lifted the now distorted face off the pavement and delivered a thumping blow with the heel of his free hand to the forehead of the attacker. The man's eyes went blank, his tongue lolled from his mouth, and he slumped unconscious to the ground.

Jake stood up and looked for his mother, who was standing close by.

'My God Jacob, where did you learn to do that?' she asked, looking at him with her mouth wide open and ready to break into a big smile.

'It's just a pity he chose the hard way mum; I'd have preferred not to hit him,' Jake said. By now a crowd had formed around the small group and they burst into spontaneous applause.

The Police car pulled up at the roadside and two Policemen emerged from the car and moved swiftly towards Jake and his mother.

'Who can tell us what went on here then?' the older of the two policemen asked.

Jake's mother replied. 'I can.'

'And who are you madam?' the younger constable enquired.

'I'm Alice Higgins, and I saw this chap,' she said, pointing down at the still unconscious mugger. 'He was stealing a handbag; my son grabbed him as he tried to escape,' she said, pushing her chest out with pride.

'Is this your son?' he said, turning to look at Jake.

'Yes, he's my son, and he stopped that man from getting away.'

The policemen looked around the quickly gathering crowd of onlookers. 'Do we have any other witnesses of the robbery?'

The young woman whose bag had been snatched appeared from the crowd. 'Yes, it was me who was attacked,' she said, in heavily accented English.

'Are you alright, you're not injured are you?' one of the officers asked as he looked at her.

'No I'm fine just a few scrapes of my skin and a small cut on my wrist,' she said, looking across at Jake as he stood silently beside his mother.

The officer sat in the patrol car and contacted his control. *'Yes, we're attending a mugging on Oxford Street, can you get an ambulance here; the mugger needs some attention.'*

They took Jake to one side, away from the main body of spectators. 'Right young fellow, come and sit in the car, we need a chat.'

The young mugging victim moved alongside Jake's mother. 'Are you alright dear?' Jake's mum asked, looking at her, concerned for her welfare.

'Yes I'm alright now, I'm very grateful to the young man, I hope that he won't get into any trouble.'

Jake's mum placed her hand on the girl's arm. 'He'll be all right. I didn't know he was capable of doing such a thing, he's always been such a quiet, gentle boy.'

The young woman looked across at Jake, then turned to his mother. 'What is his name?' she asked.

'He's called Jacob, but he prefers to be called Jake, Jake Higgins.'

'I think you said that he was your son?'

'Yes, I'm his mum; he's brought me to London for a special weekend treat. Then this happened. I hope that it will all be sorted out before the show starts.'

'I'm sorry,' she said in her stumbling English. 'My English is not good I've been here not very long, I'm still learning.'

'Oh yes, where are you from?' Jake's mum asked.

The woman was looking slightly bedraggled; she took out a brush from her bag and began brushing her shoulder length black hair.

'I'm from Italia! Italy.'

'And do you work in London?'

'Yes I am a violin player.'

'A violin player, oh you are clever, I love to hear the violin,' Jake's mum said, giving the girl an admiring glance.

'Then you must come and listen to me with the orchestra,' she said.

Jake peered out of the police car window; he'd almost finished giving his statement to the police. He looked across at his mother. She was deep in conversation with the dark haired young woman who had just been attacked. *I wonder what they're talking about?* Jake asked himself.

Chapter 26

Mick Young had recently been dating a girl from Brigade Headquarters; they'd been out a couple of times to a nightclub and got on well. Mick had taken the lead and asked her out for a date at the weekend, and she agreed to meet up with him.

Mick was a confident young man, and after some years in the army with time spent in Kosovo and Northern Ireland he thought it was time to change. He left, and was soon in the fire service. He felt he'd dropped lucky; he was posted straight to red watch at Graveton and never looked back.

'Where are we going Mick?' twenty two year old Paula Townsend asked.

'Well, when we were chatting last time we were out, you said that you'd never been to Dovedale, so I thought that I'd take you there today. Then maybe stop off at a pub for a bite to eat, how does that sound?'

'Sounds good to me, but I'm not dressed for a hike.'

'Don't worry, we won't be walking too far, it's just a very pretty area, we can see a lot of it from the car.'

The walk to Three Shires head

Jim and Maddie had driven out and parked opposite the Cat and Fiddle public house on the outskirts of Buxton. It was busy; most of the spaces were occupied by a large group of elderly motor cycle enthusiasts who all looked slightly odd all dressed in their black leathers, with their silver hair protruding from beneath their space age looking crash helmets.

'Now Jim let me guess, you're taking us to the pub, I know about it, I read that it's the second highest pub in England.'

Jim smiled and grabbed her hand. 'You are absolutely correct, it is the second highest. The highest is the Tan Hill pub in the Yorkshire Dales, and I'll take you there one day soon.'

'We may have a drink later, but for now we have a really nice walk to do.' Jim opened up the boot of the car and passed out the rucksacks. He would have preferred to have carried all of their gear, but Maddie insisted she carried her own things.

'Well I don't feel as if I've done a proper walk these days if I haven't got my rucksack on my back,' she insisted.

'Yeah OK, little Miss Independent,' Jim said as he helped her to adjust the straps of her bag.

'So what are we doing today, husband to be?' Maddie said, the giggle in her voice bursting to get out.

'We, my love, are going to probably what is the most romantic spot in the whole of the glorious Peak District,' Jim replied, his face beaming brightly.

'You've not found another cave for us have you?' she laughed, instantly recalling the spot in Miller's Dale where they consummated their relationship for the first time, not very long ago.

'Don't tempt me, you little Vixen.' Jim laughed. 'It wouldn't take much.'

They turned their back on the pub and walked along the obvious moorland track which rose gently, before dipping over the horizon about a mile away.

'I hope that this walk lives up to the publicity you've put out Jim,' Maddie said as they walked steadily up the track.

'Don't you worry your beautiful head, would I take you to places so undeserving of our attention? I only take you to the best places.'

'Yeah, but what is it like?'

Jim put his arm around her shoulder, resting his hand on the top of her rucksack. 'I looked at a picture of it in one of my magazines; it looks lovely. It's got a couple of bridges and waterfalls and a thing called the Panniers' Pool, where in the olden days the traders would stop to let the mules drink.'

'It sounds great, looking forward to seeing it,' Maddie said, looking at Jim and pulling a funny face.

The sun climbed out from behind a cloud and lit up large patches of the brown moorland. They crested the long slope, negotiated a wooden stile, and began the gradual downward path, which gave them views of the distant moors and hills. All around them was gorse and heather. There were deep channels cut into the moor from some distant human activity.

'Wonder what they were?' Maddie exclaimed.

Jim looked on his map. 'It doesn't show anything on here,' Jim replied.

'I dare say the Buxton Archaeological Society would know,' she said.

'I guess they would if such an organisation actually exists,' Jim said, a touch of irony in his voice.

'Are you being ironic, Jim?'

Jim looked at Maddie, a perplexed mask crossing his face.

'If you tell me what ironic means, I'll tell you if that's what I'm doing,' he laughed.

'Do you know Jimmy?' Maddie said as they meandered unhurried down the ever increasingly steep slope.

'Nope, I haven't got a clue,' he said.

'When I first met you; we got on really well, didn't we?'

'Yes, you liked me and I liked you much more than you liked me.'

'Is that so?' Maddie said, gently punching Jim in the chest.

'Yes, I think that, in my opinion, and given the depth of knowledge gained over the past few months, having studied you at great length,' Jim paused for effect, 'over this period I think that I can safely say, without fear of contradiction, that I liked you more than you liked me.' Jim stopped to take in air. 'And furthermore,' he said.

'Yes?' Maddie said, taking a vice like grip on Jim's skinny neck.

'You will be pleased to know that there is no furthermore.'

Maddie stopped, looked up into Jim's face, and said, 'what is the best thing you can think of about being in love with me? And you'd better be careful what you say, heather has ears,' she said, pointing at the vast beds of heather which surrounded them.

Jim laughed. 'I know; there was Heather Jackson and Heather Pickles at school, and as far as I can recall they both had ears. I'm sure they did, in fact I clearly remember seeing them.'

'Don't avoid the question, Jim.'

What was the question?' Jim replied playfully.

'I asked you, what was the best thing about being in love with me, and you seem to be avoiding giving me an answer.'

Jim looked up and smiled. 'The very best thing about me and you is.' He paused 'You're a great kisser.'

'Am I?' she said.

'Well yes, but maybe it's time to test it again, to make sure you're still up to standard.'

'Well come here then.'

'Well OK,' Jim said as he walked to her side and kissed her. Jim felt his whole body react; he was instantly hot, his body responded immediately. His heart raced, and Maddie opened her mouth slightly and pulled Jim up close, she felt the response. She pulled away. Jim was breathless.

'I could feel that you didn't like that,' she said, looking up and down his body and grinning.

Jim laughed, there had been a time when he would have turned away embarrassed. 'Well madam, how was it for you?'

'Maddie smiled mischievously. 'It was OK, but I think that we need to practice more, maybe when we get to the bridge we can try again,' she said, making Jim's blood pressure soar, and set him sweating in anticipation.

Dane valley

They descended further, soon coming to a tarmac road and saw the footpath sign indicating the route they should take. They were soon descending an extremely steep section of loose rocky track which terminated at a point close to a large stone chimney. It was now disused, but had been part of the local industrial heritage of the area.

'Where are we Jim?' Maddie said.

'You can't fool me mad woman, we're here.' He smirked.

'Yes you daft bat, but I'm interested, what's it all about? Tell me, or I'll go into a massive strop. You've never seen me in a strop, have you?'

'No, and it is not one of my ambitions to see one either.' He laughed.

'Well you can see,' he said, look at all the heaps of stones, 'it's a bit like the old pit slag heaps,' he said, pointing across to the other side of the valley. 'This whole area, I think it's called the Dane Valley, it used to be an industrial site, but I really don't know much more than that, I didn't have much chance to read up on it with all the stuff I have to read on my course.'

'Hang on, I'll have a look on the map again.'

Jim took out the map from its plastic case. 'Here look,' he said. 'Those quarries over there,' he said looking across the deep valley. 'Look there, the quarry up on the left, that's called Dane Bower Quarry, and the one down there,' he said, pointing across to their right, 'that's Reeve Edge Quarry. And look,' he said, pointing his finger almost directly down. 'That stream is gorgeous.'

The stream, the River Dane, descends rapidly. It twists and turns and plunges over a rocky stream bed, causing the water to foam and glisten in the bright sunlight.

'Are you alright to move on a bit now, there's just a bit more of this rough going, then it will be easy going all the way,' Jim said, after consulting the map again.

They moved on, continuing the descent of the steep rocky hillside. They soon reached the bottom of the valley and followed a well worn but level footpath which tracked the river. The landscape was taking Maddie's breath away; she kept stopping to take pictures.

This is Jim striding manfully along the rough path.

This is Jim in the pretty valley.

This is Jim looking at the foaming river.

This is Jim trying hard but failing to stroke a lamb.

'Come on Mad woman, your battery will be flat by the time we get to the bridge.'

'Jim! I'm taking these for posterity. In years to come, when you're old and fat and too lazy to go for a walk, I'll be able to say to our Grandkids "this was Grandpa when he was fit," and then talk to them about what we used to do.'

Jim sighed. 'OK but can we get on, I'd like to get there in daylight.'

They descended the valley with the river on their left ever present. Jim stopped. 'Listen,' he said.

'What?' Maddie replied.

'I can hear the waterfall I think.'

Maddie strained her ears. 'I think you're right, I can hear it too. Let's go,' she said, excitedly.

They rounded a bend in the track, and suddenly there was the bridge. The old packhorse bridge, built from ancient grey stone. Maddie jogged forward and stood in the centre of the bridge, turning around, absorbing the scenery which surrounded them in all directions.

'Oh Jim, it's a beautiful place,' she called back to him.

Chapter 27

Dovedale

Mick Young pulled his Rover convertible into the car park which was surrounded by trees. The horizon undulated steeply all around. The dale is located amid some of the Peak's most stunning scenery. The day was clear, but had just sufficient breeze to make the trees gently sway. They pulled on heavy jackets, and were soon walking hand in hand along a tree lined lane into the dale. The River Dove flowed almost silently alongside the track. The occasional mallard fluttered away from them, seeming to resent the disturbance by these out of season visitors. They walked out of the trees, and the dale opened up in front of them. The valley sides rose steeply, culminating in sharp-topped summits hundreds of feet above them. There were few people around to disturb the peacefulness of the valley.

Soon they arrived at the famous stepping stones, strategically placed flat topped boulders, set to allow the passage of travellers on foot across the river.

'You go first,' Mick said, 'I'll follow on behind.'

'Paula stepped tentatively onto the first stone and started to cross, but quickly became nervous; the water moved quickly beneath her feet, and created a rushing effect around the stones which was making her feel dizzy. Close to the halfway point she stopped, frozen. 'I'm sorry, Mick, I can't move,' she said, her voice trembling.

Mick moved quickly across the rocks to a point directly behind her.

'Look, don't worry, it'll be alright.'

'I'm not so sure, I'm petrified,' she said again. 'It's making me feel weird.'

'I know, don't worry I've got a plan,' he said, confidently.

Mick turned and dropped into the river, the water barely covering his knees. He walked up and stood beside her.

'Now give me your hand,' he said.

Paula looked aghast, startled by his action. She was bemused, and secretly enjoyed his display of chivalry.

'Mick.,' she said, 'you're a nutcase; you ought to have taken your shoes off before you got into the water.'

Mick looked up at her and winked. 'That's me,' he said, 'can't resist a damsel in distress.' She squeezed his hand. 'I can see I'll have to get into trouble more often,' she said, a smile appearing on her now calm face.

'Well Mick, it's been lovely, Dovedale is beautiful, thank you for bringing me,' Paula said, now feeling relaxed and happy.

Mick paddled out of the water and sat on the rock, removed his shoes and twisted the water out of his socks.

'Tell you what Mick,' she said. 'One good turn deserves another. Let's skip lunch and go back to my place. You can dry out and I'll do us something to eat.'

'Well if you don't mind, that would be good,' he said, a knowing smile beginning to cross his face. 'It would be awkward to sit in the pub with my wet trousers.'

They walked slowly back to the car park and climbed into his car. Mick put the car into gear and negotiated the narrow lane back to the main highway. After a short drive, Mick pulled the car into a farm gateway.

'It's a lovely day now; shall I roll the top back and get a bit of wind in our hair?'

Paula looked across at him. 'You're such a romantic Mick; I thought all you red watch guys were too tough to woo a lady.' Mick threw his head back and laughed aloud.

'You must be joking. We're the sensitive watch.' He paused. 'Well we are if you discount Jock and Brian; I don't think they could spell it let alone do it. And Mac I guess. well maybe Clive as well, Pete Jacks' the new guy, he's sensitive I think, and Jake's the baby of the watch and I reckon he's got a soft side to him.'

She laughed. 'And what about Taff then?'

'Oh well you know Taff, he's Welsh, and we all know they're a bit on the soft side. But I have to say in his defence, I've seen Taff riled, someone asked him to buy a round once; It was carnage. It wasn't a pretty sight.'

'I like your car, Mick,' she said, stretching out her long legs causing her short skirt to ride higher up her thighs. 'How long have you had it?'

'I bought it from new last year, my gran died and left me a bit of money so I took the plunge and bought it; I love it too.'

Mick looked across at her. 'I think my car is a thing of beauty, from its 1396 cc engine to its very pretty interior, and dashboard to die for. If I may say Paula, a gorgeous girl sat in the passenger seat certainly adds to its aesthetic value.'

Paula put her hand onto Mick's knee. 'I bet you say that to all the girls, don't you?' she said, a wicked grin on her face.

'Actually no.' Mick stated. 'I have to say, you're the first passenger I have ever had in this car, and I can't imagine having a prettier one sitting there in the future.'

She laughed aloud. 'You really know how to get your way with a girl,' she said, mischievously.

They talked loudly above the sound of wind rushing past them all the way into the city. Mick sitting uncomfortably in his still wet trousers, Paula looking at Mick, and the contours of his lower body as he sat in his figure hugging trousers. She looked with a measure of calm anticipation.

The Dane valley

Maddie took her camera out of its case. She looked around her excitedly, each view required a decision as to where would be the best viewpoint to take the picture from.

'Jim, stand on the bridge and smile please,' she ordered. Jim did as he was told. Jim was impressed too, and was glad Maddie liked it. He'd seen the pictures and hoped that they were a good representation of the place, and that Maddie wouldn't be disappointed. They both stood on the bridge and looked downstream. The water flowed and crashed over a rocky edge, forming a small waterfall split into two streams, another fall then it discharged into a quiet pool. Alongside the pool, an elderly man sat eating a sandwich, his dog happily wading in the water drinking its fill.

'Come Jim,' Maddie said enthusiastically, 'let's go and sit by the pool and have our lunch, I don't think the old fellow will mind if we join him.'

Chapter 28

London

Jake had spent ten minutes in the police car giving his version of events. 'So what did you see and do sir?' the younger of the two police officers asked.

'Well it was all a bit of a blur,' Jake said, 'I heard the woman scream and shout something in Spanish I think; then I saw this guy, it seemed he'd knocked her down and was trying to get her handbag. She was fighting hard to stop him, and the next thing he was running towards us and I just reacted, I didn't think, I just did it. Next thing really that I remember was him hitting me in the face, that was when I hit him back. That was all there was to it.'

The policeman showed no reaction to the statement; he'd written down what Jake had told him. 'Right sir, I just need a few personal details. Name, address, work etc, are you happy with that?'

Yeah, that's no problem, just glad I was able to stop the guy.'

Jake got out of the car and walked across to his mother, who was still talking animatedly to the young woman.

'Oh hello son, have you told them everything?'

'I have; so hopefully that's the end of it,' Jake said as he looked at the girl. She returned his look, their eyes held on each other for a long second. The girl was beautiful, small, slim, olive skin, dark brown eyes, long flowing black hair. Jake felt his heart swell. She was beautiful. The look of gratitude and admiration for what Jake had done was percolating from her smile. She moved forward and said in her faltering English, 'I am very thankful for you sir.' She put her hand on Jake's arm, lifted herself onto her tiptoes, and kissed him on the cheek.

Jake flushed, and his face lifted with surprise. 'Think nothing of it, it was my pleasure,' Jake said, trying not to appear over modest.

She looked up into Jake's strong features. She noticed his short, cropped dark hair and his powerful physique, she guessed him to be over six feet tall, which in fact dwarfed her. She was about five foot two and not at all powerful; she was very impressed, and struggled within herself not to show it.

One of the policemen came across to them.

'Come with us madam, we need to let the ambulance crew have a look at you.'

The young woman turned to Jake and his mother. 'Will you wait for a minute; I want still to talk for you, if it's OK,' she said.

'Don't you worry my love, we'll hang on here,' Jake's mother said, giving her a warm smile.

'I saw you talking to her, mum, what was it all about?' Jake's mum took his hand and gave it a gentle squeeze.

'You like her, don't you Jacob?'

'Oh yes! And what makes you say that?' Jake replied.

'Jacob, I've known you all of your life. I gave birth to you, I've fed you and wiped your eyes when you cried. There's not much that I don't know about you, son. And I know that you like her, I saw the way you reacted to her.'

Jake was taken aback. 'Well she is good looking, and if I'm honest I could fancy her, but that's hardly likely to happen, she's in a different league,' Jake said, looking slightly disappointed. 'And anyway, we don't even know her name or anything about her.'

'Oh yes we do,' his mother replied. 'What do you think we were talking about while you were being interviewed by the police?'

'Well are you going to tell me then?' Jake said, amazed at his mother's ability to extract information so easily from strangers.

'Well son. As you're obviously so interested, this is the information I got after applying the thumb screws.' She paused, and waited for his response.

'Go on then, tell me,' he said, getting the distinct feeling that his mother was playing games with him.

'Her name is.' she paused for a second. 'Antonella Gerardi. She's twenty years old, she comes from Rome, and plays the violin for the London Symphony Orchestra.' Jake looked at his mother. 'You don't hang about do you mum?' he said, with a smirk creeping across his face.

'Well Jacob, let me tell you this.' She paused again, for effect. 'When she saw you, I looked at her, and I can tell you that she fancies you.'

'Don't be daft mother, she doesn't know me.'

'No she doesn't, but what she does know has impressed her, remember, you've just floored the guy that attacked her, you're her knight in shining armour.'

Three Shire's Head

Jim and Maddie made their way across the descending rocky ground towards the edge of the Pannier's Pool. The elderly man with the dog looked up from his paperback and greeted them. 'Hello,' he said, 'it's a lovely day for a walk.'

Maddie sat on a rock close by the man's dog, an old Black Labrador. It waddled arthritically across to Maddie. She stroked its head, and the dog tilted it upwards and looked at her with its big soft brown eyes. 'He's a little sweetie,' Maddie said, still stroking the dog's head, its tail beating a firm rhythm on the rock close to Maddie's leg.

'Yes he's a good old dog; he's getting a bit past it now though, twelve years old and starting to get arthritis in his hips.'

'You're a lovely boy aren't you?' Maddie cooed at the dog, which was lapping up the attention.

'Here Mad; let me take a picture of you with it,' Jim said, lifting the camera to take the shot.

'Would you mind taking a picture of me with the dog as well?' the old man asked.

'No problem, let me have your address or e mail and we'll get a copy off to you.'

'That's very kind of you,' he replied, 'this is his last walk out here.'

'Oh, why is that?' Maddie asked, suddenly feeling startled.

'Next month I fly out to America to live with my son and his family, and I can't take Henry with me.'

'So what will you do then?'

'Well I think I'll have to get him to the RSPCA or a home, I couldn't have him put to sleep, just because I can't have him anymore.'

Jim jumped up. 'No problem, we'll have him,' he blurted.

The dog seemed to understand what had just been said, and walked across to where Jim was sitting and sat in front of him.

'Look,' Jim said, a broad grin crossing his gaunt face, 'he understands what we've just said.'

'I don't think so,' the old man said, 'I think he's just noticed your ham sandwich.'

Sheffield

Mick pulled the car up against the kerb alongside Paula's small block of modern apartments. 'Right then young man, or man Young should I say, let's get you out of those wet clothes shall we?'

The apartment was spacious, the lounge had a dark red carpet and was furnished with a plush, deeply upholstered brown leather suite, a pale Beech dining suite, and a pair of Van Gogh prints hanging from the wall.

'You've got a nice place here, Paula,' Mick said as they walked into the room. 'Yes, it's OK, let me show you round,' she said, grabbing his hand.

'This is my bedroom,' she said enthusiastically, looking at Mick and winking. 'Just stay here a minute, I'll get a towel to dry you off.' Mick looked around the room. It had dark blue heavy curtains, pale wallpaper with a black floral pattern, and a double bed covered by a heavy patchwork quilt. Sitting on the bed was a large brown Teddy Bear. The room had little natural light. Mick stood and waited.

Paula re entered the bedroom and walked directly to Mick, leaned against him and kissed him ferociously on the lips. Her hand slid down from his waist and began unbuckling the belt, lowering the zip, pushing his trousers down around his ankles. She squirmed and pushed hard against him, quickly pushing his damp underpants to the floor. Mick was aroused. She stepped back and looked at him, a huge smile crossing her lips.

'It's true what they say about you firemen, I see,' she said laughing.

Mick stood exposed and feeling slightly embarrassed.

'Now you just stand there Mick,' she said firmly. 'I'm going to dry you off.' She took the towel she'd brought into the room and knelt down in front of him and in a slow, sensual way gently rubbed the towel over Mick's still damp but rigid lower body.

London

The girl climbed stiffly out of the police car, and Jake noticed that she'd grazed her knees during the attack.

'Are you OK?' Jake asked, his eyes fixed like a laser on her shapely red lips.

'Yes, thank you Mister Jacob, I am always very grateful for you what you did for me.'

'That's alright, as long as you're OK,' Jake said, incapable of taking his eyes away from her face.

'I was spoken to your mum and she was telling of me that you are going to theatre tonight.' She paused for a second to collect the words she was to say. 'I am in such pleasure to have you save me Jacob; I feel that I can to repay you and your mama in some way that I only can.'

'You shouldn't worry about that, I was glad to help,' Jake said, beginning to feel a little self-conscious.

'I have spoken with your mama and I would ask you to visit London to come to a concert at which I will play.' Jake noticed the tears beginning to form in her eyes and run down her olive cheeks. She fought to stifle a sob. 'I'm very sorry,' she said, 'today was a big shock for me, I was very frightened.'

'I'm sure you were,' Jake agreed, 'but it's over now and you're OK, that's the main thing.'

Jake was still fascinated by the girl. Uncharacteristically, he stepped forward and put his arm around her slim shoulder.

'You'll be fine now. Look, if it would help, I'll give you my phone number and you can give us a call and have a chat to me or mum if you need to, how does that sound?'

She looked at Jake and gave him a weak smile. 'That would be very good I think.'

Three Shire's Head

Jim and Maddie sat with the old man for a while and talked about his migration to America. 'My son works over there, he's been there about ten years. He works in a company dealing with computers in Atlanta, Georgia.'

'That sounds great,' Maddie said. 'Will he stay over there?'

'Yes, he's married with two children, my grandchildren; they were born there, so I can't see him coming back to England now.'

'Well I hope that you settle alright,' Maddie replied, 'it's a big move for you.'

'Yes, it's a move I wouldn't have made, but I lost my wife a year ago and I don't have anyone else here to think about, so hopefully it will suit both of us.'

Jim spoke up. 'Look if you would like us to have Henry when you leave, here's my phone number, have a think about it and let me know.'

The old man stood up and called the dog over to him.

'Come here Henry.' The dog dutifully came and sat by the old man's legs. 'Well I'd better get off; he'll need his dinner soon. It's been nice talking to you. I'll be in touch soon, thank you.'

London

Jake's mother stepped up to the girl, put her arms around her, and hugged her. 'You'll be alright now, my love. And you are very beautiful. Jake hasn't said much, but I can tell he likes you.'

Jake turned away, embarrassed by his mother's attempts to fix him up.

'Awe mum, leave it out, she doesn't want to know about that.'

The girl said. 'I am very grateful to you both for my helping and please come and see me in my concert.' She paused for a long second, looked directly into Jake's eyes.

'I think that Jacob also is very handsome man,' she said her smile widening, her eyes wide and dark, her hair long black and shiny, her lips a fiery red. Jake noticed everything about her, and it made his body tingle.

Sheffield

Mick woke up, the light outside was beginning to fade. He looked at the bedside clock. '*Hell's teeth, is that the time?*' he said to himself. Paula lay quietly beside him, her hair now dishevelled. She stirred and turned over to face Mick who was about to get out of bed. 'What time is it?' she said in a tired voice.

'It's a quarter past six, time I was away from here,' he said, light heartedly. 'It's been the best day out in the hills I've ever had.'

'Well thank you Mick, it's been an eventful day, perhaps we can repeat it soon?' she said, 'I'd love to do it again.'

'How about next weekend?' he suggested.

'That should be fine, I don't think I've got anything arranged, in fact I'll make sure I've got nothing on,' she replied, a wicked smile crossing her face. Paula laughed; she liked Mick a lot. 'Well off you go young man; I'll look forward to hearing from you in the week about next weekend.' Mick put his arm across her as she lounged in the bed, and kissed her on the forehead.

'Until next weekend then,' he said as he pulled the door closed and made his way down the carpeted stairs to his car.

Chapter 29

The morning was cold, a low lying mist hung like a damp curtain across the back garden of Jane's house. Droplets of water dripped continuously from the branches of the arthritic looking apple tree that had stood unmoved and unloved for over thirty years. Jane was up and about making tea and toast. She heard the creak of the stairs as Brian slowly made his way down. 'Good morning,' she said cheerfully, 'I was going to let you lie in. How are you now, how are the burns?'

Brian was feeling much improved, most of the soreness from his scalds a few days before had receded, and he felt good. 'I feel fine, the sleep last night has really made me feel much better, do you fancy a trip out with our little girl?' he said.

Jane sidled up to him and put her arm around his waist. 'That would be nice, have you got any idea where we could go on such a beautiful damp morning,' she said, ironically.

'Oh I don't know, how about a little drive out, look at a few views, and stop off somewhere for a bite to eat?'

'Go on then, you've talked me into it,' she said smiling as she leaned forward and planted a kiss on his cheek.

'You know I'm back at work next tour don't you?' Brian said.

'Yes, why?'

'Well before then I want to get you out to town to show you something,' he replied.

'What's that then?'

'You'll have to wait and see, it's a surprise.' He laughed.

The roads were quiet as Brian steered the car out into the Derbyshire countryside. 'It looks as though the weather's keeping everyone at home,' he said as he drove down the gently sloping road, which at the bottom turned gently to the left. Fifty yards on were a set of temporary traffic lights, there to protect unfinished road works. The light turned to red; he slowed the car and pulled to a stop close to the lights. They sat for a couple of minutes, waiting and chatting.

'I know where we can go,' Jane suddenly said, 'can we go up to Monsal head? I've not been up there for years, I seem to remember it was beautiful.'

Brian pulled the car onto the small car park which overlooked the valley. The mist was still lingering, and the air was damp and cold. They sat looking at the view. The valley was cut deep by a fast flowing river. Cattle stood in the adjacent fields looked around unconcerned as small groups of hikers passed by them.

The river was crossed by lovely old bridges which created a sense of timelessness. Jane imagined packhorses crossing the river to deliver their goods to local towns. The valley sides were lush and green, punctuated by silver grey limestone escarpments creeping out of the steep valley sides, which rose hundreds of feet above the river.

'This is a beautiful place,' Brian said, as Jill stood up in the back of the car looking between them. They sat absorbing the view for a few minutes, and then Brian suggested that they do a short walk. 'Come on you two, the exercise will do us good.'

'Are you sure?' Jane exclaimed, 'in this weather!'

'It will be fine if we go to the valley bottom, I'll drive us to the other end, park up, and we can have a stroll along by the lake for a few minutes.'

He drove down the steep road into Upperdale and along by the river. He parked close by an old, semi derelict mill which was undergoing refurbishment. 'OK guys, let's get out shall we,' he said cheerfully, trying to ignore the rain which was spattering the windscreen.

They walked through an area of old stone buildings, and then passed close to a cafe, which was closed. As they walked, they came within sight of a powerful weir; the sound of the rushing water carried a long way in the otherwise silent dale. Then, the view opened up before them, high limestone cliffs surrounded a large lake on one side, the other heavily forested with the occasional rock buttress protruding from the mass of bare trees. 'Oh this is a gorgeous place,' Jane said, her voice showing her surprise.

'Is this the first time you've been here?' Brian asked.

'Yes, I've never been here before, it's lovely, it's so well hidden. It would be nice to come again in the summer.'

'We will,' Brian promised. 'Often there are rock climbers messing about on the rocks, and the lake usually has loads of birds on it. I think it's a nature reserve, it does get busy, but it's a nice walk up river. We'll come back another day in better weather.

'Right ladies, where shall we go for lunch?' Brian asked. 'Tideswell is just up the road, there must be a couple of pubs up there that do food,' he said enthusiastically. 'OK, back to the car, and we'll get there hopefully before the pub gets too busy.'

Brian drove up the steep winding tree lined road out of the dale, and they were soon stopped outside a large public house close to the huge Tideswell church. The car park was sparsely occupied, inside were just a couple of locals standing at the bar.

'What can I get you, Sir?' the attractive young woman behind the bar asked.

'We'd like to eat, have you got a menu?' he asked.

'This young lady,' he said, putting his hand on Jill's shoulder, 'would like a coke, and this young lady,' he said looking at Jane, 'would like a glass of cider, and I'll have a half of lager, please.'

Brian looked at the girl behind the bar; she seemed familiar, something about her triggered thoughts in his head, she was very attractive and was dressed casually. Then he remembered. She was the girl from the shop, where not long ago he'd tried to buy clothes for Jane. He remembered the way she walked and how being so close to her had made him catch his breath. *She's obviously earning a bit more money to make ends meet,* he thought to himself.

The food was good; the three of them sat and listened to the sound of a young man who sat on a stool playing his guitar in the corner of the lounge. After a while, the bar began to fill up and the volume of noise increased, but they were all enjoying the atmosphere. Brian kept catching a fleeting glimpse of the barmaid. *She is very attractive,* he thought.

Mac and Val had done the week's supermarket shopping. The girls were coming round tonight for tea. Although they saw them regularly, Mac still missed the close contact he had always had with his daughters when they were much younger. He'd spent much of his time and money when off duty at weekends being the family chauffer, taking them to the mass of schoolgirl activities. Saturday morning it was horse riding for Lucy, Ruth on a Saturday afternoon had a gymnastics class. Sunday mornings it was both girls to netball practise and later tennis lessons.

They unloaded the car, and Val began re stocking the shelves in the freezer and pantry, just another ordinary Sunday. Mac enjoyed these days they had time to sit, relax, and read the paper or read a book, maybe have a soak in the bath and then TV in the evening. *Paradise,* he thought.

He wandered into the conservatory with its heavily upholstered cane furniture, armed with his mug of tea and the Sunday paper; a perfect time to relax, away from the stress of work and people making demands on his time. Val came through with a magazine, and they both sat comfortably reading; the warmth of the sun through the windows belying the cool temperature on the other side of the double glazed windows.

'What's happening with the Ranger thing?' Val asked, lifting her head from the magazine and peering at Mac over the top of her glasses.

Mac sat up in his chair and put the paper down. 'Not too sure at the moment. Janet said that I can go out on patrol with her anytime I want.' He paused for a moment. 'I don't think I'll be able to fit them in before I retire though, I'll probably sign up and do all of the training patrols once I've finished with the Brigade.'

'Yeah, I suppose that would be the sensible thing, with all the other things going on in your life,' she said, almost absent-mindedly.

'Well it's going to be pretty busy the next few weeks; what with Clive getting married, and I'm not too sure what Brian's up to, but I'll know more when he gets back to work. Then we've got the funeral down near Birmingham next week. Then I'm trying to arrange Pete's trip with Trudy to Penrith, it's a miracle we've got time to go to fires.'

The phone rang. 'Hello dad.' It was Lucy.

'Hiya Luce. What's up?' Mac asked, suspecting that he was going to get a plea for help.

'No problem dad; well just a small one.'

'Yeah, what's that then?' Mac said, a knowing smirk planted on his face as he looked across the conservatory at Val.

'In a word dad, I can't start the car.' Mac sensed the young light sound of frantic desperation in her voice.

'Are you at home?'

'No,' she replied, her voice sounding vexed.

'Where are you?'

'I'm in a lay-by on the Fox House road near Owler Bar.'

'What happened?'

'Don't know, it just stalled and I can't start it again.'

'OK, I'll be with you in about a quarter of an hour, stay in the car, OK?'

'Will do,' she said, sounding relieved that her dad had been at home.

Over the last few years since Lucy had been able to drive, Mac had been out to rescue her about half a dozen times; it was usually something simple and was soon fixed.

'That was Luce,' Mac said, 'she's broken down near Fox House; I'll go out and have a look.'

Mac went to the garage and put his tool box and a tow rope in the boot of his car, and the emergency can of petrol he always kept, just in case. Val came out. 'I'll come out with you just for the ride,' she said, climbing into the passenger seat of the car.

The sun was shining, but there was a cold wind blowing. Mac felt the gusts rock the car as he climbed out of the city heading towards the moors.

'Let's hope it's the usual shall we? It's a bit nippy out there to be hanging over a car bonnet in this weather.'

Mac soon pulled up in the lay by behind Lucy's car. 'Thanks dad.' She greeted him. 'Hi Mum,' she said as her mother hugged her.

'Right, let's have a look, can I have the keys?'

Mac sat in her small red Fiesta and turned the ignition. The engine didn't fire. He looked at the petrol gauge; it was showing empty.

'Lucy, when did you last put petrol in your car?'

'Oh not too long ago, I think the gauge has stopped working; it's showed empty for a few days now.'

Mac smirked. 'Well just in case, I've brought some fuel with me.'

Val and Lucy sat in Mac's car and watched him pour the contents of the can into Lucy's fuel tank. He turned the ignition key. The engine turned for a few seconds, then it fired and continued to run.

'There you go, young lady,' Mac said, smiling benevolently at his relieved daughter.

'What was it this time, dad?'

'Fuel starvation, the same as last time,' Mac said, grinning.

'Oh! It keeps doing that,' she said, smiling sweetly at her father.

'Yes, you have to put petrol in it occasionally my love. There's nothing wrong with the gauge. Can I suggest that you go to the next garage and put more fuel in the tank?'

'Thanks dad, you're a treasure, we'll see you later,' she said, smiling apologetically at Mac.

Mac climbed back into the Volvo. 'Come on gal, back to the tea and papers.'

Brian ducked his head as he climbed back into the car. 'Back home then, shall we?'

Jane sat with her hand resting gently on Brian's thigh. She asked 'you said you had a surprise, what and when?'

Brian looked across at her. 'When; next week, the first chance we get. What? Well that's a surprise,' he said with a chuckle.

Jake had been nominated as the Mess Manager again, and had been hit by the usual quips about his as yet below standard food supplies for the Watch. He brought out the tray of tea filled mugs.

Brian was back at work, he sat next to Jake. They'd had a chat in the privacy of the locker room before the shift started, and again Brian had thanked Jake for his help at the fire.

'You don't have to say anything; it was nothing compared to what you did for us,' Jake said, still looking in awe at Brian, who he saw as his saviour in the fire.

'How was the weekend with your mum in London then, Jake?' Clive asked.

'It was fine, she loved it. Les Miserables wasn't my style, but mum thought it was great.'

'What else did you do then?' Pete piped up.

'We had a trip down the Thames on a boat and had a nice meal, it was excellent.'

Mac spoke up. 'Was there anything else you want to tell us?'

Jake flushed. 'No, it was a good weekend, mum wants me to take her again, she said she wants to go to a concert.'

'And what about you, Jake?' Mac asked.

Jake was feeling a bit unsettled at the line of questioning. 'Is there anything else you'd like to tell us?' Mac persisted.

'Well yeah, I'd like to go to the concert as well, or I wouldn't go would I?'

Mac turned to look at Jake. 'It seems boys, that young Jake here is not telling us the whole truth. Val rang Jake's mum yesterday, guess what she told us?'

'What?' Brian asked.

'Well, Jake has taken a fancy to a girl that he met in London, in fact according to his mum, he's in love.' Mac paused for a second. 'It seems that he was a hero again, weren't you Jake? Why don't you tell us all about it?'

Jake's face became flushed, his pale skin seeming to accentuate his embarrassment.

'Look guys, it was nothing. I just saw this bloke trying to steal this girl's handbag; he knocked her down and ran off. I didn't think about it, he ran near me so I grabbed him until the police came, and that's it.'

Mac smirked. 'Not according to your mum it wasn't,' he said.

'Well yeah, I had to deck him; he punched me so I hit him back. Then the police came and he was dragged off to the Police Station.'

'But it seems from your mum that you knocked his lights out, and that this girl, a beautiful Italian Violinist called Antonella, seems to like the look of you; the poor girl. And according to mum, the font of all knowledge regarding her beloved Jacob, she reckons that you've taken a fancy to her. Would that be something like an accurate summary of your dull old trip to the capital, Jacob?'

'Jake looked around the men of his watch whose faces all sported broad grins, and Jake realised that it was all good natured joshing.

'Yeah, it was something like that, but it all happened so fast I didn't have time to think about it. If it happened again, I'd maybe do what everybody else did; just ignore it. I think that was what annoyed me most. Nobody did anything to help her.' Jake stood up from his chair and walked out towards the kitchen. 'I liked London, but I was annoyed that people could just see someone, especially a girl being attacked, and not step in.' He walked into the kitchen and poked his head through the hatch. 'Does anybody want another cup of tea?'

After the boys had finished their break, Jake cleaned up after them. He loaded the dishwasher, wiped the Formica tabletops, and tidied the black plastic chairs.

Jake stopped and leaned against the kitchen worktop. He was feeling a bit weary; he knew the reason. He hadn't slept too well since his return from the London trip. The reason was the girl. During the time since they met on Oxford Street, he'd become fixated on her face. If you asked him to describe what she was wearing, or if she had a good figure then Jake would have been unable to give a clear answer. Her face was the only thing that he could recall; it seemed to have been burned into the back of his eye, and he was having difficulty getting her out of his mind. He knew when he thought about her he got hot and his heart began to race. He wondered why that was, was it love or something else? He rationalised that it was probably the excitement of the circumstances surrounding their meeting. Maybe that was the cause, as simple as that. But even now, as he stood by the kitchen window, the vision of her face talking soundlessly to him flickered in and out of his mind.

'Wakey wakey Jake, come on, let's get a move on.' It was Mac.

'We're all ready when you are.'

Jake turned round to face Mac. 'I'm sorry Sub; I was day-dreaming. Sorry.'

Chapter 30

Hubert Styles parked his Jaguar on the yellow line outside the car showroom, ignoring the Traffic Warden who leered at him from across the street. He walked lightly through the heavy double glass swing doors of the showroom. The manager raised his head from his paperwork and saw Hubert pacing briskly across the showroom towards him. He smiled a subtle smile. Hubert was an old customer, and the manager needed the business.

'Good morning, Mister Styles. How are you today sir?' he said brightly, standing up to shake his hand.

'Well, my dear man,' he said, a smile creasing his polished features, 'I need you to do me a favour and a little bit of business,' he said, sitting down in front of the manager's desk. 'If I remember correctly,' he said, 'you provide a drink for customers, would that be correct?'

'Absolutely correct sir.'

'Right, young man, I would like a dry sherry if you please.'

Forty minutes later, Hubert walked out of the showroom, a happy smile radiating from his powdered cheeks. He looked across at his car and noticed the plastic bag containing some form of written document stuck to the windscreen. Hubert wrinkled his brow and pouted his lightly rouged lips before ripping the bag theatrically away from his windscreen. He then screwed the offending document into a tight ball before looking at the concerned parking attendant who was loitering across the street.

'Thank you for that darling, but I won't need this,' he called, blowing a kiss at the pale faced and by now angry civil servant. He then tossed the crumpled notice into the nearby rubbish bin.

The twenty lengths of hose stretched out across the drill yard, testing them was almost finished, just the need to give the hose a scrub to get the last remnants of grease and mud off the red plasticised outer coating of the hose. With the exception of Mac and Brian, the whole watch were engaged in equipment testing. Mac and Brian were getting on with the monthly returns of paperwork, balancing the imprest and checking that the training records were all up to date. In a couple of weeks, the Inspectorate was due to visit the brigade, to test its procedures, make visits to the stations, and have a close look to ensure that everything was as it should be. It was always a time of frantic activity. Getting the jobs done that had been put on the back burner. This was the ideal opportunity to sort out these things.

Mac leaned back in his chair. 'How's things going Brian? We've not had much chance for a chat since you came back to work.'

Brian sat up from his desk. 'Things are good; the old war wound is fine, no after effects at all.'

Mac looked at him. 'Tell me about it, I've not spoken to either you or Jake properly since the job. What happened in the fire?'

'You know Mac, I'm not really sure, it was bloody hot and I remember we had a bit of a flashover. I got hit pretty hard by that, then I felt absolutely knackered, thank goodness Jake was up to it.'

'Yeah, well I had a little chat to Jake about it, just in case there had been anything unusual happen in there. Jake said that he thought you'd saved his life, and that's why you collapsed.'

'I don't know about that,' Brian replied, 'I remember the fireball, and after that it is all a bit of a haze.'

Mac looked on at his friend of many years. 'You know, Bry, in this job we don't crow about the good things we do often enough. Based on what Jake's told me, and having spoken to the Station Commander, I reckon he'll be talking to the Div Commander about you and recommending that you get some recognition for what you did.'

Brian tried to speak, but choked on his words. He relaxed back in his chair and composed himself.

'You know what this job's about, Mac. We go through our time doing our best, sometimes we cock up, other times it goes well, and I think like most people, I got a bit cocky. I thought I was immortal. You know; the 'it won't happen to me' syndrome.' He stopped and thought about what he wanted to say. 'I've been really lucky; I've lost my eyebrows and had my ears scorched a few times, broken fingers, had cuts and bruises like we all have. But recently I don't know. I think my luck's beginning to desert me. I had that bang on the head a bit back, and now this, I must be getting old.'

'Aren't we all?' Mac said, looking fondly at him. 'You're a really good fireman, I'm sure that what you did the other day with Jake was typical of you. I know Jake thinks you're some sort of superman.' Mac paused, he knew what he was about to say would surprise him.

'I think you need to think about moving on, beyond where you are now. Get yourself promoted or transfer into Training. I think you'd be really good at it, and I think you'd love it as well. It would be a chance to pass on the experience you've got to other young fire-fighters.' Mac looked at Brian, who was looking rather puzzled. 'Take yourself away from this, you've done this for years, you can still develop, I think you'd enjoy the change. You'd be on days, you'd see more of Jane and Jill.' Mac paused again and leaned back in his chair. 'I know you love the job, but maybe the time is right for you to think about getting promoted. You've got the exams passed and the brains and most important, the experience. Remember also, the pension is waiting a few years away in the future, hopefully you'll have a lot of years to draw on it after you retire.'

Brian looked bemused. 'I've never really considered going for promotion, I've always loved being out with the lads on the machine having a laugh.'

'Well I think,' Mac said, 'having watched you doing the temporary slot here, that it's well within your ability; it would be a shame to waste your talent.'

'That's interesting Mac; I'll give it some thought and get back to you.'

'You do that, now can you go and check on the lads, I want to have a Watch meeting after dinner.'

Mark was feeling pretty tired; the boss at Central had had them out drilling in the yard then they got a shout before they could settle to have their tea break. They'd been called to help an old lady who had slammed the door of her terraced house, leaving the keys on the kitchen table. No sooner had they resolved her problem than they were called to help the police catch a stray dog which was rampaging back and forth along the bank of the River Sheaf, close to the city centre. The police had no equipment to do the job, and it did require tricky descent down a ladder to the riverbank fifteen feet below. The Central appliance carried a dog grasper, a piece of equipment, a throw back from the seventies, used normally to restrain free running guard dogs in secure premises. On this occasion, it was perfect for getting the dog back to street level and allowing the RSPCA to remove it, and the threat to the public.

George Collier sat in his office. Over the past few weeks he'd been having a close look at Mark Devonshire, or Devo as he had become known to the watch, and now he thought that it was time for a chat. George's Sub Officer, Kenny Leonard, was sat at his desk compiling the watch training records.

'Ken, just nip downstairs and get Devo up here will you? Where is he by the way?'

'Last I saw of him George he was mopping the engine house floor with Chas.'

'Well just get him up here, and I want you to sit in as well.'

Mark knocked nervously on the Station Officer's door. Being summoned upstairs was something that was new to him. He'd worked hard and blended in well with his mates on the watch, and he thought he'd done all right at the fires, so he was a bit nervous as to why the boss would want to see him.

'Come in Mark and sit yourself down lad,' George said in his broad Sheffield accent.

Mark sat in the comfortable blue padded chair opposite George, who looked searchingly at him across the desk.

'Now then Mark, how long is it since you started here, remind me?' George said, looking over the top of his rimless glasses.

Mark looked up at the panelled ceiling.

'I think boss it's about three months.'

'And how are you finding us, up here in the frozen North?'

The sudden informality of the boss instantly made Mark relax.

'Before you answer that Devo, just let me say, this isn't an interrogation, it's just a chat whilst we have a bit of time on our hands to see how you're doing, so don't worry OK?'

'Well boss, you know I was in the Navy and I liked that, but getting married made me think I needed a job where I could have a normal life with my family, and South Yorkshire were recruiting, so I'm here.'

'And liking it so far?' George asked.

'Oh yeah, it's great, the lads are great, and I enjoy the stuff we have to do. You know the fires and the fire safety, yeah I enjoy it all.'

'That's good; all the boys seem to think you're settling in well, and you've done well at the fires we've had; so there are no problems as far as I'm concerned, other than Arsenal. Isn't it time you got over them and started going to Hillsborough to watch a proper team? Mark smiled.

'And how about the family, are they settling in OK?'

'Yes, we're in the house now, there's still a lot to do, decorating and stuff like that, and the neighbours are nice. Trisha, she's just got a little job a few days a week, so that will help her settle as well. So yes, it's all good, I love it. I really look forward to coming to work.'

'Well that's good Devo, anything you want to ask me?' George said casually.

'There is just one thing I was wondering about boss,' Mark said.

Jake knocked tentatively on Mac's office door.

'Come in Jake,' Mac called, 'Take a seat. The reason I wanted to talk to you.'

The alarm sounded, both Jake and Mac sprang from their seats and jogged down the stairs and into the sloping linoleum covered corridor and on into the appliance room. Brian had ripped the turn out sheet from the printer.

'We've got a job at Avien Electronics suppliers in Sheffield Road. Apparently it's well alight'

'Control from Alpha zero one zero, mobile to Avien electronics, Sheffield Road over.'

Barrie Wedlock the Control Operator had taken the call, and had been informed by the shop owner that the fire was severe and that his staff had managed to get out of the building unharmed.

'Zero one zero, received, for your information we have had several calls to this incident, all staff are out of the building over.'

The machine thundered down the hill towards the town centre, the smoke was visible from a distance. Mac twisted in his seat.

'Get your sets on and started up, it looks like a cracker.'

Pete Jacks and Taff began donning their BA sets; Jake sat between them looking anxiously towards the plume of smoke as it rose fiercely above the surrounding buildings.

Mac heard George Collier's voice over the radio, booking out to Sheffield Road. ADO Paul Davis was the Duty Supervisory Officer for the Division; he had just finished eating his packed lunch when the call came in. Control had mobilised three machines to the incident, and it was then automatically given to the Duty Officer to turn out.

The heavy smoke from the fire had filled the road like a thick grey fog. Mick drove slowly into the smoke, the crew unable to see its source. The road had a series of two storey terraced shop units, built around the eighteen eighties. Many of them were in a poor state of repair or boarded up.

'Pull up here Mick, there's a hydrant just back about twenty yards, get it set in,' Mac picked up the radio.

'Control, in attendance, expect informative over.'

'Zero one zero received.'

Mac jumped into the mist followed by his BA team.

'Jake, get a jet out, two length of 45 mill. Quick as you like,' Mac called out.

Jake's heart pounded with excitement and anticipation of the action to come. He slammed up the roller shutter door to the locker containing the delivery hose. He grabbed the aluminium hand controlled branch, quickly jamming it between the buttons of his fire coat. He lifted out two lengths of hose and sprinted around to the back of the machine. Mick had run off at speed with a length of 70 mill hose and the standpipe key and bar to get a supply of water into the pump from the hydrant. Jake rammed the male coupling into the gunmetal outlet from the pump, and ran out the first length of hose with one hand, whilst grasping the other length of hose under his left arm.

The visibility was poor; the smoke was thick and made breathing difficult. Momentarily, the smoke cleared, giving them all a first view of the fire. Mac's heart sank.

'Jake, do entry control,' Mac shouted. 'Taff and Pete, get the jet on it now,' Mac said with urgency in his voice.

'Control from zero one zero informative message. From Sub Officer James at Avien Electronics, a row of four two storey terraced shops alight and spread into the roof spaces. One jet and two BAs in use. Make pumps six over.'

Control responded immediately.

'Zero one zero, your informative message and make pumps six received out.'

There was now a bustling sense of urgency in the Sheffield fire control. Alan Pursglove, the Senior Controller, began the process of ordering the extra resources that would be needed at the fire.

'Yes Sir, Control here, we have just ordered six pumps to a fire in shops on Sheffield road. The informative message said four shops involved.'

'Thank you control, I'll attend.'

Ian Blain's heart raced, he hadn't had much opportunity recently to put his newly discovered ethos into practise, so today would be the day.

Alan turned to the other operators in control. 'Right folks; let's start getting machines moving, let's bring pumps from Ringinglow and Elm Lane in to cover the city OK?'

Paul Davis slammed the gear lever of his Peugeot into a lower gear and threw it around the roundabout. He looked across the skyline and saw with trepidation the smoke rising above the rooftops. *Oh bloody hell, just what I don't need today of all days,* he thought. Paul was stressed. A heavy workload, a problematic marriage, and a child being bullied at school ensured that when he went to bed at night he didn't sleep. Slowly life was becoming almost too much for him to bear.

George Collier smiled to himself. He'd heard Mac's make up message on the radio and though, this could be just like old times. *Me and Mac getting into it again,* he thought.

'Pull up here, Jacko,' George said, indicating a spot close to the back of the other machines that were already in attendance.

'Right you lot, just hang on here and I'll be back in a minute, and don't go eyeing up the local talent, focus on the fire OK?'

Mac felt a presence looking over his shoulder. 'That's you isn't it George, you old so and so?' Mac said as he looked around behind him. 'Blimey we must be desperate, it must be worse than I thought if they've let you out. Bottom of barrel and scraping comes to mind.' Mac grinned.

'Well Control mentioned that you were in charge and then I thought, bloody hell, my house is only half a mile up the road, I was worried about it spreading that far, so I thought I'd best come out with my young warriors to add some professionalism to the job and at the same time save my own property.'

'Nice one George, I presume you'll be taking over?'

'Yeah for about the next ten seconds, the ADO and DC are on their way, obviously getting bored with their knitting patterns.'

'So Mac, what's up?'

'Four shops well alight, I've got Stage Two BA being set up, three teams in at present, and three jets and two hose reels hitting it, but we'll need another team now you're here. And we'll need to bump up the water supply, the supply lines are getting a bit soft.'

'What have we got now?'

'We're into a four inch main. But just across into Moors Road that's a separate main, we could do with getting into that.'

Harry Bragg had just celebrated his Eighty Fourth Birthday two days earlier. To call it a celebration would be an exaggeration. He had no living relatives or friends. He celebrated his birthday alone, with a bottle of Rum, and a few bottles of beer.

His usual day comprised of getting out of bed and using his walking frame to get to the toilet. Then getting back in to bed for the remainder of his day either watching TV or reading one of his magazines, which were stored in an untidy pile at the side of his bed. Harry was a proud man, he'd served his country in the Second World War, working on merchant convoys delivering goods to Russia at a time when the Germans were doing their best to stop them getting through. After the war, Harry got married to the girl who had been his childhood sweetheart. Their marriage was very happy, but the one thing they wished for was children, and try as they may none came along, much to their great regret.

After the war Harry, got a job in the steelworks, working in the rolling mills. It was a tough life for tough men. After he retired, Harry was diagnosed with severe Arthritis, which over a period of time stopped him in his tracks. Harry was no longer able to do the things he had always done, either as a man or husband. In 1985 his beloved wife died.

Harry, now badly disabled and living in a squalid first floor flat above a dry cleaners, sank slowly into a well of self pity and alcohol.

He woke with a start, struggling to open his eyes. The light through the thin curtains was the only thing he was able to distinguish. The sound of a bell pierced his aching brain. He could hear raised voices and distant horns, but the alcohol which permeated his body had numbed his senses to the point where the sounds made little impression. Then there came the smell; the aroma of fire and smoke, a deadly cocktail. He smelled it, and in his confused state his mind told him that he was imagining it. Then there was the crash of splintering glass nearby. This sound in some way resonated with him; the realisation that this could be him, his flat, somehow brought him to full consciousness and his heart began to race. Still confused, he tried to climb out of his bed only to tumble in a ragged heap on to the floor. He could feel the heat of the fire, which was burning fiercely one inch below his body, protected only by that one inch of timber floorboard. He felt the heat but didn't have the strength to lift himself up from the floor to escape. At first, there were just small wisps of smoke beginning to creep between the badly fitting floorboards. Harry breathed in some of this poisonous cocktail. The smoke entered his already diseased lungs and he began coughing. In seconds, the gaps between the boards began to blacken and then turn red as the fire ate away at the combustible floor on which he lay. The smoke, now tainted with burning plastics, entered Harry's room and then his lungs. Harry coughed one last violent cough before he lost consciousness.

'Excuse me Sir,' said the middle aged Asian shop owner, his face contorted with panic. He grabbed Jake's arm as he ran past. 'Did you know that Mister Bragg is still in his flat? I'm sure he's still in there,' he said. His body language alarmed Jake.

Jake focussed on the man. 'Which flat do you mean?'

The man pointed to the first floor above the dry cleaners.

Jake looked around, he saw Mac in conversation with an officer.

Jake ran across to them. 'Sir, the man there,' he said pointing at the shop owner, 'he's just told me that there's a man still in that flat above the dry cleaners.'

Mac stopped dead. 'Right get a set on, I'll grab someone else to team up with you, fast as you like Jake.'

Jake scrambled into the back of the Graveton appliance and lifted a breathing apparatus set off the rack. He'd soon donned and started it up, and written in black China graph his details on the yellow plastic tally.

Rob Blakemoor stood by the machine with his set on. 'It looks like it's you and me then sunshine,' he said, a wry smile on his face.

Jake looked across at the building, which by now was burning like a blowtorch, he could see a team of three men earnestly throwing a ladder into the first floor window above the dry cleaners. Jake looked, saw, and shivered with tension.

'Right young fella, let's get to entry control and get this job sorted shall we?' Rob said, in an almost casual voice.

The ladder had smashed the window, and as the head crashed into the building flames were issuing from the window beneath the ladder.

The men had laid out a hose reel ready for the BA team to use on the fire.

'Right sunny Jim,' Rob said to Jake through the plastic of his face-mask. 'I'll go up and in first; you follow me when I'm inside, alright?'

Jake was astounded. The area around the ladder was becoming very hot and the flames from the window were impinging on the aluminium ladder. He looked at Rob, the old soldier. 'Are you going to be OK?'

'I'll be fine; you just back me up, alright.'

Rob slung the hose reel over his shoulder and forced his way up the ladder through the heat and smoke. He stopped briefly just below the windowsill and shot a high pressure wide spray into the gap left by the broken panes of glass. He was instantly enveloped in a vast cloud of boiling steam, then almost casually lifted himself to a point level with the window, and almost fell into the room. Jake was fast up behind him. The heat radiating from the window took Jake's breath away. In seconds, Rob stood before him in the window. Rob had hold of Harry in a bear hug, and in one movement lifted the slight old man onto the windowsill. Jake stepped up, his shoulders just below the level of the sill, the heat from below was baking him and all he wanted was to retreat. His nerves jangled, his resources stretched to his limit.

'Grab him sunshine,' Rob called as he lifted Harry's limp body out of the window and across Jake's shoulder. Jake felt the weight of the old man then quickly adjusted to the burden. He moved mechanically downwards, pleased to be getting away from the furnace at the top of the ladder. Harry's skin was turning brown, his hair was smoking, and his clothing charred. The ambulance team were waiting on the ground and the moment Jake's feet touched the pavement they took the old man's weight and put him on to a stretcher. Jake looked up at the window. Rob was standing casually at the top of the ladder in no obvious sign of discomfort, and then he slowly descended down to the pavement.

'Well done lad,' Rob said before slapping Jake on the shoulder. 'You did a good job there, that was a bit warm.'

They went back to entry control and recovered the tallies and started removing their BA sets.

Jake was impressed by Rob. 'How did you do that?' Jake said, looking admiringly at the older fire-fighter.

'Do what?' he replied, as he wiped the dirty sweat from his face.

'Stand that, it was horrendous and it didn't seem to bother you.'

Rob laughed. 'My gaffer, George, he reckons I'm too daft to notice, but I don't know. It's something that I've always done, my mother reckons she used to feed me really hot tea in my bottle when I were a nipper, and experience I guess, mind you it used to get really hot when I worked in the Steelworks, maybe that's the secret.'

Harry felt no pain, his only conscious sense was of peace, no painful joints or money worries. He drifted along as if on a soft conveyor belt, surrounded by very bright lights which flashed brilliantly in his eyes. His mind drifted back to the time when he sat on the deck of his ship with his old mate Saul Biggin; his friend, also a Sheffielder. They sat on the deck in the darkness, sharing a cigarette, the freezing weather kept at bay by several layers of woollen clothing, nonchalantly chatting about what they were going to do after the war. These were some of Harry's happiest memories. Then he remembered his wife, the lovely Dotty, and the love they shared. He remembered the trips on the charabanc to Bridlington and the walks along the beach, wading ankle deep in the cold North Sea. He thought of the days and nights sweating hard in the Rolling Mills of Steeloes, the steelworks where he toiled for over twenty years. He loved his job, hard as it was; there was a distinct form of camaraderie amongst the Sheffield steelworkers.

The flashing lights began to dim. Harry tried to brighten them, but they slowly subsided and then went out.

The ambulance crew did what they could to save Harry, but the burns and the poisonous fumes he'd ingested, along with his poor health meant that he was beyond the help of anyone. Harry passed away with a gentle smile on his face, eighty four years and two days after he was born.

The fight to put the fire out was now being slowly won. The number of teams operating both inside and outside of the shops had been increased along with the supply of water. Much of the terrace of shops was destroyed, but the teams had prevented any further spread along the terrace. Ian Blain looked at the blackened buildings, and concluded that they had done the best possible job given the nature of the fire when the first crews arrived. He was happy with the job they'd all done. Any fatality was always a disappointment, especially to the men who had tried so hard to save him. But it was a fact of life, it happened somewhere in Britain every day.

Mac climbed wearily up into the appliance and picked up the radio handset.

'*Control from Alpha 1 over.*'

'*Alpha 1 go ahead over.*'

'*Alpha 1; stop message. From Divisional Officer Blain. Stop for Avian Electronics. A two storey terrace of four shop units severely damaged by fire. Four jets three hose reels and eight BAs in use. One occupant code one removed to hospital by Ambulance over.*'

'*Control your message received and acknowledged out.*'

The canteen van arrived at the incident having stocked up with tea and sandwiches, and soon it was thronged by several fire-fighters all needing a drink and a bite to eat. George Collier sought out Mac.

'Half decent job Mac, it went well enough I thought.'

'Yeah, shame we were a bit short of water pressure early on, but the lads did well.'

'I noticed that one of your young guns teamed up with Rob to get the old guy out.'

Mac smirked. 'Yes, I spoke to young Jake, he was mightily impressed by your old man Rob.'

'Well you know Rob, he's an impressive guy.'

'Yep I remember a lot of stuff about him, a real old grafter, not many of those in the job now of course. It's all, get your exams passed, get yourself promoted, don't worry about Ops, get yourself into fire prevention; the fast track away from the muck of the job.'

'I reckon you're right. Still, it was nice to get a decent job and bump into you again George, and we did manage to stop it before it got to your house.'

'Yeah I'm glad about that. I can't see it happening for much longer now though, we'll both be on the scrapheap soon enough.'

Mac stopped a second. 'That young guy of mine you know, I think he'll do well, he's not a brain box but he's got a hell of a lot of natural nous about the job. He did that rescue while he was still at training school, he did really well there.'

'Yes I heard about that. Young Devo, Jake's mate gave us the low-down, it seems your boy is a good lad.'

'Well Mac, I'll go and round up my lot before they get too comfort-able, and we'll get away. I'll give you a bell and maybe you and Val can come round for a stale sandwich or something.'

'That would be good George, look forward to it, you take care now.'

Jake and Mark managed to find each other on the fire ground, and stood by the Canteen Van sipping tea from plastic cups and eating the last remnants of the cheese sandwiches brought by the fire fighter from central station. 'So how was that for you Mark?' Jake asked.

'Loved it, spent all the time on a jet, I noticed that you were in BA.'

'Yeah, with one of the guys from your watch, don't know his name, but Christ he was good.'

'That was old Rob Blakemore, He retires soon; he's been on our gaf-fer's watch pretty much all his life.'

'Well we were up a ladder getting the man out from the flat, it was like a furnace. I couldn't stand it. It didn't seem to bother your man at all.'

'Well from what the other lads on the watch tell me, he's the tough-est of the tough. You'd not know it; he's really quiet and friendly. He's got four grandkids you know. But bloody hell is he hard," Mark said, his voice almost in awe of old Rob.

'Our gaffer, George, he doesn't like being called boss or anything. He told Rob to look after me, he's a great boss. I'll sure miss him when he retires.'

'Yeah, Mac's due to retire soon, that's a worry.'

For the next four hours, the appliances slowly managed to quell the fire with no further casualties.

Ian Blain walked around the now burned out building; the operation had gone well, the fire was out, the casualty was removed from the fire by his crews who showed great tenacity to achieve the rescue. He was satisfied, comfortable in his own skin, something had been put to bed that had been bugging him. He was for the first time in many years content with his lot, no great desire to impress; only the men he was working with, their respect for him meant a lot.

'Well Mac, a good job I think, the boys did well.'

'Yeah they did, I thought for a while we were going to lose the whole street, so I was relieved when we got the water pressure increased and gave it some welly.'

'It's a shame about the old fella the lads brought out, but they did well enough just to get in to get him out,' Ian said. 'Anyway, I'll be getting off now, have you got all the details for the fire report?'

'Yeah, I think so; I'll just have to wait for a cause from the fire investigators, that'll probably take a day or two.'

'OK then Mac; let me have your report and the fire report when you've had chance to write it. Tell the lads well done from me will you, I'm off.'

Ian removed his fire gear, climbed into his car and slowly drove off towards the city. As he descended, he found himself looking around, something within him was changing, a sudden acceptance that this was it, what he wanted, and where he wanted it. He looked down on the high rise buildings and the wide sprawl of his city, and calmness came over him. At last he felt at home.

Mick pulled the machine to a halt under the canopy of the wash down behind the appliance bays.

'OK lads, just a quick re stow, and get the BA sets sorted, then in for a cuppa, a belated meal, and a nice rest.'

Jake jumped out of the back of the machine and threw open the locker. He removing all of the dirty hose and re-stowing with fresh hose. Pete and Taff were in the BA charging room servicing the sets and charging the used cylinders.

After lunch, Mac and the crew drove around the area. Topography, familiarising themselves with several new buildings that had been erected recently, they checked the fire alarm points and the water supplies. Something the fire service has always done. Later, after the mid afternoon tea break, they all piled out into the drill yard and had a game of volleyball, Taff managing to sprain his ankle and Mick getting Jock's thumb in his eye.

'OK lads; let's get it all cleaned away ready for the night shift taking over. Then showers and off for the night with your beloved wives, girlfriends, boyfriends etc,' Brian said, suddenly relishing the responsibility that the temporary rank had given him. *Maybe Mac was right, a change could be a good thing,* he said to himself.

Jake stood naked in the shower, relishing the warmth of the hot water and soap as it streamed down his body. He dreamed about London and the girl's face; he couldn't get it out of his mind. He didn't know why, he was captivated by it, but knew that it was just a transient feeling, something borne out of the situation that had occurred. He rationalised that it was understandable, it had been something significant for him, all of these thoughts permeated his brain and he just wished that for a while he could put his mind to something else. He was now beginning to understand how Tracy, the girl from the fire felt, how that incident had affected her and how she may feel about him. In Jake's mind it was going nowhere, initially there had seemed to be a twinge of attraction, but latterly after a cooling off period the idea of having some sort of liaison with Tracy seemed less likely, or indeed desirable. Nothing had been said, but Jake felt that she was of the same view. There had been no mention or unsaid understanding that they would be an item.

Chapter 31

Pete walked stiffly down the stairs. During the night, he'd had to lift Trudy out of bed and had strained his back. He sat at the kitchen table eating his toast and sipping on his mug of tea. He heard the letterbox bang shut, got up from his chair, and scooped up the four letters that lay on the door mat. He perused the envelopes and noticed one from Penrith. He quickly opened it and read.

'Dear Mr. Jacks. Thank you for your completed application for a place at Jubilee Court. I can confirm that following a recent cancellation I can offer your wife and family a place for the week commencing Saturday 10th April. Please reply confirming your intention to accept this offer using the pre-paid envelope enclosed.

Yours sincerely.'

Pete smiled to himself, and strode up the stairs with the letter and a hot cup of tea for his wife.

Pete knocked on the office door. Mac was on the phone but waived him to come in. Mac quickly terminated the phone call.

'What can I do for you Pete?' he asked.

'I had a letter from Penrith this morning, offering us a place there, commencing the week after next. I have to confirm ASAP, I need to sort out the time off.'

'Leave it with me, I'll sort it out, it shouldn't be a problem. The watch is fully loaded, so you get on and write the letter, or better still give them a ring today and then confirm by letter OK?'

Clive was awake early. He turned over and looked at Helen's hair as it flowed across the pillow next to him. His chest ached when he looked at her. The recent trauma of the loss of the baby had knocked the stuffing out of both of them, and despite the lads on the watch wanting to help and support them, they'd decided they'd handle it themselves with just the help of their families. The wedding was imminent, all of the arrangements were in hand. Clive had his speech written, Taff had assured him that he had the best man's words of wisdom sorted out, and promised Clive that no ill fortune would befall him on his stag night. Clive was, however, slightly reluctant to believe him.

He climbed slowly out of the warm bed and went into the en suite shower room, allowing the hot water to wash the sleep out of his system. He was so looking forward to getting married to this girl he loved so much. Prior to the accident with the bike which had brought on the miscarriage of the baby she was carrying, they'd both taken their relationship for granted, a sort of unconscious acceptance that everything would be alright. They'd never thought that something so devastating could happen to them and destroy their happiness. It had taken a huge effort on both Clive and Helen's part to recover from the trauma.

Clive put shampoo on his hair and had managed to create something akin to a bee hive on his head when the shower door opened.

'Do you want me to get you some breakfast ready?' Helen said, leaning through the glass shower door.

'No I'll do it, why don't you get in here with me? I can soap your back for you.'

'OK,' she said sliding her white night dress to the floor of the en suite. 'But no monkey business or you'll be late for work.'

'Come on in then,' he said, taking her hand and helping her to squeeze into the small cubicle.

'Close your eyes,' he said as he moved up close behind her and placed his arms around her waist. 'I love you, lady,' he said, laughing aloud, before spraying the shower hose over her hair.

Brian climbed into his car. Jane sat alongside him in the front and Jill sat happily chattering in the back.

'Right team, let's go,' he called, before driving slowly along the road, heading for town.

Ten minutes later he pulled the car up outside Jane's Office.

'I'll see you tonight lover,' she called through the still open side window. 'Bye bye Jill, you have a good day at school, no messing about alright?'

'Bye, Mum,' Jill responded, waving her hand furiously.

'OK then madam; let's get you to school shall we?' Brian said as he looked in his rear view mirror at Jill who was feigning smoking a cigarette with a pencil she'd taken out of her pencil case.

Jake came downstairs already dressed for work. He saw the letter on the mat. He picked it up and saw that it was addressed to him and had a London postmark. He put the kettle on to make the morning tea, and waited for it to boil. He ripped open the letter. He noticed the heading; it was from the Italian girl he'd met whilst in London. *Mum must have given our address to her,* he thought to himself.

Dear Jacob and Mrs Higgins, I am writing to you because since we met under the very bad circumstances, I have been all the time thinking about it. And I wanted to be thanking you again for what you did to rescue me. I thank you Mrs Higgins for your support and conversation, it helped me greatly and I am very happy to have conversed with you, thank you very much indeed.

Jacob, that is what your mother said you were called, I have been not able to forget you from what you did, I dream about you every day and night. I have put in this letter two tickets for my concert at the Barbican Theatre, I hope that you will be able to come; I would like very much to see you both again. I hope that you are not disturbed by me; my Mama always has said to me that I am impulsivo, but I am not very long in your beautiful country and I do not yet have any friends to communicate with, only my work colleagues, I hope that you can understand my very bad English, I hope it will be better in future times. I wanted to speak Jacob to tell you that I like you very much, I am sure of it, I hope that you are not very unhappy that I tell you this, and I also hope that your Mama does not be ashamed of me. I hope that you will come to the concert.

Love from
Antonella Garardi, your very excellent friend always. XXX

Jake read the letter again. His hand was shaking. He'd had the same thoughts; in his mind's eye he thought of her a lot, he visualised her wide mouth her white teeth, her brown eyes, her long black hair and her shy smile. The first time he saw her he knew he wanted to get to know her more, but didn't know how to express such a thing. It was new to him; he'd never felt this way before.

'Here you are mum,' Jake said rousing his mother. 'I've got you a nice cup of tea and an interesting letter for you to read.'

Jake's mum sat up against the headboard of the bed; Jake pushed one of her pillows up behind her.

'Oh yes, and who is that from then?' she asked.

Jake said nothing, he handed her the letter. She opened the pale yellow page and began to read. 'Pass me my glasses will you son?' she said. 'The writing is a bit too small for me to read.' Jake passed her the red plastic glasses case. 'Thank you,' she said, giving Jake a warm smile.

She began reading, a smile crossing her face, and then she let out a low chuckle, then another smile. She put down the letter on the bed.

'Well Jacob, it would seem that she fancies you, how about that then. It would be nice to have grandchildren with lovely black curly hair,' she said, a wide grin now running across her face.

'Oh come on mum, she said she likes me, that's all there is to it,' Jake said. His mother could see his face was flushed, and she smiled a knowing smile.

'Yes I read what she wrote, and I know what she meant, she fancies you Jacob. I saw it at the time, she couldn't keep her eyes off you, and the tone in her letter confirms that. So watch out, she's after you; and having watched you mooning around since the trip I reckon she's got a good chance of getting what she wants.' Jake shuffled uncomfortably as he sat at the bottom of her bed. 'Jacob, now we need to talk. Did I ever talk to you about the birds and the bees?' she said, laughing out loud.

Chapter 32

Sunday morning, 9 30 am. Dave Blakeley stopped his battered old Ford Escort outside of the old semi derelict row of terraced houses which were all destined to be demolished as soon as the present occupants could be re-housed. Some had already gone; most of the rest of the houses had been vacated and were boarded up ready for the wrecking ball.

Dave sounded the car horn twice. A minute later, his friend of many years emerged, bleary faced and unshaven, obviously the worse for wear. Saturday night in the club had taken its toll on Dennis Alder. Dennis, despite his outward grubby appearance, was a brilliant rock climber, one of the tigers of the Peaks; his slight frame giving him the exact profile for the roll of major crag rat. Today was their day. Every Sunday, rain or shine, out into the Peaks and onto the steep grit stone walls that had become their second homes these past years. When dusk fell they'd clamber, along with others, into the local hostelries to quench their by now burning thirsts.

'So what are we doing today Den?' Dave asked. There was an unofficial pecking order in their relationship, an unspoken hierarchy, all was equal, but accepted unconsciously because of Dennis's superior ability; it was left to him to decide the routes for the day.

'I've been having a look at a wall, it's never been done, virgin rock. It's been tried by a few but never done. The route looks pretty thin and unprotected, but I've got a feeling in my water that today could be the day.'

'So where is it?' Dave asked, his curiosity suddenly aroused.

'It's that wall we've looked at, just about between Goliath Groove and Ulysses on Stanage; I reckon it'll go.'

'Are we going to clean it up first and top rope it to start?'

'Yeah, probably I guess, not a lot to stop a peel so better be sensible,' Den said, a look of determination on his face.

Janet Clark was patrolling from the Stanage Ranger Station. She'd been given her route to walk and was again to be accompanied by a trainee. They set off steadily, the weather set to be dry and relatively mild all day.

'OK Pat, what is it you want to focus on today?' she asked the young female trainee.

Without breaking their stride, they talked about the programme for the day. Pat had said she needed navigation practice, map reading, and pacing.

They walked West past a plantation of conifers then cut up right, heading for the Stanage escarpment close to the old Roman Road.

'OK, let's stop here and do a bit on the map,' Janet instructed.

Pat opened the map of the Dark Peak and spread it out on the grassy track side.

'See this point here? this is where we are,' Janet said, pointing at a spot on the map with a thin piece of grass held between her fingers. 'Tell me how far from here to that spot on the horizon,' she said indicating another point some distance away.

Pat looked flustered. 'Don't worry about it, take your time, you know where we are; so orientate the map find the point on the map we're looking for, then work out how far it is between us and there.'

After some minutes Pat came up with an answer.

'OK so it's one point nine kilometres,' she said, looking relieved that she'd done something right.

'OK now, how long will it take for us to walk there?'

Pat checked the map, looked at a scale she had in her jacket pocket, and came up with an answer.

'Not too bad, that's OK for the distance, you need to adjust that for the height gained,' Janet said. 'Look at the contours and tell me how much height we gain, and then work out the extra time it's going to take us.'

Janet looked at Pat, who by now was beginning to look stressed and little beads of sweat were forming on her forehead.

'Take your time, relax. We all have had to do it, I still do it to keep my level up.'

Pat shuffled the map around, not sure if it was properly oriented to the landscape.

'OK, I'll go through it with you. You did OK on the lateral distance but what you have to do is count the contours between the points; each line is a metre rise in height, so looking at this between point A and B. We'll climb a total of one hundred and forty metres, we have to take that into account when we work out the time it will take to cover that distance, are you OK with that?'

'Yes I think so, I didn't realise it was so hard.'

'It's the one thing that we focus most on, it's so important, but it takes a while to get the hang of it so don't worry, it will all click in time, you just need to keep practicing.'

Dave and Dennis made their way along the rough path created by the thousands of booted feet that had trod the trail for the past hundred years. It followed roughly the contour of the crags which sat ominously fifty feet above them, giving them a clear view of the enormity of the edge which travelled from horizon to horizon in both directions, giving literally thousands of routes for the climbers who swarm over them most weekends.

'There it is,' Den said, looking around at Dave and pointing upwards towards the bleak grey slabs that towered above them.

The rock was about sixty feet in height, and was split its full height by a series of narrow fissures. The steep slabs located between these cracks were smooth and featureless.

'Yeah, that's the kiddie,' Den said, turning to Dave and grinning.

'Well matey it looks pretty horrible to me, I'm glad you're going first.'

'That's where the fun is, I'm not happy unless I'm halfway terrified,' he said as he strode off the path and cut uphill through the bracken to a point just below the imposing steep grey wall.

'I'll take a rope off the top and abseil down; I'll have a look at the possibilities for some belay points and do a bit of sweeping up while I'm at it.'

Den quickly fixed the rope from a large rock at the top of the face, and was soon swinging freely from his anchored rope. He checked meticulously for hold and anchor points, twenty minutes later he was back with Dave at ground level.

'Yep, I reckon it'll go, there's a couple of thin ledges I can maybe hang a couple of sky hooks from, other than that there's sweet Fanny Adams. I may have to slide off sideways and put a big nut in a crack over to the right, but you'll have to watch me, it'll be a bit scary.'

Den removed his trainers and squeezed on his rock shoes. He fitted his nylon harness tight around his waist and fixed his chalk bag onto the waist strap. Then he was ready to go.

'I'm just taking a small rack, there's not much up there to use gear on, so let's keep our fingers crossed.'

Dave smiled nervously. 'I'll cross everything else as well.'

Den looked at him. 'Don't worry; you just keep your eyes peeled once I've got something fixed.'

Den leaned against the rock, his red shorts and sleeveless green shirt exposing his slim but muscular body, both arms were locked tight, his fingers feeling the harsh texture of the cold grit stone. The muscles in his body were hard with tension, the breeze catching his shoulder length black hair. He stood a minute, rehearsing the early difficult moves in his mind. He was focussed, nothing around him had any significance, just the rock and the sixty feet of terror that he was about to embark on.

He leaned hard against the rock. He looked down at his feet and a spot on the rock where he could place his stiff rubber soled climbing shoe. He lifted his right foot about a foot, and placed it on the sloping surface of the slab. It felt as though it would stick. He dipped his hands into his chalk bag, covering his hands in the white magnesium oxide. He cautiously lifted his left foot looking for a placement over to his left. He leaned across to his right, allowing some flexibility for his left foot. There was nothing at all for his hands to grip, just some minor sense of friction against the steep slope. His left foot found some purchase on a minute bulge, and he allowed some weight to be transferred and was now balanced precariously, with his weight equally shared by both feet. 'Phew, that was bloody hard, and I'm only a foot off the floor,' he said, already breathing heavily.

Dave held on to the rope as his friend searched for some way of progressing upwards. Den waved his arms around searching the rock above his head, if he were to lean back even slightly he would fall, so progress was by touch.

Dave moved around, looking for possibilities for Den.

'Den, I think if you sway to your right you can get your left leg another six inches higher, then lean onto your right hand at shoulder height; there's another bulge you just may be able to use to get your right foot a bit higher.'

Den tried the move, his left foot came off and once more he stood in the grey dirt at the rocky base of the climb.

'Well now I know why it's not been done yet,' he said, his face a mask of determination. 'I lost concentration, in the middle of that pathetic effort; I started thinking about bacon sandwiches, what's that all about?' Den said incredulously!

'Didn't you have any breakfast before you left this morning?' Dave scolded.

Den smirked and looked up at Dave. 'No, there was nothing in the fridge.'

'Right, before you have another go, get this down you,' he said, pulling a large sausage roll out of his rucksack. 'Maybe that will help your concentration.'

'Yeah, thanks, I should have thought of that before I started,' he said, as he set about demolishing the large greasy fifty percent of Dave's dinner.

Janet and Pat sat resting on the top of the crags. Janet loved this walk, and had often wished she'd climbed herself when she was younger. Sometimes she stopped and talked to the climbers who were usually happy to chat about the climbs they'd done, and grateful also for the job the rangers did. It wasn't unusual for the rangers to get involved with the local mountain rescue team if they were needed, help transporting casualties off the rocks to waiting ambulances.

Janet sat eating her apple and Pat ate a sandwich while they rested for ten minutes.

'So are you enjoying the training?' Janet asked.

'Oh yes, it's something I've wanted to do for ages, and now I have the time to do it, I'm really enjoying it.'

'What prompted you to join up?' Janet asked.

Pat leaned back on her elbows. 'Years ago, my mum and dad brought me out here. We were coming down Jagger's Clough when dad slipped and broke his leg. We were very lucky of course, it was long before mobile phones became commonplace; my mum shouted out for help and fortunately there was a ranger within earshot, he heard us and called out the mountain rescue. I've never forgot that, and decided that when I could I'd have a go at being a ranger myself.'

'That's a really good reason to join up, I reckon.' Janet said. 'Now back to business, let's do a bit of pacing shall we?'

With renewed determination, Den stood again at the base of the as yet unclimbed slab. He rehearsed the moves in his head and focussed as he had never focussed before.

'Come on Den, go for it,' Dave shouted to his friend.

Den didn't hear him; he was in the zone. It was a place where nothing else was of any importance. Nothing mattered, only this second in this place.

He lifted his foot and placed it on the rock, his eyes fixed almost laser like on the rough grey stone he was about to confront. He stretched up his left hand; he found the bulge and rested his hand on the rough surface. He raised his right hand and laid it against the cold stone. He stood motionless for several seconds, then leaning to his left he raised his foot and laid it flat on the near vertical grit stone. He pushed with his left, raised his foot and moved steadily upwards, his mind computing every centimetre of rock, its every fault, and its suitability as a means of moving forward. Soon he was ten feet from the ground. To his right was a thin ledge, hardly the width of a piece of card. He quickly unclipped a skyhook from his waistband and hung the hook from the ledge, quickly clipping the rope through the karabiner. He inwardly sighed, *progress at last*. He moved to his left to a small, narrow vertical fissure, its sharp edges almost daring anyone to risk the flesh of their fingers in there. The crack was just wide enough for Den to insert his little finger. He leaned back testing its grip; it held comfortably. He knew he was all right. He released his right hand, swung his weight on the hand secured in the crack, and lifted his right leg placing the heel of his shoe on a small bulge. He was committed; going for broke. He had to get a placement for his other foot before his little finger popped out of the crack. Pulling hard on his left hand, he felt the flesh of his finger tear as the quartz ripped into his soft skin. He felt no pain; he knew only that the next move was critical. He had to do it or fall, he knew that his protection was flimsy. He quickly put his hand into his chalk bag, then with his finger still jammed in the crack he leaned to his right, stretched, and put the heel of his hand on the bulge occupied by his right foo. He pulled with his left, pushed with his right, and moved upwards. Den was aware of voices from below. '*Good move Den; I've got you, go for it.*'

Now twenty feet above ground and the climb seemed to get harder, but Den felt euphoric, climbing to a level he had never dreamt about, but at the same time seemingly within himself, almost in a state of grace.

He was standing on minute bulges with both feet, and the little finger now level with his waist was serving no purpose. He intensified his focus. Just level with his forehead was another ledge, maybe a quarter of an inch wide. In Den's heightened state it looked enormous, he smiled to himself. He slid his right hand slowly upward, no rapid movement, to do so would be the end. He was teetering just in balance; the slightest error now and he would fall.

'Look at that guy,' Janet said to Pat as they walked along the edge of the escarpment. About a hundred yards away the climber seemed to be glued to the wall.

'How on earth is he holding on? The rock looks flat,' Pat said, her voice exuding a certain ghoulish sort of excitement.

'I think we'll stand and watch for a while shall we?' Janet said; it being more of a statement than a question.

Dave stood transfixed, his hand rigid on the rope, watching for the slightest clue that his friend was going to fall. He'd watched Den over the years in all sorts of difficulties; this was part of the process. To be good you have to push yourself, but Den sometimes pushed a bit too hard and came unstuck, this was where their friendship and mutual trust counted.

Den was in extremis, on the edge of what was possible, and giving it everything to make it go.

His hand crept slowly upwards and eventually it reached the narrow horizontal ledge. The muscles in his legs were beginning to tire, and he fought to prevent them from shaking. His fingers ran blindly along the ledge; at the back was a narrow crack. *'I can get a little nut in there,'* he thought. He could feel the sweat from his forehead begin to run down his cheek. *Ignore it,* he said to himself. Slowly he leaned left and removed his bloodied finger from the crack. He felt totally exposed, but not allowing a single negative thought to enter his head. He held the narrow ledge with his right hand, his left fumbled blindly for the small nut with the thin wire attached to a steel karabiner. After what seemed an age he found it and unclipped it from the rack which hung from his harness. He felt elated, almost tearful. He lifted his left hand slowly and his finger, now painful, foraged with the wired nut, looking for a place where it would slot into the groove at the back of the ledge. He fumbled and then got angry. *Come on, get in there, you.* He couldn't look up, to do so would knock him out of balance. He heard the skyhook he'd placed earlier come loose and slide down the rope to the ground; he was seconds away from falling. He slid the nut to his right; the nut went in, he slid it to the left, it held. He gasped. 'You beauty, you bloody beauty,' he said, quickly lifting the rope and clipping it through the karabiner.

'Don't give me any slack, Dave,' he called down.

'That was bloody brilliant Den my boy, I think you've cracked it.' He was jumping like a firecracker with excitement. 'Definitely the climb of the year mate,' he shouted up.

'You just concentrate, the next bit leans out and I can't see anything to hold on to, can you see anything from down there?' he called down.

Dave scoured the face looking for a weakness.

'I can't see a thing from here,' he shouted up.

'Thank you friend, let's see what we can do then.'

Den was now more confident, the solid belay he'd fixed had bolstered his confidence; he was up for taking a risk. As he looked up, the wall began to lean out to just beyond the vertical. He figured that if he were to pull up on both hands he might just get a foot on the ledge, reach up with his right hand and feel around, he seemed in his mind's eye to remember a small hold from his earlier descent; he'd go for it.

His leg was becoming numb from the strain of standing on the microscopic holds for the past fifteen minutes; he knew that it would only get worse.

He summoned up all of his strength and lifted himself upward; the thin ledge was now at chest height, more effort and sweat; now at waist height. He pushed his face hard against the rock and lifted his right foot. Leaning wildly to his left, almost at the point of tippling off, he got the toe of his shoe onto the ledge. He swung his hand wildly back and forth across the cold rough grit, he was almost at the point of panic. He found it, a small split about one inch deep and a quarter of an inch wide. To Den, it felt like a cavern. He slid his index finger into the crack, twisted it; it jammed, he was euphoric. *Yes, got ya,* he shouted. There was a vocal rumble from below. Unbeknown to Den, a crowd had gathered to watch this exhibition of idiotic risk taking.

He pulled on the finger laying away from the rock, his feet now secure on the ledge and a good secure hold with one hand, the other now searching for a hold. He needed one more hold; there was nothing between his hands and feet, his salvation lay somewhere above where he now stood. The hand found two small bulges, he laid his hand on them; would they take some weight or would his hand slip? He didn't know, but he did know that he had to go for it or he would be off in spectacular style. He tentatively laid some weight onto the bulge; his hand stuck. *That's it,* he said to himself, *Shit or bust.* No time for thought now, only action. His energy was draining away, it had to be now.

Den leaned back and summoned all of his strength; he pulled hard, his finger held tight in the crack, the left hand held on the bulge. He moved upward, he leaned to the right, and placed his left foot on the bulge where his hand lay and pulled again, he was desperate but he felt no fear; he could see the top of the route three feet above his head. To fall now would be disaster. His body shook with effort, he removed his hand from the bulge and searched frantically for purchase above, he found it, a ledge maybe two inches wide, he grabbed it like a boy with a new toy. 'YES,' he gasped, 'YES,' he shouted. He took his finger from the groove which had held him so well and grabbed upwards. Now with both hands on the ledge, he felt a fantastic sense of relief.

Not far away, Janet and Pat had watched with fascination and some trepidation at the performance on the crag. When he reached safety, they both felt a sense of relief.

'The lad did well, I was scared stiff for him,' Pat said as they looked across at the group of onlookers witnessing this first ascent.

'Let's wander down shall we, have a chat with them,' Janet said.

Den fell over the top of the climb, landing heavily on his stomach, his face buried in the dirt and grit. His mouth was dry, but all he felt was elation. His body was shaking. The sudden release of emotion and relief at having survived had left him completely drained of energy. He could hear voices below, but couldn't make out the words. He lay there for what seemed an age, basking in the feeling of security that now covered his sweat soaked body like a child's comfort blanket. The feelings of normality were slowly beginning to re-appear in his consciousness. His fingers now hurt like hell; his calf muscles were close to cramping. He heard his pal Dave shouting up.

'Are you alright up there Den?' Then there was the general cacophony of voices emerging over the edge of his rock.

This climb could turn out to be his defining ascent. He knew that it had been at the very apex of his ability, and couldn't envisage being able to climb anything more difficult. That probably would have to be left for someone else. *Must think of a name for it,* he mused. Slowly, he got himself back to the land of the living. He stood up and peered over the edge of the route, raised his arms in triumph and shouted, 'piece of piss,' and something else indiscernible to the watching group on the ground below.

Janet and Pat emerged amongst the excited group of climbers. The young man who had just descended from the top of the crag was swathed in admirers, trying to explain just how it had all gone.

'Well done young man,' Janet said admiringly. 'I thought for a minute you were a gonner. I was relieved to see you finish it in one piece.'

'Yeah so was I,' Den replied.

'So is it off to the pub now?' Janet asked.

'No, I think my mate Dave over there wants to do a couple of the old classics, so we'll probably be here until it gets dark.'

'Well good luck. It was a brilliant effort,' she said; 'I hope your mate stays safe as well.'

'Right now Pat, let's move on shall we? I think we'll head up to the Cowper stone, we can practice pacing and do some walking on a bearing if you fancy that.'

'Yeah that'll be great,' she replied enthusiastically.

The sun had dipped down below the horizon, just the small remnant of daylight left to illuminate their trek back to the car about half a mile away.

It had been a good day, and Den's new route, aptly named 'The Pig,' had been the highlight. Dave had been proud to be the second man to climb it, albeit on a top rope. Then they did a few of the old Stanage Chestnuts. 'Goliath Groove' followed by 'Robin Hood's right hand buttress direct', and then the classic 'Inverted V.' This climber's menu left both Dave and Den with a wonderful afterglow as they got into the car and headed down to the pub in the village, where there would be several lesser beings keen to hear Den's description of the climb, which would in due course become part of the folk lore of rock climbing in Derbyshire.

Janet and Pat made their way slowly along the road from Higgar Tor heading for the Ranger Station at Stanage; it had been a good day for them. They'd got on well, something which Janet was always pleased about. They'd ticked all of Pat's boxes, they'd done route finding, walking on a bearing, and a lot of exhausting pacing exercises. Finally, as the light began to fade, they did re sections, something that Janet, when she was a beginner, had found difficult to master. Hence, she kept up the study to the point where she became very expert and was happy to help others master this particular skill.

They sat down tiredly in the small room allocated as a mess room come recreation room. Pat filled out her daily log. Janet made the two of them a cup of tea. Shortly after they arrived back, the other rangers returned from their patrols with muddied boots and gaiters, telling tales of dogs on the run, chasing sheep along the road, and walkers lost on the moor. It was just another day in the life of the ranger service.

Chapter 33

Jake drove his new car through town heading for work. He was still conscious of the fact he was inexperienced. He'd learned enough during his short time in the Brigade to know that new young drivers were at the greatest risk of accidents. He was also aware of the cost of insurance, and was intent on keeping his license clean. He'd spoken to Mac on one night shift just after he'd passed his test; Mac had told him that he'd not had an accident for over thirty years. Jake was impressed, and had decided he would be his target to be a really good driver.

He pulled into the station yard; a couple of the lads' cars were already there. As usual, when he got to work his heart rate increased as the anticipation of more action made his adrenaline flow.

Pete Jacks and Taff were in the locker room chatting. 'Hi Jake, how's things?'

'Great, glad to be at work,' Jake said, grinning as he opened the door of his locker. 'Aren't you and Brian at that funeral tomorrow?' he asked.

'Yep, we're off pretty early in the morning; the service is at half past ten, so we don't want to be late,' Taff said, 'then we've got Clive's wedding next weekend and I haven't got my speech sorted out yet, but I shouldn't complain, it's good to be in such demand.'

The rest of the watch came in and the crew of the night shift drifted down from the mess deck getting ready for the change over parade.

Mac sat in the office with the Station Commander and Alan Wilson, the officer in charge of the night shift.

Terry Cork, the Station Commander, said, 'we've got some manning issues coming up in the next few weeks, what with Clive needing time for his honeymoon and Pete Jacks taking the family to Jubilee Court, so we'll have to sit down and sort out who, what and where later today. We'll have a chat later, Mac.'

After parade, Mac got the watch to meet him on the mess deck and took Pete into the office.

'So Pete, you're off to Penrith tomorrow, are you all set?'

'Well I had a bunch of paperwork come the other day, we had to fill it in; it all sounds great. They have a programme they'll develop for Trudy to fit her specific needs, she'll have an assessment first thing and then she'll be into it, I'll have time with the kids whilst she's doing her physio, so we'll all benefit. I'll take the kids down into the Lakes, which will be a nice change; I've never been up there before,' Pete said enthusiastically.

'You'll love it, it's beautiful, and the towns are good, lots to see and do. So the kids shouldn't get bored.'

The morning was busy; after drills, the crew were sorting out special risk cards ready for doing visits later in the week. Brian was in the office with Mac getting on top of the usual paperwork when the alarm operated.

He leaned across to the printer and ripped off the message.

'RTA City Road, persons trapped,' Brian shouted as he jogged into the appliance room, the engine of the machine was already running. Mick the driver was dressed in his overalls; the rest of the crew jumped on board.

Mick slung the machine hard left at the end of the high street. Mac flicked the switch to turn on the siren. The road was busy, made worse by a series of road works. The siren wailed, and Mick pulled the machine to the right overtaking the queue of traffic waiting at the lights. He shot through, soon emerging at the far end of the high street with a clear road ahead. Another roundabout, first left, then right, and now steadily uphill. The traffic was stationary, tailing back from the accident.

Just one car involved, it was on its roof set against a dry stone wall, the driver was hanging upside down held by his seat belt.

'*Control from Alpha zero one zero in attendance over,*' Mac called into the radio handset.

'*Alpha zero one zero your message received.*'

'Right boys, let's have the hose reel off and laid out,' Mac called to the crew as he jumped from the machine.

Mac walked across to the wreck of the car and knelt down at the side of the driver. 'Can you hear me?' Mac called to the seemingly unconscious driver.

There was no response. Mac put his hand in through the broken side window and felt for a pulse in the young man's wrist and then his neck. He could feel nothing.

Mac stood up, his crew ready around him. 'I think he's code one, but let's go ahead as normal, do a good job OK lads?'

Mac had looked and surmised the driver was not trapped, but just held in by his seat belt.

The Ambulance crew arrived on scene, and Mac spoke with the attendant asking them to check the driver out.

'He's gone,' the ambulance man confirmed, 'there's nothing we can do to help him.'

'Yeah I thought not,' Mac replied.

The police were in attendance, and agreed that the driver needed to be removed then they could measure up and begin the investigation into the cause of the accident, before opening the road.

It's time to give Jake a bit of experience, Mac thought to himself.

'Jake come here.'

Jake loped across to Mac. 'Yes Sub?'

'If you feel up to it, I want you in the car. I think he's dead, but we still have to do it right, are you OK with that?'

Jake glanced down at the inert body in the car then looked back at Mac, realising that this was vital experience for him.

'Yes Sub. What do you want me to do?'

Jake scrambled into the relatively confined space of the inside of the wrecked car. The body hung limply in front of him, and he reached across, attempting to get to the seat belt release. The driver had taken a massive blow to the head which had bled profusely. Jake took care; he glanced at the face of the driver. 'Oh my god,' he shouted, a loud, involuntary response to the shock of seeing his old school friend hanging dead before him. He hadn't seen him for months. They'd grown up together. The shock had momentarily almost paralysed Jake.

Brian was lying on the road, peering into the car from the other side.

'What's up Jake?' he asked, having seen Jake's reaction.

'Sorry Bry, I know him, he's one of my best friends. I've known him for years; we went to school together. His mum's going to be really upset.'

Brian looked at Jake and guessed that this would be tough for him. 'Jake, are you alright, can you manage? There's no problem if you need to come out, we can get one of the other lads to do it.'

Jake steeled himself, images of his friend running in his mind.

'No thanks Bry, I'll be OK,' Jake replied, his voice giving away the struggle he was having within himself.

'If you're sure then, we'd better get on with it,' Brian reiterated.

Jake leaned across the car and fumbled with the seat belt release. Managing to place his legs below the driver's, head he clicked the release button and the young driver tumbled into Jake's lap, the blood from his head wound spreading over Jake's over- trousers. Jake looked at him, he felt as though he was locked into some horror film that he couldn't escape from. The carcass that lay inert, dead, across his legs was still his oldest friend, but somehow Jake needed to separate that fact from the job he needed to do.

'Are you ready out there?' he called out to the crew, who were all preparing to take the young driver's body.

'Yeah, when you're ready Jake, pass him through.'

Jake manipulated and manoeuvred his friend into a position where he could get his arms around his chest. Given the fact he was in a cramped position, this proved to be difficult. He persisted, and in his mind he managed to divorce himself from any other feeling than the movement of the awkward dead weight that he was attempting to remove from the car. He eventually managed to move him inch by inch to a point where the waiting crew were able to grab the driver's shoulders and haul him out of the wrecked car. Once free of the confines of the car, the ambulance crew took the body of the young driver and placed him in the waiting ambulance, where a doctor, who had just arrived on scene quickly, pronounced him dead.

Jake scrambled from the wreck; he saw the blood on his over-trousers and felt the bile in his stomach begin to rise.

'Brian spotted Jake's dilemma. 'Go round the back of the machine and have a little break, you'll be fine in a minute,' he said, patting Jake on the shoulder, 'you did a good job there, Jake.'

Jake looked across at the ambulance and the crew who were doing what was necessary before removing him to hospital. He stood at the back of the machine, away from the gaze of the rest of the crew and vomited. He'd held it back; now freed from that constraint, he lost his control.

Mac poked his head around the side of the machine. 'Are you all right there Jake?'

'Yeah I'm alright, sorry about this,' he said as he wiped the residue of vomit from his lips on the sleeve of his jacket.

'Don't worry about it, we all get like that sometimes, come and see me back at the station if you need to talk about it.'

Red Watch put the car back on its wheels and cleared the debris from the road before leaving to go back to the station, leaving the police continuing to do their investigation into the cause of the crash.

Later that night Jake, pulled his car up outside the semi detached house where he'd spent a good part of his young life playing with his friend. He had a dread of what he could be confronted with when Mrs Graves opened the door. He rattled the letterbox. After a long thirty seconds, Jake saw a dark shape coming to the door.

It was eleven thirty and Jake couldn't settle to sleep. The image of his friend haunted him. He'd had a word with Mac at the station, and he'd been re assured that these feelings were normal and, with time, they would be easier to live with. Earlier, he'd called at Eddie's mum's house. She was naturally bereft, and was pleased to see Jake. She said to him that it gave her some comfort to know that Jake had been on the crew that had dealt with the death of her son. Upset as she was, she reassured

Jake that she would be all right and he shouldn't concern himself about her.

It was two a.m. and Jake still hadn't got to sleep. He walked quietly down the stairs and switched on the TV. But no matter what was on the screen, the image of his dead friend's face was still embedded in his brain.

Chapter 34

It was seven thirty in the morning, the air was cold, and a mist lay low on the ground. Taff pulled his car up outside Brian's house. Brian was expecting him, and was soon leaving his house dressed in his best uniform.

'Good morning Taff,' he called as he climbed into the passenger seat of the car.

'Morning Brian, how are you this fine morning?'

'Perfect weather for a funeral isn't it.'

Taff gunned the car down the M1; the traffic was unusually light for that hour of the day.

'We went to the adoption thing the other day and we've started the process; it feels a lot better now we're actually doing something about it,' Taff said, looking across at Brian.

'Well it's been a problem for you for so long that I should think it's a relief just to be doing something positive.'

Nine fifteen, and Taff pulled the car into the rough dirt car park of a transport cafe.

'We're in plenty of time, we'll have a bite of breakfast shall we?'

'That sounds good to me,' Taff said, thinking a nice hot bacon sandwich would go down very nicely.

After a short stop and a quick bite to eat, they set off for the church. They were surprised to see the roads around the church filled with parked cars. Taff drove around and eventually found a spot about 200 yards from the church.

They stood along with fire-fighters from around the country, waiting for the funeral cortege to arrive. After a short wait, they saw a police car escort preceding a turntable ladder on which the coffin of the fire fighter was laid covered by the Union Flag. As the cortege approached, they could see the appliance was flanked by more men in dress uniform marching slowly alongside; their white gloved hands swinging in unison. The coffin was carried into the church, and the path up to the church was lined by men who, on a signal, saluted their dead colleague as it passed.

The service was a solemn affair; the Chief Fire Officer gave the eulogy saying what a good fire fighter he had been. Then, members of his family told the congregation what a good brother and husband he was, and how he loved his job. The hymns were traditional, sung with gusto. Some of the men in the congregation had tears running down their cheeks.

Then it was over. Everyone filed out into the cold, late morning air, and soon they were leaving on their various journeys back to their normal lives.

'Well that's that until the next one,' Brian said solemnly.

'Yep, I don't think I would want a brigade funeral, I just don't fancy it. I don't think Jane and Jill would want the stress of it all.'

Two hours later they were back in Sheffield.

'Hiya sweetie, you're home earlier than I expected, how did it go?' Jane said, putting her arms around Brian's waist.

'It was alright, a bit sad I suppose, it's the third one I've been to, I don't think I'd want all that fuss if I turned my toes up.'

'What about your family? They may want it, and it would give your friends a chance to say goodbye properly.'

'Well it's not going to happen is it, I've no intention of going for ages yet, at least not until I've won the lottery.'

'Well that could be a long wait then.' Jane laughed.

Clive stirred, disturbed by a gentle rattle of the letter box. He slid quietly out of bed, and pulled the curtain a few inches to the side. He could see a man dressed in a smart suit standing by his door. The man looked up at him; Clive acknowledged him and indicated that he'd be straight down.

'What can I do for you?' Clive asked of the middle aged man standing on his door step.

'Well sir,' he replied, 'I've got your new car.'

'New car, I haven't bought a new car.'

'No Sir, it's courtesy of Mister Styles.'

Clive was stunned. 'Why would he give me a car?'

'I don't know sir, I was just asked to deliver it and give you this letter,' he said as he handed a light coloured envelope to Clive.

'Thank you, where is the car?'

'I left it out on the road sir, I wasn't sure you would be home. I'll bring it in to your drive shall I sir?'

Clive was perplexed, he remembered Mister Styles and the fire where they'd chatted for a while, he remembered liking him, and the fact he'd been Helen's employer some time ago.

The man turned and walked out to the road, disappearing behind the high hedge.

Seconds later, a gleaming black BMW appeared in his drive.

'It's all yours sir. I'm sure you'll understand when you've read the letter.'

'My god, why would he do that?' Clive muttered to himself, 'how the hell can I afford to run a car like that, it'd cost a fortune!'

Clive shouted upstairs. 'Helen, you'd better get yourself down here.'

Soon, Helen stumbled down the stairs, still feeling drowsy. 'What are you so excited about?' she asked.

Clive smirked at her. 'Just take a look outside.'

He pulled open the timber door and Helen looked out. 'Yes, what am I looking at?' she said, a hint of sarcasm in her voice.

Clive took her hand. 'See the big silver car; well it's ours,' he said, a huge beaming smile on his face. He'd forgotten the sudden panic he felt when he imagined the cost of running such a car.

'What do you mean it's ours?'

'Well do you remember Henry Styles the hairdresser, you used to work for him?'

'Yes.'

'Well he's given us a car.'

'Why would he give us a car?' she said, her voice tinged with cynicism.

'I don't know, he's left a letter which the delivery driver gave me, I've not opened it yet.'

'Well open it you fool, it could be a joke.'

Clive ripped open the letter and began to read it.

Dear Mr. Botham and Helen.

I dare say that finding the car on your drive was quite a surprise. Well let me explain. When you, Clive, and your firemen friends came to my house to extinguish the fire in my chimney, I was so grateful to you all for your professionalism and kindness.

We spoke at length Clive, if you remember, and I explained my circumstances regarding my partner. Well the time has come for us to depart England and go to my villa in Spain for the next phase of our lives together. I will be forever grateful for your kindness and consideration toward myself and my guests. You were, and are, a credit to the Fire Service and your family.

Please accept the gift; it will please me if it gives you and your future wife a lot of pleasure.

Finally, you shouldn't worry about the expense of the car. I have set up an account, which will cover the cost of fuel, tax, and insurance, and also arrangements have been made for a garage periodically to maintain the car for you.

It only remains for me to once again thank you, good luck to you and your future wife. God bless you both.

Yours sincerely,
Hubert Styles.

Clive and Helen stood at the bottom of the stairs unable to speak, and Clive began re running the conversation he had had with Hubert. He realised now that the situation regarding his partner must have forced him to make a move abroad quicker than originally intended.

'Well,' Clive said, 'I don't know what to say.'

'Nor me,' Helen said, attempting to stifle a loud shriek.

Clive gulped down his breakfast of tea and toast, and for the tenth time walked to the lounge window, and looked out at the car which had just fallen into his lap.

'Are you ready yet?' he called up the stairs.

'Be down in a minute,' Helen's voice drifted down the stairs.

Clive drove carefully. Having spent half an hour looking through the car's manual at the multitude of features the car possessed, he felt he knew enough to take it out on the road. Prior to this, he'd always driven second hand cars, old bangers, cars, some of which driving them was considered an adventure. But this; this was driving of a different class, it was smooth, quiet and comfortable, the radio purred in the background. He turned left into a street of nice houses and pulled up outside Mac's house.

Mac came out and stood back, shocked at what Clive had told him over the phone.

'Well it's a beauty; he must have liked you a lot,' Mac said as he walked slowly around the car, examining it in detail.

'I just thought he was a nice guy, we talked a bit in his loft and he told me about his partner's condition and we seemed to just hit it off. But this, I never expected this, or anything in fact.'

'We were going to have a little drive out into Derbyshire and wondered if you fancied a trip with us for a couple of hours.'

'I think that would be nice, I'll grab Val, we were wondering what we'd do this morning, it'll be a nice change.'

Clive gently pushed the car along, braking to turn by the Fox House pub, one of his regular stopping places when he was out doing his boxing roadwork. He whipped the car left by the Toad's Mouth rock and moved smoothly through the gears, over the surprise viewpoint, and steeply down towards Hathersage. The road was quiet as he doubled back to turn sharp right up hill heading for Burbage Bridge. Then they skirted past the rocky outcrops around Higgar Tor with views down into the valley.

'Well Clive, I have to say this is better than sitting at home reading the paper,' Mac said as he sat comfortably in the crème leather upholstered seat. Clive slowed to allow the passage of several sheep that seemed intent on suicide.

He pulled the car into the side of the road by the bridge which gave good views down the Burbage valley. Val leaned forward. 'We always reckon this is one of the best views in the Peaks,' she said, peering into the slight mist covered depression that formed the valley floor.

'Shall we have a little stroll down the track as we're out here? It would be a shame not to,' Mac said, looking at Clive.

'Yeah, that would be nice,' he replied.

The valley was deserted, and as they walked they chatted about the forthcoming wedding and their plans for later, after the wedding. As yet, there were no plans to have a honeymoon. Their finances weren't up to that; just the cost of wedding had cleaned them out.

'When I'm back at work, Mac, I've decided that it's time to get stuck in. I'm going to start working at the exams and see if I can get myself qualified,' Clive said.

'Well that's a good thing to do, it's great being a fireman on the machine, but in the end it's the pension you've got to live on when you retire.'

They turned back after about twenty minutes of gentle strolling, and returned to the car.

Chapter 35

Change of watch 1800 hours. 'Red Watch, fall out,' Brian called. The crew dismissed and began doing the routine checks of the machine and the equipment stored in the lockers.

Mick made the tea. The crew sat around the white Formica table drinking and talking; that was one of the things that Jake had noticed, that there was almost always the constant hum of conversation on the watch.

Jock spoke up. 'You know lads that Fraser's in the United Reserves, well they're playing Bolton Reserves next Tuesday night, anybody fancy coming?'

'Yeah I'll come, put me down,' Jake said.

Taff said, 'I'd come Jock, but we're at a meeting with the adoption people, sorry.'

'Don't worry boy,' Jock replied, 'there are more important things than football.'

'Yep, Jock, I'll come, and Val will want to come as well to support him,' Mac said.

'Well you know I'd come,' Clive said, 'but what with the wedding and everything?' Clive said, scratching his head.

'Yeah, don't worry about it; you've got plenty to think about already, thanks boys. Fraser asked me to ask you, he reckoned it would help him play better,' Jock said, smiling.

'Right you lot, out for drill. Brian you do it, I'm up to my eyes in paperwork,' Mac called as he walked up the stairs to his office.

Mildred Gathercoal lay in bed. At ninety-four years old, and with no living relatives, she sometimes wondered whether her life had any purpose. Her eyesight was fading, and her joints gave her permanent discomfort. Her mobility over the past couple of years had reduced, almost to the point where to get out of bed was a matter of pure willpower.

She desperately needed to go to the toilet. The commode she used was at the far end of her bedroom. Squinting her eyes to focus, she looked across the bedroom at the commode. *No chance Mildred,* she thought.

Millie had been a sergeant in the WRAF during the war, and she had always maintained a strict personal discipline, the soiling of her bed was out of the question. So she devised a plan to save her from the dishonour, as she saw it.

Red Watch had just started drill when the alarm sounded. Mac tore off the message from the printer.

'Brian, you take it, I need to stay here and catch up, OK?'

'Sure Mac, what we got?'

'It's a special service. Go to 221A. Manchester Road, an elderly lady needing help to get out of bed.'

Taff swung the machine off the station forecourt and accelerated along the high street. 'No great rush Taff, I'll not use the horns.'

They drove steadily up the sloping road looking for the house they needed.

'There it is,' Jake shouted, 'it's written on the dustbin.'

Brian surveyed the house, he knew there was no point in knocking on the door, but noticed that one bedroom had a window open.

'Right lads; let's sling the nine metre ladder up to that window,' he ordered.

Jake, Mick and Taff quickly pitched the head of the ladder up against the windowsill.

'OK young Jake, you go up, and take a look.' Jake jogged easily upwards whilst Jock stood, putting his weight onto the bottom of the ladder.

He got to the top of the ladder and peered into the window.

'Can you see anything Jake?' Jock asked.

'No, do you want me to get in and have a look?'

'Yeah, but take it easy, no heroics, alright?'

Jake stood on the top of the ladder, stretched his arm, and managed to reach the catch, which allowed the window to open. Jake scrambled in. He left the small bedroom which led onto the landing.

'Hello, are you there?' A frail voice came out of a room further along the landing.

'Hello, yes, it's the fire brigade.'

'Thank goodness, I'm desperate,' the voice called.

Jake carefully made his way along to the large florally decorated bedroom. He swung open the door. In front of him was an old lady. She was stuck, half in and half out of bed and clearly very distressed.

'Thank goodness young man,' Mildred said, her voice wavering with desperation.

'I have to go to the toilet now,' she said, pleading with Jake to hurry.

'OK,' Jake said suddenly thrust into something he was completely unprepared for. 'How do I help?'

'I'm desperate to sit on my commode over there,' she said almost crying with the effort not to let go. 'Please be quick,' she said through gritted teeth.

Jake went over to her bedside, and placing one arm under her legs, and the other arm around her shoulders said, 'OK madam one second.' He lifted her easily out of bed, noticing that she was as light as a feather.

'Will you sit me on the commode please?' she gasped.

Jake carefully lowered her onto the commode. 'Just a second,' he said, lifting her nightdress away from her bottom. 'You're alright now.'

She uttered a loud sigh. 'Oh thank you, you saved my life young man.'

'It was nothing, that's what we're here for. Now you let us know when you're ready to get back in bed,' Jake said as he left the room, giving the old lady some privacy. He went down stairs and opened the front door. The crew came across. 'Was there a problem in there?' Brian asked.

'No, when I got in I heard her calling. She sounded desperate, so I went into her bedroom and she was almost falling out of her bed, she begged me to put her onto her commode, so I did, that's where she is now, waiting for us to put her back to bed when she's finished.'

'Well Jake, you did what you had to do. Normally jobs like this we need the police here to oversee our entry, and again it should be the ambulance or social services who deal with these types of thing.'

Brian patted Jake's shoulder, it had been a small baptism of fire for him, and he had survived intact.

'Well, I suppose we should go up and get the lady back into her bed; I'll get some details for the report,' Brian said.

Jake tapped on her bedroom door. 'Hello Madam, can you hear me?'

'Yes, come in young man, I'm all done now.'

They went into the bedroom and she sat quietly, slightly embarrassed by her situation. 'I'm sorry,' she said, 'I'm afraid I had to do a number one and a number two. Usually my carer helps but she's late today; she called to say she'd been delayed because her little girl was off school poorly.'

'Don't worry, we'll sort you out,' Brian said, smiling his kindly smile. 'Young Jake here will get you back into bed. I just need to ask you a few questions for my report.'

Jake lifted her easily off the Commode and noticed that he would have a little job to do with the commode before he left. He carefully placed her back in bed and fluffed up her pillows.

'Now, is there anything else we can do before we go?' Brian asked.

The lady thought for a moment. 'Well,' she said, 'I could really do with a cup of tea, how about all of your firemen, would they like a cup also?' she said, smiling with gratitude.

'Jake, you sort out the Commode; I'll get Mick to make a pot of tea.'

A few minutes later, the crew sat around the lady's bed drinking tea and sharing a packet of digestive biscuits.

'Now we'll have to go, is there anything else?' Brian asked.

'You could put the television on for me please, and there's a clue in today's Daily Mail crossword that I couldn't get, are any of you any good at them?'

Taff examined the crossword, wrinkled his brow, and sucked the end of the lady's pencil. His face lit up. 'Got it,' he said triumphantly. 'The word you want is *probable.*'

'I'm very grateful to you boys, what would I have done without you?' she said, a great look of gratitude on her wrinkled face. 'We're so very lucky to have such gentle, caring firemen.'

'You're very welcome my dear, it's been a pleasure. The tea and biscuits were lovely, as are you Madam,' Brian said, a wicked grin crossing his tough features.

'Now boys, don't forget; if you're passing, pop in for a nice cup of tea any time, my young carer lady would love to meet you all I'm sure.'

'How did it go?' Mac asked as Brian dismounted from the appliance.

'It was fine, the old lady was desperate to use her commode, so I got Jake to go up the ladder. He found her and sorted her out, he did well. And we all got a cup of tea out of it. She's a really nice old lady, she's invited us back for tea anytime we're passing; she says her pretty young carer would love to meet us all.'

Pete, Trudy and the kids had arrived at Jubilee Court after an uneventful drive up the A1 and then the A66. In reception, they were greeted by the receptionist who then showed them to their room. They had been allocated a ground floor apartment which had been designed to accommodate people with mobility problems. It had a walk in shower and beds which could be raised or lowered to suit the needs of the person occupying the room.

'Well this is nice isn't it kids,' Pete said enthusiastically. 'The lady said to meet her at reception at three o clock, and she would give us a tour of the facilities mum will be using each day.'

After they had settled in, and had finished unpacking some of their clothing, it was time for them to go to reception.

'Hello, its Trudy and Peter I believe? I'm Linda, you'll see me most days. If you feel up to it, I'll show you around.

Tomorrow you'll be starting pretty early in the morning, so I'll tell you where you need to go first thing after breakfast.'

They walked around the spotless building with its tiled floors and pristine decor.

'This is the hot pool, you'll be spending time in there every day,' she said enthusiastically, 'then we have a normal pool used for doing certain exercises, and here we have the gym. There is all of the equipment, rowing machines, exercise bikes etc,' she said, pointing out the wide variety of equipment that was spread around the room.

Linda gave them information as they walked slowly around the facilities. 'In the morning, the physio will speak to you, and work out a specific programme for you during your stay.' They walked, on amazed by the quality of the facilities. 'Every day, you and the group you are allocated to will do a nice walk, accompanied by at least one of the physios,' she explained. 'All in all, your days will be very busy and you'll find there isn't a lot of time to spare, but I'm sure that you will enjoy it.'

'Finally here, this is the mess room and bar area. Breakfast will be from 7am onwards, you will also have lunch and dinner here. Any problems, pop up to reception and we'll do what we can to sort it out.'

Back in their room, Pete said 'isn't it fantastic, Trude, I reckon you'll love it.'

'Yeah,' she replied. 'Let's get settled in, I'm feeling a bit weary now.'

It had been an unusually quiet night. There had been just the one call to the old lady, and once that was done the crew had time on their hands to do other things. Mac was busy in the office, the crew sat in the lecture room, looking for a subject in the manuals to give a short talk to the rest of the crew on the next tour of duty.

Chapter 36

Mac got home in time to take Val to the hairdressers. He dropped her off outside the salon. 'OK love I'll see you later, I'm off to do some map reading.'

Val smiled, 'so you've got the bug I see,' she said, realising of course that this was all part of Mac's coping strategy for the time after he left the brigade.

'Yeah I won't be out long; I'll be home about half past one I reckon.'

He pulled the car into the side of the road on a muddied, unofficial parking place on Clod Hall Lane. The weather was fine; he'd already decided the route he'd take. He set the map and calculated that with a steady pace the walk would be about an hour. He crossed the road and climbed the wooden stile which accessed the moor; there was an obvious track, leading diagonally across the gently upward trending moorland. As he walked, he kept his eye on the map, checking the lie of the land against what the map was telling him. Twenty minutes later he was at the trig point, the high point of white edge. He set his map using the vistas around him. The view to the front was the expanse of Big Moor, its bleak slopes covered in dense brown gorse and bracken, the moor, where only a few days before, he'd attended a fatal helicopter crash. Across to his left was Froggatt Edge. Today it was quiet. At weekends it was usually busy with climbers pitting themselves against some of the best rock in the area. He stood by the Trig point and reset the map. He'd given himself a test to get himself across the featureless moors. A mile away, marked on the map, was the Hurkling stone, an ancient meeting point for local shepherds; then he'd hike to the short distance to Lady Cross. He set his compass and began walking on a bearing of

32 degrees over a distance of a mile crossing rough rocky ground. He'd calculated that it would take him about 20 minutes, but the nature of the walk with dense heather, hidden rocks, and an area littered with water filled depressions soon put him behind schedule. He eventually arrived at the stone, satisfied that he'd been able to walk direct, despite the difficulties he'd encountered. He noticed the many ancient carved symbols chipped out of the hard gritstone. He'd heard that the famous old Clarion Rambler Bert Ward had written a lot about the stone, and he told himself that he'd try to read what Ward had written.

Next stop Lady Cross, he said to himself. Once again, the terrain was tough. Although the distance was short and relatively uncomplicated, he still found it difficult to master the skill of walking accurately on a bearing; but after some problems with the rough ground and deep heather he made it to the cross. His next target, having regained his breath, was to head for the White Edge Ridge where he knew there was an ancient Guide Stoop. This would be a test over exceptionally rough terrain. He'd listened to Janet the ranger on the day they'd spent patrolling together; she'd said that it was sometimes better to do what they call '*aiming off,*' a tactic where the walker deliberately heads to either the left or right of the target. That way, you would always know which way to turn on say a track or riverside. That was the option he chose. The walking was hard, along a steep hillside where the gorse was particularly deep and thick. Mac was battling hard to try to maintain his direction. He'd aimed off to the left on the map, the east on the ground, so knew that when he hit the track he would have to turn right. Soon, the crest of the ridge was in view, but he was sweating hard. He'd badly underestimated the terrain, however he figured that a teaching taught was a lesson learned and ploughed on. He hit the rough track, an old deeply rutted packhorse trail. Mac could picture the long trains of horses loaded up with goods travelling these routes before roads and signposts were put in place. He stopped for a minute to catch his breath; his next task was to locate the guide stoop. These signs were made from the local grit stone, and erected as directed by act of parliament in the early seventeen hundreds to act as guides for the Jaggers, the traders, some of whom died from exposure out in the wilds before the guide stones were positioned. It wasn't long before Mac found his target, set back from the trail and leaning over drunkenly, with its carved directions deeply embedded in the grey rock. Mac could imagine the relief a traveller would get, maybe in bad weather or darkness, having reached the stone, and confirmation he was on the right track for his destination.

He was now high above the surrounding countryside and looking eastwards. He could just make out his car, parked about two miles away. He walked steadily downward, certain now that navigation was a complicated subject, one that he was determined to master. Thirty five minutes later he arrived at his car. He had a feeling of quiet satisfaction that he'd done all right, however he knew that had he been tested by Janet, she would have said that there was plenty of room for improvement.

Chapter 37

Clive and Helen were now engaged in the confusion of last minute arrangements for the wedding at the weekend. The lists were done. The cake had been baked and iced; the dresses were fitted and paid for. Clive had bought a new suit. Both the flowers and the Vicar were sorted. They began to believe that it was really going to happen, and Taff, his best man, had assured him that all was well.

Jake had read the letter from the young Italian woman several times, and each time the memory of the incident and her face made his heart race. He sat at the dining table, his mother was busy with her house-work so it seemed like a good time to write to Antonella and confirm that they would indeed be going to the concert.

Dear Antonella. Thank you for the invitation to the concert, I am just writing to tell you that we will be coming and we are both looking forward to seeing you and hearing you play. Mum has not stopped talking about you; I think you made a big impression. We will be coming down quite early on the day so we wondered, if it is convenient, could we all meet up somewhere before you have to leave for the concert?

Kind regards from Jake and Mum. X

He quickly addressed the envelope and jogged down the road to the corner post box and posted the letter.

Just one more night shift and then off for a few rota days, he thought. The phone rang.

'Hello?' Jake said into the phone mouthpiece.

'Hi Jake it's me, Tracy.'

'Oh! Hello,' he replied, suddenly unsure of how he should respond.

'How are you?' she said cheerily.

'I'm fine, I've just come off a night shift, one more tonight then off for a bit,' he said, almost trying not to sound too enthusiastic about her calling.

'Well, I thought I'd give you a call, mum and dad are visiting me tomorrow, and they would like to meet you if you could make it.'

'Oh right, OK, well I suppose that would be all right, I've not got anything arranged. What time do you reckon?'

'They expect to pick me up about half past ten.'

'How would it be if we met up for a drink and a quick sandwich somewhere?' he said, already computing that he wasn't that keen anymore, but not wishing to upset or offend her.

'Yes that would be good, how about the cafe over the climbing shop in Hathersage? I think the weather's going to be OK.'

Jake thought for a second. 'That will be fine, how about we meet up there say about twelve o clock for a bit of lunch then?'

'That's a date then,' she said, cheerfully.

'I look forward to meeting them,' he said, not quite sure how he felt about the whole meeting parent thing anymore.

For sure, meeting Antonella had diverted his interest; he'd liked Tracy, but figured some of it was a spin off from the rescue. Meeting the girl in London had knocked him sideways. He knew he felt something but wasn't sure what; all he did know was that he was very keen to find out more about her and himself.

Brian had diverted his car from his planned route after getting home and changing. He showered, and decided he'd go for a drive. At that time, there was no conscious decision as to where he would go.

Almost without thought, he parked the car in the car park close to the store. He knew he had to take a chance, something in his genes was propelling him to do something he knew was a mistake, but he couldn't help it. He got into the lift and pushed the button which would take him to the floor on which women's dresses were sold. He walked slowly, all the time his mind churning, his body hot. He walked into the area where he'd seen her before, he began looking at dresses. He heard the high pitched sound of a stiletto heel touch the hard surface of the floor.

'Hello Sir, do you need any help?' the female voice said.

'Brian turned to look at the face from which the voice had emerged. It was her. His heart leapt and he sucked in hard. 'Oh hello again,' he said, trying to appear that it had been a purely accidental reunion.

'Oh hello, it's you, we meet again,' she said, her bright red lips stretching into a broad smile. Brian looked at her; he noticed every small detail of her in the first second. Her hair was pulled up tight to her head, her makeup gave her an exotic look, almost Asian. Her figure was beautifully displayed by the perfectly fitting blouse and tight short black skirt she wore over black tights. He couldn't speak; he couldn't take his eyes off her.

She knew; she saw it. It was something she'd seen many times before. It was something she'd had to live with from being a young woman, there was something about her that made her a magnet for men, and she could see that Brian was drawn to her. She smiled the smile she'd smiled a thousand times before.

'How can I help Sir?' she said.

'Well I was just looking,' he said, his mind in turmoil. He was trying to court the girl, and he knew it was a mistake. He kept on, unable to control his desire to impress her. She knew; his body language told her everything. His voice had a desperation in it. She was surprised. She looked at him; he had a rough masculinity that she found attractive, however she'd been burned before, and there had never been any shortage of men who wanted to take her out to wine and dine her; and the rest. She now usually saw men, especially the pushy ones, as predators; not nice men or charming men, but men who were on the make. She'd decided a long time ago that the man for her would be the man who didn't try; that would be much more attractive to her.

'What are you wanting sir?' she said, maintaining her friendly demeanour.

Brian squirmed. 'I wanted to look at dresses,' he said nervously.

'For you Sir, or is it for someone special?'

He wasn't sure how to respond. *Is she joking or serious?* he thought.

'I mean Sir is it for a lady, your wife?'

'Well er, yes, well my girlfriend.'

'Ha,' she said, 'the mother of your children, I remember now, the pub in Tideswell, your daughter is very pretty.'

'Yes,' Brian mouthed, almost silently.

It began to dawn on Brian that his game was up and she wasn't interested.

She smiled at him. 'You know Sir, you seem to be a nice man, can I suggest that you take care of what you have, and pay less attention to what you haven't?'

Brian was embarrassed, he realised that the girl had seen through the ruse and he felt like a fool. He was hot and beginning to sweat profusely; she was right, he had a great deal, and it was time that he started to grow up and make the best of what he had. 'I'm sorry to have wasted your time, and I'm embarrassed to have put you in this position, please accept my apologies,' he said. She smiled a forgiving smile. Brian turned and walked quickly away, not wishing to prolong either his or her embarrassment. This had been a big mistake, he knew it and she had known it, he was grateful to her for putting him in his place in such a forgiving way.

Clive's Stag Night had been a pretty low-key affair; everyone was conscious of the trauma that was still affecting Helen. It had been generally agreed that there would be no excessive revelry or gross stupidity, it just didn't seem to be the right thing to do. Helen herself had asked that her friends respect her wishes that her hen night would just comprise of a night in with a takeaway and a few drinks. Clive felt, and the guys agreed, that they should follow suit.

They did however agree that a night at an Indian restaurant with a few drinks would be a good alternative.

The Star of India was resplendent. The restaurant, brightly illuminated in the dark of the evening, made the boys hungry for food and fun. They occupied one large table in the centre of the room.

The Station Commander Mick Cork stood up before the food was served.

'Well boys, I thought I should say a few words before we start. Curry has this awful effect on my mouth, and I fear that later I could be incapable of speaking at all.' There was a muted rumble of approval from the table.

'This will be a notably short speech. Clive, tomorrow you join the ranks of the oppressed, but who among us would not wish to be oppressed by such a beauty as the lovely Helen.' Another rumble of agreement, followed along with the occasional burp. 'So as I said, this will be short. Clive, not only are you a very good and capable fire fighter, you are a decent man, a deserving man, well worthy of the recipient of the special curry we have had cooked for you, eat and enjoy. And oh, by the way, good luck and have a long and happy marriage.'

A round of applause followed. Mac stood up. 'Clive, I wanted to reiterate what the Station Commander said, or maybe tonight as we are off duty we can call him Mick.' A ripple of gentle applause followed.

Clive, it's been my pleasure and honour to work with you these past years, and not wishing to be too serious on such a happy evening, I wanted to say to you this. Have a great life, Helen is a treasure. We know you are a couple in love, and we wish you both a long and happy life. Now, we have brought you a present, I hope that you don't need it.' Mac handed Clive the large package wrapped in bright pink paper. 'These are for you; at times of stress you should wear them, with love and friendship from the boys of the Red Watch.'

'Clive, get a move on, open it will you, we're all bloody starving,' Brian called across the table.

Clive ripped apart the paper, he laughed. 'Do you think I'll need them then?' he laughed, as he pulled out a brown pair of boxing gloves from the wrapping.

The food arrived, a mixture of Baltis, Madras, and a special Vindaloo for Clive, who had often boasted that he could eat the hottest curry. The table was soon overflowing with poppadoms, naan bread, and a myriad of dishes, all of which were consumed amid a storm of laughter and Cobra Beer.

Mac stood up again after most of the food had been eaten.

'*Now Clive,*' Clive looked on for a second, but he was unable to focus both eyes at the same time. The beer seemingly had begun to take its toll as he sat with his head tilted wildly to one side, with a confused look fixed across his face. '*There is a card here for you, postmarked Spain. I'll open it and read it to all of us who gather here to celebrate your demise, sorry, your forthcoming wedding to the beautiful Helen.*' Mac paused whilst he ripped open the envelope. '*Now Clive, I know what this letter contains, I had a phone call last week from the sender who asked me to do this for you.*'

Clive tried in vain to focus his eyes and sit up straight, but failed.

'*Clive,*' Mac's voice was becoming slurred, '*this message is from your friend in Spain, you remember. Hubert. Well he remembered that you were getting married tomorrow and he sent you this. I'll read it out shall I?*' Mac sat down and instantly stood up again; along with the rest of the crew he was suffering from an excess of alcoholic beverage.

'*Dearest Clive, My friend in need. This message is my way of saying to you and your fellow fire fighters that you all fill me with admiration. Your diligence and courage are a credit to the whole fire service, and I am forever grateful that, despite the circumstances, we were able to meet, and that you allowed me to be the recipient of your kindness. Your future wife, Helen, is indeed a lucky young woman. Now I know that for your own reasons a honeymoon was not on your agenda. However, I find that for reasons which are somewhat personal I have to leave Spain for about six months to stay in the USA. I would be delighted if you and your wife were able to stay at my villa for a couple of weeks, and take that as your honeymoon. Don't concern yourself about costs, just sort out your flights and stay there. It would make an old man very happy.*

Your friend Hubert Styles.'

By eleven p.m. the food was consumed, the alcohol had had its effect, and the watch were preparing to leave. Everyone was the worse for wear, with the exception of Jake, who had taken it upon himself to remain sober. Tomorrow was a big day, and he wanted to be in control of his mind and body for the service. None of these issues seemed to have entered the heads of the remainder of the watch who were happily clustered outside of the restaurant singing 'We are the champions'. It was all good natured, and even the police who were in the vicinity seemed impressed by the choral efforts of Red Watch.

The day began, the weather was kind, and the guests were almost sober. The wedding went without a hitch, there were no great traumas, and everyone at the wedding and the reception left with a warm glow. Taff had remembered to bring the ring. His speech had gone down well, albeit longer than the guys on the watch expected. Clive had made an emotional speech, telling of his love for Helen, but also alluding to the trauma of the lost baby. He became very emotional when he spoke of his and Helen's good fortune regarding Mister Styles. It was the best surprise they could have wished for; a honeymoon in Spain.

Pete, Trudy and the boys had spent a good week at Jubilee Court in Penrith. The overall feeling was that the intense physio and general exercise regime had been of great benefit to her. Pete had enjoyed spending time with the boys, ferrying them around the Lakes doing a bit of walking and travelling up Ullswater on the steamer. Fortunately the weather had been kind, allowing them to spend long hours out of doors. Pete could see a dramatic improvement in Trudy's overall health and demeanour. But now it was back to normal, the reality of everyday life.

Jake sat in the cafe as arranged, ready to meet Tracy and her parents; he was understandably nervous, unsure of himself and how to play it. Tracy thus far was completely unaware of his recent meeting in London, so he planned to be neutral in his attitudes towards her.

'Hi there, it's nice to meet you both,' Jake said as Tracy and her parents walked up the stairs into the cafe.

'No Jake, it's our pleasure, Tracy's father said, grinning broadly. 'We're both grateful for what you did. It would have just about finished us off if we'd lost Tracy. She told us all about you and that you'd been out together.'

'Well yes, we did, after the fire. I'd been busy, and Tracy had been recovering from her injury, so it seemed the right thing to do, you know, meet up, have a chat about things.' Jake paused and sipped on his cup of tea. 'So we came out and had a drink; we did a little walk, and I know Tracy is a busy with all of her studies. I'm kept pretty busy myself with work and other things. My mum relies on me quite a bit; she can't drive, so I'm her official chauffeur. I take her to the shops and from time to time we go on trips and holidays.

'So how do you like your job Jake?' Tracy's mother asked.

'I really like it, but like your daughter, life is busy. I have to go through a probationary period which requires me to do quite a lot of study.'

They talked for almost an hour, they ordered tea and cakes. Jake liked Tracy's parents; they seemed like really nice, open, ordinary people. Jake felt increasingly guilty about covering up his real feelings, and had decided that at the next opportunity he would talk to Tracy and straighten things out. He realised that all the pointless chit chat was merely a diversion to avoid upsetting all of them. It was something that he had to deal with; it wasn't fair on anyone to perpetuate the idea that things regarding him and Tracy were bound to develop. As they prepared to leave the cafe, Tracy's dad took Jake's hand and looked him in the eye.

'I understand son, I know. Do the right thing, talk to her and explain what you feel, she'll be alright, don't worry.'

'You know? I'm sorry Mister Jameson; I didn't want to hurt Tracy. She's been through a lot, I felt a responsibility after the fire.'

'I know, I understand. You are an honourable young man and I respect you for that. You talk to her. Be honest, she'll survive, she's got us to support her.'

'Thank you sir, you're a good man,' Jake said, a look of relief now on his face.

Jake sat by the kitchen table, mulling over in his mind what to say. *I've just got to say it, bite the bullet,* he thought. He dialled Tracy's number.

'Hello.'

'Hi Tracy it's me, Jake.'

'Hi Jake, it was nice to see you earlier, my dad liked you a lot.'

'Yes, I liked your dad as well. Tracy I need to talk to you. It's difficult, and you may not like what I have to say.'

'Oh! What's the problem?' she said, sounding very concerned.

'I'm sorry, but I've met a girl in London a little while back, I really like her. I'm sorry if that isn't what you wanted to hear.'

Chapter 38

1800 hours and Red Watch took over the reins of the station from Blue Watch. It was the usual routine of checking the machines and equipment. Then a cup of tea, and either a drill or a lecture. The evening had been uninterrupted by calls. After the jobs were finished the crew sat and watched TV, Brian and Taff spent half an hour playing snooker.

Mac and Brian sat in the office, having got all of the paperwork up to date. 'I've been thinking about what you said the other day about my prospects Mac; you're dead right. I'm going to apply for a job in the training department.' He paused for a second. 'What you said was right; I can see that now. I just hope I've not left it too late.'

'I don't think so, I had a chat to the Station Commander,' Mac replied. 'He thinks that you've got a lot to offer. They have a pretty regular turnover of people in training, so get an application off and see what happens.'

Just before ten o clock, the bell on the front door rang. Mick hopped down the stairs and could see an elderly man clearly distressed standing at the door.

'Can I help you, Sir?' Mick asked.

'Can you come quickly? I think my wife's having a heart attack,' the man said, his distress obvious. Mick stepped into the watch-room and pressed the bell three times, the signal that there was an emergency. Within seconds, the watch were there at the door.

'Our house is just there,' he said, waving his finger in the direction of a row of old terraced houses about a hundred yards from the fire station.

Mac shouted, 'Brian get the first aid kit, Jake you get the ambulance moving to that address.' Brian and Mac ran across to the house. The old man had left the door open. They went quickly into the lounge. The old lady was on the floor and looking very poorly. They could hear the ambulance siren approaching. Brian knelt down at the lady's side, and spoke directly to her. He stroked her head. 'You're going to be alright love; the ambulance is here, you'll be fine.'

The siren stopped, and seconds later the ambulance crew came into the room. 'Well Mac, it looks like you're taking my job over,' old George said. 'How is this young lady?'

Mac looked up at George. 'Good to see you, George, this young lady needs a professional, she'll be glad you're here.'

'Now then you, stop being nice to me.' George said as he knelt down by the side of the woman. 'How are you doing my darling?' George said, giving her a broad grin. She smiled weakly. Already, the colour in her face was improving. 'Let's just put this mask on sweetheart, it will make you feel a bit better, and then we'll take you to the hospital and let them have a look at you.'

'Well George, it looks as though you don't need us so we'll get back to the station,' Mac said.

'OK Mac, you take care, thanks for the help, I'll see you around.'

After supper Jake sat with Mac and Taff in the rec room, talking.

'So what have you been up to, Jake?' Mac asked.

Jake stretched out in his chair. I had a really strange thing happen today. This afternoon I met Tracy, you know the girl from the fire, and she brought her parents to meet me. After the meeting, I told her that I'd met this other girl, expecting her to be upset about it, so I was quite careful how I told her.' Jake stopped for a second. 'Well I was amazed, she said don't worry Jake, I've just got myself a boyfriend, he's from Leeds and I like him, so don't worry about it.'

Jake lay in his bunk in the station dormitory; his mind turning over his feelings and thoughts about the day. His lack of experience with women had left him confused. Initially, he'd felt an attraction to Tracy. On the other hand, his recent meeting with Antonella had hit him like a thunderbolt. He couldn't exactly define how he felt, he just knew that it had affected him; there was no escaping the continued nagging feelings that the thoughts of her engendered in him.

He smiled to himself when he pictured his mother's face when he stopped Antonella's attacker; her face had been a picture. And his mother's attitude towards Antonella had been very positive; she liked the girl, almost as though it had been destined to be so.

He was glad they'd decided to see her again in London. He couldn't wait; her face was still flitting in and out of his consciousness.

He ran all of this through his mind for what seemed an age. He turned over and looked at his bedside clock, one thirty am, and he was still a long way from sleep. Everyone else was fast asleep. Jock was snoring loudly; Brian had had a confused conversation with himself saying something about a dress he wanted to wear.

It was seven o clock and the night had been quiet; Mac climbed out of his bunk and shook Brian. 'Time to get up boys,' he called as he wandered into the shower room.

Jock had dressed quickly and gone to the kitchen whilst the lads were down cleaning the machines. He was on breakfast duty today. The usual sausage, eggs, beans and fried bread. Jock had cooked this a thousand times, and he had his system developed over a long time which worked. It was five to eight. The machines were clean and the station was tidy. The lads wandered onto the mess deck. Jock was clearly happy as he sang along to Status Quo on the radio and served the boys their hot breakfast and mugs of tea. The shift was coming gently to a close.

Parade was the usual cacophony of high jinks and laughter.

'OK you lot, settle down,' Sub Officer Alan Wilson said, bringing some sense of order to the parade.

'Red Watch, fall out, Blue Watch stand at ease. Duties for the day are as follows.'

Chapter 39

Brian changed into his civilian clothes before leaving the station. He was going to drop Jake off at home en route to Jane's house where he'd promised he would start decorating Jill's bedroom.

Jake looked across the car at Brian.

'You know Bry; I'm lucky finding this job and having all you lads as my mates now. It's the best move I've ever made, thanks to you and Mac.'

Brian said nothing for a minute. 'You're doing well so far Jake; you're showing a lot of good traits. Your enthusiasm gives us a boost, it keeps us on our toes, so we're glad to have you on the watch.'

'I hear that pretty soon you're going to be looking to move; I heard Taff and Mick talking about it this morning, what's that all about?'

Brian shrugged his shoulders. 'It's about the future, I've been on ops for nearly twenty years and it's only just now, where I've been doing temporary leading firemen, that I found out about this other side of the job, and I think I like it. So I had a chat with Mac and I reckon that I'm going to try to become an instructor. It will be something different, and it's days so it'll give me more time with Jill and Jane.'

'I'll be sorry to see you go, I've not been doing this long, but the jobs we've had, well I've learned a lot from you,' Jake said.

'There'll be a time, Jake, when you're the old hand and the youngsters will come along, and you'll pass on the lessons you've learned along the way.'

'Yeah I suppose so, but that seems a long way off now.'

'It'll fly by. It only seems like yesterday that I sat where you are now, learning from the old hands. That's the way it is, and the way it should be.'

Brian pulled his car to a halt by Jake's house. 'Well Jake, you have a nice break and I'll see you next tour.'

'Cheers Bry, say hello to Jane for me.'

Jake put the key into the Yale lock and opened the door; he could smell the coffee percolating. His mother spoiled him. Every morning after nights this was her routine. Coffee and toast for Jacob.

'Hi mum it's only me,' he called into the kitchen.

'Hello Jacob, your toast is in the toaster.'

He went into the kitchen, his mum stood with her back to the sink holding a white envelope in her hand. 'Here's a letter for you Jacob! It's postmarked London,' she said, with a broad smile on her face.

Jake took the envelope, his heart beat fast. He tore it open.

Dear Jacob, thank you for your very nice letter to me. It was nice for you to write back. I'm very happy that you and your mother can come to the concert. I am very much looking forward to meeting you both again.

It will be very nice to be able to see you before the concert, we have to practice in the morning but I will be free from 2 pm for about two hours, it will be nice if we could meet then. There is a place called the Jugged Hare on Chiswell Street it is very close to the theatre, I will be there at two pm. will you let me know that you will come there. Kindest regards from your friend.

Antonella X

He gave the letter to his mother, who quickly read it. 'Well son, I think she's keen to meet you, so write and let her know. Better still phone her. I've got her number in my hand bag.

'So Jacob, what sort of a night did you have?' his mother asked.

'It was quiet, just the one shout. An old lady had a heart attack, we went to help until the ambulance got there, and she seemed fine when we left. Other than that nothing, we just did the routines and some cleaning up. I did have a nice chat with Brian though, he reckons that he's going to apply to move into training school and become an instructor.'

Jim sat watching television. He lay on the settee; he'd done an hour's revision on some technical aspect of his plumbing course and was contemplating having a bath when the phone rang.

'Mister McEvoy?'

'Yes.'

'Oh hello, this is David Parsons, we met a short while ago at Three Shires Head, and you kindly offered to take my dog Henry for me when I left for America.'

Jim was surprised, he'd almost forgotten about the conversation he'd had with the old man.

'Oh yes I remember. How are you?' James said tentatively.

'I'm very well, and I have to say how grateful I am for your offer to have Henry when I left for the States. It's just that, well, I leave for Atlanta next weekend and was wondering if you wanted to come and get him, or should I bring him over to you?' the old man said. Jim could hear the sadness in his voice.

Jim thought for a second. 'Look Mister Parsons, can I ring you back? I need to speak to my fiancé. I'll get straight back to you, OK?'

Maddie had showered, and was drying her hair. Her father shouted up the stairs. 'Madeline, it's Jim on the phone.'

'Hiya Jim,' Maddie called. 'What's this, ringing this time of night?'

'Maddie, I've just had a call from the chap we met with the dog. He wants us to have it from next weekend; I was thinking it's going to be hard, what with me out on my course all day, what do you think?'

'Mmm I'm not sure. We didn't think before we opened our mouths, did we Jim?' she said, a hint of irony in her voice. 'Just hang on, I'll get back to you, I'll speak to mum and dad.'

Five minutes later, Jim's phone rang. 'Hi, it's me. Mum and dad have said they will have the dog while you're out on your course, you'll have to drop him off and pick him up each day, how does that sound?'

'Sounds good, I'll give the man a call and tell him I'll drive over and collect the dog next Saturday.'

Antonella sat with a tray of pasta on her lap, when the phone rang. 'Si.'

'Hello Antonella it's Jake, how are you?'

'Jake! Is that you, Jake?'

'Yes it's me,' he said, trying hard not to sound too desperate. 'I thought it would speed things up if I rang to say that we'll see you at the Jugged Hare at two, we're looking forward to seeing you.'

Antonella noticed that just the sound of his voice was leaving her breathless and hot. 'It's so good to hear your voice,' she said, 'I'm so looking to seeing you soon.' She paused to compose herself. 'Jacob, I am missing you and I dying for to see you and your mama soon.' Almost immediately, a vision entered her mind of the day that Jake became her hero by felling her attacker. 'Jacob you can call me Nella if you like; it will be easier I think for you to speak.'

Jake smiled to himself at her use of the language, but to Jake it just added to the excitement he was feeling.

'Nella, my mum sends you her love, she is looking forward to seeing and hearing you play.'

'And me also, looking to be with you both soon,' she said, 'love from me to your mum and to you especially Jacob.'

Mick dialled the number and held the phone to his ear.

'Hello.' The familiar voice made Mick's heart thud loudly in his chest.

'Hi Paula, it's me, Mick.'

'Hello, how are you? I wondered when you were going to call.'

'Well, it's now,' Mick replied, 'how do you fancy a ride out and a bite to eat, after last time's failure?'

'If every trip we do fails like that, I'll be out with you every week,' she said seductively.

Mick smiled. 'Shall I pick you up on Saturday at ten? Will you be up by then?'

'Where are you taking me?' she asked, 'you know, will I need my swimming gear or walking boots? Or will we just be taking the short walk to look at my bedroom wallpaper?'

Mick laughed. 'Well with a bit of luck, maybe the wallpaper will come later. I thought a drive out to Castleton would be nice. The weather seems as though it's going to be all right.'

'Go on then, you've talked me into it,' she said, 'I'll see you on Saturday.'

Mick smiled to himself. He was surprised just how this girl had grabbed him. She made him feel happy. This was a long way from how he felt after his last disastrous relationship.

Mac pulled the car into the back of the walking shop in Hathersage. Parking was tight; the shop looked to be busy.

'Right, let's go and have a look shall we?' Mac said. Val looked at him, his birthday was fast approaching and she wanted to get him something he needed, she'd asked him a while back, and he said he needed a new compass and some heavy duty over trousers.

They walked into the shop through the back entrance, and saw immediately some members of staff who they'd met many times over the years, who gave them a friendly greeting.

Taff pulled into his drive; he noticed that the curtains were still closed. '*That's unusual,*' he thought to himself. He opened the front door; there was no sign of life.

He shouted, 'I'm home.'

He heard movement upstairs, 'Hello, it's me.'

'Hi can you come up here Emlin,' Ena's voice drifted down the stairs.

Taff put down his holdall and went upstairs. He opened the bedroom door. 'Hi,' he said.

'Emlin,' Ena said as she lay propped up in bed. 'Why don't you get in here with me, I've missed you a lot this tour.'

Taff knew this was more of a demand than a request, and in a flash he was stripped off and lying alongside his wife. They'd been through a lot together; spontaneity seemed to have passed them by as the years had progressed, the stress of trying for a child had taken its toll on them and their relationship.

Taff put his arm around his wife as they lay together, relaxed, free of stress. They made love. Love for the sake of love with no thought of a reason, just for the pleasure and togetherness that the physicality of being this close together brought.

Jock loaded his son's bag into the car. Fraser was playing for the Blades Reserves today. Jock was driving him to the ground, where the team coach would take him to Birmingham where they were to play the Aston Villa Reserves. Jock looked at his son, he was so proud. Fraser had grown and was almost the same height as Jock.

'I'm looking forward to the game today son, let's hope you have a good one.'

Since Fraser and his dad had begun spending more time together, the father son relationship had flourished. Fraser now saw his dad as a friend who gave him unconditional love and support, whilst Jock watched his son developing into a fine young man.

'Could be a tough one today son, I see that Tom Bevan and Hugh Peters are in midfield. I reckon they've about thirty caps between them; a lot of experience there.'

'Yeah, the boss says it will be tough, but just to concentrate on my part in the team and work hard and I'll be OK.'

'Yes, it's all part of your education, you should learn a lot from it. You'll be fine.'

Jock stopped the car outside the stadium. 'OK son, I'll see you after the game, have a good one.' Jock watched his boy turn and walk into the ground. Now tall and powerful, he slung his sports bag over his shoulder and waved to his dad as he walked away.

Chapter 40

Pete Jacks sat opposite his wife. He looked at her with a sense that all was not well; the past couple of days had seen an almost indefinable deterioration in her condition. She seemed to understand something, maybe female intuition. She talked to Pete about how things should be after she was gone. Pete suspected the worst was coming and wrestled with his emotions. The idea of her not being around for him and the boys frightened him, although he would never allow Trudy or the boys to know that.

She was sat in her chair asleep, breathing gently. The boys were in their rooms, reading. Pete got up and walked into the kitchen and filled the kettle with water. He heard her stir. 'Peter,' her voice sounded frail. 'Peter,' she called again.

Pete went through into the lounge. 'Are you alright love?' he said, looking at her. She seemed suddenly very sad. 'Hold me Peter,' she said. He saw a tear emerge from her eyes. He knelt down in front of her and leaned into her, putting his arms around her. He knew then that it was that time.

'I'm sorry Peter,' she said. 'Tell the boys I love them, I'm sorry.'

Pete pulled her close to him. 'I'm with you,' he said, as the tears flowed down his face and into her hair. He felt her body relax into his, heard her last breath, and remembered the good times when they were young; the birth of the boys. The hard times when she had been there for him as he struggled with work to make them a home together. Now she was gone.

Pete stood in the rain alongside his sons and both his and Trudy's parents. The bearers carried Trudy's coffin into the crematorium. The organ played soulful, slow music. The whole of Red Watch and some of Pete's ex colleagues from Halifax Road sat dressed in sober clothing at the back of the crematorium. Mac looked forward; he could see that Pete had his arms around both of his boys who were clearly upset. He felt a surge of emotion course through his body, and saw his vision blur as his eyes filled with tears. The memory of Trudy and the close relationship she'd had with Pete and her boys suddenly hit him. Life was not forever, it ends.

In the short time Pete had been with them following the traumatic start to his tenure on Red Watch, Pete had blossomed, been revitalised, a re-born man. The watch had taken Pete to their hearts, they knew and understood how hard his life was, but also saw the devotion and love that he and Trudy shared. They all thought that he was a lucky man, but life now would be tough for him. They also knew that he wouldn't be short of help from the boys on the watch.

Jake and his mother got the eight a.m. train to London and sat comfortably,

relaxed and excited about what the day was to bring.

Jake began reading his latest book. The fourth one of Wilbur Smith's that he'd read. 'What's that you're reading, son?'

Jake looked up. 'It's a Wilbur Smith, I like his books. This one's 'The Burning Shore,' it's about a woman who was shipwrecked and saved by local Bushmen, it's a great story.'

'I think I'll stick to reading the paper, it all sounds a bit heavy for me,' she said as she reached into her handbag to get out her biro to begin doing the crossword.'

Jake and his Mother scurried across to the St Pancras tube, just managing to get on to the train before the doors of the carriage closed on them. It was packed; a young black man noticed her standing, so stood up and offered Jake's mum his seat.

'Thank you,' she said, grateful that despite all she had heard about the lack of community spirit in the city, this young man had done something nice.

'We should be there soon mum,' Jake said as he leaned over whilst swinging rhythmically from the flexible handle that hung from the train roof. Jake looked at the young man who had given up his seat. 'Thanks for that,' he said.

'It's my pleasure,' he replied. 'I spend all day sitting down, so the chance to stand is welcome.' He smiled at Jake. 'Is this your first time in London? I can tell by your accents you're not from around here.'

'No, it's our second time; we're down here to go to a concert at the Barbican tonight.' Jake paused. 'Yeah, we're not local, we live in Sheffield.'

'Oh, I know Sheffield,' he said animatedly. 'I was there at the university about eight years ago, I loved it, it's a great place to live.'

'Yeah I like it, there's plenty to do, and the Peak District is just a few minutes up the road.'

'Oh yes, I had a good time there, I had digs in Walkley. The landlady was great, she did us Yorkshire pudding with everything. We told her we liked it and that was it. We had Yorkshires with almost everything; even chips and gravy, something that I would never have considered before. My wife now, well she loves Yorkshire pudding and cooks it all the time, especially with chips.'

'Do you work in London?' Jake asked.

'Yes, I'm a solicitor, what about you?' he replied.

'I'm in the fire brigade, I've not been in long but I like it a lot.'

'Yorkshire's finest, that's what we used to call them when I was up there, they often used to be around the university dealing with little fires, usually started by drunken students who thought it was fun to set fire to rubbish bins.'

'I think that still happens. Anyway it's been nice to meet you, we get off here. Come on mum, let's go. Thanks a lot for the seat,' Jake said as they made their way to the door of the train.

Jim and Maddie drove across the high moorland heading for the market town of Leek; they were on their way to collect Henry the black Labrador from his owner who was leaving to live in America. 'Do you think we're doing the right thing Maddie?' Jim asked.

'Yes I think so, what you offered was something very kind. The old man was clearly sad at the prospect of leaving Henry behind, so you did him a favour. He'll know that he's being looked after by someone who'll take care of him. So I'm sure there'll be times when having a dog won't be very convenient, but I'm sure there'll be good things as well.'

Maddie tapped on the stained wooden door of the nice detached house. She noticed the sold sign on the lawn of the house. The old man came to the door, and Henry was standing behind him wagging his tail furiously.

'Come in, I've sorted out all of his things, his basket and his lead, food etc. So you won't have to go out buying too many things for a while.'

He made them a cup of tea and spent a few minutes telling them a little about Henry and some of his foibles. Then it was time to go.

The old man knelt down alongside his dog and embraced him. Goodbye old friend. I'll miss you,' he said, his voice choking.

'We'll look after him and send you some pictures,' Jim said, also choking up. 'We'd better go. Good luck in America.'

Henry lay comfortably on the back seat of Jim's car and was soon fast asleep. They stopped briefly opposite the Cat and Fiddle public house to allow Henry a comfort stop, then they were soon on their way to Jim's place.

Jock was a happy man. His son, Fraser, had scored the winning goal to beat the Chelsea reserves by a single goal. After he scored two at Villa Park two weeks before, he'd become an integral, important part of the team. A corner from the right had found Fraser unmarked close to the penalty spot. He climbed high and headed powerfully into the net. He'd arrived late, running in fast from twenty yards out. It was something they'd practised in training.

Taff and Ena were living in a cocoon of mental stability after all of the stress and worry of the past few years. Their lives had changed, they were happy and content, nothing troubled them anymore. The map of their lives had now been drawn. They were looking forward to a satisfying future together.

Chapter 41

The restaurant was quiet; there was just a subtle glow from dimly lit table lamps. There were few windows to light up the space. Jake looked around, the bar on the left had been made from mature oak; just two people leaning against the bar talking quietly.

Then, a series of tables lay with white linen cloths which were set out ready for customers to eat their meals. Along the walls were comfortable red leather upholstered bench seats and the walls were of painted brick, giving the lengthy bar area a subtle homely style. They walked through the bar area into a small room with bench seats surrounding the room, also set with small tables.

They saw each other. It took Jake's breath away. Nella stood up to greet them; her face lit up and was split by a huge smile. Her electric blue silk dress shone in the dim light. Jake walked across the room to her. She held out her hands. Jake took hold of them and found it impossible to speak. He was again paralysed by her beauty. Her face, which had circulated around his mind, looked even more beautiful than before; her hair was a lustrous jet black, her wide smile was just as Jake remembered it.

Jake's mother came, put her arms around her and hugged her.

'It's so nice to see you again, Antonella. Don't tell anyone, but Jacob has missed you a lot, he's always talking about you.'

'And me also. I have missed you both very badly, and now I see your beautiful son, my heart wants to burst with happiness.'

Jake finally managed to get his words out. 'Nella,' he emphasised. 'It's good to see you. You look a lot happier than when we met before. How have you been?'

'I have been OK I think. Sometimes my head is thinking of the incident and I get worried but most time my thinking is of you and your mama, how kind and brave you are, and how happy I have been since then we have met.' She paused and ran her hands through her hair.

Jake noticed her small hands, the slim fingers, and the light as it struck her hair, the smell of the perfume that she had so carefully placed. He noticed everything, storing every image in his mind, the shape of her face against the light from the small lamp on the table, the way she spoke and smiled.

Unbeknown to Jake, Antonella was registering him in the same way. His short cropped black hair. His square jawline. His pale blue eyes, his strong hands, his broad chest and powerful arms. How she longed for those arms to be placed around her.

She saw the light glisten of sweat on his forehead and how he breathed deeply when he looked at her.

He noticed the rising and falling of her chest when she spoke to him and the intense look of her dark eyes which closed momentarily as she looked at him.

Jake's mum looked on like a spectator at a football game. She could see that Jacob was transfixed and Antonella was engrossed in her son.

'I'm just going outside for a breath of fresh air,' she said. 'I'll be back in a minute.' She smiled to herself. She understood. She had felt like this when she'd met her husband, Jacob's father, so many years ago now.

Mick picked Paula up from her flat and drove out into Derbyshire, descending steeply into the Hope Valley, passing through Hathersage on their way to Castleton. Mick pulled up in the car park beyond the village.

'Where are we off to next Mick?' Paula asked.

Mick turned and peered into the distance. You'll need to put your coat on, we're going up there,' he said, pointing upwards towards the huge hill behind the car park.

'The shimmering mountain or Mam Tor, that's for us today, a short stiff walk then great views and usually very high winds.'

Paula threaded her hand through Mick's arm. 'This is nice Mick, We should do this more often.'

The track led steeply up on thick stone slabs curving around the hill. Soon they reached the summit and were almost blown over by the strength of the wind.

'There you go lady, sit on the Trig point and I'll take your picture.'

This high point gives great views in all directions, and Paula was impressed. 'I've never been up here before,' she said. 'It's just a beautiful place.'

Mick took her photograph; she smiled and climbed down from the trig point. She walked over towards the edge of the cliff which falls away several hundred feet and stood almost transfixed by the panorama.

Mick walked up behind her and put his arms around her slim waist. He pulled her up close to him. 'It is beautiful, but then so are you,' he said. 'Paula, I know we've not been going out very long but.' He stopped.

'But what?' she said, a smile crossing her lips.

'I've been and seen a lot of things, in the army and other places, and this may sound corny, but.' He paused again. 'I think I like you a lot.'

Paula was stunned. She turned to face Mick, and could see that it had taken a lot for him to say what he had just said.

'You think you like me? What makes you think that?'

'I don't know, I just know you make me feel great when I'm with you. It's not sex, it's more than that; I've never felt like this before, so if it's not love I don't know what it is.'

They sat in the small cafe in the centre of the village; a sudden seriousness had come across them. Paula had never had a serious relationship with anyone. And Mick, this was all new to him. They sat and sipped their tea; suddenly they had other things to talk about.

Jake and his mother sat close to the front of the auditorium, the orchestra was settled on the stage. Jake had spotted Nella, and she them; she'd given them a secret gentle wave and a broad smile.

The lights of the auditorium dimmed, only the stage was illuminated. The music began, gently at first.

'What are they playing Jacob?' his mother whispered.

Jake looked at the programme. 'It's Tchaikovsky's violin concerto in D major. Opus 35.' Jake replied, unconvincingly.

'Oh,' she said. 'It sounds lovely. Doesn't Nella look beautiful?'

Jake smiled; clearly his mother had become a fan of classical music. He thought she would love whatever she played. He looked at Antonella, her graceful movements as she stroked the bow across the strings of her violin, and the look of peace and concentration on her face. He was enchanted; he wasn't listening to the music, his whole focus was on her face.

The piece ended with loud applause in the auditorium. The orchestra stood and bowed at the signal from the conductor. Jake saw that Nella was looking straight at him and smiling.

The light dimmed again and the music began once more.

'What are they playing now?'

Jake looked again at the programme. 'It's something called Zigeunerweisen,' he said, struggling to pronounce the title. 'Opus 20 number 1, at least that's what I think it says. It's German I think.'

'Oh right, it sounds lovely, and Nella is playing really well, don't you think?'

'Yeah she's lovely,' Jake replied absent mindedly.

Antonella was lost in the music occasionally looking up at the conductor. Occasionally, Jake would notice her glancing down at him and his mother. She swayed to the romantic rhythm of the music, her concentration absolute. Then it was over. The audience stood and applauded for several minutes, the orchestra bowed. Flowers were brought onto the stage and slowly the audience quietened, the lights brightened, and then people began to leave. Jacob and his mother sat, barely able to move. The performance had transfixed them both. It was something that had taken them both by surprise; it was far beyond any previous experience.

'Well mum what do you think to that?' Jake gasped breathlessly.

'Jacob, I have to say, it was absolutely wonderful. I closed my eyes and I drifted away above the countryside, it was breathtaking. We must do it again.'

The Jugged Hare was busy, filled with customers, many of whom, they thought had just left the concert, like them.

They found a small table toward the back of the pub and waited. Jake felt tense. Somehow, seeing her perform the way she had and amid the company she kept had sapped Jake's confidence, he felt, but he would in no way acknowledge a feeling of social inferiority. It wasn't a feeling he'd had before, and he fought within himself to subdue it.

He spotted her weaving her way through the groups of people clustered around the room. She saw him and gave a slow wave of her hand, and her face, then serious, broke into a broad smile.

Both Jake and his mum stood up to greet her.

She took Jake's arm and kissed him on his cheek.

'How did you enjoy the concert?' she asked.

'It was absolutely wonderful, we both loved it didn't we Jacob?' his mother said.

'Yes, it was great. You were brilliant. I didn't look at the rest of the orchestra, I just watched you,' Jake said, his face flushed and his heart pumping.

'I think that I felt that. I did look at you both when I could, I love playing music it makes my heart sing,' she said, waving her hands. It is so romantic. I thought of you, Jacob, when I played the slow romantic part of the concerto.'

They sat and had a few drinks, they talked, ate snacks, and talked some more. In no time at all it was late. Jake reckoned it was about time they should make a move for the hotel.

Jake's mother spoke. 'Look son, I'll get a taxi back to the hotel, why don't you and Nella spend a bit more time together on your own?'

Jake looked at Nella, and she looked approvingly at Jake and his mum.

'Well if Nella doesn't mind I'd like that; how about you?' he said, looking directly into her dark eyes.

'My accommodation is in Camden town but I would love very much to have spending time with you Jacob. We may not have more chances for a long time coming,' she said, taking hold of Jake's hand.

The taxi dropped them close to London Bridge. The night was cool, and a gentle breeze blew. It was dark, the moon was just creeping slowly from behind a cloud. Antonella had just a light blouse and a thin silk scarf. He noticed her shiver. 'Are you feeling the cold?' he asked.

'Yes, I had not considered the cold. I was so pleased to meet you again, but it is how you say? Chilly a bit.'

Jake slipped off his jacket. He wore a white short sleeved shirt. 'Here, put this over your shoulders,' he said.

'Oh Jacob, you are my Walter Raleigh, so English, so gallant. Now you will be cold.'

'No I'll be fine, I think we have thicker blood in the north, I don't notice the cold very much,' he said.

They walked slowly alongside the river, looking at the reflected light of the moon and noticing how the light framed the towers of London Bridge.

'You know Jacob, London is a very beautiful city, it seems more beautiful now you are with me here,' she said as she slipped her arm through his. They stood silently, leaning against the rail looking at the river.

She looked at Jake. 'Jacob, can I ask you a question?'

'Yes, no problem,' Jake said, wondering what the question would be.

'Jacob, I am young, Italian and I have hot blood,' she said as she turned to face him. 'Will you kiss me please?' She moved close to him, putting her arms around his waist.

Jake looked at her face; this was like a dream. *Is this really happening to me?* he thought. *Here I am with the most beautiful woman I have ever met, and she wants me to kiss her.* He felt dizzy; the blood coursed through his brain and made his head swim. 'Yes of course I will, it's all I've thought about since we met,' he said, looking sheepishly at her, 'but I don't know if I'm any good at it,' he said as his heart raced. He looked deep into her eyes, she returned the gaze.

The kiss was long and passionate. Jake felt the need to breath but Nella clung to him, holding him tight against her. Then she broke away, they both gasped for breath. 'Jacob, since we have met I have wanted this every minute of every day. I don't want tonight to finish.'

Jake leaned back against the iron railing. 'You are one beautiful woman, Nella; I can't believe what's happening to us.'

'Jacob. I don't like you, I love you! I want us always to be with together.'

Jake smiled, unable to grasp the intensity of how he felt. 'Come on, let's walk a bit more and talk, we don't know much about each other do we?'

They strolled very slowly, their fingers interlinked.

'So Jacob, who are you? I want to know,' she said, squeezing his fingers.

Jacob though about what he should say, this had happened before and it had all gone sour with Tracy, he didn't want a re-run of that.

'Well Nella, there's just me and mum. We live together in a nice area close to Sheffield. I didn't work very hard at school so I have no qualifications, so I had to work on buildings as a labourer. I wasn't very well paid. Then something happened to make me try to be a fireman.' He stopped to consider what to say next. 'Then I found that when I went to do my training it clicked, I'd found my perfect job. I love it.' He paused. 'I did well, in my training, and was really chuffed when I was voted the best recruit of the year and I got a silver trophy.'

Nella spoke. 'What is chuffed, Jacob?' Jake smiled at her. 'Oh it's just a word we use to say we're happy.' She smiled at him and looked a little quizzical. 'So, Jacob, I am much chuffed to kiss you again.' Jake lifted her hand and kissed it.

Nella grinned. 'You English people are very English, I do not think an Italian man kiss my hand if I ask him.'

'So as I was saying before I made love to your hand. One night I helped to rescue a student from her house which was on fire. We both had to go to hospital, but we're both OK now I'm glad to say.' Jake stopped and placed his arm over her slim shoulder. She noticed the powerful arm and thought that he was a man who is very strong.

'I work at the fire station with my crew mates who I admire very much. They are teaching me a lot. Not long ago, Brian, a friend, saved our lives in a fire. But Mac, my boss, is my hero. He retires from the brigade soon, he is the one who helped me to become a fireman. I like to study for my work to make me better at it. I like to go into the Peak District to walk. Sometimes I like to take my mum out for a meal. That's about it. I'm eighteen years old and now I've met you; it's the most exciting thing that's happened to me.'

'You Jacob are a very nice man and a very interesting man also. I want to find out more about you.'

'How about you? Tell me, I'd like to know.' Jake paused. 'To do what you do there must have been some very interesting things in your life,' he said, looking at her face half in shadow, half lit by the moonlight.

Antonella stopped and leaned back against the decorative iron railings.

'When I was very young, my parents moved away from Rome because of work. I was left with my grandparents who I loved very much. They were very good for me,' she said, with a wistful look in her eyes.

'Nonno Paolo was a violinist with an orchestra; he did sometimes take me to concerts.' She paused and threaded her hand through Jake's arm. 'He loved Toscanini and I was always interested and exciting when I am with him.' Once again, she had a faraway look in her eyes as though she was back as a child in Rome.

'For the entire musicians, the music was important. They were in the war, and music helped them to survive. They loved me, I was very small and pretty so they spoiled me, and they gave me sweets.'

Once again, she paused, as if reflecting on her past life. 'Nonno Paolo bought me my own violin and taught me reading music and technique of the violin.' She paused to wipe her eyes with her handkerchief. 'Nonno Paolo said the music must be a secret, not tell my parents.' She paused momentarily.

'One day I was practicing Mendelssohn and my parents heard me. I was surprised, they were not angry. They said I should go to the conservatoire and take exams. Nonno did not agree, he said that it spoils the imagination of the musician. But because of all of the orchestra's help I passed my exams and then did an audition to come to London as a scholarship, which I did, and I was successful. My grandparents were very proud of me and I was very happy,' she paused again. 'My grandpa was at the audition, I played music by Bach, something he was expert at and he loved it, he was nervouser than I.' She stopped talking and shook her head slowly.

'I did not know that the examiner was the man my mother loves and should have married. Nonno was very sad when he left, they did not get married. My mother was a very great pianist, she played with the best orchestra in Europe, but when she met my father there was no more music. So I hope one day all my family will hear me play and it will mend the breaking in my family.'

Jake was stunned by the frankness of what she had just said to him. He put his arms around her shoulders. 'What are the other things that you like to do?' he asked.

'Well in Italia when I go with my friends to holiday, I like to go into the countryside and see the lovely mountains and swim in the lakes. I like other music as well. My mama loved the Beatles so we hear that very much in our home, so I also like the rolling stones as well.'

They sat oblivious of the hours passing they talked about everything until the dawn began to break over the eastern horizon.

'Look at the time, Antonella. You'll be too tired for your next concert, let me get a taxi for you.'

Jake put his arms around her shoulders and kissed her lightly on the lips. 'I will telephone you every day. I have loved being with you.'

'Jacob, I will miss you every minute of the day and night I promise to you.'

The taxi came and she left reluctantly, looking over her shoulder every step towards the taxi. Jake stood and waved at her as she left and watched the taxi disappear into the distant early morning light.

Chapter 42

Dave and Dennis sat on a rock at the base of Curbar Edge. Den had climbed most things, but the Peapod was one of the old classic climbs that he'd overlooked. The vertical grey wall rose over sixty feet with a peapod shaped cleft set in half way up the face and was a serious challenge for any climber.

'Are you sure you don't want first try Dave?' Den said, knowing exactly what his response would be.

'Don't be daft; I'm in no hurry to kill myself, that's why I bring you, that's your job.'

'Well thank you friend,' he said as he tied the rope to his harness.

The start of the climb was on smooth rock, but access was via a narrow crack which split the crag from top to bottom. As he began, he heard the wail of a siren and the tortured roar of a diesel engine as it powered up the steep road from the village. 'See that Dave, if I ever get a job, that's what it will be, I always fancied myself as a fireman,' he said, releasing his fingers from the narrow crack.

'Oh thinking of working for a living are we?' Dave replied.

'Well yeah, I'm getting cheesed off with always being short of money, the benefits don't go very far, and I get pee'd off always having to explain how hard I look for work.'

'Oh yeah, I've seen you do that, in the pub.'

'Well I mean it; I think I'll find out about getting into it, next week.'

Den's hands were bleeding; the inside of the crack was like the edge of a file with minute crystals of quartz protruding. They did stop the accidental slipping out of fingers, but did lacerate the skin in the process. Den, after a short but violent struggle, got to the deep cleft in the face and arranged his body slightly; leaning left with one foot jammed in the crack, and his other struggling for friction on the outside face. He reached up and inserted his hand into the crack above the peapod, his body leaning out, defying gravity. He'd managed to fix a good belay at the base of the groove about eight feet below where he now struggled. He reached up, his breath now a clear sign of the strain being put on his body. As he reached he stretched, his foot slid out of the crack, and in a second he was off. Swinging in space.

'That was a pretty move, Den,' Dave said, his laughter ringing across the escarpment.

'Yeah, well you hold on to the rope, I'm giving it another go.'

Den, suspended from the belay, swung pendulum like across the front of the climb. As he slowed, he managed to jam his hand into the crack, and with renewed determination he positioned himself, both feet and hands, in contact with the rock. He shuffled in ungainly style up the deep cleft and somehow was able to clamp his body inside the depression, enabling him to get a solid hand jam above its lip. His hands hurt and he saw traces of his blood left on the rock. *A nice present for anyone following,* he thought.

He was in no position to place any further protection, and he felt very exposed. A fall now would be a long one, so he focussed his thought on the next two feet of rock. He allowed his body to swing out from the rock, his hand jammed solidly in the crack now supporting all of his weight. He swung and twisted his body, his breath rasping. He managed to insert his other hand into the crack. *That's better Den,* he said to himself. *Now get a grip and do it.* His foot was flat against the rock; he leaned out to give it some positive frictional value. He levered his bloodied hand from the crack, and inserted it another foot higher, then struggled to raise his body. He got a toe back into the crack again and removed his hand. In a second he was off; with no time to react, he fell thirty feet before the belay caught his weight. Dave didn't laugh this time. Den was livid. *Dennis you are a stupid prat,* he called to himself angrily.

'That's going to have to be it for today. My hand is wrecked, but I'll get it next time,' he shouted down to Dave.

It was 7 PM. The Robin Hood pub in Hathersage was packed. They sat bemoaning the day's failures. Several empty bottles were laid out before them.

'I bloody nearly had it Dave, but my hand was knackered. Next time I'll wrap em up in tape, that should help.'

Dave put his arm over Den's shoulder. 'Were you serious about trying to join the fire brigade.'

'Yep, definitely, if I've got to work it may as well be something with some exciting bits to it.'

Chapter 43

0900 hours, Graveton Fire Station.

'Red Watch, fall out.'

Mac pulled Jake over to one side.

'Well Jake, how was the weekend in London?' he asked.

'We had a really nice time Mac, the concert was fantastic. We met Antonella before the concert and had a drink with her. Afterwards, we sat and talked and walked for ages along by the Thames. I like her a lot Mac, and she likes me. We'll definitely be seeing each other again.

Mac felt the hair on his neck stand up, he knew what was coming.

The alarm actuated, and the station lights came on.

The crew moved fast, putting their gear on, their shoes left abandoned on the appliance room floor. The large red doors swung open. Jock hit the button and the siren wailed as he powered out of the station heading for the city.

As they crested the hill, Mac turned to his crew. 'It looks like it's a good one,' he said, as the plume of smoke interspersed with balls of fire erupted from the building two miles away.

Jake pushed his arms through the straps of his breathing apparatus set, pushed the yellow helmet firmly onto his head, and smiled the smile of a truly happy man.

The end

ND - #0081 - 270225 - C0 - 234/156/16 - PB - 9781780910796 - Matt Lamination